# EVERYONE'S A FAN OF SOMEONE...

*All I can see is you.*

My stomach somersaults as he looks up towards the back of the room, right where I'm standing.

He can't possibly see me; I'm in the near-dark here and the spots lighting the stage will be in his eyes.

He can't see me. No way.

Nobody sees me – that's the point. Nobody sees me and I've worked very, very hard to make sure that's how it is. I don't want to be the centre of attention; I can't think of anything worse. I happen to like it in the shadows, with my lists and – yes – my clipboard. It's safer here. So, no. He can't see me.

But it certainly feels like he can, because he's looking *straight* at me. Straight *into* me.

# Praise for UNCONVENTIONAL

"Deliciously slow-burning romance, with characters that demand to be adored from the very first page and the most unique setting in contemporary YA ever."
**LAUREN JAMES, AUTHOR OF "THE NEXT TOGETHER"**

"A gorgeous one-of-a-kind novel, perfect for fans of Rainbow Rowell."
**MAXIMUM POP!**

"Breathlessly brilliant – spine-tinglingly romantic, unashamedly geeky, smart and funny… It's a perfect meeting of worlds: fantastic fandoms, books you want to live inside and a completely gorgeous love story."
**MIRANDA DICKINSON, SUNDAY TIMES BESTSELLING AUTHOR**

"*Unconventional* is the ultimate love story for the age of fandom and, much like a meeting with your favourite celebrity, it will leave you breathless."
**MEREDITH RUSSO, AUTHOR OF "IF I WAS YOUR GIRL"**

"Maggie Harcourt is the UK's answer to Rainbow Rowell. *Unconventional* is original, funny and I wish I could transport myself into it, amongst all the characters who stole my heart right from the beginning."
**LUCY THE READER**

"*Unconventional* is the swooniest swoonfest."
**MELINDA SALISBURY, AUTHOR OF "THE SIN EATER'S DAUGHTER"**

# UNCONVENTIONAL

Maggie Harcourt

**USBORNE**

For Juliet and Rebecca.

Lexi couldn't have asked for a better team –

and neither could I.

First published in the UK in 2017 by Usborne Publishing Ltd., Usborne House, 83-85 Saffron Hill, London EC1N 8RT, England. www.usborne.com

Text © Maggie Harcourt, 2017

Cover illustration by Helen Crawford-White, studiohelen

Cover illustration © Usborne Publishing, 2017

Author photo © Lou Abercrombie

The right of Maggie Harcourt to be identified as the author of this work has been asserted by her in accordance with the Copyright, Designs and Patents Act, 1988.

The name Usborne and the devices ♀ 🐝 **USBORNE** are Trade Marks of Usborne Publishing Ltd.

A CIP catalogue record for this book is available from the British Library.

ISBN 9781409590156  JFMAMJJASON /16  03571/1

Printed in the UK.

# APRIL

## HOME

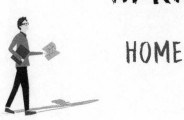

# THE WRONG SIZE TREES

There is a very specific sensation, right in the pit of your stomach, that comes from realizing that because you sent that stupid confirmation email from your stupid phone on the stupid bus while you were thinking about the stupid history essay that was due *yesterday*, you put a hyphen in the wrong place…and now, instead of having a box of inflatable three-metre-high palm trees sitting on your doorstep, you have three boxes of inflatable metre-high palm trees. You have, essentially, palm trees that wouldn't impress a toddler…never mind the seven hundred book, film and comic fans who will be pitching up just in time to look down – literally – on them.

And this very specific, palm-tree-related sensation?

It's not good.

It's not good at *all*.

There is only one person I want to talk to right now, so I dig my phone out of my bag on the hall floor and dial her number.

"Angelo!" She draws out the "o" of my surname the way she always does when she answers. "What's up?"

"Help!"

"What did you do?"

This is Sam through and through. Straight to the point.

"I did a thing."

"You did a thing."

I nod. Two hundred miles away in Leeds – and at the other end of the phone – my best friend can't see it, but I'm nodding anyway.

"Lexi…" Her voice sounds way calmer than I feel. "What did you do?"

"The palm trees."

"Yes?"

"I shrank them."

"You shrank the palm trees." Down the line, I can hear that Sam has gone very still – like someone who's just realized they've wandered into a minefield. "Shrank them… *how*?"

"I have really bad grammar?" I say, hoping this somehow makes it less bad.

"These palm trees. These are the inflatable ones, right? The ones your dad had you order."

"Yes."

"The ones that are supposed to be lining the walkway?"

"Yes."

"In three days."

"Yes."

"Shit."

Another thing about Sam. She tends to say what she thinks.

In fairness though, that was the first thing that went through my mind too.

That, and: *Dad's going to kill me.*


I kick the closest box. I hate the palm trees. I do. I hated them from the second Dad told me he wanted the first convention of the year to have a theme in the registration area. A tropical theme.

"Palm trees? It's not very…fantasy-y, is it?" I'd said, poking my chopsticks into the box of noodles between us on the table. "Doesn't exactly go with the guests we've got."

Dad had waved at me vaguely. "That's the point. Anyone can bung a couple of plastic rocks in reception and say it's the moon or Mordor or…wherever."

"As opposed to plastic palm trees, you mean?"

"Lexi." He'd put his chopsticks down on his plate and frowned. "Look. Last season, people said we were good. I heard them. *Good.* It's not enough! This year, I want people saying we're spectacular. I want people to talk about Max Angelo conventions with a look, you know. *That* look.

Awe and wonder. This year, next year…*every* year."

"You stick a load of palm trees in reception, Dad, and you're going to get them talking about you with a look. And not a good one."

"We'll see."

"Send them back. Send them back and he'll never know," says Sam.

"I can't! The courier's already gone."

*Gone* is too gentle a word for it. He dumped the boxes on the doorstep, shoved a manifest in my hand and was back in his van and zooming off in a cloud of dust before I could even open my mouth.

Sam whistles tunelessly, then makes a humming noise like she's thinking. After a long, long, long pause, she says, "Well, then. You're just going to have to own up, aren't you?"

"Thanks for your help, Samira."

"Good luck…"

I hang up on her before she can make any more helpful suggestions.

I eye the boxes.

They're still there.

I try closing my eyes, turning round three times and looking again.

Still there.

She's right.

I'm going to have to tell my dad. And it is not going to be pretty.

Hundreds of photos judge me on my way up the stairs to Dad's home office at the top of the house; pictures going all the way back to when he first started running fan conventions. I mean, *now* Dad is "Max, the boss of Angelo Events" – the best events company around – but *then* it was just him and a few friends getting together in a pub to talk about books they loved. After a couple of these chats, more people started turning up, and within a few years those little get-togethers had turned into weekend-long conventions. The whole history of it plays out across our walls: photos of Dad surrounded by writers, artists, film stars...all of them beaming out at me as I plod up to his office.

It's his life and he's proud of it, and I guess I am too. His company runs all kinds of big events now – like that celebrity wedding last year, the massive one in Venice? That was Dad's company. And the one the year before that – the one with the castle and the snakes that made all the papers? Dad's company. But the weddings and the conferences, that's not what he cares about, not really.

What my dad cares about, what he insists on planning

and arranging and running personally (with a little – or a lot – of help from yours truly)? It's still the fan conventions; the ones that run from Easter through to Halloween every year.

The first one of which is in three days.

And it looks like I've already managed to screw it up.

His office door is closed, but he's obviously heard me coming because I don't even get the chance to knock before it swings open.

"How was schoo…no, sorry – sixth-form college?" he says, stepping back so I can get inside. The floor is awash with paper. It actually looks like a paper tsunami just came through here. "Don't touch anything," he adds, hopscotching back to the desk. "There's a system."

"It was fine." Which isn't quite true, strictly speaking – but seeing as my last term report is somewhere under this lot, and he's not even opened the letter about yesterday's meeting with my form tutor (mostly because I hid it behind the bread bin downstairs), I don't think I need to worry too much about him catching me out on this one.

"Great. Look, I need you to… Wait…" He ruffles his hands through his hair like he always does when he's remembering something. "I know I had it a minute ago…" He starts scouring the piles of paperwork, looking for that one specific printout with yet another job for me to do...

This is my moment. While he's distracted.

"Dad?"

"Mmm."

"Dad."

"Yes, yes, that's definitely me."

"About the palm trees..."

"Oh. Yes. Right." He pauses; stoops and picks up one sheet, then shakes his head and puts it back down again – on the wrong pile, but I'm not going to stick my neck out.

"The courier's just dropped them off, and—"

"Could you call Davey and ask him to come deal with them?"

"Davey?" Davey is Dad's PA. His actual PA in his actual company office. The one who works for Dad because it's his *job* and he gets *paid*, rather than just because he has the privilege of sharing a load of Angelo DNA like I do. "I thought..."

"No. You were right. Scrap the palm trees. Terrible idea. What was I thinking? Davey'll take care of it." He hops over another pile of paper to reach his desk, and turns his laptop to face me, pointing at a photo on the screen. It shows the main entrance to a large convention centre, in the rain. And lined up in a neat row leading up to the doors, dripping gently are...guess what? "Besides," he says, "Comic-Con did it last month."

Huh.

"Lexi?"

"Yep."

"What's the matter?"

"Nothing, nothing." I study my fingernails intently. "Why d'you ask?"

"It's just…that sounded like a laugh."

"No. No…"

I can't hold it in much longer.

"You, umm, want a cup of tea?" I take a step towards the door. He's already back peering at his piles of paperwork.

"Tea? Yes. Cup of tea would be…" He tails off, and I could wait around till next Tuesday but it won't make any difference: he's forgotten I'm here.

I gulp down the rest of the laugh, close the door behind me – and by the time I'm halfway down the stairs, somewhere in a room on the other side of the country, Sam's phone is already ringing…

# APRIL

## HEATHROW

# ARRIVAL

Hotels built for conventions are not what you'd call glamorous, and this one is no exception. I mean, it's fine and everything: it's got a fancy automatic revolving door like they have in airports (the kind where someone always stands in front of the sensors and makes it grind to a halt so everyone trips over everybody else) and a couple of big concrete planters outside the entrance with a selection of flowers and tiny trees. Inside, it's all polished tile floors and monogrammed carpets and basically the clone of every other convention hotel I've ever set foot in.

In short, it's my second home.

Dad drives the car right up to the door, ignoring all the *No Parking!* signs.

"It's only for five minutes. Ten at most," he mutters when I point at the sign right outside my window. The boot and back seat of the car are loaded up with boxes of paperwork, registration cards, folders, name badges, lists, lists and more lists. Everything you need to run a convention.

Well. I say "everything". Most of it's in the van that he drove over yesterday, and left parked around the back. As I said, hardly glamorous.

Noon on a convention Friday. We have exactly five hours before the first of the early arrivals turn up. No pressure.

The faint *click-click-click-click* from the driver's seat tells me Dad's already back on his emails. He can plan a massive convention almost single-handedly (*almost*) but has yet to work out how to turn off the stupid keypad noises on his phone.

Someone bangs on my window, making me jump. The clicking pauses as my dad peers round me, then sighs.

On the other side of the glass is a tall olive-skinned girl my age with bright red hair. *Bright* red, like scarlet-lipstick red. She's grinning and waving madly at me, shaking her hair from side to side.

Sam.

"Go…" Dad says wearily. He knows that if I don't get out, she's going to get in. Or try to, anyway.

My hand rests on the door handle. "Do you want me to help unload the car?"

"Paul and Marie can help, I'm sure. Go. Get checked in while you're at it, but be in the lobby in fifteen minutes. We've got work to do."

I nod, and open my door.

* * *

"You!" Sam throws her arms around me like she's on a mission to squeeze all the air out of my body. Sam's hugs take some getting used to – and, ideally, enough warning to be able to brace yourself. I guess it has been a couple of months since we saw each other face-to-face; apparently Skype doesn't count.

"You!" I croak back with the last of my available oxygen.

"Sorry…" She lets me go, and suddenly I can breathe again.

"What the hell did you do to your hair?"

"New wig. You like it?"

"It's very…red?" It's the best I can do. And it is. Very red.

"I've got a different one for every day. You'll see."

"I am veritably breathless with anticipation."

"Oooh. What's got into you?" Sam narrows her eyes at me and pulls back as we shuffle through the revolving door into the lobby.

I immediately feel guilty. I shake my head. "Sorry. Nothing."

"Mmm. Nothing." She snorts. "It's either your dad or college, right? Did your tutor have a go at you again?"

"No. It's not that." I hesitate. Do I tell her? I don't know. It'll sound stupid, and sulky, and like I'm some silly kid having a tantrum…

Oh, of course I'm going to tell her. She's *Sam*.

"Dad and Bea. They've set a date," I say, hoping it doesn't sound as bad out loud as it does in my head. "It's really happening."

"Uh-huh." Sam makes an interested sort of noise, but doesn't actually answer. She's too busy looking at the floor, at the glass around us, at a bit of fluff on her top…anywhere, I realize, other than at me.

"Sam?"

"It's not like it's a massive surprise though, is it? Technically, they've been engaged for a bit, right?"

"Yeah, but…" If I close my eyes, I can still see the writing on the neat little save-the-date card Dad plonked in front of me at breakfast. His name alongside Bea's, and there in black and white: a time, a date, a place.

How can I explain to Sam that – being my father's daughter – it's always been drilled into me that nothing happens until the date is locked? If you don't have it on a schedule, it doesn't exist. It's one of our unbreakable convention rules: set the date *first*, then plan it. So when Dad originally told me a few months back that he and Bea had decided to get married, I braced myself – waiting for the when. But it never came, and as minutes turned into hours turned into days, it showed no sign of coming either. It's not like I ran away from it – I dropped hints, I left sentences hanging; gave him every possible chance to provide that crucial piece of information. But he carried on as though nothing had happened. After a while, I assumed it was just one of those Things Dad's Going To Do – like how he's going to get the leaky landing window fixed, or call someone to sort out the light in the kitchen that hasn't worked for five years…all stuff he says is going to happen and never does (because, obviously, no date locked). Nothing was *different*. Bea didn't move in, and she didn't even cut down the travelling she does for her own events business. Dad didn't mention the "M" word again, so I figured I could just forget about it.

And then: save the date, because – surprise! – Max Angelo's getting married again.

He actually thought it was funny, springing it on me out of nowhere, and a bit of me wondered whether that was Bea's idea. (The cards definitely felt like her; Dad would never have chosen that font.)

Except – and this is where I know I sound ridiculous, and much as I hate it, where I know Sam's right – it wasn't out of nowhere and I can't pretend it was. He'd told me – they'd told me – and I'd just kind of assumed the same rule applies to people as to conventions.

Obviously not.

The revolving door finally lets us out and Sam waves across the hotel lobby to her parents, unpacking a crate full of books onto a table: conventions don't just run in *my* family. I pick at a hangnail on my left thumb.

"Well, anyway… Dad and Bea are actually, really, seriously and most definitively getting married."

Sam cocks her head at me. "You okay?"

"Mmm. Yes. I'm fine. It's fine. Everything's fine." It's not quite a lie, but it's not quite true either. "Still processing, maybe?"

"What does your mum say?"

"I haven't had chance to talk to her about it yet – he literally just dropped this on me."

"But he told you months ago…?"

"He only told me they'd picked a date this morning. This morning!" I say stubbornly.

"Lexi…" She rolls her eyes theatrically, and I know what she's thinking: she's picturing me running up and down a hillside in the sunshine, picking flowers and wearing a dress called DENIAL. But she doesn't punch me on the shoulder and tell me to get a grip, which is her usual support tactic, and I can see there's something which might actually count as concern in her eyes – despite the rolling.

"I know, I know. You're right. I've been pretending it wasn't going to happen. It's fine, I'm fine. Fine fine fine. I just need more time to get my head round it. *Really*," I add, watching her watching me.

But I don't have time – not right now, anyway. Because, date or no date, this convention's happening first.

And what I do have now is plenty of work.

I give Sam a smile and poke her arm. "So, are you checked in already?"

"Of course. Checked in, unpacked and everything." She says this like it's a Herculean achievement. I suppose it is – Sam doesn't exactly travel light. Last time, she had so much stuff that I ended up carrying half of it for her. It's the costumes. Sam's cosplaying is legendary; last year, she dressed up as Spider-Man, Black Widow, something inexplicable from an anime that seemed to involve a lot of neon, and Draco Malfoy – which involved slightly less neon. The costumes are how we became friends, back when I started helping Dad. Sam had managed to glue her hand to the one she was making, and came to the convention operations centre to ask for help getting unstuck. She was hoping to find her parents, but instead she found me. The rest is history…and a *lot* of messages and online chats I never want to fall into the wrong hands.

"What room are you in?" I ask as we walk towards the hotel reception desk.

"406." She lounges back against the desk beside me. "Did you hear about Nadiya?"

"What did I miss?"

"She broke up with Ajay."

"Seriously?"

On the other side of the lobby, a couple of traders I recognize are rolling three racks of comic book T-shirts through to a massive room full of stalls. They give me a wave and point at the racks. "Last lot!"

I wave back. They already look knackered and we're not even open yet; they've probably been unloading stock from their van since the crack of dawn. For anyone selling merchandise at a convention, it's very definitely a marathon, not a sprint. Sam watches them get caught in the fire door, then carries on as though nothing happened to break her flow.

"She messaged me this morning. It happened last night."

"Is she still coming?"

"Alexandra Angelo! One of your friends is in serious emotional pain – and all you're worried about is whether she's still coming to work?" Sam wags her finger at me.

"You think Ajay is as much of a dick as I do. And anyway, we're already one staff member down from ops, and the art team had a last-minute dropout."

"Really? Who bailed?"

"Not now."

"I say again, *really*? I smell scandal."

I give her a mock-serious glare. "Samira, are you fishing for gossip? After the 'serious emotional pain' thing?"

"Shut up." She rolls her eyes, trying not to laugh.

"You shut up."

The hotel receptionist who has just appeared behind the desk blinks at me. I think I might have offended her.

"Sorry. Not you, obviously. Hi. Hello. Checking in? My name's Lexi Angelo. You should have a reservation for me under the convention booking?"

At the word "convention", the receptionist raises a perfectly-plucked eyebrow at me, then starts tapping on the keyboard of her computer.

Sam leans over the desk and switches on her brightest smile. "And if she could have the room that interconnects with 406, that would be magic."

Just like every convention hotel has the same entrance (with or without inflatable palm trees) and the same lobby and – weirdly – the same carpet in the upstairs hallways, every con's operational office is always the same. It's the nerve centre, the room where everything happens, containing several laptops, a printer that won't connect to any of them, the biggest Wi-Fi black spot in the entire hotel, a first-aid kit, a corkscrew and enough paper to make it a serious fire hazard. Which is why there's always a fire extinguisher in there too – often being used as either a doorstop or a paperweight. Or occasionally both at once. Somewhere, there'll be a clock. It's almost always wrong – not by much, but just by enough to lull anyone keeping half an eye on it into a false sense of security. There will be a trail of discarded plastic cups, crisp packets and other detritus.

Above all, there will be people; none of them sticking around for long, but all of them passing through regularly and at high speed. And – at an Angelo convention – there will be me. This is where I live. Has been ever since I can remember; from just following my dad round, or stuffing the tote bags everyone gets when they sign in and pick up their membership badge (all those flyers and bookmarks and freebies don't get in there by magic) right up to now – when I'm actually part of the crew. Running the crew, in fact. We're what Sam cheerfully calls the "cannon fodder": the ones who run around keeping the plates spinning and making sure the show goes the way it's supposed to – and that everybody comes out in more or less the same state they went in. We're the first in the firing line when there are problems, so we're the fixers and the make-it-work-somehow-ers. My crew are my friends, my tribe, my band of brothers (and sisters, obviously) and I'd be lost without them. So would Dad. And so would any of the general membership who keep insisting on asking us where the toilets are instead of looking at an actual *map*.

I push the door open. Someone, almost certainly Sam, has already stuck a Post-it note on the laminated *Convention Operations* sign taped to the outside – it's bright pink and reads *Abandon hope all ye who enter here*. My crew are sitting on folding chairs dotted around the room – all except Sam, who left me to lug my bags alone once I'd checked in and is now lying on the floor with her hands behind her head. Bede is on the chair closest to her, throwing Smarties at her face, which Sam's trying to catch in her mouth. Right at the back of the room, Nadiya is furiously typing on her phone, occasionally stopping to scowl at it and shake her head, then smooth the folds of her hijab with a sigh. Still, at least she's here.

"MORNING!" I shout cheerfully at the room.

A Smartie bounces off Sam's nose. "It's quarter past one, babe."

"Eat your Smarties."

Dad has obviously unpacked the car while I was taking my bag up to my room; several boxes' worth of paperwork sit stacked on the table. Maps, programme scheduling, staff rotas, lists of guests and attending members, extracurricular events, contact numbers: everything we need to keep the show running. It has taken me weeks to pull this stuff together…and I know that within fifteen minutes everything will change and the whole lot will need updating, and I might as well have written it in peach crayon for all the good it's going to do.

But that's life. That's conventions. Kind of the same thing to me, I guess.

I look at the to-do list Dad has stuck to the front of my clipboard, already propped on the table. Forty-two items. And at the bottom of the page he's written *Continues…*

alongside an annoying little arrow. Like I don't know him well enough to always, *always* check the next sheet.

I consider the clipboard. I pause. "He's already been in, hasn't he?" I ask the room.

Nadiya swears at her phone.

"Missed him by five minutes," says Bede, aiming another Smartie at Sam.

"So why are you all still here?"

"Wanted to make you feel special." Bede shrugs, lobbing the empty sweet packet at the bin. It misses. I stare at him pointedly until he gives in and picks it up. "Nice to see you, Lexi," he mutters.

"Yeah, yeah. Missed you too. Now shift your arse. We've got to set the registration desk up." I swipe at him with my clipboard as he slouches past me out of the room. He dodges, and blows me a kiss before strolling out into the corridor and sticking his hands in his pockets. I can hear him whistling the theme from *Game of Thrones* as he goes.

Sam rolls over and pushes herself up off the floor, throwing me a salute and a "Sir! Yes, sir!" before running off after Bede, laughing. Nadiya keeps tapping on her phone, then finally looks up.

"Hey, Lexi. Heard your dad and Bea have set the date. Big news," she says, coming over and giving me a hug.

"I only found out this morning! How do you know already?"

"You know convention staff. And this is your father we're talking about."

"Don't remind me." I stare at the clipboard. Hard.

Obviously realizing we could do with a change of subject, Nadiya clears her throat and whistles. "So where do you need me to go?"

"Didn't my dad…?"

"Assign me already? Yeah, but that'll only take me half an hour."

"Uh, hold on." I scan down the list of Impossible Tasks I'm Supposed to Accomplish Before 5.30. "Do you want to go over to the traders' room and the art show and see how they're doing with set-up? Make sure they've got everything they need, and all the stalls are ready?"

She nods. The art show and the traders' room set-up are the two real headaches: they're so big that they have their own teams and their own staff, but they always need backup if it's available. With so many different stalls in the trading space selling everything from collector cards to toys via superhero costumes and board games, and a load of original artwork to display on the specially-constructed art show walls, there's plenty of work to go round.

"Nadiya? Before you go…"

Talking to Nadiya isn't quite the same as talking to Sam. How could it be? Sam's Sam, and that makes her one of a kind (luckily for the rest of us – I'm not sure the world's ready for two of her yet). With Nadiya it's a little more awkward. Even though she only lives on the other side of London to me, I haven't seen her since the end of the last convention six months ago. She's never really seemed fussed about meeting up in the real world, and that's okay with me. Besides, at home, the people I know from sixth-form college – the ones I occasionally hang out with when I don't have coursework or Dad-work – they don't really *get* conventions, and while I'm with them I guess I'm slightly less… conventiony. So being able to turn up here and be me – *really* me – with everyone I love, it's a relief. College friends are fine, but these are my *people*. "How are you doing?"

She knows exactly what I mean. "Sam told you?"

"About Ajay? Yeah. Sorry." I try a shrug. "Convention staff, you know?"

"He keeps messaging me. Saying he's sorry, saying I've made a mistake, saying…a load of shit." She shakes her head.

"Do you want to talk about it?"

"Uh-uh." Another head shake. "He's a dick. Better off without him."

"Want me to block his number for you?"

"No. Yes. Maybe? Ask me tomorrow." Her phone buzzes again and she rolls her eyes. "Scrap that. Ask me in an hour."

"Any time. You just say the word and he's gone."

"Thanks. Sam offered to throw my phone in the fountain for me."

"That should worry me. But I'd actually be more worried if she'd been anything other than incredibly dramatic."

Nadiya tries to cover her laugh with a cough.

I smile back at her. "I mean it, though – you need anything, you tell me."

She nods – and then mutters "Dick" again, slipping her phone back into her bag without even looking at the latest message.

"Where did Daddy Dearest put you first then?" I hold the door open, then lock it behind us.

"Signage," she says, holding up a stack of laminated signs with directions, room names and arrows printed on them. I wince. Hotels *hate* convention signage. "Wish me luck?"

When she's gone I look at my clipboard.

*Item 1: unpack books for membership bags. Priority.*

The next twenty-two items all have *Priority* written after them.

Don't they always?

Thanks, Dad.

# PINEAPPLES EVERYWHERE

The relative quiet of the early registration period is over in a flash, and Saturday morning comes round far too fast – like it always does. We're well into the first full day, with breakfast already a distant and fading memory, when Bede raises an eyebrow at me from his spot behind the registration desk. "You have jam on your lanyard."

"I know. I'm saving it for later." I surreptitiously give the Access All Areas pass hanging around my neck a wipe, and he almost falls off his chair laughing.

Naturally, this is the moment my dad chooses to appear round the corner, having just walked the length of the registration queue. He narrows his eyes briefly at Bede, who takes the hint and gets on with flicking through the rack of membership badges for "Sands, J", while beside him Nadiya hands over one of the canvas membership bags we were stuffing with freebies till gone midnight. I try really hard not to notice the smudge of what looks like pizza sauce on the back of the bag as it crosses the table.

Dad surveys the queue. He's rocking back and forth on his heels, the way he always does when he's nervous. "How's everything going so far?"

"Seems okay. We opened registration at 9.30 this morning, and we're at about a hundred an hour."

I can see him doing the maths in his head, so I add: "Faster than last time, yes."

"Do you…?"

"No. I don't have the figures from last time. I was there. Do you trust me or not?"

"You know I do." He squeezes my shoulder. This is barely a step up from the kiss-on-the-top-of-the-head. In front of a queue full of people who have literally nothing better to do than stare at me. Awesome. "I'm just wondering whether the queue might move a little faster with someone else helping?"

"You mean me."

"Not necessarily. But what *are* you doing at the moment?"

"I'm standing here. Talking to you, Dad."

"Right. Yes."

"Would you like me to get behind the reg desk for a bit?"

"If you think that's the best thing to do…"

I've already lost him. He's craning his neck, peering down the queue towards the main entrance. And he's spotted someone, I can tell.

"Lexi, could you ask…"

"Sam? She's already on it," I say, clambering over the pile of tote bags – it's a lot smaller than it was last time I looked. Sam is, as usual, on guest liaison duty. Her job is to prowl the lobby keeping an eye out for any of our convention guests – anyone who's due to be on a stage over the weekend. When she spots one, she sweeps them off to a separate registration area to give them their pass and schedule. Her wig today is bright green and matches her outfit, so it's fair to say that seeing her striding across the lobby towards them, some of our guests may well assume she's cosplaying as broccoli. (Who knows? She might be. I didn't dare ask when she stuck her head round the connecting door between our rooms.)

This satisfies my father – in as much as he ever can be satisfied with the way a convention is going on the first morning. He nods and wanders off, smiling at people in the queue and stopping here and there to chat. I notice he gives the guys dressed as space marines – already getting excited about the Interstellar Terror Q&A and apparently rating Hollywood aliens on a sliding scale of scariness while they wait – a wide berth though.

"Lex? We're running low on bags." Nadiya pokes me in the side. "Where are the rest?"

"Down in the cargo bay. We only brought half of them from the storage locker this morning. I can radio through and get some brought up – how many do we need?"

She looks up and down the queue, then up at the ceiling as she rolls through the numbers in her head. "Another two hundred? But quickly, yeah?"

I grab my walkie-talkie from the desk – and promptly drop it straight into Bede's lap. He yelps.

"Sorry. Sorry, sorry, sorry…" I lean forward to grab it – and then stop. "I think you'd better pass that to me, don't you?"

He hands it back over his shoulder without even looking up from the names he's ticking off on the membership list.

"Lexi?" A voice I don't know is saying my name.

"Hmmm?" I look up from the walkie-talkie, trying to match the voice to a face. On the other side of the table, just to the left of the rapidly-diminishing bag mountain, is a woman with a friendly smile and neat blonde hair. She's wearing a beige trench coat, a white T-shirt and skinny jeans with ballet pumps. On the floor beside her is a huge leather shoulder bag, and in her hand is a phone.

*Publicist!* hisses a tiny voice in the back of my head. First rule of conventions: always be nice to the publicists. However tired, stressed or pissed off you – the convention staff – might be, the publicist has got it worse.

(Actually, that's a lie. The first rule of conventions is: always make sure the hotel knows you're coming. Because sometimes they don't. True story. A story I've heard many, many times from my father, usually late at night and in the immediate run-up to another convention…)

"Hi!" I arrange my face into my best I'm-busy-but-delighted-to-help expression. I know it's the right one. I've practised it in the mirror.

"I'm Lucy, from Eagle's Head?"

*Eagle's Head. Books. Something about books.* That's literally all I've got right now.

"How can I help?"

"I was wondering…we have a new author, and would it be possible…?"

"You need another pass?" I have a list somewhere. I know I do…

"Lexi! Bags!" Nadiya hisses at me. I glance over at the bag pile. We're down to maybe fifty. If we run out of bags, the queue grinds to a halt and everyone starts getting grumpy. Plus I get my dad breathing down my neck again. Bags. We need bags. I need to get bags. I have never needed bags as badly as I do at this moment.

"Lucy. Umm. Lovely to meet you. Yes. Pass. I don't have any extra passes here at the moment, but if you want to double back and head to guest registration on the other side of the main lobby, one of the team will get you sorted out. Just ask for Sam, and tell her I've sent you over. She's basically dressed like giant asparagus. You can't miss her."

"Great. Thank you." Lucy the publicist picks up her bag and heads back down the line.

*Eagle's Head. Why does that ring a bell?*

"BAGS, LEXI!"

"Shit. Yes. Sorry." I press a button on the walkie-talkie. "Mike? Can we get a couple of hundred swag bags up to registration, please? Yep. Now. Like, *actually* now? Thanks."

The call comes over the walkie-talkie during the late-lunchtime lull. At first, I try to ignore it. It's only half past one, and I'm already officially shattered…but one does not simply ignore the call of the walkie. It's my dad – and while I don't catch all of what he says, it doesn't matter. I definitely get the word "pineapple".

"Pineapple" is the code word.

"Pineapple" is never good.

Bede hands what feels like the thousandth bag over the desk and looks at me with horror. "Did he just say…?"

"Yes. Yes, he did. Pineapple. Pineapples everywhere." I jab the talk button. "Pineapple. Understood. On my way to the ops room now." I stuff the walkie into the back pocket of my jeans. "Can you tell Sam if you see her?" I ask.

Bede nods. "Where is she anyway? She's meant to be taking over from me on reg."

"I haven't seen her since this morning." I crawl out under the desk. It's the quickest way. Not the most elegant, but who needs dignity?

"Can you call her or something? I'm starting to lose all the feeling in my legs. Plus I'm *starving*..." he shouts after me.

I half-walk, half-jog down the main corridor, dodging between groups coming out of one of the programming halls. Marie – one of Dad's senior staff – is standing by the double doors, directing the queue waiting to go in for the next panel. She opens her mouth to say something...but closes it again when I mouth the word "pineapple" at her.

She shudders, and I hear her say, "Good luck."

The ops room door is ajar.

I take a deep breath.

My father, the hotel manager and Sam are gloomily huddled around a petite, pixie-like woman, and a slightly frazzled-looking guy who is only a couple of years older than me – which would probably make him her assistant. I recognize *her* immediately. She's one of our guests of honour – which would explain why Sam's here, and not switching with Bede. The guest is an actress; I remember seeing her check in to the hotel last night. I remember, because she had one of those incredibly tiny dogs with...

Automatically, I check the room for a dog.

I see no dog.

There is no dog.

There is no dog, and the guest of honour is crying.

Oh no.

Pineapples *everywhere*.

The dog, it turns out, is called Bangle. Bangle has – not to put too fine a point on it – done a runner from his hotel room and is now at large *somewhere* in the hotel.

Probably.

The first thought that lands in my head as Dad explains the whole sorry saga is: *the dog has its own hotel room?*

The second is: *Bangle? Really?*

Not that I'm judging or anything.

But...Bangle?

Either way, Bangle is a very small dog in a very big hotel full of people who aren't exactly looking out for a dog the size of the average pencil case. What if he gets out of the building? What if somebody *treads* on him?

Sam takes the hotel room and the upstairs corridors. The assistant takes the stairwells and lifts. Dad takes the lobby and the convention floor, giving me a stern look that says he'll be co-opting more of my staff to help with that...which leaves me with the service areas. Looks like instead of ducking into the Feminist Harry Potter panel, I'll be spending the afternoon crawling around the housekeeping storage areas, shaking a packet of dog chews. Excellent. I'd so much rather be doing this.

And anyway, *who gives a dog its own room?*

"Dad…" I grab his arm as we step back out into the corridor. His face looks ashy-grey in the artificial light. We've never had to deal with this kind of problem before. Guests getting sick, guests oversleeping, guests missing their trains or (one time) completely forgetting that they were supposed to be here. We've had all those, and over the course of his whole glorious career, Dad's had plenty more. But a Small Dog On The Loose? That's a new one.

"Just do your best, Lexi."

"It's a dog. A tiny, tiny dog. There is a *lot* of hotel here – it could be anywhere!" I hiss at him. He smiles back through the open door at the tearful actress – who is now dabbing her eyes with the corner of a handkerchief and glancing around to check who's watching. I'm tempted to tell her there are no cameras in the ops room, but I imagine that would go down like a lead balloon, so I don't.

"Exactly. It could be anywhere. So start looking."

"It's probably at the bottom of her handbag and she just can't see it." This sounded funnier in my head. Out loud, it isn't funny at all.

"This isn't a wallet, Lexi. It's her pet." He looks at me. I open my mouth to say something back, but he's right. Tiny dog. Big hotel. Lots of people. Anything could happen to Bangle – most of it very not-good. Dad knows what I'm thinking though, and he shakes his head. "We can talk about the animal rule tomorrow morning. Right now, we look for the dog."

"Bangle," I say, wondering why we even bother having rules. There's the smallest twitch at the corner of his mouth, like he's trying not to smirk. But he has his game-face on.

"Bangle," he says firmly. "Now go."

The service corridors of the hotel go on for ever. I thought the convention floor was big, but it's nothing compared to the warren of passageways and storage areas down here. There's a whole room just for storing sheets. It's like I'm Alice and I've fallen down the rabbit hole. You know, if the rabbit hole involved lots and lots of laundry. A slightly open door near the kitchens leads to a huge pantry full of sacks of flour…and two chefs dressed in checked black-and-white trousers and open white catering jackets, sitting on a pile of them, smoking. They're almost as surprised to see me as I am to see them, judging by how fast they try to hide their cigarettes. I explain the dog problem before they recover enough to start shouting at me – I'm not technically supposed to be poking around down here. They look at each other. Then back at me.

"I don't suppose you've seen him, have you?" I ask. "He's about this big…" I hold my hands up. He really is very small.

They variously frown, shrug and shake their heads. Right. Helpful.

I'm pondering the big steel doors into the hotel's massive industrial kitchen – and thinking exactly how much I don't want to go in there and tell them the convention that's already making their lives quite hard enough, thank you, has managed to lose a dog – when my walkie-talkie chirps. Bangle has turned up, unharmed…in the wardrobe of his own bloody room, which the frazzled (and possibly useless) assistant had managed to shut him in without noticing. Sam opened the door, he bounced out, crisis over. Everything is *fine*.

Fine is a state of mind. I'm starving, knackered and standing in the middle of a gloomy hotel service corridor that doesn't feel a billion miles away from something in a horror movie, flickering overhead fluorescent lights and all. I'm sweaty from running around looking for a missing pet that wasn't actually missing, I've walked for what feels like miles and – what's worse – I've absolutely no idea how everything's going upstairs on the convention floor… And when I get back up there, I'm going to have to deal with a sulky team who've had to cover for me and Sam while we've been off on our magical mystery tour. Yes, they're my friends…but friendship only goes *so* far.

As I trail back along the corridor towards the lift, I try to shrug off my black mood. I'm annoyed with Dad – for sending me down here, for letting a guest bring a dog when I could have told him something like this would happen… and also for suddenly presenting me with incontrovertible, un-ignorable proof that Bea is a serious thing, not just someone he likes going for a drink with after going to serious, business event-type conventions. (Who would have thought that conventions about conventions were even a thing – let alone romantic?)

Yep, that's what I'm really annoyed about, isn't it? The wedding thing.

It's not that I don't like Bea, exactly, it's just that I'm not sure I'm ready for her to become a permanent fixture. I mean, I like the picture on the wall in my hotel room, but that doesn't mean I want it in my *actual* room. It would feel alien. Wrong. But it's not exactly something I can talk to Dad about, is it? Conventions? Yes (provided I can pin him down long enough). My feelings? No. No way.

Like when he first announced they were getting married – I didn't even know how seriously to take him at the time. I guess I thought if he actually *meant* it, Bea would be there too, telling me with him. Plus, you know: date, schedule… all that.

"I really love her, you know."

"I know." (I didn't. Not until then…)

"And I want to do things differently this time. I don't want to make the same mistakes with Bea that I made with your mother, making her feel like I was neglecting her. I want to be better, be a better husband."

Oh, like the conversation wasn't already awkward enough.

But…a tiny little patch of fear uncurled, fernlike, somewhere in the middle of my spine.

"Does that mean you're going to stop doing the conventions?"

I wasn't really asking about the conventions. Of course I wasn't. I was asking about…life. Our life, his life, what happened next. I didn't actually believe he'd ever stop: I'm not sure he can. But maybe if he loved her better than Mum…better than me…if he wanted to *be* better…he'd consider it, at least in his casually dropped into conversation kind of way. It would be a warning bell. Or what if he said he wanted to bring Bea onto the team? Did that mean she was replacing me, somehow?

"No! Of course not. She may not care much for the fan conventions, but she's in the business too. She knows how much this all means to me."

It wasn't the most reassuring answer, but it was good enough.

"Stop doing that," he said, waving a fork at me.

"Doing what?" I swallowed a mouthful of coconut rice.

"That. With your face."

"My face?"

"You're making that face."

"There's no face. This is just what I look like."

"You know what face I mean, Lexi – I'm looking right at you. I thought you liked Bea?"

"I do!" (In small doses. And at a healthy distance…)

"Then what is it?"

"Nothing."


In the gloomy service corridor, I poke at the lift button again. It hasn't lit up, but maybe that doesn't mean anything. I bash it harder. Bea's fine – I do like Bea, I suppose – but what if getting married again makes Dad different? He is different with her, but what if it makes him different with me too? He'll still be Max Angelo – but will he still be my dad? But then what if he doesn't change, and Bea can't handle how crazy he can drive people when he's planning an event, and things go wrong like they did with Mum? I don't know how he'd cope with getting divorced again. I go cold just thinking about it.

We were doing fine as we were, him and me… Okay, so most of the time I'm the one who counts as the responsible adult at home, but other than that? I've been dealing with Dad's eccentricities my whole life; it's part of being my father's daughter. I don't understand why things need to change.

Me? If I got my life running the way I wanted it to, I'd just leave things alone – the same as anybody would, surely?

My dad isn't just anybody though, is he?

He's an Angelo. And I'm an Angelo and conventions are woven through both our lives. I love them – working at them, planning them, thinking about them – because they're where I feel safest. They're what make me feel like me. And right now I feel like that could all be about to unravel.

I poke the button again. It falls off the wall.

Umm.

Stairs. I think I'll take the stairs.

Finding Sam on the other side of the stairwell door onto the convention floor – holding out a clipboard and very clearly waiting for me – makes me wish I'd considered that decision a little longer.

"You look happy," she says.

"Appearances can be highly deceptive. What d'you want?"

"Not me. Big Boss Daddy. Can you go check the green room, he says?"

"Why? Isn't it where we left it?"

"Funny."

I sigh. "Seriously? I've been traipsing round the basement…"

"Bede's on his break and nobody knows where he's gone – and even if we did, he'd be sulking anyway – and I've had to draft one of the art team in for cover on registration because Nadiya's stuck with some crisis in one of the panel rooms…"

"What crisis?"

"Would you just chill?" Sam rolls her eyes. "Something to do with a microphone. She's *got* it."

"Why can't you do it?"

"I don't look after the green room. I only do the mics and soundcheck since…" She tails off pointedly.

"Ah." There was an incident last year involving an entire tray of full coffee cups, a table leg, and a very famous writer wearing a white shirt. "Fine." I snatch the clipboard out of her hand.

"Love you too!" she yells after me.

I stick the middle finger of my right hand up at her behind my back as I walk off. Someone dressed as Judge Dredd makes a disapproving sound. "Sorry, Judge," I mutter.

Green room it is.

# THE HIGH PRIESTESS OF THE ORDER OF THE CLIPBOARD

Our green room – the holding pen for VIPs and guests – for this convention is a small, windowless room with a large orange damp patch on the ceiling. The glamour. Anyone with the right pass is free to drop in whenever they please for as long as they like – but we ask them to definitely, definitely be there at least half an hour before any appearances they might be making. That way, we know where they are when we need them – not like the old days, when I used to get sent to the hotel bar to fetch them out…

I know. I'm a convention kid.

Because the green room is technically for people to prepare ahead of panels and events and to decompress and relax afterwards, it's off limits to anyone without an Access All Areas pass – and is therefore the one place where we have a security guy sitting outside the whole time, just in case someone decides they absolutely *have* to give their manuscript to that author, or to ask this actor to marry them.

Our guard's name is Rodney, and when he sees me coming he lowers the newspaper he's reading.

"Someone's a ray of sunshine today," he says, his Welsh accent turning it into a song.

"You've heard about the dog?" I push the door open – only to step through it and find Bangle himself sitting on the table in the middle of the room, being fed popcorn by Frazzled Assistant. "You have got to be *kidding* me."

On the other side of the closing door, Rodney lets out a cough that sounds suspiciously like a laugh.

Bangle yaps at me – then growls. Of course he does. Frazzled Assistant offers him another handful of popcorn.

This is not my life.

A quick scan of the room reveals (besides my two new best friends) four publicists, three authors, one graphic novel artist and a handful of empty bottles from the "artist hospitality" fridge… Check, check, double-check.

And a guy sitting on the sofa with his feet on the table.

I don't know who that guy is. And he isn't with anybody. I skim through the list on my clipboard. The list of names with access to the green room goes on and on – but I know most of the faces that go with them. Well, it's not like this is my first rodeo, is it?

No face. Well, all right, he has a face. But I'm my father's daughter, and as well as being brought up to be a retriever of wayward celebrities, I was taught to remember faces. And this isn't one I know. He's just sitting on his own in the corner playing with his phone. Something's not right.

"Hi." I clutch my clipboard to my chest as I approach him. "Can I see your pass, please?"

He looks up and blinks at me a couple of times – like that will somehow make me disappear. "My pass?"

"I'm afraid the green room's for our guests. The speakers, their publicists…that kind of thing?"

"Oh. Right, sure." He gives me a weird little half-smile. And that's it.

"So…your pass?"

"I don't have one."

"You don't."

"Nope."

Oooookay.

"Right. So, if you don't have a pass, and your name's not on my list" – I brandish my clipboard for good measure – "then I'm afraid you can't be in here."

He smirks, and slides his phone into his pocket, shifting slightly in his seat to look up at me. "Did you seriously just wave your clipboard and give me the 'if your name's not down, you're not getting in' line?"

"No. Well, yes. Yes, I did."

"And you're sticking to that, are you?"

"I'm sorry?"

"And now you're apologizing?"

"I…what? No. No, I'm not apologizing…"

He grins at me and unfolds himself from the sofa, standing almost toe to toe with me. He's taller than I am – my nose is level with his chin. This does not help.

I am not going to look up at him. No. Not happening.

"It's fine. I got the message. But for the record, my publicist asked me to tag along with her to this, and then there was a mix-up with badges and—"

I cut him off. "Who's your publicist?"

"My publicist?"

"Yes. Your pub-li-cist." I'm probably not at my most friendly. Across the room, Frazzled Assistant clears his throat. I turn and scowl at him. He immediately goes back to studying Bangle's ear – which makes me wonder whether he is, in fact, the dog's assistant.

"Uh, Lisa? Lois? Louise? Something beginning with L. Shit." The interloper frowns. He really can't remember. Eventually, he gives up. "I'm new at this."

"You don't say."

"You're not going to let me off, are you?"

"Sorry. Can't. I don't make the rules."

"But you do have the clipboard…"

"You can't let that go, can you?"

"Shameless sucking-up doesn't work on you either?"

"No."

"Fair enough." He reaches down to pick up a battered leather messenger bag from the side of the sofa, slinging it over his shoulder. A pair of glasses fall out, along with a vaguely familiar-looking paperback which he stuffs back in before I can clearly see what it is. "I'm Aidan Green, by the way." He holds out his hand.

"Lexi. Lexi Angelo."

One of his eyebrows shoots up. "As in Angelo Events?" He points at the floor as he says it. I guess he means, *as in this event? Here, now, where I'm making your life difficult?*

"My dad."

"No wonder they made you High Priestess of the Order of the Clipboard."

"I beg your pardon…?"

"See? You're doing it again. Apologizing to me."

A dozen withering comebacks whizz through my mind – and I'm too slow to use any of them. I mean, maybe it would sound like I was pausing for dramatic effect…but more likely it would just sound like I'm thick. So I settle for, "Out."

"Yes, ma'am," he says, throwing up his hand in a salute. It's annoyingly close to what Sam did earlier. Maybe it's the clipboard.

It *has* to be the clipboard.

I follow him to the door – just to make sure. As we step back into the corridor – now full of the audience from the panel discussion that just finished – he turns and gives me a broad, confident smile. "Nice to meet you, Lexi Angelo. Maybe I'll see you around."

"Enjoy the convention," I say – and I watch him lope off down the corridor until he is swallowed by the crowd.

"Who was that?" Rodney asks, looking up from his newspaper.

"Nobody," I say.

"Must've been somebody, or I wouldn't have let him in," he says, disappearing back behind the politics pages.

"Funny."

If I squint, I'm sure I can just make out the back of Aidan's head disappearing around the corner at the end of the hallway – and then I realize with a sinking feeling that the tapping sound I keep hearing is me drumming my fingers on the top of my clipboard.

*High Priestess of the Order of the Clipboard*, I think.

*Nobody*, I think.


"Hello under there?"

Sam's face appears below the edge of the tablecloth.

"Go away."

"Brought you a drink." She hands me the bottle of water like it's a peace offering. Or a grenade. I prop myself up on one elbow on the floor and lean forward to take it from her.

"Thanks," I say, hoping it sounds a little less grudging outside my head.

She clambers in between the table legs, pauses, then steeples her fingers together and looks at me over the top of them. "And why are we hiding under the table?"

"It's my safe place. Safe. Quiet. Happy place," I say between mouthfuls of water. Sam eyes me sceptically.

"Not that safe, babe. You realize your dad knows you're here, yes?"

Of course he does. He knows perfectly well that under the table is my happy place – just like he knows that when I'm under the table, it's best to leave me there. As for everybody else, the trick is making sure they never know exactly which table to look under. The hotel's banquet room is usually one of the first places they check, but I really couldn't be bothered to find anywhere more elaborate today.

"How did you find me?"

"I was going to go with a process of elimination," she says as she folds her legs in front of her and settles into a pose that wouldn't look out of place in an advanced yoga class. It makes the back of my knees ache just looking at her. "I did start with the registration desk, but Bede said that if he'd found you under there he would be kicking you already..."

"He's a bit pissed off, isn't he?" I tip my head back and stare at the underside of the table. I already feel bad about poor Bede, left to handle the registration desk by himself while we were all off on a mad dog hunt, and now he's having to cover for Eric from the art team – whose stomach is busy violently disagreeing with...everything. I am not Bede's favourite person right now. Hence: table.

"Almost made it through day one though, yes? That's a good thing." Sam grabs the water bottle while it's halfway to my mouth – coming dangerously close to pouring what's left all over my lap. There's a loud gurgling sound, and she clamps a hand over her stomach.

"Did you eat?" I ask. I haven't. With the best will in the world, the idea of finding time for lunch and dinner went out the window the minute I heard Bangle's name.

Sam squints at the hem of the tablecloth. "I have a vague recollection of a handful of peanuts around four thirty?"

"And that's it?"

"I did get Nadiya to bring some crisps from the green room when she went to check it earlier… Does that count?"

"Stop stealing stuff from the green room, Sam."

"Technically, it wasn't me. It was *Nadiya*, remember?"

*Green room.*

I snatch the water back and drain it. I'm thirstier than I realized. Or maybe I'm just hungry? I can't tell any more. "That reminds me – we need to keep a closer eye on the green room. I found a complete random in there earlier."

Sam's eyes widen in alarm; she takes the green room as

seriously as I do – as seriously as my dad does – even if she doesn't run it since the tray incident (of which we do not speak). "What was he doing?"

"Just…sitting." I realize this doesn't exactly make him sound like public enemy number one, but it's the *principle*.

"Did he have a pass?"

"Yes, Samira. Of course he had a pass, which is why I pretended not to know who he was and threw him out."

"Yeah, all right, Sarcasmo. What's wound you up so much?"

"He made fun of my clipboard."

Sam's laughter fills the space under the table, fills the whole of the deserted banqueting hall around us. She keeps going way, way longer than I'm happy about.

"You finished?" I mutter. Of course she's too busy laughing to hear me. I think those are actual tears I can see.

"He made fun of the clipboard? Oh my. What did you *do* to him?"

"I told him he wasn't allowed in there."

"But you did it with your characteristic charm?"

I blink at her. "What's that supposed to mean?"

"You know. You can be a bit…" She stops. She considers. She is suddenly very interested in a loose thread dangling off the tablecloth.

"Go on…" The words come out with all the warmth and approachability of a cobra with a really bad headache.

"A bit, you know, bossy." Sam bites her lip and gives me

the side-eye as she says it. I swear she's actually scooted further back from me than she was a minute ago.

"Bossy?"

(Is that really my voice? I didn't realize it went so high. I sound like an angry chipmunk.)

"A little bit. When you're stressed, I mean."

"A little bit?" I ignore the "stressed" comment.

"A little bit too much, is what I'm saying." She squeezes my arm. "I get it. You're under a lot of pressure and you don't want to let your dad down. I know. And I know you're not okay with the whole 'wedding' thing yet – believe me, I do. And that's okay." She sighs. "But we're your friends, Lex. Me and Nadiya – and, yes, even *Bede*. And you've been kind of snappy today. With all of us."

She won't meet my gaze at all; I can see her looking at her shoes, at the carpet, the bottom of the table legs, the tablecloth. Anywhere but at me. Again.

Sam is my best friend and she's trying to tell me that I've been a bit of a bitch today.

Sam is my best friend…and she's probably right.

The whole day plays back in my head on fast-forward, slowing down so I can get a really good look at all the times I've been crabby with my friends. Now I know what I'm looking for, there are more of them than I expected. Certainly more than I'd like. No wonder Bede's pissed off with me.

"Oh." It slips out before I can stop it, and Sam panics.

I can see it all over her face.

"It's not *that* bad. I mean, no one's on the verge of walking out or anything."

"No, no. It *is* that bad." I can see myself from outside, snapping at people for the slightest thing; running around like a headless chicken when what I really needed to do was stop and breathe and take a second to remember that it's a convention – nobody's going to *die* if a panel starts five minutes late.

I'm being a drama queen. I don't want to be that person – I'm *not* that person.

I groan and throw myself backwards dramatically – and manage to smack my head against one of the table legs on the way down. There's an almighty great clang that makes my ears ring and my teeth rattle.

"Wow." Sam leans over me. From my spot on the floor, it looks like she has tiny spangly little stars dancing around her head. Or maybe she's got glitter in her wig. It's hard to say with Sam.

"So that's what karma feels like."

She holds out her hand and heaves me up while I rub the back of my head. I can already feel the lump coming up under my hair where skull met table. They didn't get along. "Ouch."

"You thought it wasn't going to happen. The wedding. But it is."

"I never said that – not *exactly*…"

"You didn't need to. I know you, Lexi – and if you'd thought they were really getting married, we'd have had this conversation back in December when he told you. Except we'd be having it over Skype, not under a table."

"Sure. Whatever."

"You thought that because he didn't give you a date, a seating plan and a minute-by-minute breakdown of his wedding day, there wasn't going to be one…because how could a control freak like your dad even consider getting married without a million bits of paperwork, yes?"

And although I pretend I'm not listening, I notice she lowers her voice to a whisper when she calls Dad a control freak. At an Angelo convention, you can never be sure if he'll pop up from nowhere, having heard everything you just said.

Or maybe it's just me he does that to?

Sam crawls out from under the table and stands up. She is reduced to a pair of boots and bright green tights – and a voice.

"You know what you need?"

"To be examined for concussion?" I say, crawling out after her.

She ignores me. "The big book party's on. Right now. It's Saturday night, and we've officially clocked off for the day as of…" She looks at her watch. Like the rest of her outfit today, it is bright green. I don't know how she does it. "Now!"

"Lexi doesn't want to go to a party. Lexi wants to go and lie down in a dark room. A dark, quiet room."

"There'll be food…" she says in a sing-song voice. There will be. There's always food at convention parties. Sometimes, it's even stuff that isn't crisps.

And it *is* a while since I had anything to eat – I'm starving.

The book party is always one of Dad's favourite parts of the convention, and this one's no exception – I can just about see him over by the coconut shy. The hotel's ballroom has (for one night only) been turned into an old-fashioned fair – with candyfloss machines, hoopla games, hook-the-duck stalls and a fortune teller. Dad picks the theme, and all the publishers chip in. It's meant to be relaxed; it's both part of the evening entertainment schedule, and kind of a nod back to how these conventions all started. Everybody loves it – even the people who don't care so much about books. There's a New York Times bestselling author over there, handing out buckets of popcorn and signing books…while on the other side of the room, a couple of the hotel's waiting staff are in a tight huddle at the end of the drinks table with two publicists, Nadiya's uncle and Sam's mum. Instinctively, I take a step forward – then stop myself. I am not working now – it's the parentals' shift. And besides, the parties, as Dad likes to tell me with a smile, are "out of my league" – like I'm seven, not seventeen.

He never used to smile like that, slightly insincere and ever-so-superior. It's a smile he's caught from Bea; I recognize it. It's not a real smile – it's the facial expression equivalent of a sticker for opening your mouth wide at the dentist. And maybe it's weird to notice it, but…he's my dad. How can I not?

I'm just helping myself from a passing tray of tiny, tiny pizzas when I spot *him*.

Dark curly hair, wire-rimmed glasses. An air of smug self-satisfaction that wafts across the room like the smell of blocked drains.

"Sam. *Sam!*"

"Wha'?" She looks up from her candyfloss.

"It's him! Clipboard guy!" I hiss at her.

"Where?" She's beside me in a heartbeat, peering across the floor with absolutely no subtlety whatsoever. If he even slightly looks this way, he'll see her staring and me trying to pretend I'm not staring and he'll know that I was talking about him. *Thinking* about him.

Which I wasn't. Not at all.

"So? Which one is he?"

I'd forgotten Sam was there for a second.

"There. With the dark hair. In the navy blue jumper."

"Talking to Lucy?"

"I don't know – I can't see." I lean sideways, but my view of whoever it is he's talking to is blocked by a waiter with a tray of wine glasses.

"Curly hair?"

"That's him. And the chin."

"Chin?" She peers at me, then at the figure on the other side of the ballroom.

"You don't think his chin's kind of huge?"

She pats me on the head. "I think you've had a long day."

"Yes, Mum… Oh, no." I turn away quickly.

"What?" Sam shuffles even closer. She's actually standing on my foot, but I'm not going to draw any more attention to myself.

"He saw me."

"Huh?"

Because just as I stared at him the hardest, he frowned like something was bothering him…and then he looked straight across the ballroom and *right at me*. And to make it worse, he saw me watching him.

And he smiled.

"*Move!*" I try to hide behind Sam, or make myself invisible, or something – anything – to not be here.

"I think he's coming over!" Sam's voice is suddenly far too loud. It's like a foghorn, blasting through the music and the voices that fill the room.

"Shitshitshitshitshit. I'm not here. I've got to…" I eye the nearest table. It's draped with a long white cloth, and I've never seen anything so welcoming. "You've not seen—"

"Hello again," says a familiar voice.

Reluctantly, I turn around.

He's younger than I thought he was in the green room; maybe nineteen? And – irritatingly – he's better-looking than I remembered him. He takes his glasses off and slides them into the back pocket of his jeans, and he's studying me with eyes that are the same colour as clouds reflected in the sea. Maybe his chin isn't so big after all.

"Just to check, am I allowed in here? I wouldn't want to get in trouble…" He flashes me a grin and pulls a standard membership lanyard out from under his jumper, letting it drop onto his chest.

"The parties are open entry to members." It comes out of me automatically, like I'm programmed to say it when someone presses my button.

*He's* pressed my button, hasn't he?

I can feel my teeth grinding against each other.

Followed by a sharp elbow in the ribs.

"Hi!" says Sam brightly. "I'm Samira. I'm one of Lexi's staff."

"Aidan," he says, smiling at her. "Nice to meet you." He waves at the room. "So this party, this is all you guys, is it?"

"God, no." She shakes her head and laughs. "We're the

daytime grunts. Cannon fodder. The parties are mostly our parents, hers and mine." She pauses, but then sees his blank expression. "Lexi, me, Nadiya, Bede – basically, anyone you see wearing one of these lanyards, we're all staffing the convention." She tugs at hers to make her point. "Some of our parents have been doing these for years, so we're kind of keeping it in the family."

"I see." He nods appreciatively. "I've never been to a convention before. I didn't know what to expect."

It's the strangest thing, because although he's clearly talking to Sam, he's looking at me. Not uncomfortably, it's not like he's staring or anything…but it's like he's curious. Like I'm some kind of display in a museum.

They make small talk about the convention – which I mostly tune out of as I catch sight of my dad across the room. He's having a whale of a time chatting to a guy in a leather jacket who looks like he might be an actor from last year's big superhero film. Or maybe not. I'm not sure; it could be the light…

"I've been trying to work out what's different," says Aidan – and I realize he's talking to me.

"Different?" I peel my gaze away from my father.

"About you." Aidan smiles…and then it's obvious why. He can barely keep a straight face. "And I just realized – you haven't got your clipboard with you. No wonder I didn't recognize you at first."

"Gosh, you're funny." I very much hope my tone of voice tells him just how much I don't believe this.

"So I'm told."

"And you listened to whoever told you that, did you?"

"What's that supposed to mean?"

"Oh, never mind."

My relatively good mood has soured. I don't know why he's annoyed me so much; it's probably not even him. All right, I *know* it's not him – not all of it, anyway. But his snide little clipboard comment earlier, combined with Sam calling me out, and that tone of voice: over-friendly, over-familiar… I'm over *it*.

"Sam?"

"Yup?"

"I'm going to…I'm really tired, okay? Tell my dad I've gone up to bed and I'll see him at breakfast?"

"Wait, what? Seriously? It's only… Oh." She looks at her watch again. "Wow. That hour went fast."

Aidan is still standing there, right in front of me, but I don't care if I'm being rude. I just don't have anything left. Anyway, technically he started it with the clipboard jibe.

I walk away without saying goodbye, leaving the two of them staring after me.

\* \* \*

Closing the door to my room feels like shutting an airlock. Outside, there's the convention. There's all the people and the fussing about lanyards and schedules and lost dogs and the endless running around – the stuff I'm normally fine with (lost dogs aside, maybe). Outside, there's Dad and Bea. Everything changing, saving the date. College. Outside, there's the Lexi I seem to have been today; someone I don't really recognize, the one who snaps at her friends. And they *are* my friends – my real, proper, can't-live-without-them friends.

It's not that we spend a lot of time together, a few weekends a year, maybe. But those weekends are *intense*. They say a convention weekend is the equivalent of six weeks, real time – especially if you're one of the staff. It's how Sam can be my best friend even though we live a couple of hundred miles apart; how I can know everything about who she really is, and how she knows everything about me – more than anyone from college, even.

I did try, at college. One lunchtime, we were all sitting around because it was raining and no one could face going outside, and Oscar, who sits next to me in history, asked what it was about conventions I loved so much.

"How much do you know about them? Conventions, I mean?" I asked. He shrugged, and after a bit of nudging he admitted that he thought they were just places where people went to dress up for the weekend. And that it was all a bit "weird".

"There's nothing 'weird' about conventions," I said, laughing, and because I just happened to have some of my planning notes in my bag that day by chance (this is a lie – I always have my planning notes in my bag, in my pocket or under my pillow), I showed him some of the panels we had planned for the next one.

"But what about all those people who dress up as comic-book characters?"

"Not everyone dresses up – but they can if they want to. It's…celebrating stuff. It's cool."

"Cool. Right." He pulled a face, and I rolled my eyes.

"Okay, so you don't like anything? There aren't any books or films or songs you love – nothing?"

"I love Aston Villa. Doesn't mean I want to run around pretending to be one of the squad at weekends though, does it?"

"So what's that shirt you were wearing last week, then?"

"That's different. That's, like…a replica home shirt."

"Uh-huh. Sure. Different." I grinned at him, but he got my point – and since then, everyone at college just files conventions under the list of things people do in their spare time. Oscar plays FIFA; I "do" conventions. And that's as far as their interest goes.

But Sam…Sam's the one who understands it, for good or bad. Understands me. And if she reckons I'm off, she's probably right.

I close the interconnecting door between our rooms. We normally leave it open, but tonight I want to be left alone. I push open the door to the bathroom and flick on the light. In the mirror, my reflection manages to look both grey and a sort of unhealthy beigey-yellow. Appealing – but nothing a soak in the bath and a good night's sleep can't solve, hopefully.

With the bath running, I pick through the mess of things I've dumped on my bed and find my phone, flicking through the contacts until I reach M.

"Hello?" The voice on the other end is crackly, and sounds further away than it really is.

"Mum. It's me."

"Lexi! I wasn't expecting to hear from you this weekend. It's a convention weekend, isn't it?" She immediately flips into panic mode. "What's happened? Is it your father? Is everything all right?"

I laugh. Five years they've been divorced – but she can't help herself. "Dad's fine, Mum. Everything's fine."

"Oh. Good. Of course. I'm sorry, Lexi – you don't usually call when you're working, and I thought…"

"Sorry. I needed to talk."

"Is something the matter?"

In the background, I hear another voice; a burst of music like a door has opened and closed, and Mum whispering something in rapid French to the other person in the room with her.

"How's Leonie?" I ask.

I can actually hear Mum light up, the way she always does when I mention her. "She's fine. She sends her love – and she's asking when you're going to come out and see us. You could come for the summer? You always have a room here, any time you want."

"I know. This summer though…"

Mum sighs. "They've set a date for the wedding. I know. He called me last night. I suppose I should feel honoured he managed to squeeze me in between whatever panels or parties you had running." She always knows what I want to talk about, even if I haven't quite worked it out myself when I pick up the phone. "He wasn't sure how you'd taken it."

"Oh, you know…"

"Lexi. Don't try and pretend with me."

"It's fine. Bea's okay – honestly. You'd like her…" I hope she didn't notice the tiny, tiny, quarter-of-a-heartbeat pause in between "Bea" and "okay". I didn't mean to put one there, but I just ran out of breath all of a sudden.

"You'll have to forgive me if I'm not completely convinced by that 'fine'."

"No, I am, really. It's just been a long day…" I pause. She waits for me to say more.

Oh, what the hell.

"It's taking a bit of getting used to, that's all. You know Dad."

"I do." She pauses again, and I can't decide whether what I hear is a sigh, or the wind in the background at her end. "And what about college? How's that going? You're not getting behind, are you? It's an important year..." A creaking sound tells me she's now out on the back terrace of the farmhouse in Brittany she and Leonie bought two years ago. The night they moved in she sent me a photo of the two of them, huddled together on an old wicker sofa with a wine glass each. I don't think I'd ever seen her so happy before. "Be honest, Lexi."

"College is good. Really. There's just so much to do right now – start of the season and everything. A lot of work." I scuff the carpet at the end of my hotel bed with my toe. Like hell I'm going to be honest. We'd be here till next April if I was...

"School – sorry, *college* – work, or father-work?"

I laugh at the dip in her voice when she says "father". "Both."

"Listen to me. Your father has his own life. He's made his own decisions and choices – for better or worse. I know. I was there for most of them. What you need to do is make him understand that you have to do the same, and you need the *time* to live your life too. There's more to it than conventions, you know."

"I heard that somewhere. Not sure I believe it." I laugh.

"You sound just like your father. Just because he regularly

does the im-bloody-possible, he thinks everyone else can do it too."

"It's fine."

"You keep saying that."

"Because it is."

It *is* fine. Ish. It could definitely be *worse*. But I could very much do without all the extra wedding stuff in my head right at the start of the season. I know, I *know*, that it would kill Dad to think I feel this way, but…

"Sam said I was being a nightmare today." I feel better as soon as I say it, like I'm confessing.

"Were you?"

"I don't know. Probably."

"Lexi," she sighs. "Like it or not, you *are* very like your father. And that means you do have some of his…less appealing traits. Don't treat people the way he does."

"He's much better now…"

"Oh, stop defending him, darling. I lived with it for much longer than you have. As long as I could."

"I know…"

"I didn't leave him because I didn't love him. I left because…"

"Because you couldn't cope with him any longer."

"Exactly. I needed to come first in my life, Lexi – not second in somebody else's."

I don't have an answer to that, so I twirl my hair round

my finger and peer through the bathroom door. There's a grand total of about three centimetres of water in the bottom of my bath. At this rate, I'll be able to go for a paddle before I go to bed.

"Are you still there?" she asks.

"I'm still here."

"Think about what I said, Lexi."

"First in your life, yes."

"That's not what I meant and you know it. I meant that your father has always had a tendency to put things – his career, his business and, yes, his conventions – above people. Don't make the same mistake. College, your friends, your *future* – they matter too. They matter more." She says it so gently that if I really wanted to, I could almost pretend she isn't saying the same thing Sam did earlier.

Almost.

"I'm not sure that makes me feel any better, Mum. Besides, these guys *are* my friends."

"Who says I was *trying* to make you feel better? I'm just telling you what you need to hear."

"I'm not sure that was what I needed to hear right now."

"Did you eat?"

Mum may have removed herself from the world of conventions, but she still remembers.

"I had some very small pizzas?"

"Get something from room service. Tell your father I

told you to, when he complains about the bill."

"I'm not really that hungry. I'm just tired. I think I'm going to go straight to—"

"Nonsense. Have something to eat – I don't care what. You'll feel better for it."

"Yes, Mum," I say, wondering whether she can hear me rolling my eyes.

"Lexi, I may be in another country but I am still your mother."

(As it turns out, she can.)

"Love you, Mum."

"I love you too, Lexi. Look after yourself."

I hang up and, mess or not, I throw my phone onto my bed – and myself after it.

# OH, BROTHER

"See? This is what I'm talking about. Just look at that."

My father has skewered a sausage with his fork and is holding it aloft, peering at it. The whole breakfast table is trying to ignore him.

"You can always tell a hotel by the sausages they serve at breakfast. A good venue *has* to pass the sausage test."

Next to me, Sam snorts into her glass of orange juice. I kick her under the table. She nudges me and winks.

"Sausage test."

"Zip it, you." I turn my attention back to my bacon. I don't particularly feel like eating it – breakfast isn't really my thing – but on convention time, who knows when the next meal's coming...or what variation on dried potato it will be? Sam keeps sniggering; it's never too early for innuendo where Sam's concerned, but the way I see it, innuendo – like breakfast – is best dealt with from the other side of at least three cups of tea. I give my rubbery bacon one more poke with my fork. It bounces.

Yeah, no thanks.

"You going to eat that? Swap you a hash brown if you like?" Bede doesn't even take his eyes off my plate from across the table.

"Oi. My eyes are up here, dude…"

"I'm not interested in your eyes. I'm interested in your breakfast meats."

It's all too much for Sam, who turns a lovely shade of purple and dissolves into hysterics, resting her forehead against the edge of the table.

"Give us it." Bede leans forward and shuffles my abandoned bacon onto his plate, while a couple of seats along Nadiya pulls a face. Being the most sensible of us, she's got a massive plateful of fruit and cereal with yoghurt, and is stuffing croissants into her bag when she thinks nobody's looking.

The 7.30 breakfast meeting is one of Dad's convention rules; as unbreakable as…an unbreakable thing. The theory is that they're meant to be some kind of team bonding exercise – you know, everyone breaking bread together and sharing a meal as a group. In practice, they're where Dad runs through the list of everything that went wrong yesterday, everything that could go wrong today and grumbles at us for both of the above. Pre-emptively, in the case of today's list. It's how he shows he cares. Or something…

There are a lot of dog jokes around today's table. Or our

end of it, at least. The other end is all paperwork and technical specs and serious faces and what I'm fairly sure is a printout of a wiring diagram. Which my dad appears to be holding upside down.

"Get your own!" Nadiya smacks Bede's hand as it creeps towards one of her croissants. "These are mine. Mine. All mine." There's the very faintest hint of mania in her voice – in all our voices, probably. I don't think anyone except me went to bed before midnight, and when I got down to open up the ops room an hour ago, both Nadiya and Bede were already sitting on the floor of the corridor outside, waiting for me.

I shush them both, elbow Sam in the ribs (she's stopped laughing, but I have a nasty feeling she's actually trying to go back to sleep – Sam can sleep anywhere; last year, she disappeared during one of the evening parties and I eventually found her asleep under the sink counter of the VIP toilets) and pull the clipboard out from under my chair.

Everybody groans.

"Oh, piss off."

"All hail, my Lady Clipboard," Sam hisses and before I know it, she's right back to the hysterics. Bede looks at her blankly.

"What's this?"

"Nothing," I snap – but not before Nadiya leans ever so slightly sideways and whispers "Tell you later…" to him.

"Not you as well?" I try to look wounded. "How do *you* know about that?"

"Oh, I hear everything. That, and Sam couldn't keep a secret if her life depended on it."

Sam takes enough exception to this to stop laughing. "Hey. Hey, hey, hey," she says, resting her elbow on the table and wagging a finger at Nadiya. "That's not fair and you know it. I mean, I never told anyone about you and Charlie at last year's Easter con ball now, did—"

She's cut off by Nadiya's shriek, and it takes her a second to work out what she just did. "Oh. Oh shit. I just did that, didn't I? Sorry."

"Sam!" Nadiya throws a croissant at her. It bounces off Sam's shoulder and straight back at Bede – who snatches it off the table. Nadiya holds out her hand. "Mine, thank you?"

Bede looks at Nadiya. He looks at the croissant. He looks at Nadiya again…

And then, before she can stop him, he licks the croissant from tip to tip – before holding it out to her. "Want it back?"

"You're revolting. On every level – including a few that science hasn't even discovered yet."

Bede grins and takes a bite out of his hard-won pastry.

It's going to be one of those days…

\* \* \*

I've managed to get the only seat in the whole breakfast room with a clear line of sight right through the lobby to the registration desk, so I can see that there's already a queue loitering in front of it by the time we finish eating. Lucky me. This also means I have a perfect view of the guy we not-so-fondly refer to as "the Brother" when he saunters over and starts picking through the piles of bookmarks, chapter samples and postcards on the freebie table, like the swag-hunting vulture he is. I lean back in my chair, and hiss at my dad behind Sam's head. Down at the far end of the table, he can barely hear me but I can see him doing that pulling-his-eyebrows-together thing that means he knows I need him.

"What…?" he mouths.

I shake my head, hold up a hand…and give him the signal we've developed over the course of several years. It's clear and concise and can only mean one thing – and he recognizes it immediately.

The Brother has arrived to check out the competition: us.

I don't need to be able to hear my dad to know what he says next.

He pushes his chair away from the table, smoothes his hair back and pulls his T-shirt straight; shuffling all his papers together into a pile, he looks at us all. "Everyone set? Any problems, I'm on the walkie."

There's a murmur from round the table as everybody

starts picking up their stuff and Nadiya tries to shoulder her handbag as normal. It's so full that she can't actually put her arm down over it properly, so she sort of rests her hand somewhere behind her ear as though she's scratching an itch at the back of her neck. This is apparently the funniest thing Bede has ever seen.

"Lexi?" Dad is pointedly waiting for me. "You're with me. Let's go say good morning."

"Whassup?" Sam grabs my elbow before I can move.

"The Brother's here," I whisper, trying not to look in his general direction. Never make eye contact with the Brother. Eye contact is how he saps your very soul.

"Oh, shitbiscuits." Sam immediately adopts a rabbit-in-the-headlights expression. "He isn't, is he?"

"Right there, by the reg desk. Waiting."

"Like shingles."

"Huh?" I blink at her and she rolls her eyes.

"Or like one of those old plague pits – you know the ones? Any time there's archaeologists going into burial pits, they always have to be bio-suited up in case there's still Black Death germs or spores or whatever knocking around down there. Lurking."

"I think you've finally reached peak zombie apocalypse. Lay off the undead for a while, maybe." I pat her arm and trail off after Dad, taking a couple of deep, pre-emptive soothing breaths.

* * *

The Brother is still poking through the freebie table as we get within earshot. He's talking to himself as he holds up a three-chapter sample booklet from one of the publishers by its corner at arm's length, like it's a desiccated frog, examining it with an expression to match.

"...sort of quality..." is all I catch before the Brother spots us and drops the sampler back on the table.

"Damien! What a lovely surprise – we weren't expecting to see you at this one!" Dad has his business smile on and his hand held out in greeting.

The Brother – or Damien, as anyone he doesn't piss off on a regular basis would call him, I guess, seeing as it's his name – sniffs and wipes his nose on the back of his own hand. Dad's smile doesn't dim even a fraction. Say what you like about my dad, but he's a professional.

"Max. Still running your little old conventions yourself then?"

There's the slightest emphasis on the word "little". Anyone else would miss it, but neither Dad nor I do. I make a mental note to temporarily lose the Brother's membership badge when we register him later. The Brother himself, meanwhile, has put his hands on his hips and is fake-casually looking around, making sure we get a good look at the New York Comic Con logo on his souvenir T-shirt.

"For now." Dad adjusts the paperwork under his arm.

"I always say the next convention is the last one…you know how it goes."

"I do, my brother. I do indeed."

And there it is. Even by his standards, that was quick. Sooner or later, Damien calls everybody – everybody male, at least – "brother". Usually sooner. Hence the nickname.

I tune them out while they run through the usual shop talk. The Brother – as usual – is name-dropping like a sailor throwing ballast off a sinking ship.

*Clang!* A-list Hollywood actor!

*Clang!* Major director!

*Clang!* Super-reclusive graphic novel writer!

*Clang!* Ridiculously famous author!

*Clang! Clang! Clang!*

The names hit the floor and pile up, one by one, in a giant steaming heap of show-offy-ness.

He's been doing this for years, I think. The Brother goes to everyone's conventions. *Everyone's.* I've no idea how he affords it, but it's what he does. And then he goes scurrying back to advise the conventions he's involved in, based on what everybody else is doing.

Dad gives up on trying to hold onto the papers and hands them to me. I am demoted to "assistant". The Brother beams at me.

"And – hey! It's Laura!"

"Lexi."

"You get prettier every time I see you."

Because that's not creepy at *all*.

"Thanks?"

I catch the sideways glance Dad gives me as he clears his throat and swerves the conversation away, presumably in an attempt to stop either of us from smacking the Brother in the face with a lever arch folder.

"Lexi's running ops for me these days. I'd be lost without her."

I know it's for show. I know it's the sort of thing you say to the sort of guy the Brother is. But even so…my heart feels like it doesn't quite fit in my chest any more. Because even though it is true (and I know it is, because last year he managed to lose the entire guest list somewhere on his computer, and it took me four hours when I should have been writing an essay on Henry V to recover it), to actually hear it *out loud, during a convention*. When he's usually too busy bossing me about to get even *close* to a compliment…

It means something.

But now the Brother's getting to the real reason he's loitering by the desk. All that name-dropping was just the warm-up…

"Did you hear about our little coup for June?"

"Mmmmm?" It's pretty obvious that Dad isn't really listening though; he's fumbling in his pocket for something – and pulls out his phone, frowning at it.

"We just announced…"

Dad holds up a hand, then points to his phone, which is already halfway to his ear. "Sorry, Damien. Going to have to take this – lovely to see you. Lexi?" And he sets off at a brisk stride across the lobby. It's only when he's halfway across it that I realize I'm supposed to be following him…

"You know your phone screen lights up when you're actually on a call, as opposed to just pretending to be on one?" I say when I catch up with him. He sighs and holds out his hands for his papers.

"If I never have to stand in another hotel lobby, listening to him tell me about yet another glittering career he has *personally* launched, or someone else he *hand-picked all by himself* right before they got huge…well, it'll be too soon. That's all I'm saying." He ruffles the top few sheets of to-do list. "Sounds like sour grapes, doesn't it?"

"Sounds like you care about what you do."

He smiles. "This is why I pay you the big bucks, kid."

"Yeah, about that… And don't call me kid, old man."

"Don't push your luck, Lexi. Here." He hands me the second sheet of today's list. It's single-spaced and double-sided…and he's written extra points in horrible black spider writing all along the margins. Before I can even protest, he's gone, "I'll be on the walkie…" lingering on the air behind him.

From the safety of the other side of a pillar across the lobby, I watch the Brother take a quick look around him…

and then, when he's relatively sure nobody's watching, he sweeps an arm across the table and sends flyers, badges, postcards and bookmarks scattering across the floor. What a charmer.

"Bit early in the day to be under there, isn't it?" Sam's shoes stop beside the table as I crawl out with the last of the bookmarks.

"Sabotage," I tell her, dropping them on the top of their pile. It's taken me ages to put the table back together; time in which I have planned increasingly elaborate and unpleasant "accidental" deaths for the Brother. Several of these deaths are even theoretically possible to arrange within the walls of this very hotel. The last couple, though, probably not. I'm not sure where I'd be able to find a large enough jar of gherkins or three bald eagles at this kind of notice.

"Did your dad check him in already?"

"Nope. We have that joy ahead of us later. Who's on registration for the day tickets this morning?"

"That's kind of what we're all waiting for you to tell us." Sam gestures to the others, loitering behind her. Whoops.

Today's list is already pretty scruffy from being shoved into my pocket while I crawled about the floor. "Should be floating cover from Eric…" I look around and see only an absence of Eric. "But I guess he's still throwing up from yesterday?"

Nadiya nods – and when Bede opens his mouth to ask her something she just shakes her head. "I don't want to talk about it."

Bede closes his mouth again…and catches me looking at him. He shakes his own head so fast that his whole face just becomes a blur. "No. No, no, no. You can't make me."

"I can, actually," I say.

"Please. Please, please, please. Not after yesterday."

"What was so bad about yesterday?"

"You left me on reg for hours. Hours."

"I did not *leave* you."

Bede raises an eyebrow at me.

"All right, I left you. Fine."

"And what do we say, Lexi?"

"We say 'shut it or I'm putting you back on registration again'?" Before I've even finished speaking, I can hear Mum's voice over the phone from last night. I groan. "Fine. How about I take the first shift on the desk? It'll quieten down after that and we'll close it at noon anyway. Will that make everyone happy?"

"Delirious." Bede – satisfied that he's getting revenge – heads off to do the early-morning checks on the panel rooms, Nadiya disappears in the direction of the ops office and Sam scampers back to her room to change into today's costume, leaving me to open up registration.

Which is precisely what I'm doing when...

"We should stop meeting like this."

"If only we could." If it sounds heartfelt, it's because I mean it to.

This morning, Aidan is accessorizing his smug face with a grey T-shirt and a pair of faded old black jeans. His outfit, however, is the only thing about him that *has* changed.

"Listen – I just wanted to apologize. For yesterday. I was a dick."

...Or is it...?

I make a polite non-committal sound that also manages to show I emphatically agree, then turn my back on him and step behind the reg desk, heaving the archive box with all the remaining day passes and paperwork in it up onto the table.

"Let me help..." he says, reaching for the box. I knock his hand away accidentally-on-purpose.

"Thanks, but I don't need your help."

"I'm just trying to—"

"I said I don't need your help!"

"You *really* don't like me, do you?"

I lean on the box and take a good look at him. It's hard to see the expression in his eyes behind his glasses, and I can't tell if he's joking or not. Fortunately, I don't have to –

as Sam's dad arrives to help with the heavy lifting.

He looks Aidan up and down. "Everything okay there, Lexi?"

"Fine, thanks. Just telling this…visitor…where to go." Sam's dad nods and heads off to check the storage cupboard, and I give Aidan a smile that isn't a smile, hoping he gets the message. He's unreadable, but I can *feel* him reading *me*; those grey eyes measuring every part of my face. It feels like the moment stretches on for ever, hanging by a thread and spinning endlessly with just the two of us locked inside it… And then he makes a sound that could be a laugh or could be a cough or could just be the sound that asshats make in their natural environment – I don't know.

"Thanks for the directions, Lexi." His lips curl like he's about to say something else; something balanced right on the very tip of his tongue…and then he shakes his head and smiles and he's gone.

"*What* an arse," says Sam, appearing from behind one of the lobby pillars. She's changed out of the clothes she was wearing at breakfast and is now Clark Kent, even down to the glasses (and the Superman T-shirt showing underneath her shirt and tie).

"He really is," I mutter – and she laughs.

"No, I mean…look at him go. In those jeans." And she actually leans around the pillar to watch Aidan walk across the lobby to the lifts, passing her dad on his way back –

thankfully still just out of earshot. "Oh, Lexi," she says when he's gone, "your face!" Still laughing, she takes the last tray of membership badges from her dad and starts arranging them on the table.

"Sam?"

"Mmm?"

"Shut up and help me come up with an excuse for the English assignment I haven't done for tomorrow...?"

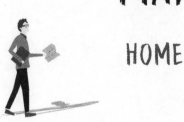

# MAY

## HOME

# BROUGHT TO BOOK

I can hear Dad shouting in his office, even with the door shut.

Even though I'm standing in the hall holding the packet the postman just gave me for him, and he's all the way up at the top of the house.

Even the *postman* could hear him, based on the smirk he gave me when I signed his delivery sheet.

It's entirely possible that whoever he's on the phone to up there could probably hear him without the actual phone – and who do we have to thank for this?

Bea.

Now there's a date, there's a wedding to plan. And that means Operation "Pay More Attention To The Wedding Plans, Max" has begun…and, wow, is Max unhappy about that. I don't know who it is he's yelling at up there, but a tiny (actually quite sizeable, if I'm honest) bit of me really, really hopes it's Bea.

Of course it's not Bea.

It's never Bea, is it? She's just the one who *causes* the shouting; usually because she's rung from an airport somewhere demanding…I don't know…tap-dancing alligators wearing Chanel jumpsuits or something – and then, oh look, they're calling her flight and she's got to run… She's never the one actually getting shouted at as Dad's stress levels rise. That's mostly me today. Or whoever happens to be the next person to call. Or sometimes both simultaneously.

It's not even that I blame her – not really. If I were her, and it was my wedding and everything, I'd want it to be the way I imagined. It's just that…it might be nice if everything was a little less traumatic for everyone else. And by "everyone else" I mean me, obviously.

The volume increases exponentially the higher up the stairs I go, until it feels like he's shouting inside my head. The pictures on the walls are rattling, and I don't even bother knocking; he'll never hear me over himself. Story of my life with dad, really. I stick my head round the door and catch him mid-pace across the floor, phone to his ear and his work Blackberry clutched in his other hand.

"Look, I know what the standard F and B rate is, and I'm telling you that you can do better. No, I don't want to speak to…don't you put me on hold…I…"

He makes an exasperated noise and shakes his head at me. "They put me on hold." He tosses his phone on the pile of roughed-out schedules for the next convention at the end of the month. "Can you give that publicist a ring for me from the landline? Anna something? I need her to confirm her people."

"A surname would help?"

"In the Rolodex. She's the only Anna." He points at the groaning contacts wheel on his desk. I swear he's the only person in the entire world who still uses one of those things – but ever since his last phone went nuts and spontaneously deleted all his emails, he won't even use the contacts app. I drop the package on his desk and reach for the Rolodex.

"This just came for you," I say, pointing to it.

"What is it?"

"Feels like a book."

"Another one?" He eyes the teetering stack of book proofs on the floor under the window. They've been arriving thick and fast for the last week. If a publisher thinks they've got something coming out that would fit an Angelo convention, he gets an advance copy. He even reads some of them...

He tips the book out of the padded envelope and skims the covering letter clipped to it with a few "Hmmmm" noises, idly picking up his phone again and tucking it between his ear and his shoulder.

"Sounds like your kind of thing – like that one you love with the wizards."

"Jonathan Strange is *not* a wizard, Dad. He's a *magician*."

"Mmmm. Want to take a...hello? Yes, yes of course I'm still here. Where else would I be?"

Now he's not on hold, I've lost his attention – but I've gained two whole jobs, as he thrusts both book and letter in my general direction and waves me out of the room, along with the Rolodex. This keeps happening – every time I set foot in that room, I seem to end up with more to do. I should just boycott the whole top floor of the house. Or barricade myself in my bedroom and pretend my coursework ate me.

Before I tackle the hell that is Dad's Rolodex, I need tea – and while I wait for the kettle to do something, I read the letter that came with the book from Eagle's Head. It's the usual PR stuff: hype, hype, more hype.

Big money, debut author, multi-continental auctions. Pre-orders, film rights, Hollywood. Blah blah blah. But beyond that, it looks like Dad's right. This could be *exactly* my kind of thing.

The Brother's snide little comments from last month niggle away at the back of my head. He's always so pleased with himself, finding the Next Big Thing before it actually gets big.

What if this book – even through all the hype and the usual hot air – is *it*?

And we've got it first.

I drop the letter on the counter and actually look at

the book. It's only a proof, an early copy sent out for review, so the cover is pretty simple: dark blue, swirled through with grey like a mist curling across it – and on the front, just a couple of lines of silver text. I run my finger over the title.

*Piecekeepers.*

"Weird title," I say to the kettle, slinging a teabag into a mug and pouring hot water over it. While the tea's brewing, I flip to the first page – where there's a quote.

*We have ripped the world apart – and that? That is the scar our magic has left upon it.*

And I don't know how, and I don't know why…but the second I read that line, I can tell that this book is going to change *everything*…

Dear Max,

*Da Vinci. Titian. Caravaggio. Rembrandt. Some of the greatest artists the world has ever seen…but what if their paintings are concealing a secret – and what if it could destroy us all?*

I'm delighted to enclose a proof copy of PIECEKEEPERS: the thrilling debut novel by Haydn Swift.

Meet Jamie, an ordinary History of Art student who is shocked to discover there is magic hidden in the world's greatest masterpieces, put there by an apprentice magician at war with his teacher. After a fierce duel across the canals of Venice, neither the teacher nor apprentice was heard from again – but the magic remains. Only a select few are even aware of its existence: the Piecekeepers, a magical organization dedicated to keeping the secret.

But either the magic was unstable or the spells are decaying, because the magic is getting out. The smallest leak will cause untold damage, as Jamie – who sees it first-hand in London's National Gallery – is only too aware. The magic must be returned to the paintings and held there…whatever the cost.

Recruited by cool-headed Lizzie, under the watchful eye of the Piecekeepers' Curator, Jamie is drawn further into their world. But then he hears the story, passed down from Curator to Curator, that one day, another apprentice will come; someone able to control the magic. And just as there were an apprentice and master who destroyed one another before, that too could once again come to pass…

*"PIECEKEEPERS is the best book you've never read – Swift's talent is a powerful magic that will bind readers young and old." – Non Pratt*

*"They say the eyes of the best portraits follow you around the room. PIECEKEEPERS shows you just how true that really is." – Will Hill*

THE GOLDFINCH meets JONATHAN STRANGE AND MR NORRELL, with sumptuous world-building sure to appeal to fans of THE SIN EATER'S DAUGHTER, PIECEKEEPERS is set against the backdrop of the world's most recognizable and prestigious galleries and supported by a global marketing campaign. With an international release set for July and a film adaptation already in development with a major Hollywood studio, this eagerly anticipated debut is sure to be one of the most talked-about books of the year.

Haydn Swift has created an electrifying story that will bewitch you, and one Eagle's Head Books are thrilled to be publishing.

For further information, please contact:

LUCY SPIEGEL, Eagle's Head Books

# MAY

BRISTOL

# HAYDN SWIFT

"Oh my god, Lexi – if you don't stop it, I'm going to nail your feet to the floor. I'm not even kidding."

"Sure you are, Sam. Except you don't have a hammer, do you?"

"Don't need a hammer. Pixie from the art show team has got a nail gun. She let me use it when we were building the main stage yesterday."

"She does know that you've managed to superglue your hand to a costume before now, right? And she still put you in charge of a nail gun? Jesus."

"Mock all you like. I was badass. Bad. Ass."

"How long is it till eleven?"

"Still another fifteen minutes."

"Maybe I should go now, just in case…"

"What is *wrong* with you?" Sam growls at me. "He's just a guy who's written a book, all right? It's not like you've never met one of those before." To illustrate her point, she waves an arm around the hotel lobby. Melinda Salisbury –

who has just collected her author lanyard from a beaming Bede – ducks out of the way and raises an eyebrow at all of us. Sam looks mortified. I *am* mortified.

"Sorry," I mumble, watching said author walk off into the convention swinging her lanyard. That went well.

Sam has retreated behind the registration desk. I perch on the side of it before I pace a hole in the hotel's carpet.

"And he's not just *a guy*, Sam. He's Haydn Swift."

"Sounds like a guy to me."

"That's not what I mean and you know it. That book. *That book.* I can't…I just can't."

Bede rolls his eyes, ticking off another name on the membership list. "Are you still on about that bloody book?"

"Yes. Yes, I am. Because it's amazing. I want to live in it."

"This is the one with the magic, right?" Sam squints at the ceiling, and I can't tell whether she really can't remember or whether she's trying to wind me up. I decide not to rise to it either way.

"*Piecekeepers. That* one. The one where the paintings are full of magic and now it's all trying to get out and there's a whole—"

"Oh, that one," Sam and Bede chorus. The family collecting their membership badges laugh – we're essentially part of the entertainment at this point. I don't care – it's eleven o'clock.

"It's eleven!"

"Thank god for that," mutters Sam through her teeth.

"How do I look?"

"Like a fangirl. Probably not quite the professional image your dad's after."

She's right. I need to tone down the over-excited twitching and be calm personified. Calm. Professional. Like this is no big deal...even though it *is* a big deal; a huge deal. After all, I was the one who told my dad we needed Haydn Swift here: this could be *our* coup. The Brother could take that and suck on it, because he didn't get there first. *We* did. "The book's going to be huge," I said, when Dad found me sitting in the kitchen that afternoon a couple of weeks ago, right where I'd been for the previous four hours – ever since I'd opened it to the first page. "You need to find a space for him. Now. *Before* that happens."

"You're sure?" And he flipped through the pages so carelessly that I wanted to scream, because as far as I was concerned that book was suddenly everything.

"I'm sure."

"I'll give his publicist a call."

And he did.

I check my hair in the mirrors of the lift on my way up to the third floor.

*Hi, I'm Lexi Angelo. I'm your guest liaison for the convention – and can I just say how much I loved your book?*

*Hello! I'm Lexi. I'll be looking after you for the weekend. And your book is amazing!*

*I'm Lexi and I love you. I love you and I love your book and did I mention I love you?*

*Can I have your head in a jar? Because it's clever. Your head. Because it makes words. I love words.*

The lift pings as it reaches the third floor and the doors slide open.

I check the room number I'm looking for, then tuck my clipboard under my arm and walk down the corridor towards room 319, where I'm supposed to collect him.

"Just a guy, Lexi. Just a guy who wrote a book."

Jenna, one of the publicists from Swift's publisher is pacing up and down the corridor, talking rapidly and quietly into her phone. She freezes when she sees someone approach, then realizes it's me and relaxes, tipping the phone away from her face to smile and whisper, "He's all ready. Door's open – just knock and go in." And then she's back to her call again.

"Just a guy who wrote a book. Professional. Lexi Angelo. Guest liaison. Loved your book. Lexi Angelo."

I knock, and push the door open.

He's standing at the window, his back to me. Haydn Swift.

I clear my throat. It feels like my heart has somehow wedged itself up there, which isn't exactly helpful, but still.

"Hi. I'm Lexi Angelo…"

My voice evaporates as he turns to face me with a broad smile, all my carefully planned words dissolving into thin air.

"Still carrying that clipboard, Lexi?"

Haydn Swift…is Aidan *arsing* Green.


"You?!"

I want to be outraged and eloquent and angry and – above all – smart. I want to be so smart that not only is he obliterated but he remembers my cutting comment for the rest of his life. But instead: "You?!"

"How's it going?" says Aidan-Haydn in the smuggest of all smug voices, with his smug mouth in his smug face. And I was right about his chin. It's far too big.

And smug.

"*You're* Haydn Swift? *You* wrote *Piecekeepers*? That was *you*?"

"Yes?" He glances down at his shoes. Even those are smug. Smug face, smug hair, smug shoes. There's a silence, then in a lower voice he adds: "Please don't tell me you thought it was shit."

This is…not what I was expecting him to say. Not this guy, with his crashing the green room and his clipboard-mockery and all the rest of it…and suddenly, he doesn't seem smug and annoying, he seems kind of, well...nervous. He's nervous. Maybe he's joking? I can't tell.

He has to be joking, right?

Because otherwise, it would mean that he really is nervous; nervous I didn't like his book. *That* book.

Of all the books in the world, Aidan Green wrote *Piecekeepers*, and now he's asking me if I thought it was bad?

"I...didn't. I thought it was kind of the opposite."

"Kind of the opposite?"

"You know. Kind of not shit?"

He doesn't move fast enough to hide the smile.

"'Kind of not shit'? Can we put that on the cover?"

*Eyes the same colour as clouds reflected in the sea, looking right at me.*

"Depends." I shrug, pulling out the clipboard and looking at the schedule list clipped to the top – anything, as long as I don't have to meet those eyes, because they're stopping me thinking straight. Or using words properly.

"On what?"

There's a click behind me as Jenna comes in and closes the door behind her – and suddenly I don't have an answer, because how can this guy be who I thought he was? How can *this* guy, annoying Aidan, be the same person who wrote *that* book? That book, which was everything I ever wanted, which I wished I could somehow climb into and live inside for ever.

That book.

This guy.

How?

Because with every page I'd turned I'd felt – no, more than that, I'd been *sure* – that I knew who that person was; the person who'd created that world. I could feel them inside my head.

And they didn't feel like Aidan Green.

Jenna clears her throat. "Lexi?"

And I'm back in the room.

"Hi. Yes. Sorry. Aidan – sorry, Haydn – is down for a spot on the one o'clock New Voices panel, and we've scheduled him to do a reading from the book at half past three. Hopefully there'll be a couple of people who come along to the reading off the back of the panel."

"Remind me who else is on that?" Jenna peers over my shoulder at the schedule and I read off the names of the other panellists. Aidan fidgets, looking increasingly pale as I list them.

"Seriously?"

"Aidan, you'll be fine, honestly." Jenna smiles at him, then looks over at me. "He's a bit nervous. Not done anything like this before – this is the start of our big publicity push for *Piecekeepers*, so we really appreciate you fitting us in at such short notice."

"Of course! I...my dad loved the book."

"He did?" Jenna brightens. "Fantastic! I'll make sure I follow up with him."

Aidan clears his throat, then clears it again. And again. It's a dry, hacking cough that doesn't sound entirely real. Peering round me, Jenna frowns at him. "Aidan? Are you all right?"

"Sorry, Jen. Can I maybe have some water or something? I feel a bit sick…"

"Oh, right. Yes. Of course. I'll get you some. Anything else?"

"No, thanks. Just some water."

While Jenna's rummaging in the minibar for a bottle of water, Aidan's eyes lock onto mine.

"You liked it? You promise?" he asks, and now I'm sure he's not the same person he was back in April. He *wasn't* joking. All the swagger's gone and it's like I've never met him before.

Now I think about it, I suppose it makes sense; last month, he was just here as a passenger. He could do and say whatever he wanted, keeping the knowledge of who he was and what he'd done close, like a secret. It meant he could be superior. This time, he has to stand up in front of people and say things; things about the book he wrote, about who he is and why he writes and what he thinks. He has to go and be an author. Judging by the shade of grey he's gone, this is not a fact that is lost on him.

He gulps the water Jenna hands him gratefully, then blows out a long, slow breath.

"You okay?" I ask, wrapping my arms around my clipboard. He nods.

"Right, Aidan, I've got to run down to reception to meet another author. Will you be okay with Lexi? She'll get you where you need to be – won't you, Lexi?"

Before I can even answer, Jenna is gone – leaving me to babysit Aidan.

The silence in the room is so thick you could cut it with cheese wire. It's chokingly awkward.

"So."

"So."

"What's with the name, then?" I try to lean casually against the edge of the little desk – but somehow, I get it wrong and end up sitting on the tiny tea tray on the top and tipping the whole thing over. There's a horrible clatter as very small mugs fall over and the kettle hits the carpet. "Shit. Shitshitshitshit. Sorry. I'll tidy that up."

"It's okay," he says – and there's the slightest hint of that smile again. "This is Jenna's room. I'm over the road in the other hotel. Last-minute thing."

In the lift, I try again.

"So – the name?"

"Why'd I write under a fake name, you mean?"

Well, obviously, yes. Because that's exactly what I just asked, isn't it? I make a vague "Mmmm" noise. He checks his hair in the mirrored wall and pushes his glasses further up his nose.

"Art's the family business. My dad's a curator for a gallery, and Mum's an Art History lecturer. I didn't really think a book written by their son about how there's magic that can kill people leaking out of some of the paintings would go down so well. Not with them, anyway. And I didn't want to...you know, embarrass them. They have to deal with some pretty serious art people. Collectors. The types who don't really like the idea of people having fun writing about paintings. Or having fun in general," he adds.

"But they do know about it, right? Your parents. They must have read it?"

"Yes – and no."

"They haven't read it?"

"Not their kind of book. They aren't really interested – they're more into big literary novels, not so much what I want to write." He checks himself; corrects himself. "What I *do* write."

Oh. That got serious quickly, didn't it?

"And Haydn? Where'd that come from?"

"Just sounded, you know, good?" He doesn't sound sure about that.

It does sound good though. I was picturing what Haydn Swift would look like, sound like, from the second I put *Piecekeepers* down. Trying to imagine who could write a book like that.

Turns out it's not quite who I was expecting.

The lift pings as we reach the ground floor, and even before the doors are all the way open I can see Sam looking fraught across the lobby. She spots me and starts waving at me to get my attention. Like she'd need to actually wave for me to know there's a problem.

I roll my eyes. "Can you wait here a sec?"

"Sure." He sticks his hands in his pockets and leans against one of the lobby pillars, and if I hadn't seen it with my own eyes, I wouldn't believe the change in him that has taken place in the time it took to walk out of the lift. The swagger is back.

"I need you in ops for a sec. And what are you doing with him?" Sam asks when I reach her, having dodged round a group of seven Batmans (Batmen? What's the plural of a Batman, anyway?) all having their photo taken together. "I thought you were going to fetch your author?"

"That's him," I hiss at her, grabbing her arm and towing her towards the ops office. "Haydn Swift is Aidan Green."

"You. Are. Kidding. Me." Sam emphasizes every single word. "It's a pseudonym?"

"It is."

"Oh my god! That explains last time – he must've come for—"

"Yes, yes, I know. And now I'm stuck with him for the weekend."

"How come?"

"I asked to be his liaison, didn't I? Before I knew who he *bloody* was!" I slam the ops room door open and haul her inside, throwing my clipboard on one of the tables. Across the room, Dad's friend Paul looks up from monitoring the social media feeds on his laptop, but decides he's best off pretending he can't hear or see us.

Sam is enjoying this far, far too much. "So it's really him. It's not some kind of elaborate practical joke?"

"No, it's really him."

"And how many times have you read that book now?"

"Three times in a fortnight."

"Wow." She can barely speak, she's laughing so hard.

All I can do is shake my head. And then pick up the clipboard again and bang it against the edge of the table twice. Paul blinks a couple of times, but he still says nothing.

I can't hang around, so in one quick motion, I grab a bottle of water from the stack by the door and check the message board for any surprises from Dad. Nothing – which either means everything is running perfectly, or he's so busy firefighting that he hasn't had a chance to leave a message for me. I'd prefer the former, but I'll take the latter.

"You didn't actually…you know…do the whole, 'I love you' thing, did you?" Sam asks from behind her hands.

"No, thank god. I saw him before I said anything."

"Because that would have been embarrassing. No – that would have been humiliating. Especially after last time…"

"Yes, thank you, Sam."

"I mean, more than just normal-level humiliating. That would be ground-opening-up—"

"Yes, all right, *thank you*. This is my actual life we're talking about."

"Well, yeah. That's what makes it so brilliant! I've had you going on about this guy on Skype for the last week. Haydn this, Haydn that…and now you want to deny me this teeny tiny joy?"

"Yes. Yes, I do."

"Oh, bog off." Sam shakes her head.

"Bog off? What are you – six?"

She's too busy laughing to answer: whatever it is she wanted me for, it's clearly not so urgent that it can't wait until she's done mocking me.

I suppose she's got a point. I have been driving everybody crazy about this book. Because…magic. In paintings. And chases and secret societies and history and art and *MAGIC*. It's like someone came along and poked through the inside of my head and found a list of all the things I love that aren't conventions and made it into a story – for me. I felt like that book was *mine*, and that somehow, Haydn Swift could see inside me, see everything I was and everything I cared about – everything that makes me *me* – and he said "Okay".

And then I was able to bring him to a convention.

And then…this.

If I were Sam, I'd probably be laughing too.

And just like that…I am.

"What were you flapping at me for, anyway?"

"Oh, sorry. The chairperson for the four o'clock comics panel, the one who was supposed to be asking all the questions – she's bailed. We need a new one."

"Does Dad know?"

"Who d'you think took the call?"

"Oh no. He didn't start another 'You'll never appear at another convention again' vendetta? Because last time he did that, I had to make a grovelling phone call three weeks later to persuade someone to be one of our next guests of honour. You can imagine how much fun that was, can't you?"

"Your future stepmother had just walked through the door when the call came through." The mention of Bea puts me on full alert. She's not supposed to be here! What's she doing? This is Angelo territory. This is fan conventions and cosplayers and…our stuff. Not her kind of event, all suits and sales and Powerpoint presentations. But then she's becoming an Angelo soon, too, isn't she? Too soon…

Oblivious to my racing thoughts, Sam is still burbling away to herself. "I've never seen him smile like that. Is she drugging him? It was like watching a bulldog blowing bubbles."

"Bea's here? She's in the building?"

"I don't think she was staying – said something about just passing through?"

*Thank god.*

"Right. Okay. So we need a new moderator to run the comics panel."

"Yes."

"Aaaargh. I can't do this now. I've got to get back to my guy. Who's already here that might do it?" I spin towards the membership list, which is printed in tiny, tiny font and pinned across the entire wall, because of my father's trust issues with technology, and scoop up the walkie-talkie from the table. "Bede! Bring your comics head to ops."

"What do you need?" On the other end of the radio, Bede is ready *instantly*. It's like he has some kind of magic password to activate him, and that password is *comics*. He's through the door less than a minute later.

"Here." I chuck a highlighter at him. "Find me anyone – *anyone* – who can moderate the four o'clock comics panel. Artist, writer, inker, colourist, letterer, editor…anyone. Anyone who's here and not booked for that time slot."

"I could do it?"

"Nice try, Bede. But remember what happened with the guys from 2000AD?" I shake my head in mock-disappointment.

"That was *one* time. *One*." He points the highlighter at me.

"Hey, Bede!" Sam pipes up. "How do you spell 'restraining order'?"

"Shut up," he says – but he knows none of it means anything. And they were all okay about it in the end, once Dad had offered to pay the bar bill...

"Sam? Help him. Give me a shout when you've found someone so I can run it past Dad." I snatch up the clipboard...then, on second thoughts, drop it again. "I've got to go and wrangle Aidan Two-Names."

I'm sure, as the door closes behind me, I can hear Sam making kissing noises at my back. If I didn't love my best friend as much as I do, she'd be long dead by now.

# SELF-CENSORSHIP

Having escaped Sam's mockery, I head back to the lobby to collect Aidan. Exactly what I'm going to do with him for the next half-hour (which is how long it'll be before I can dump him in the green room – where he's actually meant to be this time) I don't know. If he'd been the Haydn Swift I imagined, the glamorous, magical, superstar debut author, I'd probably have shown him around the convention a bit and made sure he knew how marvellous it all is, and by extension, how marvellous I am. But he isn't…at least, he sort of isn't, and anyway it's all a bit theoretical now because when I get back to the lobby, there is no sign of him.

I've lost Haydn Swift.

Well, that's just spectacular, isn't it?

Aidan Green, I can live without, and it's him I can't seem to get away from, somehow or other. But I actually need Haydn Swift because it's my job to be looking after him; a job I *begged* my father for. And now I've lost him, which leaves me standing in the middle of the hotel lobby with the bustle of the convention crashing around me and over me like waves, not sure what to do. I feel a little…odd.

"…don't really think that's appropriate, Max."

I know that voice, and I slam back against the nearest pillar, desperately hoping its owner hasn't spotted me. I almost knock over a toddler in a Jedi robe on my way, but other than that I think I'm in the clear.

"We agreed, Bea…"

"I didn't think you were serious about that! I know it's the only weekend, but I'm really not sure about having our wedding reception as part of the convention…"

"And I keep telling you, it's not part of the convention. It'll be a private party, just *at* the convention."

"Max. Max, I'm trying here, but all I keep hearing is 'convention convention convention'."

"It's how it works. It's how I work. You knew that when you met me. They're not just a job to me."

"But it's not—"

"Look, love. It's not till August. We'll change the date of the wedding, postpone it, postpone the honeymoon – whatever makes you happy. But that weekend, I can't just leave the convention all night. Besides, isn't the whole point of a wedding reception to invite your friends?"

"Well, yes…"

"Most of mine will be *at* the convention – not to mention Lexi."

"Are you sure about this? It's what you want?"

"Love. I've been talking to the hotel up in York, and I promise it'll be fine – better than fine. They'll take care of us. They know me, remember?"

So Bea's not as obsessed with conventions as Dad? She thinks they're just a job? Maybe hers *are*: I don't imagine putting on a skirt suit (I'll take my leggings and my skinny jeans any day, thanks) and dealing with business conventions is anywhere near as…interesting as running an event where it's perfectly normal for everyone to turn up dressed as zombies. To be honest, I can't imagine many people wanting their wedding at either kind, but it doesn't really surprise me that Dad does. I peer round the pillar to see the two of them, right there. Bea couldn't look more out of place in her white shirt and big clankety bracelets, standing there in front of the queue for the toilets, but she might as well be the only person in the world as far as Dad's concerned. He closes his hands around hers and presses her fingers to his lips and it's like she melts. I've never worked out what they see in each other; you certainly wouldn't think they'd make a couple. But *they* see something.

"Didn't anyone ever tell you it's rude to eavesdrop?" says Aidan in my ear, and he makes me jump so badly I think I actually make a squeaking sound.

"Jesus. And didn't anyone ever tell you it's rude to sneak up on somebody?"

"I didn't sneak. You were just so busy listening you didn't hear me coming." He leans out to look around the pillar, following my line of sight. "Who's that then?"

"My dad and Bea." The words just fall out of me. I could never be a spy – I'd be no use under torture at all.

"What's a Bea when she's at home?"

"They're getting married in a couple of months."

"Ah. Like that, is it?"

"It's like nothing. Where did you go, anyway? I'm supposed to be herding you to the green room to get miked up."

"Oh, I'm allowed in there now, am I? Have you got my name on your clipboard this time?"

"I've got *Haydn's* name on my clipboard," I say pointedly – and I'd show him, if I hadn't left said clipboard with said list on it in the ops room. Not that he's listening, anyway. He's too busy smiling at someone on the other side of the lobby.

*Sam.*

He's smiling at Sam.

And she's waving at him.

*Traitor.*

"Aidan?" I lay a hand on his elbow to steer him towards the green room, and he yanks his arm away and touches it like I've burned him.

"Sorry. Sorry, wasn't expecting that." He glances back over at Sam, but she's already deep in conversation with a knot of fans looking for the big comics signing. "It's Sam, isn't it? Your friend."

I check my watch. "Samira."

"She's nice. We got talking at that party last time."

*Nicer than me, clearly.*

"Yeah, Sam's great. We should really make a move to get you ready."

If I didn't know better, I'd think he couldn't hear me. But there's the faintest sheen on his forehead, and his glasses keep slipping down his nose. First-time panel nerves, and I can't say I blame him. I'm not sure I can think of anything more terrifying than having to stand up in front of a room full of strangers and convince them you're worth listening to. The couple of times I've had to introduce a panel (and we're talking "Hello, the fire exits are here, here and here. Please welcome to the stage..." – not exactly the last act of *King Lear*), I've very nearly forgotten how to *speak*. Most of the guests get nervous ahead of a panel, whether they want to admit to it or not; the actors are usually better at it – it's what they do, after all – but the authors are generally a bit rubbish at coping with the pressure. I guess that's what comes from sitting behind a computer all day and listening to the people in your head – and then having to go and talk to *actual* people. More than one time I've had to drag a writer out of the toilets where they've been throwing up out of sheer nerves. (I now carry mints at all times.)

Aidan falls into step alongside me as we thread our way through the hotel towards the green room. The lobby and corridors are filling with people heading to the next event. As we turn a corner, I see Nadiya shepherding a group of live action role-players, all of them in character and acting out whatever scenario they've agreed on today, into one of the rooms set up for their workshop. She catches sight of me, spots Aidan and starts drawing heart shapes in the air – which earns her a funny look from one of the goblins she's holding the door for.

I mouth the words "shut up" very clearly, with a variety of associated hand gestures – just in case she can't read my lips. She can, of course, and I can see her laughing…but then I realize she's not looking at me. She's looking just to my right. I follow her gaze – and there's Aidan, his head cocked slightly to one side, his arms folded across his chest and that smug little smirk plastered across his face, watching me. Nadiya, of course, disappears into the workshop space.

"Come on," I mutter, and shoulder my way through the bodies ahead of us. The green room is right at the far end of a long, sweeping corridor lined with stalls selling books, comics, trading cards, art and replica costumes, so getting from one end of it to the other is a cross between an assault course and shopping in the sales. The people who recognize me get out of my way; the others get trodden on. Politely. "'Scuse me, excuse me. Mind your backs, please.

Coming through. Thank you, yes. On your left, thank you."
As the crush gets thicker between the main panel rooms,
I have to turn back every couple of steps to check I've not
lost Aidan. He's still there – increasingly pale and sweaty –
but at the rate we're going, I'll be lucky not to lose him.

"You'd better walk in front of me. I'll steer you."

"Is it always like this?" he asks, edging between the stalls.

"Not usually." I sidestep a slightly wonky Dalek. "There
was a pipe leak above the room we were going to use as
the traders' space – like a big marketplace for this lot – and
the hotel didn't have anywhere else that was big enough.
All these guys had already paid for their tables, so we had to
put them somewhere!"

He says something back, but I can't hear it over the
general noise. A burst of static from the back pocket of
my jeans means someone's trying to get hold of me on the
walkie, but that's just going to have to wait, isn't it? There's
some jostling directly ahead and a couple of students barge
their way in between me and Aidan – who chooses that
moment to turn around and look panic-stricken.

He looks so different when he's not being smug.

More like I imagined Haydn Swift would look, I suppose.
Interesting. Even the chin's not so bad from this angle.

I manage to edge my way through to him and rest my
hands on his shoulders from behind, pointing him at the
green room door. "The one with the sign on it."

"What?" He leans back to catch my words. My hands are still on his shoulders – and at that moment, someone shoves me from behind, pressing me up against his back. There's a sharp "Sorry!" but I can barely hear it over the buzzing that fills my head.

"That way!" I practically shout it into his ear.

And my hands are still on his shoulders, and I'm still pressed up against his back.

The crowd opens up around us…and I pull away. "Come on, while there's a gap." I half-guide, half-shove him forward, and suddenly we're free of the crush and in front of the green room door.

Inside, Sam's mum and Marie are checking microphone battery packs and clipping them onto guests ahead of the next set of panels. Marie spots me and holds up a finger, meaning it'll be a minute before she can deal with Aidan.

"That felt like being perp walked," he says, ruffling his hands through his hair and adjusting his glasses. "You know, being marched off in handcuffs and thrown against the wall of a cell?" he adds – like I didn't know what that meant.

"Maybe you can tell people we met in jail…"

It's my voice saying it, I'm sure. And it's my mouth moving, my lips making the words. But I definitely, definitely did not mean to say that. Not at all.

I've just quoted *his own book* at him. I have. I've just

quoted the line the main character uses on the girl he's interested in.

Oh. My. God.

I just did that.

I did.

I want to die.

But instead of smugface, or a snarky clipboard comment, his face is completely unreadable, and it feels like I'm going to be stuck in a little humiliation time-bubble for ever. And then one corner of his mouth twitches into a smile.

"Deal," he says.

"Everything all right?" Marie hurries over carrying a tangle of wires, headsets and microphone cables. "I just need to get your battery pack clipped on, then we'll mic you up right before you soundcheck."

"There's a soundcheck?" Aidan sounds flustered.

Marie blinks at him. "Yes?"

"He's a newbie, Marie. Be gentle?"

She leads him over to the far side of the room, where she starts feeding wires down the back of his shirt and checking whether the pockets of his jeans are deep enough for the battery pack.

"Mmm-hmmm."

Sam has materialized beside me.

"Shut up."

"I see you looking. You like him."

"I'm doing my job, Sam."

"Mmm-hmmm."

"Don't you have something to do? Because if you don't, I can always find something. There's a stack of membership bags to come out of the store…"

"I am very busy indeed, thank you very much. I come bringing suck news though."

"Suck news?" I stare at her. Occasionally, Sam could do with having some kind of phrase book to help people translate her. Sadly, I think it would probably be me that had to write it.

"Tonight's a bust."

She can only mean the gig. The secret gig we've been looking forward to for ages; the one you can only get tickets for today, on the door…and then, only if you know the password. My heart sinks. "You're kidding?"

"Nope."

"Arse."

As one, the room – which is much quieter than it was a second ago – glares at me. Especially Sam's mum.

I clear my throat awkwardly. "Sorry, sorry." I turn back to Sam and lower my voice. "They're completely sold out? Already?"

"Yep. No fun for Sam and Lexi. No singing. No dancing. Only sad."

"What's this?" Aidan wanders back over, tugging at the

mic wire Marie has fed down the back of his shirt. She snaps her fingers and barks at him to leave it alone, and he drops it like a kid who's been caught pinching sweets. "Hi, Sam. Nice to see you again."

"Ai-dan." Sam makes his name bounce. "You've met your biggest fan then?" She bats her eyelashes and jerks her head towards me. I can *feel* my face heating up.

"Lexi's been looking after me before my panel." The last word sticks in his throat. Automatically, I grab a plastic cup from the water dispenser and hand it to him. He takes it and sips at it, and I wonder whether anyone else has noticed how much his hands are shaking.

"The other authors on your panel should be here in a minute. We'll introduce you and then you can chat and get ready, then about fifteen minutes before start time, Marie will take you through for soundcheck. Can I get you something else to drink? Or something to eat?"

"I couldn't eat anything. That would be a bad idea."

"You wouldn't be the first, you know."

"The first to what?"

"To throw up."

"Right. Yes. No. Okay."

Sam clears her throat. "So. I'm still here?"

"And?"

"Tonight. Where do you need me, seeing as I'm not going to be at the Carveliers gig?"

Aidan looks up from his plastic cup. "The Carveliers?"

"Sam's favourite band." I take the empty cup from him and lob it at the bin. It misses. Whoops. "They're playing at the Fleece tonight, and Dad said we could go."

"But it's sold out. So." Sam pouts. "Like I said, no fun for us. Sam is sad. Sad Sam."

"Oh. Sorry." He frowns.

"*Anyway.*" All this is just prolonging the agony. I need to get away from the source of my humiliation. "You're all set here, and I've really got to go and..."

*Be somewhere else. Be anywhere else.*

"Be doing something else. And I absolutely know what that is. Yes. So." My hands are clenching and unclenching all by themselves, and my feet are doing this weird sort of shuffle and Sam's looking at me like I'm insane – but Aidan doesn't notice because he's staring at a fixed point somewhere just in front of the green room door, where the rest of his panel have just walked in. It looks, in fact, like he's mouthing the word "Shit" to himself over and over again, and I am forgotten. Which is the way it should be.

"Come on, Sam. Got to get back to work!" I loop my arm through hers and tug her towards the door. "Good luck on the panel!"

Aidan's attention snaps back to me. "What do I do afterwards? For the reading?"

"Come back here, half an hour beforehand. I'll take you over."

He nods. "Will you let me back in, or…?" He's only half-joking.

The sound that leaves my throat is a very unhappy one because I am *not* in the mood for more clipboard jokes, but something makes me stop at the door. Maybe it's knowing this is his first panel and he's nervous – and part of my job is to make sure he relaxes. Maybe it's because I want to say it. Or maybe it's because I can still feel his eyes on me, all the way over here, and somehow it's like stepping into the sunshine when you've been in a dark room. "By the way – the book's amazing. I really did love it."

I run away before he has the chance to reply. Abandoning Sam, I run all the way down the busy corridor, all the way through the lobby and past reception, down the stairs to the creepy basement banquet hall and sharp right into the ladies' toilets, where I slam the door shut behind me and lock it, leaning my forehead against it and listening to my heart pound in my ears.

Right.

*Right.*


Aidan looks much happier when I see him in the green room before his reading. I feel a little guilty when I see him actually.

I'd meant to stick my head into the panel room and see how he was doing, but the hour disappeared thanks to an air-conditioning crisis in one of the workshop rooms, where everyone was sitting huddled in their coats like they were about to go ice-fishing – not that the hotel's maintenance guy seemed too bothered. To start with, he tried the usual I'll-get-to-it-when-I-get-to-it line they all trot out when it's a girl (me) talking to them. I'm used to it – although I can't help but wonder whether they'd pull the same bollocks with my dad… Still. After a bit of "persuading" – mostly me threatening to withhold part of the convention facilities bill in my most righteous voice – the air-con problem is resolved, and I'm doing a round of the green room with my clipboard (of course) and not at all checking every time the door opens in case it's Aidan.

And if I *were*, it would only be to make sure he isn't late for his reading.

Naturally.

When he does walk in, he's talking to someone behind him – Will, another author and the moderator from Aidan's panel, who also blurbed his book in that press release. They're in the middle of a conversation by the look of it, and Aidan almost walks right past me. He does, at first, stopping dead three steps past me and swivelling on his heels.

"Hi."

"Hi." I drop the clipboard onto the table. "How'd it go?"

"Good. I think. I mean, I don't feel like I made a complete idiot of myself, so that's probably good, right?"

"Generally. Did you get any questions?"

"A few. Not so much for me, because nobody knows who the hell I am, but the others were pretty nice and made sure I wasn't just sitting there grinning like an idiot."

"They're a good bunch." I smile at Will, who's helping himself to a beer from the green room fridge and sitting down to check his phone. He's an old hand at conventions now; this is at least his third season, so he doesn't need any babysitting. I catch his eye and he gives me a smile back, raising his beer in acknowledgement. "So," I turn back to Aidan. "Reading."

"Reading." He makes a gulping sound.

"There's nothing to worry about, I promise. No radio mic for this one – there's a static mic on the lectern."

"Mmmm?"

"So I'll take you in, and I'll give you a signal when it's time – after that, you can start when you're ready." I pick up the clipboard again – reluctantly – but he doesn't seem to notice. "There's water in there for you if you need it."

"Mmmm."

"One thing – we really have to keep to time, or everything ends up running late and I get yelled at. I'll be at the back, and I'll give you a five-minute signal."

"Sorry – five-minute signal?"

He hasn't been listening to a word I've said, has he?

"Five minutes before the end. If you're coming up to the end of your reading, you can ask if there's any questions – or you can always finish early. Up to you."

"So…I just…read?"

"That's generally how a reading goes. Jenna went through this with you, right?"

He ignores my question. "Out loud. Read."

"Ye-es?"

"To people."

"That's the idea."

"Any chance no one will turn up?" He sounds like he's only half-joking, and I can't decide whether an empty room is his greatest wish or his worst fear – or both at the same time.

"No." Not if I have anything to do with it, at least. Aidan or Haydn, I don't care; there are going to be people in that room, listening to him read from that book – even if I have to drag them in by their toes.

Aidan fidgets with the strap of his watch. "Has anyone ever…you know, forgotten how to read?"

"Forgotten how to read?"

"From nerves or whatever."

"No."

"Right."

"Still, there's a first time for everything…"

"Oh." His eyes widen and I swear I can see pure, distilled terror spinning in them. Great. I was trying to be funny, but now I feel even more guilty than I already did.

"I'm *kidding*. Everybody's nervous before their first reading, but you're going to be great. I promise."

"Mmmm." He shakes his hands down by his sides; tips his head from side to side.

"Almost time. Have you got your book?"

"My book?"

"Or script – whatever you're reading from."

"Oh. Sure. Yes. Going to need that, aren't I?" He reaches into his pocket and pulls out a narrow sheaf of papers. They're pages, torn from a book and folded to fit into his jeans.

I stare in horror at the paper he's holding. "Is that…did you tear up a *proof*?"

He looks at me blankly. "Yes?"

"You tore up the proof for your book? Your first book?"

He turns them over in his hands. "I've got a couple of them. And it's a big book. *Heavy.*"

I have never seen anyone tear up the proof copy of their first book before. Never.

But then, I don't think I've ever met anyone quite like Aidan Green before.

* * *

The author reading rooms are two small meeting rooms, opposite each other across the main corridor. Both doors are open, and Bede is changing the "Reading Here…" sign on room two, where one of our Big Names is about to read. Aidan spots the name on the door and shakes his head.

"I might as well give up and go home now."

I steer him into room number one, where a handful of people are already settled into their seats and waiting – probably off the back of his panel appearance this morning. I pull the last reader's sign off the door and stick up Haydn Swift's. Aidan stares at it as though he's forgotten who that is.

"Go make yourself comfortable at the lectern if you like. You've got a couple of minutes."

But he's not listening to me. He's in that place they all go to in their heads: unfolding his pages (torn pages, from a proof – wait till I tell Bede!) and scanning them, his lips moving along with the words as he gauges his speed.

"Wait – Lexi!"

"Yep?" I stuff my ball of sign-sticking Blu-tac back in my pocket.

"There's swearing. In the bit I was going to read. I didn't even think about it until…" He gives a pointed glance around the room. Well, there's no kids there, but it's a whole different thing dropping an F-bomb on your computer to doing it in a roomful of strangers.

"See how you go. It depends on the actual swearing, really…" I glance at my watch. I need him up at the lectern, ready to start. A couple of stragglers slip past us and take seats at the back of the room. "My dad always says it's the *words* people get offended by – not the intensity or the emotion, you know? So maybe just censor it if you're worried. Can you do that while you're reading?"

"Censor it?"

I really, really need him to start – or we're going to fall behind. Bede's already shut the door to the other room, which means they've started. I practically shove Aidan at the lectern. "Think about it this way – they bleep out swearing on television sometimes, don't they? But you don't lose the feel of it. You still get everything behind it."

It's like a light bulb goes on in his head. "Right. Thanks."

The second he steps behind the lectern, Aidan vanishes and Haydn takes his place. It's the strangest thing, because I don't know what happened, or how. I just know that the guy standing there taking a sip of water from the glass isn't the guy who was panicking about forgetting how to make sounds in public. This guy is confident and smiling and – not to put too fine a point on it – ever so slightly arrogant. I find myself wondering whether there were seedlings of Haydn when I met him that first time; sure as hell feels like it.

I decide against closing the door. The corridor outside is fairly quiet (at long last) and Aidan's voice carries well:

an open door might just entice a few more people in. He starts his reading and I recognize this section of the book – it's the confrontation between Jamie, the main character, and one of the Piecekeepers. It's a good choice and, sure enough, another couple of listeners appear in the doorway. They pause; then Aidan reads a joke and they edge into the room and sit down. And even though it's not me reading and it's not my book and it's not like he's my friend or anything…I feel a swell of pride because in a tiny way, this is down to me. I brought him here.

I'm good at this. The picking guests, getting them in front of an audience who may never have heard of them, but who might just leave as devoted and lifelong fans. The planning the panels to put people on, who to put them with… I know I can do this. I'm better than I would be at anything else, and I know it. And I won't let someone like Aidan Green throw me off balance.

Aidan's crowd grows – slowly but surely, a steady trickle of people come in and take a seat. We're ten minutes into a twenty-five minute slot, and he's found his stride. His words flow; sentences wind their way around the dull beige walls of the meeting room and paint them with colour. The hotel we're sitting in becomes the Piecekeepers' headquarters – all ancient stone walls hung with oil paintings and tapestries: art from across time and around the world. His pace picks up as he reaches Jamie's argument with the Curator, and I take a second to check the rest of the afternoon on my clipboard.

"'Give me the *bleeping* key.'"

The spell is broken with a jolt. I look up. Did I imagine that?

He's still reading. "'What did you say?'"

"I said, 'Give me the *bleeping* key!'"

Then it hits me. He's censoring himself. He's *bleeping* himself.

Just. Like. I. Said.

I did this.

Oh. My. God.

Sam scuttles across from the door; I didn't even know she was there, but she must have stopped to listen. She leans over the back of my seat in the last row.

"What the hell's he doing?" she hisses. "He sounds like a shit grime track!"

"He was worried about swearing…" I mumble from behind my hands, which are now clamped over my mouth. It doesn't stop her (a) hearing, and (b) figuring out what I've done.

"This is *you*?!"

"No. Yes. Oh god." I hide behind my clipboard. "Is it really bad?"

We both look up at him – Sam from behind my chair, me from behind my board. We look at the room, at everyone listening. None of them seem bothered. More importantly, none of them seem *bored*. Nobody's got up and left and nobody's checking their phones or whispering to their mates.

They're *listening* – and so are we. Without even meaning to, Sam has slipped into the seat beside mine and is leaning forward as though it will help her to hear better, get her closer to what happens next.

I can't blame her; Aidan's a natural. It's like he was made for this, and I could listen to him read for *hours*.

I mean, it *is* my favourite bit of the book. Of course. That's what it is.

# SUNG IN A MINOR KEY

"Yeah, but they didn't make you dress up, did they? It's not like someone held you down and forcibly dressed you as an elf."

Bede doesn't look impressed – although I can't tell whether it's Sam's piss-taking or the fact he's currently dressed like a stray from Middle Earth that's causing it.

"They were one short."

"I thought that was the dwarves," Nadiya says casually, walking past with a boxful of power cables. She doesn't even break her stride when Sam and I both applaud her – but she glances over her shoulder at us and grins. "Thank you, I'll be here all weekend!"

Bede looks even less impressed.

"That's what you get for offering to help out the LARPers." I can barely breathe, never mind get the words out. Bede's legs were not designed for tights. Let alone shiny ones. "Are you sure they weren't just messing with you?"

He shakes his head sadly. "This never happens to any of you lot."

"Because," Sam chimes in from her spot on the empty registration table, swinging her legs back and forth, "none of us actually *join in*."

"I'm sorry – much as I'd love to stay and carry on this little team bonding exercise, I have to go and give an elf his tights back." Bede stalks off with his head high, and the sounds of our deeply unsupportive and desperately unsympathetic laughter in his ears. His dignity remains intact(ish) most of the way across the lobby – right up until the moment he steps into the lift just as Aidan steps out. They collide smack in the middle of the lift doors, and Bede swears in a most un-elfish way. Sam laughs so hard I worry she'll pull a muscle somewhere – but as usual, she goes one better. She somehow manages to fall right off the table, backwards, in a shrieking cloud of laughter and swear words.

Aidan raises an eyebrow at the carnage. "I'm missing something."

Sam rolls onto her stomach under the table. "Aidan!"

He leans sideways and peers down at her. "Evening…"

"Loved your reading. Seriously. It was aces."

"Seriously?"

"Seriously." She nods.

"Thanks. That means a lot."

A fist clenches tightly shut somewhere in the pit of my stomach. It's like someone has tied my insides into a knot and there's a person pulling on each end of the rope.

Well, that particular train of thought can…umm, get knotted.

"Anybody going for dinner – oh." Nadiya is back from dumping the stuff in the ops office. "Why's Sam under the table? Isn't that usually your spot, Lexi?"

"You are on *fire* tonight, aren't you? All this comedy."

I'm aware of the quizzical look Aidan is giving me, but I ignore it for just a couple of seconds longer than I need to – and then I panic in case he thinks I'm ignoring him. Which I kind of am.

"It's a long story," I mutter in his general direction.

"You like sitting under tables?"

"Turns out it's not so long after all."

With his usual timing, my father breaks the tension – choosing this exact moment to summon me via the walkie-talkie currently tucked under my arm. "Lexi? Where are you?"

I fumble for it, drop it (twice) and finally manage to stop it howling with static at me. "Here!"

"Which is…?"

"Registration. We've just closed the desk for tonight. I figure if any day members aren't here by now, they're not coming."

"Oh. Right."

He's using his Just-One-More-Thing voice.

I reply using my You-Can't-See-Me-Rolling-My-Eyes-

Over-The-Walkie voice. "Is everything okay?"

There's a long, long pause.

"Dad?"

"It's fine. Nothing to worry about – I'll deal with it tomorrow."

"That doesn't sound good…"

"No, no. It'll be all right. You and Sam go have fun at your gig."

"But the…" I stop.

"Lexi?"

"Nothing. Thanks."

"Don't be out too late. Come find me in the bar when you get in."

"Will do. See you later!" I click off the walkie and put it on the reg desk, pretending not to see Sam staring at me as she clambers out from under the table.

"You didn't tell him the Carveliers is off?"

"I did, but he's forgotten. You know my dad. Besides, if he thinks we're not going, he'll only give us something to do."

"About that." Aidan is leaning back against the table, and he has something in his hand. Sam turns to say something to him – but her eyes skip his face entirely and lock onto the strips of plastic he's holding.

"Are those…wristbands?" Her voice climbs to somewhere vaguely operatic. I didn't think it could actually get that high.

Aidan's got his smug chin face on.

"They are."

"Not to…?"

"Yep."

"Oh. Migod."

"Lexi?" And he actually holds the wristbands out to *me*.

"You're kidding? Are those for the Carveliers? Tonight?"
He nods.

"How did you get those? It's completely sold out! They're not even putting people on a waiting list!"

"I'm with the same agency as them. After you said it was sold out, I gave my agent a call and asked if there were any hospitality passes going in the music department. Turns out there were three."

"Three?" I look at the pair of wristbands he's holding out.

"These are guest bands, which means you have to be signed in. By me. Sorry."

I'm in the middle of thinking up a cutting (yet gently witty and reasonably grateful) reply when Sam leaps forward and snatches the bands out of his hand with a grin. "Thank you! That's amazing! You're amazing! I…" She freezes mid-dance. "These are…these… These are VIP bands. They…they…"

"Did I forget to mention? These bands come with an invite to go backstage after the show."

The sound that comes out of Sam's mouth is like nothing I've ever heard before. It's a sort of yelpy squeaky hiccup-cough. She looks like she's about to burst into tears any moment too. I've never seen her so *happy*; it's like seeing a kid version of Sam in front of me – and in that second, in that heartbeat, I want to hug Aidan for doing this for her. I really, really want to – particularly when she starts running laps around the lobby, narrowly avoiding one of the hotel staff on his way out of the bar carrying a tray of cocktails. (Whoops. Dad'll hear about that.) I can't be grudging about it at all.

Instead, I look Aidan in the eye. "Thank you. I mean it – really. Thank you. She'd been looking forward to the gig for *months*. You've made her weekend. Year. Life."

"It's no problem," he says with a shrug – and maybe it's the lighting in here, but I could swear he looks a little more flushed than he did a minute ago. And over Sam, dancing around the lobby, and the noise of a group of Musketeers meeting up ahead of dinner, I'm not completely sure whether he actually says anything else or whether it's a trick of the acoustics. But – for one insane second – it almost sounds like he says, "Besides, I didn't do it for Sam."

The Fleece is – not surprisingly – packed. It smells…warm. Sweaty – but in a good sort of way. It smells like dancing;

like hundreds of feet attached to hundreds of people bouncing up and down on the floor and trying not to bash into the narrow pillars holding up the ceiling. Sam hasn't stopped grinning all night – not since we walked past the long, long line at the door and flashed our wristbands while Aidan signed us in with a casual, "We're on the list."

"You hear that?" Sam squeezed my arm so hard I thought she was going to break it. "We're. On. The. List."

"Sam? You are the least cool person I know. The very least cool."

But it *was* cool, and so is being here, surrounded by people who aren't about to turn around and ask me for something. These are just people. There's nobody here I have to look after – apart from Sam, who's pogoing like her life depends on it somewhere in the middle of the floor.

I pick my way through the wall of People I Am Not Responsible For to find Aidan, lurking at the back where it's quieter and the air's cooler – not that it smells much better.

"Everything okay?" He has to raise his voice over the music and the crowd's singing (shouting).

"It's great! I just needed a breather."

"Sam's still out there?"

I give him something between a nod and a shrug.

I lean over the bar and shout to the barman for a couple of bottles of water. He nods to show he heard me, and carries on pulling pints of lager for people who have already ordered.

Aidan sidles up alongside me. "I meant to say thank you – for today."

"What do you mean?" The barman bangs two sealed bottles of water down in front of me and I pull out a handful of change – but Aidan shakes his head.

"I've got this."

"No – you got us *in*."

"It's a couple of bottles of water, Lexi," he says as he pays. "It's not like you're stinging me for a magnum of vodka."

"I thought only wine, champagne and stuff, came in magnums?"

"Sounds like you know more about it than I do." He raises an eyebrow at me like he's trying to be provocative. "Get through a lot of magnums, do we?"

I snort, picking up the bottles and tucking one under my arm for Sam. "I've been helping my dad on these conventions since I was a kid. One of the first proper jobs he gave me was to check the F&B orders."

Aidan frowns. "Eff and bee?"

"Food and beverage. It's what the hotel charge for…" I catch myself right before his eyes glaze over. "Wow. Sorry. This is the most boring conversation in the world, right here. It's hard to switch this stuff off sometimes."

"Do you like it?"

"Like what? Checking the F&B? God, no. That's a nightmare."

"I meant the conventions. Helping your dad."

"I do. It's hard to fit it all in sometimes, but I really, really do." I gulp down half my water in one go.

"Fit it in?"

"Around sixth-form college. Apparently, running a convention doesn't count as a good enough reason to get off doing essays. I've tried."

"Why don't you ask your dad if you can do less?"

I choke on the mouthful of water I've half-swallowed.

"Do less? For the conventions, you mean?"

"Uh, yes?" He looks puzzled.

"No way."

"Why not?"

"Because I love it." I ponder this, then decide I need to explain a bit more coherently than that. "At least, I love it when everything goes right."

"And when it doesn't?"

"Then I love it a bit less, maybe? But I do still love it." I cock my head to one side and look at him – and even though his face is neutral, scanning the crowd, I think what I've said makes sense to him. "I imagine it's a bit like writing, from what I've heard authors say."

"Funny," he says. "I was just thinking the same thing. On a good day, it's the best thing in the world, but on a bad day…" He winces. "Can't seem to stop doing it though." His pained expression turns to a grin. "I guess you know how that feels."

The room is suddenly hotter than I imagined a place could ever be. I am standing on the *surface of the sun*.

I am *changing the subject*.

"Talking about writing...I know you said your book wasn't your parents' sort of thing, but they must be pretty proud of you, right?" I wave my bottle at Aidan by way of punctuation – and slosh water all over his shoes. "Oops. Sorry."

"Proud? Why?"

"You're an *author*. You write books, and then you get to go and read things you made up in your own head to other people and they *listen*. That's pretty impressive."

"You think it's impressive?" His eyes narrow, and somehow they look warmer, lighter. Almost mischievous.

Ah. "I was theoretically saying that *some* people might find it impressive."

"But you don't?"

"I'm my father's daughter. You've got to be a *pretty* big deal to impress me."

"Like my book did, you mean?"

I don't know how to answer. Is this a game? Is it a way to avoid talking about his parents – because don't think for one second I didn't notice that particular conversational swerve?

Am I supposed to have a clever comeback? Or am I meant to tell him the truth?

And what if I get it wrong?

*"I didn't do it for Sam…"*

*What if I imagined he said that; and what if he actually* did?

"Where did you go? I'm dying out there! Oh, water. Amazing."

Sam saves me.

Sam always saves me; sometimes from other people, more often from myself.

But this time, do I even want to be saved?

She snatches the second bottle of water from under my arm and downs the whole thing.

"How good are they? HOW good? Are you coming back or what?" She grabs my hand and starts towing me into the middle of the crowd – then stops. "Hold up." She drops my hand. "Did I just…were you guys…what *was* that?"

I shake my head and laugh. "I don't even know."

Even in the dim light, I can see her eyes narrow at me.

"Lexi Angelo. You *like* him."

"I do not."

"You. Do." Her whole face lights up with it, this shining realization she's had. "And you know what? You are going right back over there to—"

A loud squeal of feedback from the stage makes everyone comedy-groan.

"We're almost done for the night, but we've got time for one more song."

A round of applause. Cheering, and a few shouts for more.

"And we actually want to dedicate this one to somebody here tonight, kind of a friend of a friend of the band – can we have the house lights on, maybe?"

The lights around the bar fade up a little – and Elis, the Carveliers's singer, peers out into the crowd.

"Sam? Where are you?"

I feel Sam tense. "It's not me," she whispers – more to herself than to me.

Nobody answers.

On the stage, Elis shades his eyes with the flat of one hand, the other keeping his guitar slung behind his back. "Samira?"

Nobody answers.

It feels like the silence drags on for ever. She's shaking. She's actually shaking; I can see the great lion's mane of her (natural, for once) hair moving.

I crack. I stick one hand straight up and wave it madly, pulling at her arm with the other. "She's here!" I yell. Elis looks right at us as I half-drag, half-carry her through the crowd as it parts in front of us. "Sam's here!" I risk a glance back at her face midway to the stage and she looks totally dazed; she's either about to burst out laughing or into tears. It could go either way. I get her all the way to the front and park her right in front of Elis, who beams down at her.

"Nice to meet you, Sam. You having a good time?"

"'s." She nods, but you'd have to be standing where I am to hear her.

"Do you know 'Sung in a Minor Key'?'

"'S." Louder this time – loud enough for him to hear.

"You want to hear it?"

She doesn't even manage to make a sound this time. Just a nod, and a smile so wide it could blind the moon.

As the Carveliers launch into their last song of the night and Sam beams and sings along, I look round – and right at the very back of the room, behind all the faces and through all the voices, I'm sure I see him.

He's smiling, and he's looking right at me.

# JUNE

## HOME

To: <Max Angelo>
From: <Lucy Spiegel>
Date: 7 June; 14:32
Subject: Haydn Swift / PIECEKEEPERS launch confirmation

Dear Max,

Lovely to speak to you yesterday – and thank you again for all the support you've been giving us with the PIECEKEEPERS publicity push. Our commissioning editor Rebecca has asked me to let you know how much she appreciates it, and she'll be in touch directly soon.

In the meantime, can we go ahead and confirm that launch slot for Haydn at the convention at the end of this month? We'd really like to do something with you in Brighton – the book isn't officially released until just after the convention, but we can arrange for stock to be shipped to the venue as an exclusive.

Haydn's asked me to pass on his thanks to Lexi for looking after him so well during his events – and to you for inviting him. I understand from my colleague Jenna that you've asked him to take part in one of the larger author panels next time around – when are we likely to have a time for this?

(Obviously, I don't want him to have to rush between the launch and panel events if at all possible…)

   Very best,
   Lucy

---

To: <Lucy Spiegel>
From: <Max Angelo>
Date: 7 June; 15:25
Subject: Re: Haydn Swift / PIECEKEEPERS launch confirmation

Hi Lucy,

Thanks for your message. I'm happy to confirm the
8 p.m. slot on the Saturday for the PIECEKEEPERS launch –
you'll have the main signing room for an hour. If you have
any associated publicity materials to display (posters, cut-
outs, bookmarks and so on) please send them direct to the
hotel CLEARLY MARKED FOR MY ATTENTION and labelled
PIECEKEEPERS LAUNCH – or alternatively, bring them along
to the convention operations office AT LEAST three hours
before the event is due to start.

   For a launch of this size, we would generally suggest
providing a glass of wine/soft drink with every book
purchased; it does seem to help bring in the crowds –

and more importantly, gets them in the mood for book buying!

I attach the hotel's F&B sheet, which – as you will see – has a range of catering options from the hotel's house wine (red/white/both) and orange juice through sparkling wine up to champagne and canapés, depending on your budget.

Please complete the form as appropriate and send it back to Lexi at the usual email address no later than June 15th. Either Lexi or Marie will be in touch in due course regarding general programming.

We look forward to welcoming you, Jenna and your author to our convention later in the month.

Max

# JUNE

## BRIGHTON

# PIN-UP

"Are we sure proper clothes are compulsory? I really do have a gold bikini in my suitcase…"

"Leia's slave bikini? I don't think so." I glare at Sam across the top of the copy of *SixGuns* magazine she's using as an impromptu fan. "And that's mine," I add, yanking it out of her sweaty hands.

"Take it. It's not even helping." She slumps across the ops office desk, peeling her T-shirt away from the back of her shoulders with one hand. "And those windows really don't open?"

"Nope. I tried."

There are windows along one entire wall of the ops room in this hotel. They don't look out onto anything more exciting than the grimy concrete of a blank wall – and while they're all sealed shut "for security purposes", the one thing they do let in is the sun, even with the feeble, tissue-thin curtains drawn – which is in full-on June heatwave mode. I have never been so hot in my entire life.

Across the road from the hotel, the beaches of Brighton and Hove are packed with people in varying shades of crimson; this morning, the traditional "heatwave" photo of them spread across the pebbles was on the front pages of all the newspapers. This did not go down well with a convention crew stuck in the un-air-conditioned bowels of a hotel for two days, getting increasingly sticky and sweary and sweaty. It may be great weather for sunbathing, but it's pretty miserable for a convention that takes place entirely indoors. Thanks to Dad's…*robust* conversation with the hotel manager, we've managed to get additional fans installed in all the panel and screening rooms, but the author's reading room is like an oven, and a couple of them have already gone rogue and led their audiences outside and across the road to the seafront and read there. I don't blame them at *all*. Even if it did seriously piss Dad off.

"Is that your boyfriend's cover?" Bede slides the magazine down to his end of the desk.

"He's not my boyfriend."

"Mm-hmm." He turns it face-up, and there is Aidan. The photographer has put him on the steps to the National Gallery, and obviously told him to look "moody", because he's half-scowling, half-squinting at the camera. Naturally they've got him holding out his hand and photoshopped some kind of weird glowing ball into it – because, *magic*. And I'm relatively sure that moody squint is because he's not wearing his glasses, so he can't even see the camera.

"Look at it. There's no glowy magic balls in *Piecekeepers*," I mutter.

Bede makes a snorting sound that could have been a rubbish attempt to hide a laugh. "At least they didn't put him in a cloak with one of those big floppy hoods. You know – Traditional Fantasy Book Cover Number One."

"Hooded Man With Sword?"

"Hooded Man With Big Shiny Magic Glowing—"

"Stop." I hold up my hand. "Can't."

"Well, I think he looks good," Sam says, perking up and spinning the magazine back along the desk, away from Bede. "And there's a massive interview inside. They loved the book too." She flips it open to the start of Aidan's feature: a full-page photo (thankfully without the ball) and a three-page interview. "Oooh. Have you seen who's been cast as Jamie in the film?"

"Mmm." If I rest my forehead on the desk and then lift it ever so slightly, there's a second when it feels like my skin is stuck to the wood and peeling off my face. It's the weirdest sensation. I do it again.

"Hey! Look! There's a thing about us in the event reviews page! Well. Not *us*, exactly..."

"Where?" Bede scrambles round to her, peering over her shoulder. "'Last month's convention...blah blah blah... big names...yaddah yaddah...but the procession of Angelo's greatest hits…" He stops suddenly. I know what that means.

"Hit me," I tell the desk.

"No, it's…"

"They're being bitchy about Dad again, aren't they?"

"Really, it's fine. Just the usual boring stuff."

"Who wrote it?"

"I dunno. There's no name – it's just the regular convention column."

"Give it here?" I click my fingers and Bede slides the magazine back to me. Peeling my face off the desk again, I sit up and focus. He's right; there's no byline on the article, but a quick flip to the contributors listing confirms my suspicions.

"There." I plant my fingertip alongside one name and put my head back on the wood. It's cooler than the air.

"Damien Woodman?"

I actually *hear* Sam pull a face. "The Brother."

"Bingo."

"So what's that about?"

"One: he never misses a chance to get a dig in, not when it comes to that column. Two: I bet you any money he's going to try and book Aidan for one of his autumn events. Any money you like. And I bet he'll do what he always does and make it about the film adaptation – there'll be a panel with someone from the studio, and a couple of the actors and the screenwriter…"

"I heard someone say it was going to be Joss Whe—"

"Quite. And Aidan will be tacked on the end like a crap show pony with ribbons in its tail."

We all take a moment to ponder this particularly vivid mental image.

"It's the heat," I mutter. Too late; they've already judged me to the full extent of their judginess.

Bede hauls himself out of his seat. "I've got to go check the water supplies in the screening room."

"Last time I was down there, it was the coolest place in the building. The guy with the short horror film event was ecstatic – he had a full house."

I really, really don't want to leave this room. Outside that door is a world where I have to be organized and polite and sensible and responsible – and actually, all I want to do is lie down on the floor and have someone pour ice on me. At this point, I don't even have any preference as to who that would be. Anyone – as long as they bring lots and lots of ice.

"I'll swap you the screening room for the cosplay workshop?" Sam asks hopefully. Bede frowns, then shakes his head. "Hot glue? Today? No thanks."

"Coward."

The door closes behind them, and there's the faintest hint of a draught. It smells of feet. Nice.

I peel my face off the desk again and my legs off the plastic chair. My shorts feel ever so slightly damp. Also nice.

I paste my most professional attempt at a smile on my face, open the door, step out into the main corridor and…

"I thought you must be hiding in there – your flying monkeys passed me on the way over. Oh, hey – is that my issue? I haven't even seen it yet."

Aidan snatches the magazine, which I only now realize I've rolled up and brought out with me. He unfurls it and studies the cover. There's a pause.

Then… "Wow."

"Wow?"

"Glowy magic ball. Right there."

My stomach lurches in a way I don't quite understand. It must be the heat. Maybe I'm dehydrated.

"It's a good cover. Very…" I fumble for the right word and eventually settle on: "Moody. Very moody."

"I was going to go with 'gimpish'."

"That's not even a real word."

"It is now. I made it one. See how that works?"

"Doesn't count until it's in a book."

"Is that so?" He tips his head to one side.

"You are not going to put it into a book just to prove a point."

"You don't know what I'm capable of. I could do *anything*."

"You could. But before that, you've got a panel and… oh no."

Out of the corner of my eye, I spot *him* midway down the hall. He must have come out of the screening room and spotted Aidan – and now he's bearing down upon us with the inevitability of an iceberg; the difference being that an iceberg would actually be pretty welcome right now.

"It's the Brother. He's seen you. And he's coming – you don't want to be here when he arrives, because you'll never get shot of him."

"What? The who?"

"Walk with me. Quickly. Walk with me this way."

Without thinking about it, I loop my arm through his, the way I would with Sam, and I start walking.

"Where are we going?"

"Just keep walking, okay?"

"Can I keep the magazine?"

"Will that make you walk faster?"

"No, but like I said, I haven't had a chance to read it yet."

"Fine. Keep it."

The doors to the service corridor are directly ahead – and if I know the Brother, he won't follow us there. Service areas are always off-limits to general members; back there, it's hotel (and if they're looking for, say, a missing dog… convention) staff only. And Damien Woodman may be a prick, but he knows the rules. I shove Aidan through the double swing doors and peep back through the porthole window – as I thought, Damien stops dead in his tracks.

He stares at the door a moment longer, then shrugs and wanders off, pulling a convention schedule from his pocket as he goes.

"You can thank me later," I say – and I turn round, bumping right into Aidan, who is standing much closer to me than I realized. "Umm. Sorry."

Even in this unbearable heat, at this distance I can feel the warmth from his body radiating out of him. Close up, he smells of deodorant and...I don't know, some kind of cologne or aftershave or *something*. He smells like the sea, like he's just stepped out of the sun.

*I smell like crap.*

*Maybe he won't notice.*

Why is he so much taller than me? I hate having to look up to people, like they've got some kind of...moral superiority over me – which Aidan Green absolutely does *not* have.

I follow the line of his jaw, his chin – that chin. Still not over that chin. His mouth, his lips...

All the way up to his eyes, which meet mine. And they're laughing, but somehow it's not *at* me. Not like it was before. He's looking right into me.

All the way into me.

I have to say something.

I don't want to say anything. I just want to stand here and...smell him.

I have to say something. This whole situation is making me look creepy. Creepy, creepy Lexi.

I say the first thing that comes into my head.

"How come you're not wearing your glasses?"

*Well done, Lexi. Smooth. First you drag him into a service corridor, then you ask about his glasses.*

He shrugs, but his eyes never leave mine. "It depends how vain I'm feeling. I can't wear contacts, so it's a choice between looking like a nerd or bumping into things I can't see."

"They're not nerdy."

"That comes direct from someone who never got called 'Four Eyes' at school."

"Did you? Get called 'Four Eyes', I mean?"

"What do you think?"

"Umm…yes? How about now?"

"Nobody's called me Four Eyes for at least three weeks, no."

"No!" A stray hair glues itself to my clammy cheek. I peel it off and tuck it back somewhere behind my ear. My hands feel wrong, like I've not eaten in too long or like I've just been running. "So how vain would you say you're feeling right now? On a scale of, say, one to a million?"

He looks at me quizzically, so of course I keep on talking. Of course I do. "And you really can't see that well? How many fingers am I holding up?"

*Who is this idiot other Lexi who has taken control of my mouth and can she please just…not?*

I hold up three fingers, because what the hell else am I going to do?

"I don't know." He doesn't even look. Instead, he tilts his head forward, just a fraction of a centimetre, just the breadth of a hair, as he whispers it: "All I can see is you."

"LEXI!"

Sam's voice fills the service corridor and we jump apart as though someone's lit a fire between us. My heart is pounding hard enough to bruise my ribs.

"Sam?"

"I think your shorts just yelled at you," Aidan laughs, pointing at the walkie-talkie aerial sticking out of my back pocket.

"Oh. Shit. Yes." I pull it out and press the talk button. "Hi, Sam."

"Where's Ai…Haydn? I need him in the green room for his mic check and his publicist is *freaking out*. Send him over, will you?"

"What makes you think he's with me?"

"Oh, please. Nadiya saw you guys disappearing into the service corridor behind reception." She drops her voice to a guttural whisper, but in the bare concrete corridor it's still foghorn-loud. "*I have eyes everywhere.*"

"I'll…I'll bring him right over."

It's just as well there's already a heatwave going on out there, because hopefully nobody will notice the extra heat from the small super-fiery sun that used to be my face.

"Come on, come on, come on..." Sam is actually standing in the doorway to the green room, holding the door open and shouting at me as I hustle Aidan inside. Our little detour to avoid the Brother has left precious little time to mic him ahead of the panel – let alone soundcheck.

"Sorrysorrysorry..." I mutter.

"Never mind that. Stand here," she tells Aidan through the mic leads she's holding in her teeth, as she turns him round by the shoulders and runs a cable down the back of his T-shirt, clipping the battery pack onto his belt. "Mmm. Clammy," she laughs. "What *have* you been doing?"

"Shut up, Sam," I snap, ducking round in front of Aidan to make sure his mic is resting in the right place. "Did you check the levels?"

"I stood in for him at soundcheck – just don't say anything in too manly a voice, 'kay?" she adds to him, before grabbing him again and pointing him at Bede, who's waiting by the exit. "Go."

\* \* \*

The green room slowly empties; I wait for the door to close and then I go and hug the tower fan in the corner, draping as much of myself over it as I possibly can.

It's coming. I know it is. It's just a question of waiting.

Wait for it…

Wait for it…

Any second…

"So…you two seem to be getting cosy."

"I'm doing my job, Sam. He's doing his."

"Mmm-hmm."

"What? Just because he did one nice thing, it doesn't mean I'm crazy about him. Not like *you*, clearly."

"Mmm-hmm." She bats her eyelashes at me as I let go of the fan and perch on the edge of one of the sofas.

"I like his book, okay? It's a good book. And maybe I *was* a bit harsh before – I mean, a *complete* jerk couldn't write like that, could they?"

"They probably could." She throws herself at the sofa beside mine, and lands with a mid-level *thud*. "Ow. Are sofas supposed to thud?"

"This one's just as hard." I rap on the cushion with a knuckle. It clonks. "These are definitely not the seats they promised us."

Sam squints across at me from her position face down on the sofa and I give her a sarcastic look, just to let her know I'm not thrilled with her line of questioning. I can almost see it bounce off her and ping towards a photocopy of today's schedule, stuck to the wall. Sam's superpower is some kind of Teflon coating – everything just slides off her. Or is that Kevlar? I think we had an essay question on them in GCSE science, but I was in the middle of a guest cancellation crisis that week so I can't be sure. It's one of them, anyway. Maybe both. Hard to say.

To prove my point, she wriggles over onto her back and holds her hands up in the air to examine her nails, which appear to be painted yellow with tiny Batman logos on them. "You know what your problem is, don't you?"

"Does it matter? You're going to tell me anyway."

"You're worried you like a guy who doesn't exist."

"I'm not worried I like anybody." (Which is true. I'm not even going to like Sam much longer if she keeps this up...)

"You like Haydn Swift, except he's just as much a figment of Aidan Green's imagination as those bloody wizards you keep banging on about."

"*Magicians.*"

"Them too. But you know I'm right – even your mum agrees with me..."

"Woahwoahwoah. You spoke to my mum?" I stand up. This is new. This is...unsettling. "Why did you speak to my mum? How do you even have her number?"

"She gave it to me ages ago, remember? And I was calling Leonie, actually. I needed help with my French project."

"So you rang *my mum's girlfriend*?"

"She's French, isn't she?" Sam rolls her eyes at me, missing my entire point. "*Anyway.* Your mum thinks I'm right."

"My mother's affection for you has clearly clouded her otherwise sound judgement," I mutter. "What did you say to her?"

"Not much. I just told her that you were conflicted." She sits up and crosses her legs on the stupidly hard sofa. "I didn't start it – she asked how you were," she adds, looking wounded. Maybe she didn't miss my *entire* point after all.

"What she was really asking was how I'm handling the Bea thing."

"She was?" Sam looks genuinely surprised. She's never been good at working out what people mean – what they *really* mean – when they ask things. My best friend always says what *she* means outright (at the time, at least – she's also the mistress of I-changed-my-mind-what's-your-problem?) and expects everyone else to do the same. It's one of the reasons I love her.

Sam rearranges the platinum silver wig she's wearing today. It can't be cool, not in this heat. Maybe it's boiling her brain? That would explain a lot, come to think of it. "Is she coming this weekend?"

"Mum?"

"Bea."

My future-stepmother's appearance at the hotel last time did not go unnoticed – or unmentioned – by most of the con staff. Little whispers curled their way around the bar, the ops office, the lobby like smoke; *it's her, she's here, is that Bea?* She's become this mythic presence over the last few months, heard about but rarely seen. Like the Loch Ness monster. Or Bigfoot.

I keep having to stop myself from wondering whether she was testing the waters, deciding whether she wants to get involved in this part of Dad's life, just like she's wormed her way into all the other parts...

*No, Lexi. That's not fair. You're being unfair. It's his life, it's up to him who's part of it.*

*But what about me?*

*I...should probably stick to thinking about schedules right now.*

*At least with schedules I know where I am.*

*Schedules don't let you down; it's people that let you down. People can seem like they're one thing and then turn out to be something else. Schedules are easy. People are hard.*

I shake my head at Sam, who's still waiting for me to answer. "Is she coming this weekend? I don't think so. Not with the wedding so soon, and apparently she's got a load of work to finish up before then – so Dad says, anyway."

"When I get married, I'm going to do it somewhere sunny. On a beach. And everyone will have to come in costume."

"York can be sunny." Even when my father's getting remarried, I can't seem to stop defending him. There's something wrong with that equation, somehow; it feels all backwards, like I'm the parent and he's the kid.

"Imagine Bea's face if everyone turned up in cosplay…" Sam's eyes glitter.

"No. No, no, no." I am picturing that very thing, and it doesn't end well.

A bead of sweat tracks slowly down between my shoulder blades. "I'm going to go stick my head into panel room one and make sure they're not dying in there."

"You mean you're going to check how Aidan's doing, don't you?"

"Haydn." The name slips from my lips before I even feel it coming. Sam tilts her head to one side and eyes me thoughtfully.

"Mmm-hmm."

"I'm trying to be professional," I say, pushing the door open. "You should give it a whirl sometime."

And as I walk out into the corridor, I trip over the step I had totally forgotten was there.

"Mind yourself, love," says Rodney from behind his newspaper.

On the other side of the door, Sam's too busy laughing to say anything…

\* \* \*

The panel room is dimly lit, and – given the fact it's packed out and standing room only – surprisingly cool, thanks to those extra air-con units we brought in. Aidan…Haydn – whoever he really is – is at one end of the panel table, listening to another author – a woman with long hair and a big hat, even in this temperature – answer a question. He looks relaxed and happy; all hint of the nerves I saw last time have disappeared. Maybe it was Aidan who was nervous; Aidan the writer, the behind-the-scenes guy who got called names at school. Haydn; what does he have to be nervous about? Haydn's halfway to being a rock star. One who writes books – which makes him better than any rock star, really.

*All I can see is you.*

My stomach somersaults as he looks up towards the back of the room, right where I'm standing.

He can't possibly see me; I'm in the near-dark here and the spots lighting the stage will be in his eyes.

He can't see me. No way.

Nobody sees me – that's the point. Nobody sees me and I've worked very, very hard to make sure that's how it is. I don't want to be the centre of attention; I can't think of anything worse. I happen to like it in the shadows, with my lists and – yes – my clipboard. It's safer here. So, no. He can't see me.

But it certainly feels like he can, because he's looking *straight* at me. Straight *into* me.

# JUNE

He smiles – just to himself – and lowers his gaze to the panel table, and I tell myself that it's absolutely fine because even if the lights aren't blinding him, without his glasses he doesn't stand a…

Something metal glitters at the side of his eye. *Glasses.*

Typical.

# LOCK-UP

"And how do you spell that? D...O...R...I...E...? Brilliant. Can I just open your book? Yep. That page. If you pop that on there...great. Thank you!" I smooth the neon Post-it note on the title page of the *Piecekeepers* hardback, and move down to the next person in the queue. "Hi there! Are you here for the signing? Great – can I jot your name down? How do you spell that...?" And on we go.

To their credit, the publishers have thrown a lot of money at this launch. I spent most of the evening putting up all the giant artwork posters and even propping a slightly-larger-than-life-size cardboard cut-out of Aidan in the corner behind the signing table. Bede kept taking selfies with it and giggling – I do worry about him sometimes. Then there were the books; boxes and boxes of them, shipped straight from the printer. By the time we'd unpacked them all and stacked them in neat piles along the table, with Lucy the senior publicist from Eagle's Head lurking behind us to oversee things the *whole* time, I barely had a chance to run up to my room to change out of my book-dust covered, sweat-soaked shorts and top, shower, and change into slightly less sweaty shorts and top. In an ideal world, maybe I would even have had time to *choose* said clothes, rather than grab the first things that came to hand – but that's just not my life, is it? Besides, these sort of go together, if you shut one eye. Sort of. Anyway, I made it back downstairs just in time to start queue duty, which means I am winning at my job. Just not at fashion.

The signing line is long, and it moves slowly. All the hype behind Aidan's book means lots of people want to see what the fuss is about – and they want to do it before anyone else. Aidan…Haydn…whoever he's being tonight, as far as I can tell, is having the time of his life; posing for photos and writing elaborate essays in each copy he signs.

That may be an exaggeration, but it feels that way from where I'm standing.

To pass the time, I tune in and out of the conversations in the queue around me.

"He is, though," says a girl somewhere near me. "Do you think he's single?"

I risk a casual glance around, waggling my pen like I'm counting the numbers in the queue, and I spot her. She's a few places further down the line, with two friends. All three of them are staring at Aidan's photo in the magazine, and each of them has a copy of *Piecekeepers* tucked under their arm.

"I'm going to ask him to follow me on Instagram," says one.

"Is he even *on* Instagram though?"

"Is he on Snapchat? I know he's on Twitter. I follow him," chirps another one.

"This doesn't say anything about Snapchat, but he's on the others." The first one pokes at the magazine; it must have more in there about his social media profiles than there was in the proof letter. Those profiles were just the Eagle's Head ones. (I checked, okay?)

I scan the room. Bede's mum and dad are over by the wine table – keeping an eye on it and waving under-eighteens towards the soft drinks while talking to Jenna, the junior Eagle's Head publicist. Otherwise, I'm in the clear. No Sam to see what I'm doing and mock me. I slip my phone out of my pocket and open Twitter, tapping *Haydn Swift* into the search box. My screen fills with mentions of the book, the article, the signing right now (which will please Dad – he might not understand Twitter, but he definitely understands buzz) and a stream of selfies people have snapped with Aidan. I scroll through them. There's a *lot*…and it strikes me how many of them are with girls just like those three in the queue. Do they *have* to lean in so close? Do they *have* to have a hand resting on his shoulder? Do they have to…

Sam's voice echoes in my head: *You're worried you like a guy who doesn't exist.*

I'm not. I don't. I *don't*.

The problem is I don't know him – not really. Pieces of him, sure – like the piece of him that wrote his book. But that still leaves a lot of him I *don't* know. Haydn, Aidan… they're the same but they're different. That kind of reminds me of my dad, how he's both "public Max" (friendly, genial, laughs a lot) and "home Max" (grumpy, can't work the washing machine, always losing his phone in his office). I mentally push that comparison away. This is about Aidan, not Dad.

But who *is* Aidan? Could I get to know more of him than just pieces?

*I didn't do it for Sam.*

*All I can see is you.*

Stomach flips and sweaty palms; eyes the colour of clouds in water and he smells like the sea.

I could (probably) ignore it all – if only I hadn't read the book.

I wish I could unread it… No, I don't.

*Am I daydreaming about a guy who doesn't exist?*

But Aidan wrote *Piecekeepers*, didn't he? Aidan's the real Haydn – it's Haydn who doesn't exist. He's just a name; the window dressing, the one posing for photos and signing books. *Aidan*, on the other hand…he is the one I see.

I search again, and there's a Twitter account box, marked with the little blue and white "verified" tick logo. *The official*

*Twitter account for Haydn Swift, author of* Piecekeepers *(out this summer from Eagle's Head Books).* I click the "follow" button…and instantly realize that I'm still logged in under the convention account instead of mine. I panic-unfollow, then figure that he's one of our guests so it doesn't even matter. I re-follow.

He has an Instagram account, does he…?

"Seems to be going well, doesn't it?"

Lucy is beaming at the queue – which is still going strong.

"It's a really good turnout." I stick my phone back in my pocket and shuffle my Post-it notes. "Definitely one of the best signings we've had in ages."

"Between you and me," she whispers, "I think the casting announcement for the film last week has made a huge difference. We're already into the second printing for the hardback, and the official release date isn't for another two weeks."

"Wow. You must be really pleased!"

Up at the signing table, a girl is asking Aidan to sign straight onto her arm. I can hear her telling him she's going to get it tattooed on permanently, and he looks like he's trying to work out whether he can say no.

Lucy spots it too. "Oh, lord. Excuse me." And she strides across to rescue her desperately uncomfortable author.

He doesn't even look over at me.

Back to work then.

"Are you here for the signing? Great, can I just check how to spell your name? And that's A...N..."

It took less than an hour for us to shift all the copies of *Piecekeepers*. It took significantly less time for the free drinks and snacks to disappear, but that's conventions for you. As the last of his fans leave with their signed books – *Are they fans? I guess so. Haydn has fans. Besides me, I mean. That's...weird* – Aidan caps his signing pen and stretches.

"Not so fast, cowboy," Lucy says, putting a hand on his shoulder and pushing him back down on his seat before he can get out of it. "I need a photo."

"I've been sat here for the last hour – you didn't get one through all that?" Aidan groans.

Lucy is unrepentant. "No, I need a good one of you signing a copy. One we can use on the appearances page of the website." She plonks one on the desk in front of him and pulls out her phone to take the picture. "Lexi – how about we get you in it too? You could pretend to be a fan!"

I ignore Aidan's cough of amusement: my lanyard has got tangled with my necklace. "Me?" I say, trying to separate the two. "Oh, you don't want me in it. I'm all sweaty and..."

"Come on, Lexi. It'll make me look like less of a loser if someone else is in it." Aidan beckons me over to the table and my insides are suddenly more tangled than my jewellery.

"We can both be losers," he adds as I stand next to him, really hoping he can't hear how fast my heart is beating at this distance.

"Bit closer, Lexi," says Lucy, pointing the phone's camera at us. "Otherwise I've only got half your face."

I can just *imagine* how awkward this photo's going to be...but I duly oblige. Satisfied, she takes the picture.

"Great. I'll put that up on Monday. Thanks, Lexi – and thank you so much for all this." She waves a hand at the emptying room. "We really appreciate all the effort."

"It's no trouble. Really."

"Hey, Lexi!"

Just the sound of him saying my name raises goosebumps down my spine.

*Aidan Green. Haydn Swift.*

*You heard those girls in the line. Do you want to be stood there with them, giggling over him? Do you want to be fighting them over him? I don't think so. Here be dragons.*

*No way are you sailing over that line. Nope. No chance.*

"What do you think? Good for a photo?" Now the signing's over and it's just him and me and a couple of the other convention staff left tidying up, he's clearly starting to relax. He has an arm slung around his cardboard cut-out's shoulders – and he has to stand on tiptoe to do it. Just like I would have to do to put my arm around him. Not that I would want to, obviously.

"I think you make a beautiful couple," I say. He stretches up and plants a kiss on the figure's cheek, and it's so ridiculous that I can't stop myself laughing.

"Hang on. My phone."

He's patting his pockets, over and over – that panic-pat that everyone does when their phone or wallet isn't where they thought it was.

"Everything okay?" I tug the largest poster down from the wall and roll it up with the kind of grace, ease and skill that only comes from years of experience; which is to say I get it all rolled up, then drop it and have to catch it as it unrolls across the floor. My words barely filter through whatever he's doing.

Pat-pat-pat.

"It was in my back pocket earlier."

Pat-pat-pat.

"Have you lost your phone?"

"Yes. I had it before the panel…"

"Did you give it to Lucy or Jenna?"

"No, no. And I definitely had it before the panel. I remember checking it was off when I sat down at the table."

"And you've not used it since?"

"No. I…it must have fallen out."

He looks thoroughly depressed – but at least he has managed to lose his phone in front of the best possible person. If anyone knows how to find a lost phone, bag, book

188

# LOCK-UP

or coat – or dog – at a convention, it's definitely me. Or, you know, Sam. But Sam's not here right now, so yes. Still me.

"Don't panic. It's probably under your chair from the last panel. We'll go back and check – yours was the last event in that room for today, so it should still be there."

"Shit. Shitshitshitshitshit."

I cross the room and hand my walkie to Bede's dad, who is folding up the cloth from the drinks table. "Haydn thinks he dropped his phone in panel room one – I'm just taking him back over to check."

"Are you finished for the day then?"

"Yep. That's me."

"Have a good evening." He glances at his watch and frowns at the time – nine thirty. "Well…whatever's left of the evening anyway. See you at breakfast – the weather's supposed to be cooler tomorrow, so that should make life a bit easier." He takes the walkie and tucks it under his arm along with the tablecloth, heading in the direction of the ops room. This section of the convention is slowly shutting down for the night. Now, it's all about the evening entertainment – karaoke, parties, the cosplay catwalk… Thankfully, as always, I get to stop work. I could go and catch up with the others, but I'm too tired to be good company. And too sticky. No, once we've tracked down this phone, I'm going to go and sit under a cool shower until I finally stop sweating.

Aidan pats his pockets – apparently at random – all the way back to panel room one, as though he thinks his phone is going to miraculously appear somewhere he's already checked fifteen times. The main corridors are deserted now, and I can hear someone vacuuming one of the workshop rooms. Sam always complains it's spooky, walking around a convention after-hours, but I love it. It's not spooky at all; it's peaceful. Calm. It feels like a completely different place to the one we've been running around all day, which I guess just goes to show it's the people that make a convention. You can set up all the art shows and book stalls you like, but without the people coming to see it – the people wandering the traders' room and arguing about whether this comic is better than that comic, the guys in the corner of the bar drinking so much coffee they vibrate and play-testing the new tabletop game they've designed – without them, it's not a convention. It's just a load of *stuff*.

The lights are all off in panel room one when we push the doors open. Admittedly, it does look a *little* eerie inside; there's only the green glow from the emergency lighting and what's filtering in from the corridor. My shadow sprawls across the chairs – and as I stand there, another one joins it. Aidan's.

"Where's the light switch?" he asks.

"On the left, beside the door." I set off down the central aisle while he looks for the switch.

"You're not going to wait?"

"I know where I'm going."

As the door swings shut, the lights flicker on with an electric hum and I scramble under the table on the stage. There's no sign of a phone here – not hidden by the convention banners between the table legs, not under the chair…not anywhere.

"Anything?" Aidan shouts from the back of the room.

"Nope. Not here." I clamber out – and realize as I look back across at him that he's standing exactly where I was earlier…and I'm where he was. I wonder whether he *did* see me… "I can try calling it, if you tell me your number?"

I look at my phone. No signal. I should have thought about that; the signal on my phone is rubbish in this building, but it's not a problem when I have the walkie – which I usually do.

"On second thoughts, that's not going to work. The reception's too crappy."

"It's off anyway. I don't know where else it could have gone…"

"There's one more place I can look – the stage is hollow, so maybe it's fallen under."

"How?"

"If it fell out of your pocket, it could've got kicked off the edge and somehow got stuck?" How am I supposed to know? I'm just trying to help. "It's a bit dark under there – can you come hold my phone for me? I'll put the torch on."

He hops lightly up onto the stage and edges around the table as I jump down behind, pushing the black backdrop curtains aside on their runners. I toss him my phone, the flash lit up to act as a torch. "Here. Point it that way." I point at the black hole under the stage.

"Are you sure?" He wrinkles his nose. "I wouldn't want to go in there."

"I'll have to check it after the convention anyway – we always do, just in case something's fallen back there and got lost. You know, like an author's phone?" I add, and immediately wish I hadn't, because it comes out sounding a lot more snarky than I intended. I cough, like this makes it any better. "It's fine as long as you don't wriggle too much."

I crawl into the gap, shuffling forward on my hands and knees and peering ahead of me into the shadows. There's a lot of dust, a handful of paperclips and absolutely nothing else. No phone.

"Bugger," he says when I crawl out and tell him. The dust has stuck to my sweaty legs, and there are grim grey stripes down the front of my shins. I brush the fluff off my hands as best I can.

"It'll probably turn up in the ops room tomorrow – don't panic. Maybe Nadiya picked it up straight after your panel finished. We find phones all the—"

There is a loud grating sound from the other end of the room. I stare at the door.

Aidan follows my gaze. "What's the matter?"

"No. No, no, no." Ignoring him, I scramble across the stage and run down the central aisle; my fingers close on the door handle and I turn it and...

Nothing.

The door is locked.

"Rodney? *Rodney!*" I bang the flat of my hand on the solid door, hard. If only there was a window, a glass panel, *anything*, he'd have seen us. But as it is...

Nothing.

"Lexi?"

"RODNEY!" I bang again, repeatedly.

Nothing.

We're locked in.

As that knowledge takes root, the lights click off.

"What the...?" In the darkness, I hear Aidan trip over a chair leg, then another, then bang into the door. Finally he makes it to the lighting panel and starts flicking switches. It stays dark.

"There's a master switch for these function rooms at the end of the corridor. Rodney must have turned it off when he locked up," I tell him gloomily.

"Wait – did you say 'locked up'?"

"I did."

"You mean we're locked in?"

"Yep."

"*How?*"

"We lock the convention areas when they shut down for the night – it's the only way to guarantee the art show and the traders' room stay secure." Sometimes, I wonder whether Dad swapped me for a parrot at birth. This stuff just *comes out* of me.

"But…aren't you supposed to check whether there's somebody inside first? So this doesn't happen?" Aidan can't believe it. Neither can I actually; I'm going to have a word with Rodney when I see him next, that's for sure.

"I guess he forgot."

"But you can get us out, right?"

"In what sense?"

"You must have a key?"

"Why would I have a key?"

"Because you…you're staff. You work here, right?"

"On the convention, sure. Not at the hotel. They let us have one key and it stays with our certified security guard. And last time I checked, I couldn't magically unlock doors with the force of my mind, so no. I can't get us out. Although…" I snatch my phone back from him and point its pathetic little light at the far end of the room.

The backdrops.

I'm sure I remember…

"This way," I say, and walk into the dark. "I've got an idea." Keeping to the side of the stage, I move round to the back, making sure Aidan's still with me. "Through here." I reach behind me and it's only when I've done it that I realize I've grabbed his hand. His fingers twine through mine and at any other time I would be considering what this actually means...but right now, all it means is that bloody Rodney is so worried about knocking off for his dinner that he didn't do his job properly.

With Aidan's fingers locked into mine, I move along the curtain until I find the edge of the fabric panels. "Here we go. It's somewhere here..."

I fumble at the wall, and then I find what I'm looking for.

A door handle – and it turns.

The door swings open, and with a whoop I pull Aidan through it and into the light.


A couple of hours ago, we couldn't have stood here without either being trampled or swept away; we are in a vast, galleried room packed with tables selling books, trading cards, plastic figures, T-shirts, toys, cosplay weapons, wigs, outfits...and right now, it's totally deserted. As it's on a different lighting circuit (one Rodney has clearly forgotten about), it's also still lit – so unlike the panel room, we can actually see what we're doing. Even if the light is horrible and fluorescent and makes me feel like my eyes are bleeding.

"This is amazing," Aidan says, turning in a full circle.

I am, admittedly, less amazed. And my phone still has no signal because my network is useless here. "Yeah. It's just swell."

"Nobody says 'swell'. Not unless they're in a black-and-white film."

"I happen to like black-and-white films, thank you." Maybe a text message would get through? I start tapping one out to Sam – it's worth a try.

"You do?" He's stopped turning.

"Look, Aidan. I'm kind of busy trying to get us out of here, so can you maybe leave taking the piss until I've sorted that, please?"

"What made you think I was going to take the piss?"

I'm about to remind him of the first time we met when I realize he's serious, standing there watching me with his head tilted to one side and his thumbs tucked in the back pockets of his jeans. He blinks at me through his glasses. He suddenly seems surprisingly calm about our situation. I point this out to him and all he does is shrug.

"I didn't have anywhere else to be tonight – did you? Might as well make the best of it."

I picture the shower in my hotel room. The pile of notes from college that need to be turned into something I can actually hand in. "That's not really the point…"

"You just need to look at this the other way around," he says with a wink.

"We're locked in the convention complex, with no way of telling anyone we're here – and probably no way of getting out until the morning. Please tell me what the other way of looking at this is," I snap. I check my phone again – my text didn't send. Bollocks.

"We're not locked in. *They're* all locked *out*." He spreads his arms and spins around once more.

"Who's they?"

"*Everyone.*"

"Or, to put it another way, I'm locked in here with you."

"Yes! It's an adventure." He pokes at a display of carved wooden wands on the stall closest to him, shooting a quick look over his shoulder at me.

"But it's…weird."

"You think I'm weird, is what you're saying. I'm weird and you don't want to be stuck in a big room with me."

"Noooo…"

"You read my book, didn't you?"

"Well, yes…"

"Then you know me. And you know that I am definitely *not* weird." He picks up one of the wands and waves it around, muttering something that sounds suspiciously like "Swish and flick".

"Put that down. What happens if you break it?" I pull the wand out of his hand and set it back on the velvet cushion on the stall.

"Then I'll pay for it," he says. "I'm not as much of a prick as you think I am, I promise."

"Who says I think you're a prick?"

"Sam."

"What?" When did he talk to Sam about me? More to the point, is there *anyone* Sam hasn't spoken to lately?

"That first time we met – when you threw me out of the green room. Remember?"

"Vaguely." Like I could forget…

"You stormed off."

"I did not storm off!"

"And she stayed at the party, and she told me exactly what you thought of me. Believe me, she didn't hold back."

I try to hide my smirk. "She usually doesn't." I relieve him of the imitation elvish dagger he's picked up. "Besides, you *were* a prick."

"My writer brain notes the use of past tense there."

"Don't push it." I shake my head.

"All right. But you said I was being a prick – how so?"

"You took the piss out of me. About my clipboard."

His laugh bubbles up and out of him and echoes around the empty hall. But it doesn't feel like he's laughing *at* me, somehow – even though he is.

"You're joking. You have to be joking. That's *it*?"

"What do you mean, 'That's it'?"

"Come on, Lexi. I was *embarrassed*, and I was trying to make you laugh. It wasn't supposed to mortally offend you!"

"You what?" *He* was embarrassed?

"You looked so fed up."

Did I? Maybe I did; after all, that was the time we were all running round after that little dog, wasn't it?

"It was because of the dog," I say, and he opens his mouth to ask what I mean. I cut him off. "I don't want to talk about it. Besides, who says I wanted someone to make me laugh? You're like one of those van drivers who roll down their windows and shout 'Cheer up, love!'"

"Have you finished?"

"No. Yes. Shut up." I turn away from him, hoping that's enough of a sign I am actually finished.

There's a rustling sound from behind me, and when I turn back around he's wearing a long blonde plaited wig from the next stall along. It looks *ridiculous*. And – despite being locked in, despite having no walkie and no working phone and not being able to have my shower, despite the fact my dad's not spoken to me all day but I've seen him outside on the hotel steps talking to Bea on his mobile every time I've walked through the lobby – I can't stop my sudden giggle-snort, any more than I can stop it turning into something bigger, something that cuts off my breath and wraps its arms around me and won't let me go until I'm actually crying with laughter.

"How do I look?" he asks, twirling one of the plaits – which catches on the frame of his glasses.

I press my lips together, hard. I try to breathe through my nose and just end up making a sort of spluttering snort.

"Mmm. You'd have thought there'd be a mirror here somewhere," he mutters, peering over the back of the stall to look for one. He's actually holding the plaits back so they don't catch on anything on the table.

"Aidan. Here." My voice comes out in a squeak as I get control over my body. I point my phone at him and take a photo, turning it round so he can see the screen. He beams as he examines my shot.

"Oh, yes. Sod the glowing magic balls – here's my next cover shoot, right here."

He takes the wig off, slipping it back over the stand it came from with surprising care. I watch his fingers smooth down the plaits, and all of a sudden it feels like someone has sucked all the oxygen out of the room. Because that's what's happened, isn't it? The air feels thin and flat and as though it'll never be enough to fill up my lungs no matter how much of it I breathe in, and my head is spinning and spinning and spinning.

When he looks up at me, his eyes lock onto mine and don't let go. "Can we start again?"

"Start what again?"

"Everything. Us."

"Us? Yeah, no. You mean you…and me." I turn my back, pretending I'm suddenly very, very interested in a stage make-up kit – when really I just can't quite tell what my face is doing and I'm not sure I want him to find out before I do.

"You know what I mean."

"Nope." I had no idea you could get special kits just to cover tattoos. I wonder whether that girl from the signing would really have got his signature tattooed on… What makes me so very different from her, when you think about it?

*What makes you different*, says a small voice somewhere between my ears, *is that everyone else has it backwards. They've only met Haydn. That's who they get to see – they don't even know Aidan exists. He's a secret; something private and quiet, a figure standing behind the curtain.*

And right now, I'm talking to Aidan. Blonde plaits and all.

Because however much I try and talk myself out of it, I know it's true. I do know him. I know him because I read his book, and I know who really wrote it. I saw him threaded through every line of it and I can see him even now. I could hear his voice there, I could feel it; I could feel *him*. And it's the same voice that seems to be lodged in my head, playing back on loop when I least expect it. Aidan's voice, echoing in an empty corridor. Aidan's voice, raised over the sound of a band and their crowd. Aidan's voice that follows me around.

I'm not with someone I barely know, I'm with someone I want to know better.

I look back towards him just as he pulls his glasses off and wipes them with the hem of his T-shirt – I glance away again, but I'm too slow to miss the flash of skin beneath his shirt. "So we're seriously stuck in here till morning then?" he asks, pushing his glasses back up his nose.

"There's…"

Something makes me stop. I was about to say that, actually, there is a fire exit – right at the back of the space, and most likely alarmed so that opening it will end up triggering the system for everything on this side of the building. But it opens onto an alley at the back of the hotel, so we could definitely use it to get out…

But Aidan doesn't know that.

This is my chance. Maybe my only chance; my chance to see if I'm right. To find the fault line between Aidan Green and Haydn Swift once and for all.

"There's what?"

"Hmm?"

"You were saying something?"

His eyes through the lenses of his glasses. A tempest reflected in water.

His hair an unruly dark cloud.

He makes my skin prickle, like an oncoming storm; one I want to walk right into.

"You said 'There's' and then you stopped."

There's a door, there's a way out, there's an exit…

It'd probably cause a massive problem anyway. Fire brigade out, people standing around on the pavement in their pyjamas, all that. And they'll probably pass the cost on to the convention (and Dad)…

"There's not much we can do. That's what I was about to say." Can he hear the lie? I don't know. Would he tell me if he could? Would he be angry? He doesn't exactly seem upset, trying on wigs and swishing wands around – but how would I know?

"Right then." He tilts his face up to the ceiling, staring at the glass roof high above us. The sky outside is dark but clear, and the glass reflects us standing below it: two tiny strangers, staring at ourselves. It gives me an idea.

"Aidan?"

"Mmm?"

"You said I was looking at this wrong. You said it should be an adventure."

"I did."

"All right then. You want an adventure? Follow me."

# LOOK UP

"This was not what I was expecting," he says, peering over the edge of the roof. We might not have been able to get out without setting off a load of alarms, but the roof access is always open. Just a shame it doesn't go anywhere *but* here, really. Although, maybe it's not all bad...

If I look behind us, I can see the spot where we were standing five minutes ago – far down through the glass skylight. But up here, all around us is the night. Ahead is the darkness of the sea, edged with the lights of the coast like amber jewels sewn onto black cloth; an occasional lighthouse sparkles in the distance. To the left of us, the wild neon and swirling rides of the funfair blaze at the end of the pier. The occasional scream drifts over from one of the rides: a giant arm that swings out over the sea, turning riders upside down and right way round (and probably inside out). Even up here, the air smells of chip fat and doughnuts – and sea salt and waves.

Or maybe that's just him. (The smell of the sea, I mean.

I don't think he smells like chip fat.)

"It's not so hot up here – must be the breeze off the sea. I didn't think I was ever going to feel cool again." Suddenly, he points at the horizon out past the stem of the i360, and his voice changes, urgent now. "Look!"

"What?" All I can see is the night. Dark water, dark sky, a handful of stars slowly disappearing behind a veil of cloud.

"There. Right out there. Did you see it that time?"

I can't see anything. Just darkness. "Nope?"

"You're not looking in the right place. Come stand here." He closes his fingers around my wrist and gently, so gently, pulls me towards him, stepping back and standing me in his place. "Now, look. Right there." He raises his hand again, and his fingers are so long, so slender. Writer's fingers.

I stare at the space just beyond the end of his fingernail so long and so hard that I start seeing spots – and I don't think that's what I'm supposed to be seeing. Although as he steps closer again – right behind me so I can feel his body pressing lightly against my back, feel his chin brushing against the edge of my jaw as he tucks his face close in to mine so he can see what I'm seeing – the spots get brighter.

And my heart…my heart…

"There. You had to see it that time!"

"Maybe?" I saw *something*. Something blurry and white, far off the coast.

"Look."

I don't know what I'm looking for. I can feel his arm pressing against mine; feel his breath on my cheek.

A white flash, way out in the darkness. Barely more than a flicker, and it's gone.

"A ship?" I ask.

"Lightning. It's a thunderstorm coming in."

There's another flash – and maybe it's my imagination but I'm almost sure I hear thunder rolling somewhere far off. Or maybe it's just my heartbeat in my ears.

I wrap my hands around the metal safety railing running at waist height around the edge of the parapet; all of a sudden, I need somewhere to put them, and there seems as good a place as any.

Aidan's still staring out at the horizon – I can feel the rise and fall of his chest against my shoulder as he breathes. "If it was daytime, we'd be able to see it coming. Everything behind the rain would disappear and the world would get smaller and smaller the closer it got."

I'm used to small worlds. For six or seven weekends of the year – every year as far back as I can remember – my world has been the walls of a hotel, and the only people in it have been the people attending a convention. And even when there isn't a convention to run, there's one to plan. We're always running towards a future we've already left behind, thinking about the next thing and the next thing and the next thing after that. Being a part of this small world *does* something to you. When you make friends, they become your best friends because everything about it is so intense. Everything is busier, more urgent, more exhausting; time stretches and compresses and somehow, by making the outside world less, what you're left with becomes *more* – becomes all there is – and only the people who've lived that understand it. It's why Sam's been my best friend for so long, even though I only see her for those seven weekends a year. It's why Nadiya's deadpan jokes always work – because we know each other so well. Because we were *made* in conventions. The first time Bede's parents brought him along and I saw him sitting on the floor in the hotel lobby, reading, I knew. The first time I met Nadiya – who'd dragged her uncle to an event because there was a big panel for one of her favourite television shows but she was too young to come by herself – I knew… And now her family – just like Bede's, just like Sam's – is part of ours. Dad's and mine. Just like everybody else who comes to these things, because coming to a convention feels a little like coming home.

Reading *Piecekeepers* felt like that. It felt like coming home, like hearing someone telling me a story they had made up just for me. It felt like meeting a friend I'd never realized I had.

# JUNE

Haydn.

Aidan.

I'm looking at the horizon – at the flashes of lightning, at the storm coming our way – and all I can see and feel and hear is him. And it's like he was made for me.

"Should we go back inside?" I don't fancy spending the night in sopping wet clothes if we get caught in the rain up here.

"Nah. We've got plenty of time – and that's if the rain even makes it this far. It might move back out to sea, or along the coast, or anywhere."

Over on the pier, the rides are still spinning, the riders still screaming. On the promenade below, the pavement between the hotel and the beach, a hen party heading in one direction meets a stag party going the other way and there are shrieks and cheers and laughter. Everything is carrying on exactly the way I'd expect it to outside the walls of the convention…and yet something in the world has shifted, somewhere deep inside the earth. Deep inside *me*.

He is the oncoming storm…and the lightning flashes and the clouds part, and I walk right on in.

Having paced around the entire roof – leaning way too far out over the railing for me to be happy about it, and crouching so close to the glass skylight that I genuinely expected to have to lunge forward and save him from plummeting to a messy death surrounded by trading cards and LARP equipment – Aidan finally stops on the side overlooking the city. From here, the streets and buildings spread out below and before us, unfurling in every direction; climbing the steep hills to the suburbs and sprawling out along the beaches and cliffs to either side. "It all looks different from up here, doesn't it?"

Maybe things do when you get a different perspective on them. Places, events…even people. All of them look like something else when you see them from another angle. Bigger, smaller, softer, sharper; you never know until you see it – and once you have, you can never unsee it.

A train winds its way out of the station, high enough up one of Brighton's hills that each carriage window is a light disappearing into the unknown.

"Wonder where they're going?" Aidan murmurs next to me – right as the breeze catches my hair, blowing it into his face. So much for that particular moment. It's hard to be magical and make deep, meaningful comments about life, the universe and everything with a mouthful of someone else's sweaty, dusty, convention-scented hair. He recovers pretty well though, considering, and leans back against the railings. "Shame the cloud's come in so fast. I bet the stars are brilliant over the sea."

I shake my head. "You don't need stars. Look over there."

I point at the side of the next hill along from the station. "There's a kangaroo."

"A kangaroo?" He hasn't figured it out yet – but I don't think it'll take him long. I hope it won't; partly because I suppose I'm testing him, and partly because if I have to explain it I'll sound like a lunatic.

A lunatic he's stuck with on a deserted rooftop.

Hmm.

I try again, picking out a spot further west. "And there's a cat. See it?"

"A cat? What the hell are you looking…?"

"And right next to it, there's an umbrella – it's open," I add after a second's thought.

Silence.

He doesn't get it. *He doesn't get it.*

*OhgodohgodohgodhethinksI'manidiot.*

And then… "The street lights. You're talking about the street lights. There's shapes in them – like constellations." He glances at me, unsure. "That's it, right?"

*He got it. I knew he would.*

*Well…sort of.*

"I see it," he laughs. "The umbrella. And the cat."

"And the kangaroo?"

"Where was that?"

"Over there." I point at the curving row of orange lights. "There's its tail, and its stomach…"

He squints into the night in silence, then shakes his head. "Nope. Don't see it."

"You're not looking in the right place..."

I tail off – because that's exactly what he said to me earlier...and because he's not looking at the lights at all. I can see him in the fluorescent glow through the glass skylight, against the backdrop of the pier. He's not looking at the lights. He's looking at me.

"You'd better show me," he says, and his voice has dropped a level. It's quieter – barely more than a whisper.

"There." I lean past him and point at the outline in the streets.

Our positions reversed, now it's my body pressing against his back; *my* arm outstretched around *him*, my chin pressed against his shoulder...

And maybe he doesn't mean it; maybe he's just turning his head to see the outline better, or perhaps his glasses catch in my hair...but when his cheek brushes mine, he doesn't move away.

I am on a roof with a guy who just got asked to sign a girl's *arm*, and I barely know him but I *know* him.

*WHAT DO I DO NOW?*

I'm afraid that neither of us are ever going to speak again. I'm afraid I've lost my voice; that he's lost his. That somehow the world has fallen silent, and nobody will ever be able to talk again – although I guess the yells from the pier and from the street below do kind of spoil that illusion. And then:

"You know it isn't a kangaroo, don't you?"

"What do you mean, it's not a kangaroo?" I ask, trying to sound both casual and offended at the same time. It's the kind of thing Sam would be able to pull off – the kind of thing she *does* pull off all the time – but I'm not Sam. I just sound…vaguely bored.

"It's a crocodile. Look. That's not its tail – that's its mouth."

"It's not a crocodile."

"It is."

"No."

"Remind me never to ask you on an Australian tour," he laughs, and he wraps his fingers around mine (which is still pointing, because, *idiot*), and starts drawing pictures in the air.

If we were in his book, our hands would leave trails of light like sparklers through the sky, glowing against the night; they would crackle and fizz with magic. But we aren't, so they're just mildly clammy and soundtracked by someone throwing up against a lamp post on the promenade (loudly).

It's so hard to pull away from him that I feel it all the way through every fibre of me. It feels like someone has ripped off a layer of my skin – but I can't stay like that, leaning into him. I can't, because if I do it a minute longer, I'm not sure I'll ever be able to step away again.

"So maybe it could be a crocodile. *Maybe*. I'm not saying you're right."

"That's funny, because I was absolutely going to say you were wrong."

His voice sounds like a grin.

The wind is turning cooler, blowing more strongly now. If there's rain coming, it won't be long before it gets here.

I point to the door. "We should go back inside."

"Fair enough. Besides, there was another wig I wanted to try on that stall – I've always thought I'd look awesome as a redhead."

Hands in his pockets, he moves away from the railing and heads for the stairs back down to the traders' room without a second's hesitation, and without a single look back.

I could tell myself the dull ache in my ribs is just because I haven't eaten, and not because he didn't so much as glance over his shoulder at me.

I *could*…

# LIGHT UP

The tiny tower of empty pistachio shells topples over, scattering across the carpet. I lean over to scoop as many of them up as I can, scraping them back into a heap in front of me. "I told you it was going."

"You were playing safe."

"You weren't." I throw a stray shell at him. His hand snaps out and catches it. Smugly. He drops it back on top of the pile and I start picking at bits left behind on the carpet; I can't imagine Darknight Comics will be too happy if they come in later and tread on a load of half-eaten nuts, scavenged from a leftover crate of event supplies.

"Is there a reason we're hiding under here?" He flicks at the edge of the white cloth draping the trader's table above us.

"The lights are giving me a headache." The fib is surprisingly easy to tell, falling from my mouth with worrying speed. I suppose it's partly true – the fluorescent lights are getting to be a bit much after a whole day running around under them, and now getting stuck here. But more than anything, it just felt...right. Ever since I read *Piecekeepers*, since Aidan told me that I knew him *because* I'd read it, I've felt that I somehow have an unfair advantage – like I've been spying on him. Bringing him under the table seemed fair. This is my safe place – however stupid that sounds – and somehow, the idea of showing him that, showing him me, letting him *see* me...it suddenly feels like the right thing.

Besides, Rodney may decide that tonight is the night he actually *does* his midnight rounds, and now we're here, it's probably a better idea to stay put until morning and slip out when everyone else starts coming in. Fewer questions, fewer problems. And if it gives me more time with Aidan... let's just call that a bonus.

"Isn't your dad going to worry about you when he can't find you?"

I was so busy thinking about Aidan that I hadn't even noticed he was talking to me. I shake my head; a bit of pistachio skin falls out of my hair. (Always glamorous, this life. I wonder, if I wasn't Lexi Angelo, if I was someone else – someone who'd never even been near a convention or who had never even touched a clipboard – would I have beautiful hair that was always shiny and glossy and never had bits of dust or cardboard or pistachio in it?) He watches it glide to the carpet and raises an eyebrow at me. Well, he's never going to get that at any of his big publishing parties, is he? I provide dinner *and* a show.

"I doubt Dad'll even notice I'm not around. He'll be busy all night, and he'll probably assume I've just gone to bed." Even if he's not doing convention stuff, the wedding seems to be taking over his head; not the actual planning – he's got somebody else doing all that – but the Bea-wrangling. That would probably make him a Bea-keeper. Huh. Funny.

I realize Aidan has been watching every centimetre of this train of thought chug through my head.

I pick at my hair.

"He doesn't check in on you?"

"No. Why should he?" I don't know who's more puzzled right now – me or Aidan. It's like the idea of my dad not needing to know where I am every second is completely alien to him. I mean, it's a hotel. How far could I have got?

"You don't think that's weird?"

"I'm a big girl, thanks. I don't need my daddy to hold my hand, if that's what you're saying."

He pulls a face. "That wasn't what I meant."

"So what *did* you mean?" I try to keep it light, but I'm not sure I want it to be.

"It's just…you're telling me he wouldn't be bothered about this?" He waves a hand around, presumably to illustrate the two of us, alone in a convention centre, under a table. Surrounded by pistachios. "About us?"

I ignore the "us", even though it makes my fingernails sweat and fills my ribs with butterflies. "As long as all the merchandise is fine, no. Why should he?"

Aidan gives me a long, hard look and opens his mouth like he's about to say something – but then blinks and obviously changes his mind. He starts stacking the shells again.

It's suddenly got surprisingly chilly under our table.

*Our* table.

*Us.*

I try to break the silence again and grab a couple of shells from the pile to lean against each other. "You'll never get them to balance like that," I say, carefully letting my two go. They immediately fall over. "And apparently, neither will I."

"What about your mum?" He picks up my fallen shells and gently, so gently, stands them upright; his fingertips hovering a hair's breadth from them until he's sure they'll stay. "You said your dad was getting married soon, but she's not your mum, is she?"

*He remembers that?* "Aren't we full of questions, Mr Green?"

"Writer. It comes with the job," he says with a grin. "And you didn't answer."

"Mum lives in France. She and Dad split up years ago and got divorced when I was twelve, and I think they're both happier with it that way."

"And you?"

"What do you mean, *and me*?"

"It didn't sound like you're a big fan of what's-her-name…"

"Bea," I reply automatically. "She makes Dad happy. She's fine."

He opens his mouth again, and I know where this is going. It's the *how-do-you-feel?* conversation again; the one Mum keeps trying to have with me – the one she's apparently been having with Sam on my behalf. I shut him down, shaking my head again.

"No more questions – not unless I get to ask you some."

He laughs. It's an easy sound – and for a second I picture him slouched on a sofa somewhere, guard down and feet up. All Aidan, no Haydn, and not a signing queue in sight. Except in my head, he appears to be shirtless.

I stare very, very hard at a small hole in the carpet.

"Go on then. Ask away."

"Where did *Piecekeepers* come from?"

"Jesus, Lexi," he groans. "I didn't realize it was an interview – you could've read that in the magazine…"

"No. Not the magazine answer. The *real* answer."

"How do you know the magazine answer isn't the real answer?" Suddenly, I have his attention; he looks up at me from beneath half-lowered lids, the start of a smile on his lips.

"The magazine answer is *never* the real answer. So?"

"That's not fair. You have me at a disadvantage."

"It's completely fair. And you know you want to tell me…"

*That was absolutely not what I was planning to say. Not even slightly.*

I'm this close to panicking when he laughs again. Apparently, my accidental and terrible attempt at witty banter worked.

"You win. It was for a girl."

And that's when it happens, when I'm least expecting it – he plunges his hand into my chest, rips out my heart and tears it to pieces. Or he might as well have, anyway.

"A girl?"

Look at me. I'm so casual. Nothing hurts. This doesn't hurt. Not at all.

"I know, I know. It's pathetic."

"Not. At. All. Tell. Me. More." I enunciate every word like I'm biting pieces off a rock.

"It was ages ago, but there was…this girl. Ali. And she was into all these fantasy books, you know? Magic and secret doorways, proper Narnia stuff. And I'd always written stories, and I thought how hard can writing a whole book be? So I started writing this one to impress her."

Ali. There's a character called Ali in *Piecekeepers*. "And that was it? That's how the book started?"

"Christ, no. *That* was a piece of shit. But it had magic in it, and that idea gave me another one – about magic trapped in paintings, and what would happen if it ever got out and nobody could control it."

"So you wrote *that* story."

"Yep." With a well-aimed flick, he knocks the whole pistachio tower down. "And when I was halfway through, Ali started going out with my mate, Nick."

"Does she know about it?"

"The book? Probably."

"No – I mean, does she know it's *you*?"

"Don't know, don't care. Not any more. Besides, she's another one not really into…this." Another hand-wave. I'm going to assume "this" means "conventions" rather than the nebulous "us".

*Us.*

"Well, if she doesn't know yet, she will soon enough. It'll be everywhere in a couple of weeks, not just at a convention. Your publishers are pushing the book hard – you're lucky."

"I know." He smiles again, but it's a sad smile somehow, not the full beam I've seen him give – the one that lights up his face and makes him glow from inside. "And don't get me wrong, I'm really grateful. There's probably a million people who'd give their right hand for it – it's just that, you know, the publicity stuff? It's all him."

"Him?"

"Haydn. Not…you know, *me*. I just want to write. All this" – he gestures out at the World Beyond the Table again – "it's intimidating, you know?"

"Are you serious? Intimidating how?"

"Intimidating every-how. Maybe not to *you* – you're used to it. But this" – another wave: isn't he supposed to be good with actual words? – "is pretty new to me. *Me*-me. Aidan-me. I'm still catching up."

Where does Aidan stop and Haydn start? That was what I wanted to know, wasn't it? And now I can see the seam where he's stitched them both together. Haydn is the lighter one, the one who grins at the spotlight. Aidan is the one who told me his own parents haven't read his book. They're different, but they overlap. Two versions of the same guy. So which one am I falling for? Or am I falling for both? Because it's pointless trying to pretend I'm not falling – I am. My name is Lexi Angelo, and I am falling hard. I was falling before tonight, before I even realized. But now I know and I'm sure of it and there's no way I can hide from it any more.

I try another approach. "I don't believe that your parents aren't proud of you. I *can't* believe that. They must know what a big deal this is!" I want to say *what a big deal you are*, or *how good it is*, but this feels safer.

There's that smile again, the sad one – and this time it comes with its very own Aidan-shaped laugh. "Maybe they would be if I'd written a 'proper' book. Maybe one about a tortured artist who has to cut off his own thumbs or something. Or maybe a book about a middle-aged art historian – one with big words that only fifteen people in the world actually use. But not so much a book about magicians…" He stops abruptly. "Let's not go there, okay? Not now."

*Well done, Lexi. Kick a guy while he's down. That's absolutely the thing to do.*

"But it *is* a proper book. It has a cover and pages and words. Proper book. And anyway, I liked it."

"You did."

I more than liked it.

"More than that – you got it. And you got all the stuff about Venice too. That meant a lot."

"I…what?" An alarm bell goes off somewhere in the back of my head. I haven't said anything to him about the bit of the book set in Venice. I'm sure of it. In fact, the only time I've mentioned it is in an email…

…An email to his publicist. Thanking her for the proof copy she'd sent Dad.

…In which I gushed like a screaming fangirl about how amazing the book was and how amazing the author was and particularly – *particularly* – about the whole section at the start of the book where the magician and his assistant have a duel in Venice.

...An email Aidan has clearly read.

...Oh. God.

It doesn't come out as a question. It isn't a question. It's more a statement of mounting horror. "Lucy showed you my email."

"She forwarded the comments, said they were from a reviewer. There wasn't a name – I didn't know it was you – until..." He stops as though he can't find the words. Ironic, that.

"Until what? I made a massive idiot of myself in May?"

I want to disappear. I want the ground to swallow me, the sea to dissolve me. I want to step off the roof and float away into the clouds – possibly riding on a kangaroo made entirely from embarrassment and the light from streetlamps.

"Until earlier. On the roof."

What did I say? I said something, I must have done.

"On the roof?"

"I don't know exactly what it was, okay? It just felt the same. It felt like you. It sounded like you do. It's stupid. I just...it *was* you. I *know* it was." He doesn't sound quite so sure of himself now, not at all. "It was, wasn't it?"

"Mayyyyybe...?"

"You just asked me if Lucy showed me your email!"

"I could've been talking about another email?"

"Fine." And his smile is back, the real one. "What I meant to say is that I hope it *was* you."

In my head, I flick my hair back and give him a dazzling but carefree and enigmatic smile and say something deeply witty.

In reality, I mumble something about him being clever and what time is it anyway and manage to almost elbow him in the face checking my watch.

2 a.m.

Even Dad will be winding down by now; has he noticed I've not been around all evening? Will he be looking around in case I walk through the bar? Text me? Try my phone?

Why would he?

Why *wouldn't* he?

As Aidan picks up the pistachio shells in great big handfuls, saying something about needing to stretch his legs, I wonder why I've never asked that question before. Why it's taken Aidan turning up to jolt it out of me.

He crawls out from under the table and groans as he straightens up – and then a hand appears back under the edge of the tablecloth. "Come on," he says from outside.

He's waiting for me to take his hand.

I slide my fingers into his, half-expecting there to be sparks.

There aren't – at least, none that anybody could see – but I feel them all the same.

"What's up there?" He points up to the galleried walkway running around the upper half of the room.

"It's the gallery."

"Well, yeah – but what's up there?"

"No, it's *literally* the gallery. It's where the art show is."

"Oh. Oh? Can we get to it from here?"

He's looking right at the open stairs against the wall. Maybe he thinks they're some kind of Escher-inspired installation...?

"It's not locked or anything. If you want to..."

I don't even get to finish, because by the time I'm halfway through saying it, he's striding towards the stairs with those long legs of his in that way that makes it look like he knows exactly where he's going. Even when he doesn't. What's that like? I wonder. Being able to give the impression that you know it all and nothing can bother you and you're absolutely in control; *making* yourself be in control.

Oh, of course I know. I do it all the time; it's what the clipboard's for – to give the impression I know what I'm doing...

Ah.

That's what he was doing in the green room, the first time we met, wasn't it? He was doing it then, pretending he knew what he was doing, pretending he was in control. And the stupid comments about the clipboard were his way of telling me we're the *same*. And I thought he was being a prick.

Ah. Oh well. Nobody's perfect, I guess.

"Come on!" He leans over the rail of the stairs and waves

down at me, impatient, and I'm torn between running to catch up with him and standing beneath him and stopping, just to look up at him with his glasses sliding down his nose and his hair curling wildly after the day's heat and humidity – even in here, even in the middle of the night.

He was right.

We're not locked in here.

Everybody else is locked out.

And I could leave the rest of the world locked out, if only it meant I got to stay in here with him a little longer.

"*Lexi!* Come on! What are you standing there for?"

So I stop standing still, and I run.

The fluorescents aren't as bright upstairs – most of the lights are below our feet up here – and Aidan peers into the relative gloom of the art show with a disappointed face.

"Wait here," I say, pointing at the floor to make sure he knows where "here" is (sometimes there really is too much of my father in me). I duck round the corner behind the stairs. "Ready?"

"Lexi…"

I flick the switch on the lighting panel and a hundred tiny white spotlights flare into life; each of them carefully positioned to bring out the best in the art they're illuminating. The boring grey of the gallery floor is suddenly a wash of vibrant reds and blues. Fairy-tale castles shimmer on canvases, blown-glass sculptures in every shade of the rainbow glitter on stands. Across the void, a life-size ceramic hooded man stands frozen with his hand on the hilt of a sword tucked into his belt – and behind him, a sea monster's tentacles crash out of a painting onto a beach made from pebbles that Nadiya and Bede helped a local artist collect across the road yesterday morning.

I'm not sure I've ever seen anyone's jaw actually drop before – but Aidan's does. "Wow."

"Impressive, isn't it?"

"I was thinking this afternoon that I wasn't that bothered about the art show so I'd give it a miss."

"Seriously?" I think I'm offended on behalf of the artists who've put so much into their work – not to mention all of us who spent hours getting splinters and blisters setting it up…

"I've spent a *lot* of time in art galleries, Lexi," he says with a wry smile. "But I'm glad I missed it anyway." His whole expression, his whole face, softens. "Because if I hadn't, I wouldn't get to see it like *this*." He turns away from the art as I walk back over to him; looks right at me. "With you."

This is too much for the tired, overworked bit of my brain – which immediately takes control. I hear a voice – my voice – replying to him. And what do I lead with? "Do you want to see the insects?"

Snap me in half, and you'd see ROMANCE written all the way through me like a stick of Brighton rock.

He blinks at me. "The insects?"

"They're much better than they sound. Honest."

"You really know how to sell them, don't you?"

"Just…shut up and come see them."

"Mmm-hmm."

"Aidan."

His name feels different in my mouth – heavier and lighter at the same time – and it's all I can do not to keep saying it over and over.

Of course, it has been a long time since I slept, so there's always *that* to consider…

We pass a large painting of superheroes fighting Vikings; another of a ballroom filled with waltzing skeletons, the wisps of fabric drifting behind them so real I want to catch one and run it through my fingers… And then we reach the corner, where the wood backdrop has been covered in plain white fabric, blinding in the spotlights. Suspended in front of them, hanging on almost invisible nylon threads, are what look like hundreds of tiny dots.

I make a dramatic arrival sound. "Ta-da. This is it."

"This?" Aidan looks a bit nonplussed. I don't blame him; it's completely nonplussing until you *see* it.

"Here. Look closer." I hand him an oversized magnifying glass hanging from a chain and he peers through it at one of the dots – and then his eyes open so wide behind his glasses that I'm almost afraid they might drop out.

"Holy shit."

"Everybody says that."

I know what he's seen, but I stand beside him and peer round his shoulder to see it the way he is, right now. It's a bumblebee in mid-flight…and on its back is a tiny skeletal fairy with wings like a fly's.

Aidan steps back – the way everyone does when they realize what all those little dangling dots really are – and treads on my toe. He spins around – "Sorry, sorry" – and we're so close that our noses are almost touching. Or, you know, my nose and his chin.

He doesn't move away.

Neither do I.

My skin buzzes as though someone's run a current through it. As though Aidan has. Like he's lightning.

Close up, his eyes are somewhere between blue and grey, flecked with tiny silver specks.

He still doesn't move away…and I can't.

I can't move.

It comes from nowhere. I have no idea it's about to happen until it does.

I look deep into his eyes and breathe in the smell of him – that salt and ocean, sunshine and late-night smell…

And I yawn in his face.

I clamp my hands over my mouth...but it's too late. The damage is done, isn't it?

I look into those sea-grey eyes in horror...and to my surprise (delight? Shock? Relief? All of these things and a hundred more?) he starts to laugh. And I start to laugh with him.

"Maybe you're right – I wasn't prepared for an all-nighter either. When did you start work this morning?"

"Umm, seven? Maybe." Well, that's a lie. I was in the ops office at half past six, but that sounds like the kind of thing only a crazy person would own up to.

"You've been up since seven this...yesterday...morning?"

"What time is it now?"

"Three. Although I don't think that changes the time you actually got up, does it?"

I try to do the maths in my head and work out how long it's been since I got out of bed.

Nope.

First time I try, I get fifteen hours. The second time, it's thirty-two. Neither of which feels quite right.

"It's twenty. Twenty hours," he says. "You were trying to work it out, weren't you?"

"No. Yes. How could you tell?" I stifle another yawn.

"You were counting on your fingers."

Oh.

I put my hands behind my back. They're safer there

anyway; they can't accidentally brush his chest or his hips or reach for his shoulders or his jaw or...

Hands. Behind. Back.

"Is there anywhere to sit, maybe lie down? A couple of sofas?" He sounds hopeful but I shake my head.

"Not in the trader's room – only the standard chairs for them at each table."

"I guess we'll have to make do, then."

When he reaches around me, I freeze. When he takes my hand, I burn. Together, we walk down the stairs from the gallery and my feet are so heavy all of a sudden that I can barely lift them, barely put one in front of the other.

Aidan steers us to a corner at the back of the traders' room, away from the brightest of the fluorescent lights.

"Here. Sit down. You need a rest."

I feel his hands guide me as I lean back against the wall and slide down to the floor.

"If I had a jacket, this is the point I'd give it to you for a pillow. But I don't. Sorry."

"'S all right."

He sits down beside me, his back to the wall and his legs stretched out in front of him – and suddenly it's the most normal thing in the world to rest my head on his shoulder, and it's not awkward at all.

"You said you've been in a lot of galleries – tell me about your favourite." I keep waiting for him to shrug me away, to move, anything – but he doesn't. If anything, he edges closer.

"The Holburne at home."

"Home?"

"Bath. I live in Bath."

"Oh." If I wasn't so tired, I'd be disappointed – part of me has been hoping he's a Londoner like I am. The same part of me that has been half-hoping I'd run into him on the street – any street, any day – every day since May. I lift my head and settle it again, more comfortably – and still he doesn't move. "How come you stayed in the hotel in Bristol? You could've gone home…"

*I'm over the road… Last-minute thing…*

"Yeah, I could have done," he says softly. "But then I wouldn't have got to spend that time with you, would I?"

Before I can answer, or even really think, sleep turns out all the lights.

# CLEAN UP

"Rise and shine, Sleeping Beauty..."

At first, I think the voice is part of my dream – but no part of my subconscious has ever called me "Sleeping Beauty", mostly because it knows well enough it would get kicked in the head if it did. It's too deep a voice to be Sam's, and I don't remember setting my radio alarm...

I open an eye.

Rodney.

*What?*

Why is Rodney next to my bed? And why do I have such a god-awful crick in my neck?

I'm not in bed, am I?

The thing I'm resting my head against, the thing that up until a moment ago I thought was my pillow, groans and shifts slightly – and everything comes flooding back.

Aidan. Pistachios under the table. Wigs and streetlights and lightning.

*Aidan.*

Which means…

I blink and straighten, only to see Rodney standing in front of me, his arms folded over his newspaper and the biggest shit-eating grin I have ever seen on his face.

"Morning, Lexi. And friend."

"Morning?"

"Mmm-hmm. Your dad's looking for you, young lady."

"What time is it?"

"Seven thirty."

"*Thewhennow?*"

I scramble to my feet, knocking into bleary-eyed Aidan and trying to ignore Rodney's laughter. "Where is he?"

"The top room."

"Right." I sprint for the main door – unlocked at last – and risk one quick backwards glance at Aidan, sitting up and blinking in the bright sunshine pouring in through the glass roof. "I'll find you later!"

In the corridor outside, the early risers among the traders are already making their way up from breakfast, ready to open their stalls for the last day of the convention. None of them seem particularly surprised to see me running past them – why would they be? Most of them are regulars, and have seen me racing past them in one direction or another for years. One of them – a woman from the biggest trading cards stall – even shouts "Morning, Lexi!" after me.

"Morning!" I take the grand staircase down to the hotel's

main lobby two stairs at a time and skid to a halt in front of the narrow cargo lift beside the reception desk. It's the fastest way up to the meeting room at the very top of the hotel, half a dozen floors up. I hate this lift – it rattles and creaks and is generally crotchety and awful and crap – but it's still faster than me trying to run up all those stairs right now. Besides, if Dad's already looking for me, it means he actually wanted to see me ten minutes ago; he only ever starts looking for me when I haven't magically appeared by his side fast enough.

Being a cargo lift, there are no mirrors in there – which means it feels even smaller than it is, a little like standing in a tiny metal coffin, and I have to attempt to make myself more presentable using guesswork alone. Nothing's going to help the morning breath though; my mouth feels like someone came along and lined it with mouldy carpet during the night. And then the lift jerks to a halt and the doors rattle open, and there – against the backdrop of floor-to-ceiling windows looking out over the sea and the ruins of the West Pier with the observation tower holding up the sky above it all – is my father. He's checking the water jugs and glasses for the Q&A session in here later, and even across the room I can tell how angry he is. It's coming off him in waves.

"You wanted to see me?"

"Where've you been, Lexi?"

"The lift's really slow, and—"

"Nobody saw you last night. Anywhere. You didn't answer your phone, and Samira tells me you didn't go back to your room."

He noticed.

"You called me?"

"Sam did. When she didn't get an answer, she called me."

I should have known.

"Oh."

"Well?"

"Funny story, actually." I raise my hand to shield my eyes from the glare coming off the water. "Do we need to pull the curtains across, do you think?"

It's not enough to distract him – but it was worth a try.

"Lexi. Where were you?"

There's no point in trying to hide it. "I got locked in the convention centre."

"All night?"

"All night."

"How on earth…?"

"Haydn Swift thought he left his phone in panel room one. We went back to check, and Rodney locked us in."

"Stop." Dad holds up his hand. "Back to the beginning. Who?"

"Haydn Swift."

"I know that name… Oh. The *author*?"

"Yes?" My voice is suddenly a five-year-old's.

"You managed to get yourself locked in the convention space overnight with a male author who is several years older than you are?"

"He's nineteen, Dad."

"And you are seventeen. Which makes you not an adult."

"It's not like—"

"Ah. No." He holds up a warning finger. "It *is* like." Finger still raised, he rubs his face with the other hand. "What were you *thinking*? You don't know him. *Anything* could have happened!"

"But—"

"Why didn't you call? I could have let you out – Sam could have, anyone on the staff could have. Were you embarrassed? Was that it?" He's started pacing up and down in front of the window. "I mean, if any of the traders find out, they'll start asking about insurance – did anything get damaged?"

"No, Dad. We were really careful, I promise…"

He doesn't seem to hear me. "There's the artists in the art show, all the book traders, the collectible traders…" He stops dead in his tracks and spins to face me, narrowing his eyes. "Lexi Angelo. If I thought for one minute you had done this on purpose…"

"What? Why? Why would I do that?"

"To spend time with a…a boy…"

"Jesus, Dad."

"Lexi…"

"I tried to call, okay? But my phone didn't work in the panel room or anywhere else – there's no reception. What was I supposed to do?"

*It probably would have worked on the roof. If I'd tried…*

"Use the fire exit."

"Set off the alarms and get the whole hotel evacuated? Yeah, you'd have loved that, wouldn't you?" I grumble.

At first, I don't understand why I'm so annoyed; why everything he says grates against the inside of my head – and then I get it. It was *Sam* who noticed I was missing. It was *Sam* who told him. My own father, who tells me how indispensable I am during a convention, who tells me how much he loves me, who I've always been so desperate not to disappoint; *he* didn't notice. And now he knows, his first response isn't that something might have happened to me overnight, it's that we might have broken something in the traders' room.

"I don't have time for this." He's stopped looking at me, and is now furiously straightening the already-straight pads and pencils at each space around the table. "I have a convention to run."

"Like I hadn't noticed. And as we all know, the conventions are what matter most, aren't they? Never mind what anybody else needs. 'What's that, Lexi? You have an essay on Napoleon and a project on modern English drama due in on Monday? Well, instead of doing those, you can send all these emails! You need to talk to me? Sorry – banquet seating!'"

"Lexi…"

I ignore the warning in his voice. I don't care. I don't. What can he do to me? He's already shown me how much he takes everything I do for granted; all the juggling, all the fitting everything – life, school, feelings, *everything* – around what he needs. Around what the conventions need. And now he has Bea, and that's great…but where does it leave me? Who can I turn to? Sam? Nadiya? Bede? Who's *my* Lexi? Who has my back? It's supposed to be my dad. It's supposed to be him – but it never has been, has it? And I've let him get away with it.

"What's this about, Alexandra?" Dad bangs his hand on the table, and even though I'm watching him – even though I see him raise his palm and bring it down again – the sound still makes me jump.

"It's not about anything," I lie – and even to me, I sound petulant. Or maybe it's only half a lie – it's not about anything; it's about *everything*. It's about the fact I've spent my whole life fitting in with Dad's plans, Dad's life, Dad's job, Dad's conventions. That's always been my world, whether I wanted it to be or not – I never got a choice. And right now, it feels like my entire relationship with my father revolves around whether the next hotel has enough space, or whether they've confirmed our banquet reservations or whatever.

The scary thing is, though, that I can't really imagine my life being any other way. I'm not even sure who I am – *what* I am – when I'm not being "Max Angelo's daughter". It's never really been an issue before – I thought everything would just carry on the way it always has for ever, and that was fine. Now, though? I can't be as certain. Is that really what I want? To always stay the same? Same old Lexi, same old clipboard, for ever and ever.

This world is where I belong, and I know that. I'm good at it and I love it – but I don't think I've ever really looked *beyond* it. I never wanted to, I guess, because I feel like here's where I'm most me… But things are changing…with Dad and Bea…and now with Aidan…just the memory of the scent of him, the feel of his shoulder under my cheek, sets off fireworks underneath my skin. Suddenly it feels like *everything* has changed.

Dad sighs and shakes his head like I'm the worst daughter in the world. Maybe I am. How would I know? How would he? All I know is how to be this version of me – and this morning, me has had enough.

"Lexi, just so you know, I've never doubted you before, but this…episode is making me question your judgement."

"Excuse me?"

# CLEAN UP

"Try to see it from my point of view, hmm? You've never even been on a date, and now – this. What would you think if you were me? If you were Bea…?"

I can't believe he's brought her into it – not Mum, who would actually have a right to a point of view. "Talk about bad judgement," I mutter – but not quietly enough.

His eyes narrow down to lasers, boring straight into me.

"Go to your room."

"What?"

"You heard me. Your room. Go there, now – and stay there. I don't want to see you on the convention floor this morning. Maybe some sleep will adjust your attitude."

"But—"

"No." He turns his back on me. "I'm not listening to another word. Room. Now."

I think my dad just grounded me. In a hotel.

I make sure I stamp on every single stair on the way down to the floor my room is on. When I pass one of the hotel's housekeeping staff admittedly I stomp a little less hard, because housekeeping are intimidating and once you've had to stand in a guest of honour's trashed hotel room begging them not to charge you for the damages, you gain a certain level of respect for them. (The housekeeping staff, that is. Not the guest of honour. She's been banned from every convention in Europe now; it's quite an achievement.) But once he's gone past, I carry on stomping just the same – and slam the door to my room for good measure. If my father is suddenly going to start treating me like a kid, I'm going to behave like one. That'll show him.

While he's three floors above me, unable to hear me or see me and probably not even thinking about me at all.

Umm.

But at least I won't be there, running around at his beck and call, will I? And that's down to him. I'm just doing what I'm told, for better or worse.

And that? That'll *really* show him.


I try Sam's mobile; it goes to voicemail. She probably wouldn't have time to talk anyway – especially if I'm not allowed down to the convention floor this morning. Even though Sunday mornings are pretty quiet, she'll still be picking up the slack, which means she's going to be annoyed with me – and that means I'll have to give her a minute-by-minute account of last night before she'll let me whinge about Dad.

My fingers curl around my phone; I could try Mum. Maybe she'd listen…or maybe she'd agree with Dad. Not about the convention and the risk of damaging the traders' room…but about getting myself locked in there with Aidan. And staying locked in there. I can even hear her voice in my mind, picture her shaking her head at Leonie across the room…

Besides, I already feel bad about that Bea comment – I just wasn't expecting Dad to bring her into the conversation, especially after that *dating* comment. Like it's any of her business. Like it's any of *his*. It's not that I've not *wanted* to go on a date, maybe even – gasp! – have a boyfriend…but I've not really met anyone who made me feel like they'd be worth the trouble, or worth spending the pitiful amount of precious spare time I actually *have* with. And that's fine. Or at least it was until my own father decided to *weaponize* my choices…

No. I won't call Mum.

But I *will* have that shower…

I don't hear the phone when it rings the first time, mostly because I went to sleep with my head under both the hotel pillows and it's a better version of the world under here. It's like being eaten by a giant marshmallow, which is comforting because if I were to be eaten by a giant marshmallow then all my troubles would be over, and it feels like a fittingly ridiculous way to go out.

But apparently my phone has something important to tell me, because when I do hear it and drag it under Marshmallowpillow Mountain, there are a stack of missed calls from Sam. There's been a crisis – of course there has. Even as I'm holding it, it rings again – although thankfully no one's there to hear me squeak.

"Sam?"

"Sorry to wake you, Lex…"

"I wasn't asleep."

"Oh. But your dad said…"

"I bet he said plenty."

"Is everything okay? You sound all muffled."

"I'm confined to quarters, so I'm under my pillow."

"What? Why?"

"Why pillow, or why grounded?"

"Either."

"Long story."

"Oh." She doesn't seem to quite know what to do with this.

"It's fine – I'll be down later. What's up?"

"It's Aidan. He was looking for you."

"Aidan?" I move so fast that the pillows bounce halfway to the door.

"Yeah, he was leaving and wanted to say goodbye, I think."

"Leaving?" No. No, no, no. He can't leave. Not yet. I was going to look for him. Why didn't I try his mobile, see if he found it? Anything, rather than just flop around here? I'm an idiot. A pure-grade, solid gold idiot. Being eaten by a marshmallow is too good for me. "When? When is he going?"

"Soon? I don't know – I saw him about five minutes ago."

"Did he find his phone?"

"I don't *know*, Lexi!"

"Stop him."

"What?"

"Just…oh, staple yourself to his leg if you have to, but don't let him leave!"

I can't find my shoe. One is right where I left it, at the end of my bed. The other should be next to it.

It isn't.

I hang off the mattress, scooping the shoe I can see up and peering underneath the bed. Nope. Not there. I can't go down with only one shoe, can I?

Can I?

I could say it was some kind of cosplay?

No.

I hobble round the whole room – twice – one shoe on, the other off (obviously), looking under the bed, in the wardrobe, under the dressing table, everywhere – until I spot the very end of a trainer lace poking out from behind the bathroom door. I lunge for it, grab it…and the bathroom door swings all the way open, knocking my make-up bag off the edge of the sink with a crash, the contents scattering all over the tiled floor.

*Aaaaaaaaargh.*

I slam the door on the whole mess and half-hop, half-run to the end of the hall, slamming my thumb onto the lift button so hard it hurts – and it's only as I hop into the lift, still doing up my second shoelace, that I remember I left my wallet, my key *and* my phone in my room. All I have is the clothes I'm wearing and my convention lanyard, tucked into the pocket where I stuck it after my shower.

Oh, arsebiscuits.

The lobby is full of people checking out of the hotel, milling about with their bags and saying goodbye to friends…but none of them is Aidan. Not one. Across the floor, Sam spots me and waves a hand above her head, pointing at the revolving door out onto the street. "He *just* left," she yells over the burble of voices. "His train…"

Train.

Train.

Right.

I make the kind of dash that usually gets you a sportsperson of the year award and throw myself at the revolving door. Just before it spits me out onto the pavement, I hear Sam shouting, "Where are you going?"

I am going to the station, Samira.

If that's where Aidan's gone, it's where I need to go too – even if it's only to say goodbye. Because after last night,

I can't just let him go; I have to see him one more time. So I am going to the station.

Somehow.

As if by magic, a taxi pulls up at the entrance to the hotel and the door opens. It's an elderly couple with a mountain of luggage. I try to make my shuffling from one foot to the other as discreet as possible and even help them with their bags – and as soon as they're halfway up the steps, I throw myself into the back of the taxi.

"Station, please. And if you could, you know, be a bit brisk about it?"

The cabbie turns round in the seat and stares at me. "You what?"

"I need to get to the station. Now!"

"All right, love. Calm down."

Every light is red. Every single light. Every junction is blocked by buses or cars or what appears to be a tricycle towing a small cart behind it.

"Shit."

"Your mother know you talk like that?" He stops at yet another red light and turns around to grin at me, draping an arm around the back of his seat.

I'm so extraordinarily not in the mood.

"My mother's a literature professor who lives in France with her girlfriend. I imagine the only comment she'd make about my language would be if I punctuated it badly." While he's been busy gawping at me, the light has turned green. Someone behind us hoots impatiently. "Can we go?"

He opens his mouth and closes it without a sound and before I know it, the station is directly ahead.

And I have no money.

It would have been great if I had thought of this before I got in the taxi.

"Five eighty, love."

"Right. Small problem."

His face shifts; he is no longer the chirpy, banter-loving cabbie of a minute ago. He's now a heavy-set middle-aged guy I've just tried to rip off (as he sees it, anyway). "How small?" he asks, right after he locks all the doors.

"So, I have to catch someone before they get the train – will you wait?"

"I'll charge you for it. And you pay upfront."

"Umm."

"Still a problem?"

I pat my pockets, just in case there's a miraculous ten pound note in there (I live in hope). There isn't – but there is my lanyard.

"This!" I wave it at him like it's made of pure gold. "Take this…"

"I ain't going to a convention."

"No, no. It's mine – and I need it."

"No cash? No waiting." He folds his arms and glares at me.

"Not even with collateral?"

"No." He pauses – and for a second I think he's about to change his mind. I look as lost and helpless as I possibly can, and then he says, "Five eighty. No waiting."

Not changing his mind, then. Fine. I can walk back, but first, I have to get *out* of here.

"Okay. Okay. Right. I don't have the cash, but if you go back to the hotel where you picked me up and ask for…" I skim through the list of Dad's staff – there's no point sending him to Sam, is there? – "Marie, she'll sort you out. I swear."

"I'm not—"

"It's the best I can do! Please?"

"It'll be a return fare," he says reluctantly.

"Yes, yes."

The doors unlock, and I'm out.

I have not thought this plan through. I don't know where Aidan is, where he's going, whether he's still here. I don't even know what I'm doing.

Departure board. Yes.

I scan the list of trains, looking for anything that might be the right thing. Most of them go to London. Would he be getting a London train? Maybe. Maybe not. I don't—

"Platform four for the train to Bristol Temple Meads. Will any passengers planning to travel to Bristol Temple Meads please board the train immediately, as it is ready to depart."

Bristol.

I look up at the board.

*Bath. I live in Bath.*

The stop before Bristol Temple Meads is Bath.

The gates for the platform are almost directly ahead of me. I run for them, hearing the train's engines rumble into life. The guard is pacing up and down the platform, waiting for the last stragglers to get on board...

And there he is. Halfway up the platform, walking away from me; grey T-shirt, jeans and a scruffy backpack. Hair like a thundercloud, and I would know that walk anywhere. I would know *him* anywhere, across the biggest room or in the biggest crowd, because I *know* him.

I can see him.

"Aidan!" I lean over the ticket gates, and I can't tell if the ache under my ribs is from the gate digging into my stomach or from the thought of him leaving before I...what? Have the chance to say goodbye? I don't know, but I need to see him. I need to leave some kind of mark on him, the way he's left a mark on me. Because all I can think is that he has left his name tattooed across the inside of my head and I have to—

The last door slams and the guard blows his whistle, hopping onto the train at the very last moment.

With a rumble that grows to a roar, the train pulls out of the station and Aidan is gone.

\* \* \*

# CLEAN UP

Having served out my morning's grounding, I spend the afternoon closing down registration and helping the traders pack up their stuff and cart it down to the hotel's loading dock. It's a relief not to be with Sam or Nadiya, not to have to listen to the chatter of a hall full of people or smile and give directions to this room, that room, the toilets, a coffee shop, somewhere-I-can-get-some-rock-as-a-souvenir. I even volunteer to help dismantle the art show, where the empty galleries are haunted by Aidan. He is everywhere I look, everywhere I turn.

Dismantling the art show keeps me out of everyone's way until we're officially closed – which is exactly what I want. By the time I come down from the gallery and head to the lobby with the last bag of rubbish, the hotel has started to take on a ghost-ship feel. As I'm on my way down the corridor, someone turns off the traders' room lights and the cavernous space is left dark and deserted…except for one table, still draped in a white tablecloth and lit by evening sunlight fractured through the glass roof. If I look carefully enough, I wonder whether I'll still see a handful of pistachio shells under there?

I drop the rubbish bag off with the hotel porter, who gives me a nod. "All done then?" he asks, disappearing the bag into his cupboard.

"All packed up. You can have your hotel back now." I try and make the smile look real, but I think it probably misses by a long way.

"You say that, but we've got a political lot coming in tomorrow." He rolls his eyes – whoever they are, they're clearly not his political party of choice.

"Well, hopefully they'll be more trouble than we were," I say brightly – then stop. "I mean," I try, "hopefully we'll have been less trouble than…?"

He leans on the edge of his desk, eyebrows raised and clearly enjoying my ineptitude.

I give up. "I want you to like us best, okay?"

"Will do." He gives me a mock salute as I turn towards the bar, where Dad and everybody else are sitting around a couple of the large booth tables in various states of exhaustion. Sam has her head down on one table and Nadiya and Bede are comparing notes on who had the worst problem to deal with. (From what I can tell, Bede's was the more depressing – after spending two hours setting all the candles up in the banqueting hall for the gala dinner, he accidentally turned off the extra air-con. The room got so hot they melted and turned into A+ gothic dribbly candelabra – onto the white linen tablecloths and napkins.) Meanwhile their parents and the other staff all stare blankly into their drinks, knackered. Marie, sitting a few seats along from Dad and nursing a large rum and Coke, gives me a smile and slides my lanyard across the table at me.

"Sorry," I say, sheepishly. "How much do I owe you?"

"Don't worry about it."

Dad looks from Marie to me, and back to Marie. "Anything I need to know about?"

"No, Max," she says firmly, and takes a sip of her drink. I love Marie a bit.

Dad pats the cushioned seat next to him. "Sit down, Lexi."

I sit. But I do it in a grudging way – obviously.

"Did I ever tell you about my first convention?"

I don't know what I was expecting; he's not the kind of dad who carries on a bollocking he started giving you earlier – his attention span's too short, for one thing. But the trip down memory lane is still a bit of a surprise.

"You held it in the back room of a pub in Waterloo and there were three—"

"Not that one," he says, from behind the glass of wine he's drinking. "My *first* convention. The first one I ever went to."

This is new.

"No…?"

"It was a comic convention. Not like the ones today though." He puts his glass down, and I don't think he even knows I'm here any more. "Not much more than a couple of collectors in a village hall, with a few boxes of books. My father – your grandfather, but you never met him, he died before you were born – took me on a Saturday afternoon. I've always remembered the way it smelled, the feel of the comics and listening to those men talking about the stories in there and who had which issues…"

I've never heard this story before. Not in all the times I've heard him talk about how he got into conventions; he's never talked about the first one he *went* to. He never talks about when he was growing up, not to me, not ever. Not until now.

"…and I've never forgotten how it made me feel. Like I was part of something, connected. Like I'd found another family – one that went beyond my flesh and blood. One that shared the things I loved, even if the people in it weren't the people I'd have imagined I could be friends with. It made me happy. I walked home with my dad, and I felt like I was glowing inside. When he passed, that was what I remembered. We'd not seen eye to eye for years by then – even after we'd patched things up, it was never quite the same between us. But that convention – if you can call it that – he took me to that because I think he knew it would make me happy, and it did. And ever since then, I've wanted to make other people feel the same way. That's why I started the conventions, in the back rooms of pubs. I was doing it for that feeling, for other people – and for me. They got bigger, and then bigger again, and then suddenly it was a business and it was what I did all the time. It went from being a part of my life to *being* my life."

Now, *that* I can identify with.

He lowers his voice so it's barely more than a whisper.

"I didn't realize the impact it was having on my relationship with your mother, the impact it was having on *her*. Not until it was too late."

"You know I never blamed you for Mum leaving."

He blinks at me as though I've surprised him. Then he smiles. "You don't blame her either though, do you?"

"No."

"I don't. I loved your mother. Still do."

"I know."

"And in her way, she feels the same…"

"Ummm. That's debatable."

"But I won't make the same mistake again."

*Bea*. That's what this is about. I should have known. He looks me right in the eye, as though he thinks he'll be able to see whether I understand by peering into my eyes. All he'll see is that I need a good night's sleep, preferably starting before midnight.

"It's okay, Dad."

"I always thought that about me and your mum – thought it was okay. And then…" He shrugs. "I just don't know where the time went. And now, with you, you're almost grown up – and I still don't know where it goes."

"Here." I tap the top of the table. "The time goes here. I can show you the paperwork to prove it." I sigh, and pick at the edge of the table. "I didn't want to let you down. I'm sorry if I did."

There is the longest, longest pause, and I'm so afraid.

And then, at last...

"No, Lexi. *I'm* sorry." He pushes the glass away from him, then slides it closer again, staring at a wet ring on the wooden surface. "I've never been the best parent, I know."

"Daaaad..."

"No, let me say this. When you were little, I was away and I was working and I let your mother do it all – and then suddenly, she was gone and you weren't a baby any more. You were a whole person, a person I didn't know. And if I'm honest about it, I don't think I ever really tried to work out what being a parent was. I was just me and I thought if I was me and you were you we'd muddle through somehow. Doing the conventions together, I hoped it would be our thing. It would bring us closer together, make us a team."

"And they have. We are."

"I thought so. But then you go and lock yourself in an empty convention hall with a boy and—"

"I said I was sorry! Anyway, I told you, we got locked in."

"Lexi." He gives me a withering look – the one he uses on suppliers who won't cut a deal. "You and I both know that's a lie. At least give me that, would you?"

"Mmmmphgffllfkkmaybe." I doodle my finger through a puddle on the tabletop, only realizing I'm drawing a heart when I finish. And then wondering what, exactly, I've just

stuck my finger in. I *think* it's just condensation, but…
I wipe my finger on the edge of the booth.

"This boy, then."

"Aidan."

"The writer."

"Author."

"He wrote that book, didn't he?"

"Authors usually do."

He laughs quietly. "You're so like your mother."

"Good."

"And so like me."

"Umm."

"This Aidan. You like him?"

"I think so."

"You think so? That doesn't sound like my daughter.
She's usually so sure of herself, even when she shouldn't be."

"All right, all right. I like him, okay?"

"Would you like to invite him to the wedding?"

"What?"

"The wedding. Would you like him to come?"

"I can ask him? Really?"

"If you like him…"

"Thank you!" I throw my arms around him in an awkward
sideways hug, and feel him hug me back. "Thank you! Are
you sure? I mean…"

"It's not me you should be thanking. It was Bea's idea –

she thought you might want to bring someone along. I spoke to her last night – before all this, I should add. I'm not sure I would have even considered it otherwise."

*It was Bea's idea?*

He must have felt me stiffen because he leans back and looks at me sternly. "I know you think... Look, Lexi, I know Bea and I haven't been together that long, but this feels right. It *is* right. You should give her a chance."

"I have. I mean, I am."

"She makes me happy."

"Good. I know."

"And she's very fond of you."

"She hardly knows me, Dad. She hardly knows *you*."

"She knows me perfectly, Lexi. She knows who I am – she sees me, for good and bad." He pauses. "Maybe you should give her the chance to see who you are too?"

There's no answer to that, is there? I stare at the edge of the table, feeling precisely eight years old.

This is clearly enough of a heart-to-heart for my father, who drums both hands smartly on the table. "We should be getting some dinner. Are you hungry? Marie and Paul were saying the fish and chip place down on the beach is pretty good if you fancy it?"

"I'll just go change my top. Give me five minutes?"

He nods as I slide out of the booth – but when I reach the lobby, I stop and double back.

# CLEAN UP

"Dad?"

"Hmm?"

"I get it from you. Being sure of myself. I get it from you."

He smiles – even though he tries to hide it by looking at his watch. "I thought you were getting changed?"

You'd have to know my dad as well as I do to hear that his voice cracks as he says it.

# JULY

## HOME

To: \<Convention.info\>
From: \<Aidan Osian Green\>
Date: 7 July; 03:47
Subject: Missed call

Hey Lexi,

Sorry I missed your call earlier – I'm in Detroit for a meeting
with the film producers. No idea what exact time it is at
home, but I'm pretty sure it's night-time-ish and I didn't
think you'd appreciate a wake-up call ;)
    Speak soon.
    Aidan

---

To: \<Aidan Osian Green\>
From: \<Convention.info\>
Date: 7 July; 07:45
Subject: Re: Missed call

Authors aren't allowed to use the Winky Face Of Idiocy. If an
actual real-life, properly published big-shot writer can't
express himself without resorting to a bunch of random

punctuation marks then I don't know what kind of world this is.

Btw: was calling to ask if you want to come to my dad's wedding.

Lexi

---

To: <Convention.info>
From: <Aidan Osian Green>
Date: 7 July; 07:49
Subject: Re: Missed call

"Random punctuation marks"? You do know using them to express yourself is LITERALLY what they're FOR, yes? As in, the difference between:

Today I helped my uncle, Jack, off a horse.

And...

Today I helped my uncle jack off a horse.

A

---

To: <Convention.info>
From: <Aidan Osian Green>
Date: 7 July; 07:50
Subject: Re: Missed call

Btw: are you asking me out?

A

---

To: <Aidan Osian Green>
From: <Convention.info>
Date: 7 July; 07:52
Subject: Re: Missed call

You're SUCH a loser

;p

L

---

To: <Convention.info>
From: <Aidan Osian Green>
Date: 7 July; 07:54
Subject: Re: Missed call

But you still called me a big-shot writer, didn't you? x

---

To: <Aidan Osian Green>
From: <Convention.info>
Date: 7 July; 07:58
Subject: Re: Missed call

Shut up.

And you didn't answer my question.

---

To: <Convention.info>
From: <Aidan Osian Green>
Date: 7 July; 08:02
Subject: Re: Missed call

You didn't answer mine. x

---

To: <Aidan Osian Green>
From: <Convention.info>
Date: 7 July; 08:10
Subject: Re: Missed call

My dad's wedding is hardly a date though, is it?

Although if you're weird enough to think it is, then FINE.

So are you coming, or what?

---

To: <Convention.info>
From: <Aidan Osian Green>
Date: 7 July; 08:12
Subject: Re: Missed call

Well, in that case I'd love to. A x

---

To: <Lexi Angelo>
CC: <Aidan Osian Green>
From: <Convention.info>
Date: 7 July; 08:14
Subject: Re: Missed call

Lexi, might I remind you that other people have access to
this email address and use it for actual work purposes –
not just for flirting?
Dad

---

To: <Aidan Osian Green>
From: <Convention.info>
Date: 7 July; 08:15
Subject: Re: Missed call

Whoops.
L X

---

[12 messages have been moved to the Bin. Undo?]

# AUGUST

## YORK

# GET ME TO THE CHURCH

Sam looks from me to the rubbish skip and back again.

"Nope. You're on your own."

"Sam…" I have tried pleading. I've tried begging. I've even tried bribing her, but it's no use. She cannot be bought. Even though *technically*, this is kind of her fault. I open my mouth to tell her this, and all she does is fold her arms across her chest and nod at the skip.

"You're up, Angelo. Tick-tock – it's half past already."

"You're going to make me climb into the hotel rubbish bins on the day of my father's wedding. I'm his best-person-thing, and you're making me go through the bins."

"Mmm…yep." She pulls at a strand which has escaped the giant bun she's forced her hair into.

I try again. "My father's wedding."

Nothing.

Clearly my best friend has as much mercy as she does conscience.

"You know, you could at least offer to help." I grab the

top of the rubbish skip, level with my shoulders, and pull myself high enough up it to swing a leg over and drop into knee-high hotel garbage in my brand-new leggings. Luckily it's not the kitchen bins that get emptied into this one, so it's mostly bags of shredded paper – but still.

Sam's voice is annoyingly clear over the sound of rustling paper and plastic as I start sifting through junk. "I *could* offer to help, but then you'd be missing the chance to really work through your issues."

I kick a yellow plastic bag full of what looks like yesterday's newspapers up and out of the skip. "I don't have any issues. Other than the fact I've – no, wait, *you've* – managed to throw out all Bea's schedules. That's a pretty big issue right now."

"It's called an order of service when it's for a wedding, Lexi."

"I don't care what it's called. I don't need to care what it's called. I just need to find a bag full of them."

There was something sticky on that last rubbish bag I picked up. I force myself not to retch. A bright blue bag, that's what I want; a blue bag that I safely tucked under a table in the ops office, all ready to take up to my room last night. At least, it was safely tucked under a table until Sam picked it up and *threw it out*. This, however, is not the story that Sam tells. Oh no. In Sam-world, I asked her to throw out the blue bag and give me the orange one.

GET ME TO THE CHURCH

Which I did not.

At least...I don't think I did.

Did I?

The look on Sam's face when I discovered a bag full of used stationery and Bede's crisp packets at the end of my bed, instead of Bea's beautifully laid out and printed service sheets for the wedding, suggests that perhaps I might not be remembering that conversation as clearly as I'd like.

What can I say? It was late. I was tired.

Neither of these will cut it with my dad. Or Bea.

Hence: the skip.

"You found them yet?"

"Oh, yes. Yes, Sam. I found them straight away. It's just that it's so relaxing in here I thought I'd, you know, hang out for a while." Was that a flash of blue? Right down at the bottom of the pile of bags?

The further I go down through the layers, the worse the smell gets. It's not "rotten" bad, but it's not exactly nice. More like...mouldy metal with a hint of stagnant pond, mixed with that weird smell you get on buses in the summer. Something damp falls sideways against my ankle and I make a mental note to throw my leggings in the bin the instant I get back to my room. If I didn't have to walk all the way back through the lobby, I'd make the whole process several stages shorter and just leave them here – but I think that might be pushing our luck with the hotel staff a little too far.

Another glimpse of blue.

"I think I can see it!"

I burrow down through the rubbish…and there it is. My bag. Well, Bea's bag. And it's still tied shut and it's not wet and it doesn't have any non-specific ooze on it or anything.

"Victory!" I hurl myself at the side of the skip, waving my prize above my head. Sam reaches up and grabs it, leaving me peering out at her. "Hey!"

"I think I'd better look after that, seeing as you're clearly set on sabotaging your dad's wedding." She says it with a grin, but it still stings. She was kidding. Of course she was kidding.

"I'm not sabotaging anything. You picked up the wrong bag, Sam."

"Did I? Or did you *tell* me the wrong bag?" Somehow she manages to narrow her eyes and raise one eyebrow at the same time.

"Oh, go find someone else to practise psych on. What about Bede? He's a writhing mass of neuroses – do him. You'd be able to get a whole essay out of him at least." I shake my head at her and lean on the top of the skip. Mistake. So that's my top going in the bin too then. "Any chance of a hand out of here, maybe?" I hold my arms out to her, but all she does is shake her head and clutch the bag closer to her chest – which is brave because, ooze or no ooze, I know where it's been. She eyes me over the top of it.

"You said, 'They've only been together a year, and they don't even live together.'"

"You're bringing that up now?"

"Well, you did."

"And they had. And they don't. And that was a couple of months ago, so…"

"It was the way you said it. I *know* you, Lexi."

"I didn't say it like anything! Jesus, Sam…"

She watches me, and I watch her watching me and I know what's going through her mind. I'd probably be thinking exactly the same if I were in her position and she was the one rifling through a rubbish skip. Although, come to think of it, I'd probably be too busy laughing.

Which Sam isn't doing.

"You really believe I'd do something to spoil my dad's wedding?" My voice comes out small and fragile because I don't even want to give the words shape, never mind weight. "You're not serious?"

"No. Not, like, on purpose."

"Sam!"

"I just think…" She pulls at another strand of hair. If she's not careful, that whole topknot is going to explode like a firework and there'll be hair *everywhere*. "I just think that maybe, on some level, you kind of wish it wasn't happening so soon. That's all."

"Sam?" I half-climb and half-fall back out of the skip.

It's not elegant, but at least it gets the job done. "I promise, I'm okay. I know everyone thinks I have to be a bit not okay, but I really, really am okay. The wedding's okay, my dad's okay, Bea's okay. It's all okay. Okay?"

"You have...something...in your hair." She reaches for it, whatever it is, to pull it out – then changes her mind. "No. I think I'm just going to...mmm."

"D'you think I've got time for another shower?" I ask hopefully, and watch as she looks me up and down, sniffing.

"If we have to, we'll *make* time for you to have another shower. It's not optional." She pats the bag under her arm. "I've got these. You get" – she waves a hand in my general direction – "that."

Back in the shower in my hotel bathroom for the second time in an hour, I scrub my hair to remove all lingering echoes of Eau de Skip. But that look on Sam's face still bothers me. She really is sure she picked up the bag I asked her to – and it's not like her to get something like that wrong.

I've tried and I've tried...but I can't remember what I said.

Maybe it *was* late. Maybe I *was* tired. Maybe I was just distracted?

Maybe, however much I try to talk myself into it,

subconsciously I'm just not ready for Dad to get married. *Will I ever be?*

By the time I'm showered, dressed and ready and have tracked my father down in the hotel lobby, one of my shoes is already rubbing. I can feel it every time I pick up my foot. That doesn't bode well. I clear my throat and tap my watch – which, being bright pink rubber, doesn't go with the blue-dress-and-big-swooshy-net-petticoat Bea has somehow persuaded my dad I should wear today – but it's no use. Dad's still engrossed in his conversation with the director in the middle of the lobby.

"Dad."

Nothing.

"*Dad.*"

He laughs at a joke the director makes, then starts telling the story about the time he lost a rubber prop head at a photo shoot… I know this story. It goes on for *ever*.

And all the while, his future wife – the second Mrs Max Angelo – is waiting for him at the registry office ten minutes' walk away.

"DAD!"

He glances at me the way he always does when I shriek at him during a convention – a quick look to make sure my hair's not on fire and I'm not on the verge of death –

and then blithely back to his chat…except then he does a double-take and looks back again. I think the lack of clipboard and the presence of the floofy petticoat probably did the trick.

"Sorry, Johan. Lovely to chat, but I've really got to get on. Give me a call next week?" He pats Johan's arm like he's got all the time in the world; like he's not wearing a suit and tie and like I'm not standing there looking like an enormous blue cake.

"Daaaaa-aaaaad."

"All right, Lexi. I heard you."

"Really? Because I'm sure you said that five minutes ago, right before you went into screening room two to adjust the projector."

"It needed doing."

"That's why I spent quarter of an hour last night showing Nadiya how to do it." And believe me, she wasn't happy about it.

"Well, now it's done and I don't have to worry about it."

"You didn't have to worry about it before – that's why Nadiya was looking after it. See the pattern?" I attempt to flatten the net petticoat again. I fail. I hate this dress – I hate most dresses, but Bea was insistent that I had to wear one for the wedding…and then picked out one that makes me feel like I should be stuck on top of a Christmas tree.

Aidan's going to see me in this thing.

Aidan's going to see me.

I'm going to see Aidan…

*Focus, Lexi.*

Oh, and Bea has also made me personally responsible for making sure Dad gets to the registry office on time.

Fail.

He starts patting down his suit pockets. "Did I give you the rings?"

I try not to roll my eyes. I fail. "Yes. They're in my bag. And you've asked me that twice already."

"Just checking. Do you really need to bring that bag? Don't you have one of those little clutch things, or…?"

*"We need to go!"* I hustle him down the steps and out of the hotel's front door, onto the sweeping gravel drive outside.

"Lexi. They can't start without me."

"Knowing Bea, I wouldn't be so sure…" I link my arm through his – mainly because I'm in heels and I never wear heels, just like I never wear dresses, and the gravel is unbelievably awful to walk on and I don't want to roll up with a broken nose or ankle or both – and tow him through the hotel gardens to the gate.

"Is it this way?" he asks, immediately trying to go the wrong way down the street.

"No. This way – we've got to cross the river." I pull him in the opposite direction.

Unbelievable.

This is a man who can plan a year's worth of conventions in a phone call; a man who can chat with film stars and huge directors and artists and authors…but who, this morning, has quite clearly lost his grip on reality.

My dad all over.

I did ask why they couldn't get married in the hotel, seeing as they're having the wedding reception there – but this was apparently the trade-off. Bea agreed to the reception, but she wouldn't budge on the actual wedding. I guess the threat of a bunch of LARPing wizards charging through the middle of their vows was probably a deal-breaker. Personally, I'd have thought it might liven things up a little. But instead, Bea insisted on the registry office, which means peeling Dad away from the convention while it's *actually running*. Bede laughed so hard when I told him that his face turned purple. It turned an entirely different colour when I told him that seeing as he and Nadiya weren't coming to the wedding, it meant they were going to be in charge of the convention's ops for the day, though…

Hurrying across the footbridge over the river, a gust of wind pulls at the petticoat of my absurd outfit. I slap it back down with my free hand – and almost twist my ankle. I cannot wait to get back to the hotel and change into my usual clothes. Shorts and a T-shirt, that's me. Trainers, not heels, thank you very much. Right now, I feel like I'm in fancy dress; like I'm pretending to be someone I'm not – like I'm going to be found out any moment. By the time we've made it over the bridge, through the car park on the other side and onto the street with the registry office, Dad's actually starting to look nervous.

"Lexi?" he asks as we reach the white-painted porch. At the end of the road, I can just make out the tops of York Minster's towers peeping over the roofs.

"You look great, Dad." I straighten his tie. It doesn't really need straightening, but it feels like something I'm supposed to do anyway. Ceremonial, somehow.

"Thank you. For being here. For being…"

"Dad. She's waiting."

He reaches out a hand like he's about tuck my hair behind my ear – but then he stops himself. Instead, he just stands there, looking at me – and then he takes both my hands and holds them between his. It feels like there's nobody else for miles around; there's no traffic, there's no convention, there's no Bea. Nothing. Just me and my dad.

And then he lifts my hands and drops a kiss on the back of my knuckles, squeezing my fingers and smiling at me.

"I suppose we'd better get on with it."

"Don't let her hear you talking like that. You'll be divorced before you even finish getting married."

Through the glass in the door, I can see Sam lurking in the entrance. She spots Dad coming up the steps and flaps wildly at someone just out of sight. Dad pauses on the top step, right before he pushes the door open…and his back straightens and his head lifts and there's so much joy in the next step. I can feel it, even from the pavement.

My dad is getting married, and he's happy.

Which is just the way it should be – so my floofy dress and I follow him inside.

"Come on, come on, come on…" Sam practically shoves me into the ceremony room after Dad.

"Where's Bea?" I hiss, plastering a smile across my face as everyone turns in their seats to look at us. Dad nods like this is exactly how he planned it and strolls calmly down the aisle to the registrar's desk where his buttonhole – a cornflower – is sitting waiting for him.

"She's in the garden, having a cup of tea."

"Is she annoyed?"

"You're only five minutes late. I'm disappointed – I had a fiver on you being at least ten minutes late."

"You were putting bets on it?"

"We've got a book running."

"Whose idea was *that*?"

She nods at Jules, one of Dad's long-time convention

friends, who's looking at her watch and grinning. I should've known.

"Hang on. Five minutes? But we're…"

Relief washes over me in great big, warm waves as I remember setting my watch ten minutes fast last night for *exactly* this situation. We might have had a hiccup with the service sheets, but I have managed to deliver my father to his wedding on time (more or less). I am a *genius*.

Sam looks me up and down, and wags a finger at the dress.

"I know…" I mutter.

She shakes her head. "No. This. This is good. You should…" She waves a hand at my outfit again. "…This… more often."

"I feel like a loser."

"Maybe. But you look *amazing*."

"Shut up."

Sam holds her hands up. "Truth. Now, I'm going to tell the blushing bride that you've managed to get him here."

"I can't believe you were betting."

"Don't tell your dad, but Bea had him down for being twenty minutes late."

I'm not sure if that reflects worse on me or my dad…or whether it just means that, actually, Bea really does know exactly who he is – and she's marrying him in spite of it. Because of it.

"Sam!"

She sticks her head back through the door. "'Sup?"

"You look pretty amazing yourself, you know." She does; the wrap dress she's wearing is bright, acid yellow and – with her beautiful curly hair and scarlet lipstick – she looks like she belongs on the cover of a magazine.

"Oh, sure I know," she says – sticking her tongue out at me and disappearing through the door to fetch Bea.

When I turn around – still laughing – there he is, looking back at me from the third row.

Aidan.

My heart leaps from my chest and wedges itself halfway up my throat. I haven't seen him since that day in June; since I chased him to the station and missed him anyway. Not in *person*, at least – because between then and now, Aidan's face has been everywhere. Or Haydn's has, anyway.

I've seen him in magazines; on posters pinned to the ends of bookshop shelves and alongside tables piled high with brand-new hardbacks with his name on. I've seen online fan art of him, of Jamie, Ali, Lizzie and the Curator and all the other Piecekeepers. And I've seen endless selfies people have taken with him at signings. I've read the reviews as though my life depended on it, and I've sworn at any of them that didn't give him…his book…a good rating. I've even read the fanfics – and sent him links to the good ones.

I might not have seen him in person, but Aidan has been in my head and in my dreams and in every single beat of my heart. I've felt him under my skin, and heard him in every line of every email, every message. I've seen his smile in every voicemail he's left; and if I closed my eyes when I talked to him on the phone, I could almost feel him whispering into my ear. And now, after seeing him and not seeing him for so long, he's here, in the same room as I am, and we're breathing the same air, and somehow it doesn't feel real.

His eyes lock onto mine across the room and he smiles and everything else in the world is just a blur.

He's wearing a suit. I've never seen him in a suit before.

I've never even imagined him in a suit before. Not actually wearing it, anyway...

He winks at me and gives me a thumbs up, then points at his tie – which is exactly the same colour as my dress.

Suddenly, the floofy blue monstrosity doesn't feel so stupid. But how did he know what I'd be wearing?

Bea.

Bea and my dad.

That's how.

I'm equal parts embarrassed and...something else. *Happy*, I think.

I almost skip down the aisle to stand beside my father, and I can sense Aidan's eyes on me the whole way. As I pass him, I can feel the touch of his fingers on my arm before they so much as brush my skin.

And I try really, really hard not to notice what appears to be a tea stain on the front of the order of service sheet in his other hand...

When she comes, Bea doesn't walk down the aisle, she practically floats. With every step closer to my dad, she seems to glow a little brighter. I've never seen her like this – not *Bea* – and I poke Dad to make him turn round and see her, but he won't.

He doesn't need to, does he?

He already sees her like this.

That's why we're all here – because to him she looks like this every single day.

Finally, when she's almost reached him, he takes a deep breath and he turns and he sees her and he smiles.

It should be weird. It should be wrong-er, somehow, than it feels. Because she's come out of nowhere and he's fallen head over heels for her – my dad, who's all about control and planning and lists and being organized, and never taking risks. This should be a risk, but to him it isn't.

Or maybe she's just worth taking the risk for.

They smile and laugh the whole way through the ceremony. And then suddenly it's over and everyone applauds.

# GET ME TO THE CHURCH

Dad and Bea hold hands while they sign the register – and they're only halfway back down the aisle before Dad sweeps Bea up into his arms and carries her the rest of the way, to cheers from everyone in the room. I half expect him to wince and complain about his back – but I guess thirty years of lugging big boxes of books up and down hotel stairwells have paid off.

The newlyweds disappear outside to the garden at the back of the registry office for photos, while – true to convention form – most of their guests make a beeline for the trays of champagne.

"Hello," says that familiar voice behind me. There he is, holding an empty champagne glass. "Nice dress."

"You have to say that, seeing as you're dressed to match." I slip my finger under his tie and flip it up to make my point. I can feel the warmth of him through his white shirt.

He looks good. He really, *really* does.

"Not great with compliments, are you?"

"They make me suspicious. They're normally followed by someone asking for something."

"Oh." He looks away. "That's a shame."

"What's a shame?"

"Because now I feel like I can't ask you if you want to go out sometime. Properly – seeing as you pointed out that your dad's wedding didn't count."

"Oh."

*Oh.*

"Well, I mean, asking *that* is fine. Obviously." I eye the tray of full champagne flutes the waiter's carrying – and then I get a full-colour mental image of me lunging for one and falling over my stupid shoes, knocking over waiter, tray, glasses and everyone in the room like some kind of human domino run. I stay right where I am.

"So?"

"So what?"

He laughs and everything about him softens and warms. His face is the most familiar face in the world and I can't imagine what my life was like before he was in it. "Not good at answers either, are you?"

"Oh. Sorry. Yes. Yes."

"Yes?"

"Yes."

"Well, all right then." He twiddles the stem of the glass between his fingers, then sets it down on a shelf and sticks both hands in his trouser pockets.

I raise an eyebrow at the glass. "You drank that pretty briskly. Anything I need to know?"

"What, that? No, there wasn't anything in it. I asked for an empty one."

"*Why?*"

"Needed something to do with my hands." He pulls a hand out and holds it in front of him, palm down. It's trembling –

a lot. When he's sure I've seen, his hand disappears back into his pocket. "Didn't think I could pull off asking you out like that, you know? Shaking hands don't exactly suggest cool, do they? Anyone would think I was nervous or something."

"And that would be totally the wrong idea, would it?"

"Obviously."

"You could always have tried shameless sucking-up first." I try not to smile. Not too much, anyway.

"I thought that didn't work on you? Or are you helpless without your clipboard to shield you?" He grins at me.

"Don't push your luck, Mr Big-Shot Writer." I give him a playful shove, and he steps back to catch his balance – and I wonder what we look like from the outside, to other people. To the kind of people who would post their photos with him on the internet; the kind of people who would ask him to sign their arms so they could get his mark tattooed on them for ever.

But he's already left a mark on me, hasn't he?

"There you go again, calling me a big-shot."

"Oh, shut *up*."


Dad had wanted to get a car to drive them back to the hotel, but Bea told him not to be so daft – so we walk, in convoy, back the way he and I came earlier. They're in the lead, arm in arm, and people stop in the street to congratulate them and smile and wave – which does make me wonder whether that's precisely the reason Bea refused the car...

Aidan walks with me, holding my hand, and at first I panic, thinking it'll be so uncomfortable, especially with all Dad's old friends who've known me since I was a kid watching us... But that isn't how it is at all. It feels so perfectly the opposite of that. Perfectly comfortable. More than I ever thought it could. And all those thoughts about what we look like from the outside, they vanish like smoke. I am here with Aidan, and everything else evaporates.

"What's this?" Sam buzzes up alongside me, beaming.

That lasted. "Go away, Sam."

"You two are so *cute!*"

"Go. Away. Sam."

She holds up her hands innocently. "I'm just saying..."

"Well, can you go and say it somewhere else?" I manage to tell her without moving my mouth. I don't know whether this makes me sound serious or insane. Probably both.

Sam gives me a smile made almost entirely of teeth, screwing her eyes shut for comic effect; I haul her out of the way of a guy walking his dog and steer her around a lamppost, although if I had any sense I'd let her crash into them. It's what she deserves. Aidan smiles and shakes his head, releasing my hand so the poor dog-walker can get past. My palm aches from the loss of his touch.

"What's the plan when we get back?" she asks, completely oblivious to the fact I've just saved her from certain death – or a nasty trip, at any rate.

"I'll pick up the walkie from ops, but other than that Nadiya and Bede have said they'll take care of anything needed. We've got a couple of extras covering for health and safety, that kind of thing…"

"Not the convention, you loser. The reception party. Is there food? I'm starving. And then there's you, isn't there?" She nudges me. "You and Aidan. What's the plan there?" Thankfully she's lowered her voice, because Aidan's right on the other side of me, staring out at the river.

"I…don't know."

Because I don't. There's no schedule that tells me how this will go, this me-and-Aidan thing. No lists of names and times. No clipboard can save me now – not from this. Just for once, I have no idea what comes next.

# QUITE A RECEPTION

Considering this has all been done by Dad's company to make up for the "convention-ness" of their wedding weekend, I can still sense the hand of Bea everywhere in the reception room at the hotel, from the blue uplighting on the pillars to the swags of ice-blue fabric tied into giant bows around the chair backs, and the towering vases of lilies and tiny blue fairy lights in the middle of each table. She and Dad are as bad as each other when it comes to handing over control, clearly (although the plus side is that at least I didn't get drafted in to help). Aidan stops in the doorway and sniffs.

"Ah."

"Too much?" It does look vaguely like a princess exploded in here.

"No." He sniffs again. "Lilies."

"You're allergic?"

"Mmm." He nods towards a table all the way across the room, beside an open French window onto the hotel terrace.

"I'll be all right over there though."

This suits me just fine; that table is about as far away from Dad and Bea and the centre of attention as it's possible to get – and there's even a well-placed white voile curtain wafting about in the breeze to shield us too. This is good. Dad's always been pretty happy with being on show, but I can't think of anything worse. Put me in the spotlight and I shrivel up and turn to dust.

I flap at my dad and catch his eye, miming an elaborate display about me sitting at that table instead of with him and Bea. He looks puzzled, then points at me and gives me a thumbs up. So that was easy. Now all I have to do is catch Sam – who is already flirting with one of the waiters.

"Sam. Sam. Sam." I try to draw her attention to me, to the table, to Aidan, to the room…

Nothing.

She's curling a strand of hair round and round her finger and waving her other hand around in what looks like her standard You-must-be-so-strong/important/clever gesture. I shouldn't take the piss; she's used it to get us an extra hand building an art show before now. She finally realizes I'm waiting for her and grins, then shrugs, then heads towards me. I point to the table and she nods. "Good pick."

I move my pointing finger towards Aidan. "Hay fever."

Sam winces, and then winks at the waiter – who winks back.

"Sam!"

"What?"

"Leave the poor guy alone!"

"He's pretty."

"It's my father's wedding."

"And weddings are so romantic," she says, leaning around me to stare at Aidan.

I hold my hands up. "I surrender. And I'm going to get the walkie."

I thread my way across the now-crowded room congratulating Dad and Bea, and kick off my shoes, throwing them under the table where Aidan is checking his phone. "I've got to run over and get the walkie-talkie. Back in a minute."

"Want me to come?"

"Want me to write your next book, seeing as you're apparently up for switching jobs all of a sudden?"

"Is that an offer? Because this whole writing business is actual work, you know." He leans back in his chair.

This is the clipboard all over again, isn't it? Well, if that's how this is going to be… "I'll be two minutes – and then you can tell me just how hard it is to be you, okay?"

Aidan picks up a napkin (which has been folded into some kind of bird – or possibly a bear, it's hard to be sure) and throws it at me.

Fair. But I still think I win.

\* \* \*

When I step through the heavy wooden doors and into the hotel corridor, it feels like slipping underwater. The floor out here is marble tiles, smooth and cool under my bare feet, and with the convention mostly happening at the other side of the building, everything seems calm. One of the guests of honour for the event is waiting for the lift up to her room and gives me a smile as I walk past. "I love your dress," she says. "Who are you cosplaying?"

"A dutiful daughter."

She looks puzzled – then her smile widens. "You're Max's kid, aren't you? Give him my love for today. We go way back. *Way* back," she says again, for emphasis…and I try not to let my smile slip. I know what "we go way back" usually means and I don't want that in my head, thank you very much. Also: kid? No.

"I'll pass that on to him. And his wife."

The lift pings. She gets in, and I shove through the fire door and into the stairwell down to the back of the convention area. To say the floor here is slightly less clean would be the understatement of the year, and I can practically *feel* the soles of my feet turning grey as I jump down the stairs. On the other side of the stairwell door, the convention is running at its usual level of cheerful insanity. A group of guys in matching *Zombie Hunter* T-shirts look me up and down as I pass them, and one of them stage-whispers,

"Is she supposed to be Cinderella or what?" at the others. I turn around and drop them a curtsey. They immediately huddle together for safety, and I head on towards the ops office – where I walk into a full-scale argument.

Nadiya and Bede are yelling at each other from opposite sides of the room; Nadiya holding a sheaf of printouts, Bede standing with his hands on his hips and scowling.

"Woah." I close the door behind me. "What's going on?"

"That stupid kid…" mutters Nadiya, before shaking her head and pressing her lips together under Bede's glare.

"What stupid kid?"

"It's nothing," Bede groans. "We're handling it."

"What. Stupid. Kid?"

"One of the temp staff we brought in to help cover this afternoon. He's bunked off."

"He's *what*?"

"He didn't show for his second shift after his break, and now he's not coming back."

"Did he say why?"

"Apparently," Bede says with so much eye-rolling it's a miracle his eyeballs don't just keep on spinning, "he told Eric to tell Marie to tell Nadiya that he wasn't feeling well and was going to lie down."

"He didn't speak to either of you in person?"

"No."

"And he didn't ask anyone to cover him?"

"No."

I'm not sure what my face does, but both Bede and Nadiya take a step back. In Nadiya's case, this means actually having to step around a chair, but she seems to think having something between her and me might not be the worst idea.

I breathe in. I breathe out. And when I'm calm enough, I try again... "Has anyone checked on him?"

"That's the thing," Nadiya mutters. "We just saw—"

"*I* just saw him," Bede interrupts. "He's at the big book launch in event room three, chattering away to a couple of the guests."

"Oh, you're *kidding*." This is not what I wanted to hear.

"Yeah," Nadiya chips in, waving her paperwork. "And now Bede wants to pull his membership, and cancel the payment for his room and make him pay for it himself."

"And *Nadiya* won't let me," Bede mutters, folding his arms across his chest. Nadiya clutches the paperwork closer and sticks her tongue out. It's like refereeing a fight between a couple of toddlers.

"Okay. Okay. I'm just here for the walkie." I pick it up from the nearest table.

"Lexi!"

"Fine." I hold up my hands, walkie and all. "Give me the rota sheet, Nadiya."

She hands it over and I spread it out on the table, running a finger along one of the columns. "Pen?"

Bede fishes a pen out of his pocket and hands it to me.

I look up at him. "It's green. You know only psychopaths write in green ink, right?"

"Not true. The head of MI6 signs letters in green ink."

"I rest my case." I'm not in the mood to get into a fact-off with Bede – I'd lose anyway. "Look. If you move *them*… here" – I circle one name in green ink and draw a big arrow across the sheet – "and switch *these* two…"

"Oh," says Bede, peering over my shoulder. "That kind of works."

Behind me, I hear Nadiya thump his back. "See? Told you Lexi would fix it."

"Any other disasters I need to know about?" I hand Bede the amended schedule…then change my mind and give it to Nadiya.

He glares at both of us. "The backdrop in the green room fell down?"

"That's not a disaster. That was inevitable. I only stuck it up with drawing pins."

"We know. The sword-fighting guy sat on one."

"Ah."

"He was fine about it – he thought we were pranking him."

"He did?"

"I told you he was weird when I checked him at registration."

"Weird, yes. You were right. I get it. So, before I go – any other *actual* disasters?"

Nadiya flutters her eyelashes. "How's Aidan?"

I side-eye her. "I'll see you later." And I leave the pair of them to it; right now, they deserve each other.

Dad raises an eyebrow at me from beside Bea when he spots the walkie-talkie – it's his usual way of asking-without-asking whether he needs to start panicking or looking for fire extinguishers, bags of dog treats or a shovel (true story). He doesn't need to know about the staffing hiccup, so I give him a thumbs up – but at the exact same moment, Bea takes hold of his elbow and steers him on to the next group of guests. I'm left signalling to his retreating back. It's for the best. I've seen him smile more today than I think I have done in the past year. He looks younger too; he's standing straighter and seems less…tired.

Back when he realized it was serious with Bea, he insisted we all go out to dinner together. It wasn't great. She picked where we went, and it was a very Bea sort of place, with starchy tablecloths and eighteen knives and forks and at least three glasses for each person. She was wearing a long white dress and she had all these bangles stacked up her arm so she jangled every time she moved. The whole evening, all I could think about was the White Witch from

Narnia. How could my dad like *her*? She was so different from Mum. (Even now, I can't see a single thing about them that's alike except that their birthdays are both in August. Maybe Dad's just really into Leos?)

Then, I was scared about what it all meant for the future, for Dad and me: who wouldn't be? But watching them now, I feel different. Bea's touch drops from Dad's elbow, and suddenly they're holding hands. I can see his finger sliding across the new wedding ring on her finger, as though he can't quite believe it's really there. As though he can't believe his luck.

Mum always says it isn't luck, being happy. It's about being brave. Being brave and letting the right people in; the people who make you better just by knowing them, people who make you stronger for loving them. I think she's right. She went through all those years with Dad, and then she left. She didn't have to take the job in Nantes, and she didn't have to let Leonie in…but she did. And sure, you could say that maybe it was all down to some alignment of the stars – but I like to think that she *knew* somehow; that some part of her knew Leonie was one of those people who are worth the risk. She took that risk, and I don't remember her ever being as happy as she is now. Looking at Dad and Bea now, I think I can see the same.

If you believe all happiness is just down to luck, you might as well give up – because you'll never be lucky enough or happy enough. Not if that's what you really think.

I think we make our own happiness – and this is Dad's way of making his. Maybe we have to *choose* to be happy. Maybe we have to take that risk.

Maybe I should just…be brave.


"Lexi." Aidan's nose is decidedly redder than when I left, and the whites of his eyes are looking a bit pink.

"Hmm?" I tear my gaze away from Dad and Bea.

"Over there." He leans in close beside me; his chest pressing against my shoulder, one arm around me, the other hand pointing at something across the room.

"I see…people?"

"Look. Over there. In front of the big wooden panel thing. With the green shirt."

I look.

Ah.

"Is that who I think it is?" he asks – and there's something thin about his voice. Something nervous…

*Aidan Green is a fanboy.*

This could be fun.

"You like his books?" I ask, casually.

"I have *all* of them, even the crazy rare ones. He's pretty much my favourite author. Ever. It was his books that made me want to write."

"Huh."

"Huh what?"

"Oh, nothing. Just never had you down as a fan of his."

"You're joking, right? He's amazing. People think his books are just horror, but they're not – there's so much—"

"Do you want me to get Dad to introduce you?"

"*What?* God, no. No. Yes. No."

"He'd love to – he loves showing off. And anyway, Steve's lovely."

*Is he going to take the bait? Is he?*

"You *know* him?"

3…

2…

1…

I turn to face Aidan. "You do *know* he's my godfather, don't you?"

Aidan, the big-shot writer with the lily allergy, pulls his glasses off and wipes them on the end of his tie. He blinks at me with grey and pink eyes, and opens his mouth…then closes it again and puts his glasses back on.

"Godfather."

"Mmm-hmm."

"Right. Did not see that one coming."

"Should have."

"Should have. Yes." He tips his head slightly. "You're not winding me up, are you?"

"Nope. Want to meet Steve?"

"Steve your godfather."

"Steve my godfather, yes."

"Absolutely."

I guess everyone's a fan of someone; even Haydn Swift.

# SURFING THE EDGE OF CHAOS

The grandfather clock in the corner of the reception room must have chimed before now, but I swear the first time I hear it is when it strikes two.

2 a.m.

Maybe the ribbons and the lilies and the napkins and the people and everything else drowned it out or sort of swallowed the sound. I can sympathize. But two in the morning comes and it rings out clear and sharp.

It's always two in the morning at convention parties. It's like the centre of gravity, only for time.

Dad and Bea have settled at the big round table in the middle of the room and they look pretty comfortable. It's littered with wine bottles and empty glasses from the hotel bar, and all Dad's long-time convention buddies have pulled up their own chairs and are trading stories about The Old Days. Bea's friends and family disappeared hours ago, but she's still here and listening to them all talking about conventions from days gone by. Even if she's not got much love for a fan convention and all its trimmings, she looks pretty happy…but then I guess she would, wouldn't she? Not only is it her wedding day, she's getting to hear all these stories about who her husband used to be. It's the best of both for her – she gets to laugh at the past and look forward to the future.

"Your dad looks happy," says Aidan from across our table. His eyes seem to have gone back to normal – as has his hair, which he'd tried to comb back earlier but which is now just as wild as it's ever been. His tie has also disappeared.

"He does," I say, studying them. Marie has just finished telling Bea about the time the whole convention committee got stuck in a hotel lift and had to be rescued by the fire brigade. Dad is wiping tears of laughter from his eyes with one hand while the other rests on Bea's shoulder. Not only do they look like they belong together, they look like they belong *there*, at the centre of that little knot of people. Maybe if she can see that; maybe if Dad doesn't make the same mistake again with work…

"You, on the other hand, look knackered."

"Too much to do. And you're *full* of charm, aren't you?"

"Don't need charm with a face like this, do I?" He beams at me and sticks his chin out even further.

"Hmm." Before I can stop myself, I've lifted my hand – and it's like I'm watching from behind a thick sheet of glass because there's nothing I can do… It's another Lexi who curls her fingers around his jaw; another Lexi who traces the dimple in his chin with her thumb. Another Lexi altogether who runs the very tip of her finger along the bottom line of his lip.

Another Lexi does it all...but it's *my* heart that starts beating out of rhythm. *My* pulse that races, *my* lungs that suddenly can't get enough air.

He looks at me and I look at him.

*It's the suit. It's the suit. It's the suit.*

Last time this happened, I managed to yawn in his face – and as soon as I think it, the urge to yawn becomes overwhelming. In fact, if I don't yawn right now, the top of my head's going to fall off.

I'm not going to yawn. Not this time.

And if I don't...what then? Where do we go from here? I feel like we're dancing around something, around each other. Around the obvious – at least to me – which is that he's him, and I'm me; I'm in the shadows and he sort of is too...but then he's not. When we're alone and it's just him and me, somewhere in the shadows – on the roof, or even falling asleep in a corner; that's when I feel like we fit. But when he's in the spotlight, signing and having his photo taken? I don't know. I've watched him on the stage, and while he was up there, he was someone else. He was Haydn. And there'll be more panels, more conventions, more *Haydn* for him... But it's Aidan I want, and I don't know how to

handle that other side of him, his life, his world. It isn't me
– and how could I compete with that?

Right now, I don't care.

My fingers are still resting on his face, creeping into his
hair. I'm breathing him in like oxygen. And when he slides
his hand into my hair, running it through his fingers, it's *my*
hair – I'm not some other version of myself any more. I feel
it, with every nerve I have, like a current beneath my skin.

It isn't luck or chance or fate or whatever it's called;
that's not what makes us happy. *We* are. *We* do it. We make
the choice.

Take the risk.

Step into the storm.

Aidan leans in so close that his jaw grazes mine, his skin
hot against me as he whispers in my ear. "Who's the guy
sitting next to your dad?"

That's not what I was expecting. I flick a quick glance
over my shoulder at the big table. "It's his friend Alasdair.
Why?"

"Because Alasdair doesn't approve. Look." He draws
away from me, slipping his fingers out of my hair, and the
space he leaves between us is suddenly the size of the world
– while in the seat beside my father, Alasdair is sitting with
his arms folded and one eyebrow sardonically raised,
looking right at Aidan.

"Oh, come *on*. It's like having another dad." The bad

thing about conventions being a family: even when your actual parents are busy, there's always another one just hanging out in the room, watching you…

Aidan laughs quietly, and although there's still a gap between us, suddenly it feels like nothing at all. His hand finds mine under the table, squeezes it once…then lets go.

I wait for him to say something – anything. He doesn't.

Right.

Okay.

Time for sensible-Lexi to take control again.

"I should go to bed. Some of us have got to pack up a convention tomorrow – especially seeing as *someone else* probably won't be on top form." When I stand, it feels as though someone has stolen my feet. It's like I'm drifting just above the ground.

Aidan reaches under the tablecloth and emerges holding my shoes. He passes them to me; when I take them, both his hands close around mine. "Got them? I'll walk you back to your room."

I'm so tired that I'm shaking. At least, that's my story and I'm sticking to it. "I think I can remember my way around a hotel." It's sensible-Lexi's attempt to distract him from the shaking. I wouldn't want him to think he was causing it, now would I?

"Great – then maybe you can help me find my room? I think I left it somewhere on the second floor…" He tails off when he sees I've gone scarlet. My cheeks are on fire, and not in a good way. "Oh boy. That came out horribly wrong, didn't it?" he blurts out. "Not like that. I'm not that guy."

"Not the guy who'd try to invite me to his room, or…?"

"No. And definitely not the guy who'd try quite such a sleazy line, either." He jerks his head towards Dad and Bea and Alasdair (still watching, still eyebrowing) and everyone else. "And most definitely not in front of your father. And company."

"Well, my room's on the second floor too, so we might as well go together," I say, more to my shoes than to him. I can't quite bring myself to actually say it to his face. "Otherwise it'll just look like we're making a big deal out of leaving separately, and Dad'll be all over that – Bea or not."

Alasdair swivels in his seat to watch us walk out.

It probably doesn't help matters that just before the door closes behind us, I turn and blow him a kiss…

The staircase winds around the lobby at the end of the hall, marble and wrought iron and deep, soft carpet that tickles my feet when I step on it. I can't help checking the stairs behind me, just in case I'm leaving a trail of grubby footprints – but it looks like I'm in the clear. The stairs are lined with mirrors all the way up – small ones framed like pictures, each with its own little light above it – and as we walk up,

I catch glimpses of us; Aidan and me. Our doubles walk up a staircase just like the one we're on, with all the same twists and turns but in reverse. They're dressed the same and their hair's the same and their faces are the same and she's even barefoot and he's missing his tie – but they don't feel like they *are* us. Maybe they aren't. Maybe these aren't mirrors but tiny windows into a world beyond the wall – somewhere else, where we are something else, some*one* else. Maybe he's Haydn, and she's that other Lexi – the one who's started taking control of my brain when he's around, the one who doesn't care. Maybe.

Or maybe they're just mirrors.

"We should have taken the lift," groans Aidan – who's dragging himself up the stairs like someone tied weights to his ankles.

"Feeble," I laugh.

"It's all right for you though, isn't it? You're used to this two-o'clock-in-the-morning running-around-hotels business."

"And you aren't?"

"Nope. Like I told you, I grew up in a *respectable* house. Cup of cocoa, hot water bottle, tucked up in bed by nine o'clock every night."

Doubtful.

"Are you saying I'm not respectable?" I spin to face him, skirt whirling out around me – and for a second, a heartbeat, the time it takes to breathe in, I can picture how it goes

310

through the looking glass; how he sweeps me off my feet, how he pulls me to him...

On the step below me and leaning on the bannister rail, he's shorter than I am – just. I hold my shoes in one hand and put the other on my hip, standing on tiptoe to make myself as tall as I can – and repeat my question. "I said, are you saying I'm not respectable?"

"You, Lexi," he says, putting his hand on top of mine so his fingers rest against my waist, "are..."

Somewhere further up the stairs there's a clatter of metal and crockery; the sound of someone putting a room-service tray outside their bedroom door.

*I'm what? What am I, Aidan? Finish your sentence!*

Except he doesn't. He leaves it; a butterfly in mid-air and me with no net to catch it. Instead, something in his expression shifts and he looks past me, up the stairs, to wherever the sound came from.

"You know the best thing about hotels at two o'clock in the morning?" he asks. His hand is still resting on mine and I can still feel his fingers against my waist through the fabric of the dress. He doesn't wait for me to answer, but snatches my free hand in his and bounds up the stairs, towing me with him. One of my shoes slips from my grip and falls, bouncing down the stairs behind us, but I don't care. I leave it there, like a glass slipper.

"Everything," he says.

# AUGUST

The second-floor corridor is deserted. Of course it is; it's the dead hours of the night, when it's too late to stay up any longer but too early for anyone to even consider getting up. People talk about midnight being the witching hour, but anyone who's been up all night knows that the witching hour starts at one thirty and ends at dawn.

We are deep into magic time.

The corridor stretches ahead, like hotel corridors do. Long and narrow, softly lit and deeply carpeted; punctuated by closed doors. "See that?" Aidan points to a dinner tray outside one of them, about halfway down.

I'm not sure I follow. "Somebody's washing-up?"

"Come on," he whispers, and tiptoes up to it.

"What are you doing?"

"Shhh." He presses a finger to his lips like a toddler, then crouches down in front of the tray and carefully and quietly starts unloading everything from it onto the floor. Two plates and their metal covers, two glasses, cutlery, napkins, an empty wine bottle, a bowl with some crumbs in and the cloth it was all standing on (complete with sauce stains), which he folds up and drops on top of the lot.

And then he picks up the tray.

"What are you *doing*?" I hiss again, seeing as he didn't answer last time. "We'll get in trouble! Are you even allowed to do that?"

"Technically, I'm not taking anything – am I?" He brandishes the tray – it's large and round and made from stainless steel polished to look like silver. I can see why they put a cloth on it. "It's not like I can fit it in my bag."

"So?"

"Up a floor."

"What now? One tray's not enough for you, so you want to look for another one?"

He rolls his eyes. "So we can disappear if someone catches us, and they won't know which rooms we're in."

"And you think this will make a difference?"

"Obviously. And would you shush? They'll hear you!"

Magic time.


"You want me to stand on the tray."

It's not a question. Why would it be a question? It's a statement of idiocy.

"Trust me, Lexi…"

"On. The. Tray. Where people had food. You want me to stand on it." I look from Aidan to the tray on the floor in front of me.

"Just try it."

"*Why?*"

"You'll see."

"But…*tray*. I haven't even got shoes on!"

"Doesn't work with shoes. Well, maybe with trainers but not with…" He looks at the shoe I'm still clutching. "You lost one."

"Rather lose a shoe than my *mind*," I say pointedly – all at the volume of a loud whisper.

"This is not what I expected from someone who climbed out on a roof just to look at the stars." He folds his arms across his chest and it somehow makes him look both younger and older at once. Or maybe it's the combination of the suit and the hair, and the way his glasses have slipped halfway down his nose…

"That had nothing to do with the stars. I needed the air."

"Bollocks. Now get on the tray, will you?"

"Fine." I step onto the tray, not quite believing I'm actually doing it. "Happy?"

"Right." He pulls off his jacket and throws it on the floor…then looks at it and scoops it back up again, folding it carefully over itself and placing it in a neat pile. "Put your feet flat." He undoes his cuffs – I hadn't even realized his sleeves don't have buttons at the end but cufflinks. He's wearing cufflinks. He palms them both, drops them into the pocket of his trousers and rolls up his shirtsleeves.

And I'm standing on a hotel room-service tray.

Right.

This is…odd.

"Feet flat, and try to keep your weight even between them, okay?"

"We're seriously not going to talk about my weight."

"I didn't…I…you know what I mean."

"I don't know *anything*."

He smirks. "You're the one who said that, not me." He steps behind me – and I turn around. "No," he laughs, putting his hands on my shoulders and turning me back around. "That way. Ready?"

"But what…*woah*."

Suddenly I'm flying down the corridor faster than I could run, the tray sliding along the carpet like a surfboard on water as Aidan pushes me along. His hands are spread across my back and the sound of my own laughter bounces off the walls and the closed bedroom doors.

My tray veers wildly left – and I only just manage to jump off before it crashes into a side table with a sculpture of a horse on top of it.

"That was amazing!"

Aidan leans over to sweep up the tray and is upright again in one easy motion. "Told you."

"Smug."

"Want to go again?"

"Yes!"

He drops the tray and I wince, expecting it to clang – but the carpet is too soft and too deep, and all it does is make a low *fmmmfff* noise. This time, I don't need to be persuaded.

This time, I feel his hands drop away from my back halfway along the corridor – I'm on my own, surfing the corridor. The panic makes me wobble, makes me throw my hands out either side of me to try and keep my balance… and in the process, somehow I manage to spin the tray around so I'm going backwards, facing the way I've come.

And there he is, in the middle of the corridor – looking smaller and taller and younger and older; Aidan and Haydn all at once. Watching me as I glide to a stop.

Around the corner behind him there's a muted *ping* from one of the lifts.

Someone's coming.

Aidan races up the corridor, past me, snatching up his jacket as I hop off the tray – and we run for the stairs, back down to the second floor, trying not to laugh…and failing. We leave the tray in the middle of the third-floor corridor.

He stops beside the third door on the second floor; our floor, but *his* room, checking over his shoulder in case. "Quick, get in."

"No one's around, Aidan…"

"Sure about that?" He leans back to look at the stairs; a shadow flickers across the wall.

"Okay, whatever."

The electronic lock buzzes as it registers his keycard and he throws the door open; the handle bangs against the wall as we half-fall into the darkness – and then the lights come on as he slots his key into the cardholder.

"Wow."

"Errr, sorry. I wasn't expecting…"

"Did someone break into your room and go through all your stuff, or…?"

Aidan has the sense to look ashamed – and quite right too, because his hotel room is awful. Not in the sense that it's a bad room, but it's a *tip*. There's clothes piled on the bed, on the back of the chair, on the floor. A towering pile of paper is balanced by the kettle, topped off by a red pen and a load of what look like biscuit crumbs. An opened multipack of crisps is half in, half out of his bag on the floor and the bin is full of empty packets. The door to the bathroom is ajar, the light on…but I'm just too scared to look inside. If he's done this to a bedroom in twenty-four(ish) hours, what could he have achieved in a bathroom in that time?

"You are a massive slob!"

"No, no. I was just, uh, in a rush." He bundles up the clothes from the floor, the bed and the chair and hurls them into the bottom of the wardrobe – which, as it's one of those completely open cupboards with a couple of hangers in it, does absolutely nothing. We both watch as his jeans roll straight back down the pile of discarded clothing and flop onto the floor in front of the door.

"Yes. Yes, that's so much better."

"You want something to drink?" he asks, looking around the room. He umms a bit, peers into a cupboard, looks under a discarded T-shirt and – eventually – points at the thimble-sized kettle.

"Tea? It's the middle of the night."

"All I've got. Sorry. English Breakfast?" He holds up the little paper-wrapped teabag with a flourish.

"I repeat – middle of the night."

"You're right. Something moodier. Which I, umm, don't have. There's instant coffee?" His voice drifts out from behind the bathroom door as he turns the tap on to fill the kettle.

"I don't drink coffee. It gives me panic attacks."

"You what?"

"Caffeine." I shrug.

"I'd never have finished the book if I didn't drink coffee. I drank a lot of coffee in the last third. You should have seen the state of the edits when I got them back. Apparently I went three whole pages without using any punctuation at one point."

"Saving it for winky faces, were you?"

"Winky faces." He shakes his head and rummages through the little bowl full of teabags next to the kettle again. "Seeing as you mocked my breakfast tea, there's a herbal one. Want that?"

"What kind is it?"

He holds it up suspiciously and peers at it. "You don't want it."

"You're making decisions for me now, are you?"

"Trust me," he says, dropping the still-wrapped bag straight into the bin. "Nobody wants that one."

"Fine."

I watch him fiddle with the cups and rub a slightly grubby spoon with his fingers, like that's going to help, then turn back towards me with one eyebrow raised. "Winky faces, though. What did you call it? The Winky Face of Idiocy?"

"Nicked it from Bede." I plonk myself down on the end of his bed and flop back along it, staring straight up at the ceiling. Messy or not, his room is way better than mine. For a start, my kettle's somehow been glued to the base so it's impossible to take into the bathroom; I've been using the tiny little mugs to fill it, scuttling to the bathroom and back.

"Really?" Aidan finds another teabag and rips the little paper wrappers off both of them, dropping one into each of the two mugs. "Umm...I used this one earlier, but I did rinse it out after. You don't mind reusing a mug?" he adds hopefully.

I prop myself up on my elbows. "As long as I'm not reusing a teabag. Because Haydn Swift or not, that's pushing it. And that's another thing – you never told me about your Detroit trip."

"Detroit trip?"

"Your email, when you said you were in Detroit for a film meeting or something?"

"Oh, yeah… Shit." He's spilled boiling water all over the place while pouring, and now he's using the discarded T-shirt to clean it up.

There's a towel on the bedside table – of course there is. I stretch across the bed for it and throw it at him. It wraps itself elegantly around his head. "Are you actually house-trained?"

"House-trained, yes. Hotel-trained…not so much. Oh, *shit it*."

The little milk-carton thing for the tea has exploded all over him.

"How come when you try and pour it, there's never enough? But get it on your shirt…" He dabs at it with the towel. He makes it worse and somehow manages to smear it all over his suit trousers too. "Excuse me a sec."

And he dives into the bathroom, shutting the door behind him…

Except the latch doesn't click, and the door ever so slowly creaks open again. Not much – maybe a couple of centimetres.

But from where I am on the bed, if I were to lean forward just a tiny bit, through the crack in the door I could see the reflection of his back as he moves around the bathroom.

I try not to.

I really, really do.

I lean forward.

He doesn't bother unbuttoning most of his shirt; instead, he pulls it up and over his head and drops it out of sight. His muscles flex under his skin as he moves around, picking up a T-shirt from the side of the sink and shrugging it on – and even though it's only a glimpse, only a second, I shut my eyes and try to get the picture to stick.

The hinges of the door squeak, and when I open my eyes he's standing in front of me wearing a pair of black joggers and a T-shirt with a hole near the hem.

"And they say writing's a glamorous job," I laugh.

He shrugs, stretching an arm awkwardly round behind his neck to scratch his shoulder.

"So, Detroit?"

"Mmm. They want to move a scene of the book to Detroit for the film. There's this house there that's been taken over by artists and—"

"Which scene?"

"What?"

"Which scene do they want to move?"

"I keep forgetting that you probably know it as well as I do," he says with a quiet smile. "The scene in the Flaxman Gallery. The one with the windows."

"And the statue?"

"That's the one."

"But it's perfect as it is! *Actually* perfect. I mean, it's not quite as good as the first scene – the one where that Piecekeeper, Lizzie, meets Jamie in the gallery and there's all the dust and stuff, and she's completely amazing and he's…" I stop. It's too much. Be cool, Lexi. Be. Cool. "So, umm, yeah." I clear my throat. "Perfect."

He cocks his head to one side and looks at me carefully, as though he's about to say something, and then he changes his mind. Instead, he turns his back and finishes making the tea, handing me a mug. "They can do what they want with it – it's in the contract."

"But they still ask you?"

"It's more to keep me onside than because they care what I think. They don't want me turning around and telling people they've ruined the book."

"They haven't though, have they?" The thought of Jamie, of Ali and Lizzie, of Lancelot and the Curator being… *mangled* by someone who doesn't understand and doesn't care and doesn't care that they don't understand…it makes me feel sick.

"They haven't."

He takes a sip of his tea and I take a sip of mine, and the air in the room changes. It's like someone has drawn a thin curtain, a grey veil, right across the middle of the room and I'm on one side and he's on the other.

"Lexi…"

His voice is different, and I can already *hear* it.

Trips to Detroit. Meetings with producers. Coffees and lunches and drinks with his agent, with his publishers. Press conferences and signings and all the things that Haydn Swift takes in his stride…

*How could I compete?*

I can't, can I?

I'm just the girl with the clipboard and the Post-its, checking the clock and asking people how to spell their names. I've always been okay with that; more than okay with it. I'm happy out of the spotlight. I'm not the show, I *run* the show.

His world is the reverse of mine, isn't it? His is signings and photo shoots, mine is hotel service corridors and soundchecking other people.

"Mmm?" I am casual.

"I'm sorry, but…"

I gulp down all the rest of my tea in a single swallow and burn every part of my mouth, tongue and throat.

"…I'm going to have to miss the next convention. I know I'm supposed to be on a panel, and I know this is going to be a pain and I really *am* sorry." He pauses; frowns. "I meant to tell you earlier, but…I didn't want to."

"Oh."

How can so much fit into such a small word?

My "Oh" is everything – it has to be.

It has to be "Oh really?"

It has to be "Oh no."

It has to be "Oh, that wasn't what I thought you were going to say."

It has to be "Oh, what does this mean?"

It has to be "Oh…when will I see you again?"

It has to be "Oh, is this it already? The moment where we find we aren't such a good fit after all?"

But all I say – and all he hears – is "Oh."

"It's for the book. There's a bunch of festivals and stuff in Italy in September, and my Italian publishers need me to go."

"Oh."

"It's only one convention though – I'll be back for October's. And I'll call you. Maybe we could do something in between…?"

He'll call me. Sure. I thought he understood me, but with one breath, I feel like he's dismissed everything – my whole world. Because it's too small for him. With one easy shrug, a handful of words, he's swept aside what was left of the defences I was already dismantling, the walls I was ready to let him inside…and he has turned me to dust.

I stepped into the storm and it has crushed me.

Funny things, words. Big words, small words; words that are bigger on the inside and packed tight with feeling. They can make us fall in love, and they can break our hearts and we're powerless against them.

I thought it didn't matter, that it was okay to not be in control of this *one* thing. That it would not burn me from the inside out and that I didn't have to be afraid of it. I'd met someone who actually understood my world, someone who got how much all this means to me and wanted to be a part of it – a part of my life – but now it turns out that other things come first. Of course they do. They always do, don't they? For everyone.

Maybe Aidan had it right the first time after all; I'm just the one with the clipboard. Maybe that's all I can ever be – maybe that's *why* I've never looked beyond it. Maybe that's all I'm meant to be. Maybe it's better that way. And he's better off with his signing queue and his spotlight. That's what he wants and what he's worked for, even if it's leaving me behind. Because how could I keep up anyway? He jets off to Italy, and I'm in the back rooms of a convention centre.

I'm just not brave enough. I want to be. I want to be brave enough, but I can't. It turns out I care just a little too much.

"Lexi? Lexi? Are you okay?"

The mug has slipped from my fingers and is lying on its side on his bed. At least it was empty.

Am I okay?

"I should go. It's late." I pick up the mug and pass it to him. "Thanks for the tea."

"Lexi? Is everything…did I do something wrong?"

"Night, Aidan."

I can't look at him as I move for the door. I can't. I can't let him see how hard this is, how much it hurts already…

My fingers close around the handle, press it down, and I pull the door towards me. It starts to open and I'm almost there, almost safe – and then I can *feel* him behind me as he leans over me, his hand stretching past me to push the door shut again – gently, softly. And I can smell him; that scent of warm skin and the sea. I can hear him breathing… and I want to turn around and I don't want to turn around. I want to run away from him and I want to run *to* him. Into him.

"Lexi?" His voice is barely a whisper and I can't bear to move. He is a spell that has been cast on me and I don't want it to break, but already the illusion is coming apart.

We stand there for ever, him and me – and if I turn around, I'll never be able to leave and his name will be etched even deeper into me and when the end of our story comes – and it will – it'll hurt even more than it does now.

Because he is Haydn Swift, and I am not enough.

"Goodnight, Aidan."

The spell shatters. He drops his hand and steps back.

And maybe he doesn't understand what just happened and maybe he does. I don't know, but all he says is: "See you around, Lexi."

I can barely see my way back to my room for tears – and when I close the door on the world, I turn to find the connecting door between our rooms open and Sam sitting on my bed in her pyjamas, reading.

"So? Tell me everythi—" She looks over the top of her book; sees me, drops it. "Lexi. Lexi – what happened?"

And I tell her, because of all the people on this planet, Sam is the only one who will understand. She is the only one who won't make it seem crazy when it comes out of my mouth: that in the end I didn't just walk away from Aidan, I ran. I ran because I'm just *Lexi* and my world is all I am. And all I am isn't what he wants.

# SEPTEMBER

## HOME

**LEXI**

So, he sent me another email. Do I reply?

**SAM**

You really want me to tell you what I think?

Yes.
Actually, no.
I want you to validate what I think.
You're not allowed an opinion.

No change there.
Well, what do you think?

I'm thinking...no?

OK.

"OK I agree", or "OK I'm saying this because you just told me to validate you"?

Yes.

Yes the first one, or yes the second one, or just plain yes to be annoying?

Yes.

SAMIRA!

[SAM is typing…]
[…]
[…]
[…]

Question: do you like him?

What's that got to do with it?

Everything. It's got everything to do with it.

You know I like him.

So why are you asking me?

Because…I don't know. It's AIDAN.

And he's...him and I'm me.
And I'm just not...you know?

Sometimes, the things that are worth fighting for, the things that matter, are the things that could hurt us the most. But they hurt because they make us FEEL.

You've been binge-watching GREY'S ANATOMY again, haven't you?

No.
Maybe.
You don't know me.
Now stop being such a loser and go reply to that email...
Before I do it for you.

# SEPTEMBER

CARDIFF

# SCAVENGERS

"No, you have to hold it higher! We all have to be in the picture or it doesn't count!"

"And to think you picked me for this honour. How very, very lucky I am." Sam's voice rings with sarcasm, but she sighs and lets the scavenger hunt group crowd around her for their photo. As soon as they have it, they huddle round a phone muttering about the next clue, then they snatch their team sign back from her and trot off down the corridor in search of another victim. She scowls at them until they're out of sight.

"That's the ninth group this morning. *Ninth*. How much longer is this game running?"

"Apparently, until tomorrow morning. Sorry. Not my call."

"Your dad's letting an unofficial scavenger hunt run over the *whole* convention?"

"What can I say? He's been surprisingly mellow since he and Bea got back from their honeymoon."

"Yeah, well. I'd be pretty mellow if I'd just spent ten days in the Seychelles too." She flicks a piece of rubbish into the bin under the registration desk. "Oh no…"

Another little cluster of scavengers appear around the corner, clutching their team sign. This lot appear to be called *Team Mothers of Dragon*. Not "Mother of Dragons", which would actually make sense, but "Mothers of Dragon". I don't even know where to start.

"Don't make eye contact, don't make eye contact…" I whisper as they close in – but it's too late, and they swarm around her. Above the chatter and noise, I hear her growling "Touch the mask and I will end you", and then they freeze for their picture and just like that, they're gone.

"Ten," she mutters.

"You're dressed like Eartha Kitt's Catwoman, and I only have my incredibly exciting staff lanyard. Of course it's you they're going to want their photo with."

She groans and pulls at the plait of hair she's wound around the top of her forehead. "How many have you had to do?"

"One. Apparently I look too miserable." It makes me laugh just saying it.

"Who said that?"

"Your group number three. They spotted me first, but decided against it." I shrug and toss the folder of membership notes into the box under the registration desk as two late arrivals wander up. Apparently, Bede has implemented a new and exciting filing system for the remaining registration packs, so I have to go through the whole lot searching for "Emma and Rosie". I'm going to kill him this time, I really am. The two of them look Sam up and down as I rummage, and it feels like an age before I can finally hand over their badges; Sam smiles and says "Miaow?" and they smile back at her.

"Your costume is awesome," says Emma – which of course makes Sam smile even more. After they've gone, she hops up onto the desk and sits there, swinging her feet back and forth and carrying on exactly where she left off.

"What I don't get is why it's only us – by which I mean *me* – they're asking for photos with. If it's supposed to be a picture with any of the convention staff, why aren't they asking my mum and dad – or Bede, or Nadiya?"

"Because – apart from the fact that, as you just heard, your costume is pretty cool – parents are intimidating, Bede threatened to insert the phone of the last one who asked him into their bodily orifice of choice—"

"Ouch!"

"—sideways, and the last time I saw Nadiya, she was going to check on the water in the quiet room and loudly telling everyone within earshot that there's no cameras allowed in there. So."

Sam tips her head to one side and adjusts her mask.

She looks too thoughtful for my liking, and I shake my head. "No. I need you here. I'm not losing you to the quiet room too."

"Ten, Lexi. Ten."

"Sorry, Sam. They're asking permission – and as long as they don't break the rules there's nothing I can do. You know that. Dad's given them the okay."

"I miss your bachelor dad. The mean one."

"Mmm."

I do too, in a way. He's been so happy since he and Bea got back from their trip and Bea finally moved in properly. Most of her stuff's still at her old house, and they spend half their time there; supposedly they're sorting everything out and cleaning it ready to rent, but I suspect they're not actually getting that much *cleaning* done. It makes me feel a bit queasy, so I try not to think about it. What it has meant, though, is that I've been left to pick up a lot of the last-minute convention crises – and maybe it's my imagination, or maybe the universe thinks I've had it too easy over the last couple of events and been slacking off with Aidan, but there seem to be more of them than usual:

Entire crate of freebie comics disappearing somewhere between the warehouse and here? Check.

Film panel pulled at the last minute because the cast

all got called back for reshoots? Check.

Hotel losing all the banquet confirmations? Check.

Guest of honour getting trapped at airport by hurricane while returning from overseas research trip *the day before the convention*? Check-checkity-check.

Thanks, Dad. I did vent about this to Mum on her flying visit to see how I was doing on my own (not burning the house down, getting arrested or running off to join the circus – like my life isn't close enough to the last one already?). After we got the usual "don't fall behind with your coursework" and "how are you feeling about LIFE?" business out of the way, things were pretty normal – by which I mean that we mostly talked about Dad.

"Lexi, your father is like a small child," Mum said, stirring the pan of tomato sauce she was cooking. "Picture him as a toddler, if you will. A toddler with a Rolodex."

"That would explain a lot, wouldn't it?"

"And, like a toddler – or a dictator – he's used to people doing what he expects them to do."

"A benevolent dictator?"

"Well, I might not go *quite* that far…"

"I don't get it! He tells me he doesn't want to make the same mistakes he did before, and that's fine – but how's it okay to just dump everything on me? He has an actual assistant he pays for this stuff. And to think I believed all the 'better parent' bollocks he gave me."

"As I said, sweetheart. A toddler. He doesn't like doing things differently. Remember, it's *your* life. And he'll respect you for standing up for yourself. You should be proud of who you are – we're both proud of you already."

I snorted.

There was a pause, then she cleared her throat. And then, quietly: "Did he really say that? About making mistakes?"

"Yes…?" I wasn't quite sure why it mattered; they've been divorced so long already.

She rested the spoon against the rim of the pan and rummaged in her pocket for a tissue. There was something that sounded almost like a sniffle as she dabbed at her eyes. "Well, now. Those onions," she said, and then she was stirring again and telling me all about some art project Leonie has got involved in. Something to do with old cooking pots – *very* Leonie – but I wasn't really listening. Because Mum was right. She usually is. She comes over from France, puts her bag down and, within an hour, she's filled the freezer, fixed the boiler and sorted my life out – or at least told me what I should do to sort it out myself.

The crate of comics turned up – like they usually do. We found a substitute film panel. I had copies of all the banquet reservations (of course I did – what am I, some kind of newbie?). And between us, the stranded guest of honour, his publicist and I managed to charm him a seat on the first

available flight and all four of its connections… The worst
disaster I've had to manage onsite so far is Sam's panic when
she couldn't find one of her Catwoman gloves this morning
– which she announced at 5 a.m. It turned up inside a book
in her second suitcase. Of course it did. But the net result of
all of this is that I am *tired*.

Tired…and trying very, very hard not to think about
Aidan. Or to keep going over the last time we were together.
It's not like we haven't been in touch since the night of the
wedding, but it's mostly been by email. I think we're both
telling ourselves it's because of schedules: it's too hard to
find time to talk…but really I wonder if it's because it's just
too hard to find anything to say. And I can't decide whether
I was an idiot, or whether I was right – or whether it's
possible to be both at the same time. Sam, naturally, has
Many Thoughts about this, and has only just got to the point
where she doesn't feel compelled to share every single one
of them with me. Mostly because I threatened to come into
her room and stuff a sock in her mouth if she carried on.

"Uh-oh." Sam swivels on the table and slides off, dropping
into the chair next to mine.

"What?"

"It's that guy. From the magazine."

"Super-specific Samira strikes again. That should be

your superhero name – and you've already got the outfit, so—"

"No, look. *Him*." She puts both her hands on my head and turns it so I'm looking straight into the lobby.

"Oh, shit. Not him."

"See? That's what I'm saying."

"No – not magazine guy – that's Andy from *SixGuns*. *Him!*" I jerk my head at the figure behind Andy, bearing down on him like a tidal wave. Editors, I can handle this morning. The Brother, I cannot.

I pull the walkie-talkie off the desk and press the button. "Bede? Nadiya? I'm going to need a carton of pineapple juice in the lobby, please? That's *pineapple* in the main hotel lobby now, thank you."

Sam raises an eyebrow, and the walkie's speaker crackles with static, followed by Nadiya's voice. "Pineapple? Are you sure? Not…like…tropical, or mango?"

"Yes, quite sure, thank you. *Pineapple*." From the other side of the lobby, the Brother looks right at me and pauses. He's weighing up who to irritate first – me, or Andy the editor. His eyes lock on. Target acquired. I give him a smile and jab at the walkie button again – still smiling. "*Urgently*, ladies and gentlemen."

"What's it worth?" asks Bede – but I can tell from his voice that he's already running. My knight in shining armour…for a price. I think better of telling him how much

# SCAVENGERS

I enjoyed his handiwork at the registration desk.

"Later. Just…get here!"

As I set the walkie back on the desk, the glow from the hotel's lights is slowly blotted out and a great darkness falls across the registration area.

"Well, hello there, little lady! If it isn't Laura…"

"Lexi."

"Sure, sure. You'd have thought I'd get it right first time by now, wouldn't you?" The Brother beams at me.

"You'd think."

"Your name's always there on the very tip of my tongue… And then it's gone." He makes a blowing sound. Sam sniggers. I stamp on her toe under the desk.

"Always lovely to see you, Damien. Are you here for the whole convention?"

"Ah, no. I've got to head out to Atlanta tomorrow morning – but I thought I'd just pop by and see how you were doing."

"That's so *nice* of you!"

It's surprisingly easy to say this through gritted teeth and a dazzling smile. If you get it right, you don't even need to move your lips.

"Actually – now I think about it – I was hoping I might catch a word with your young man, if he's available?"

"My whatnow?"

"That writer friend of yours – Haydn Swift. I understand

the two of you are…close?" I don't like the weight the Brother puts on that last word, the way it sounds on his tongue.

"I know him a bit," I say, aware that Sam is staring at me and her back is stiffening with every word. "We were lucky enough to host the launch of his book in June, and he's been a guest on a couple of panels."

"Yes, yes. Of course – I'm forgetting you had that little launch for him…"

*Little. Launch.*

I think you'll find that was the worldwide first launch, thank you very much.

And then, as if I haven't already predicted every single word to come out of his mouth, the Brother ploughs on. "Of course, we'll be having an American launch next month, with some of the cast from the movie there too. Shame you weren't able to bring them over, really, as it's always such a boost to attendance. It sounds bad because the book is the thing, but it's always the movies that people really *care* about, isn't it? That's what…draws them in."

He holds his arms in front of him in a loose circle, then sweeps them wide open to make his point – almost giving editor Andy, who has been loitering behind him and pretending not to eavesdrop the whole time, a black eye in the process.

"Oh, I'm sorry – I didn't see you there, brother."

Andy holds up his hands. "No, no. My fault entirely. I'll catch up with you later, Damien – I was actually after a quick word with Lexi?" He looks from the Brother to me and back again, pointedly. The Brother doesn't move but continues to stand his ground, beaming. I glance at Sam. She glances back at me.

Nobody moves, nobody says anything.

And then, trainers screeching on the tiled lobby floor, Bede comes pelting around the corner…and freezes. "Oh. So you won't be needing me then?"

"Not right now, thanks… Although…" Inspiration hits. "Damien, have you had a chance to look in on the art show?"

The Brother looks puzzled. "The art show? No, I…"

No. Of course, he never goes to the art show, does he? Because an A-list artist isn't quite the same as an A-list actor in his stupid mindset.

(Or a big-shot writer.)

The thought of Aidan again makes me ache all over. It *hurts*. He should be here. And instead he's in Italy.

"We've got an amazing installation from a really exciting new concept artist. You have to see it – Bede will take you across, won't you, Bede?"

"I…" Bede is floundering – but then he takes a good look at me and sees a future that holds only pain if he doesn't get a move on. "Yes. I was just heading that way now. If you'd like to come with me…?"

Bede's charm, when fully deployed, is an irresistible warm glow; a siren song that leads anyone within earshot to follow it…and tricks them into getting involved in a fact-off about ambergris. Which he will always win.

And so it comes to pass that the Brother, with little more than a "Well surely, brother", finds himself being led – ever so politely – away from registration and towards an art show he has no interest in seeing, but which is far, far, far away from me.

The three of us – me, Sam and Andy from *SixGuns* – watch them go.

"So," says Andy.

I wait for the rest of the sentence.

There doesn't appear to be one.

"Picking up your press pass?" I ask – and he nods.

"Yes, that's it." He takes the lanyard from me and drapes it round his neck. "How's married life treating your dad, Lexi?" Andy and Dad have known each other for years – although perhaps not quite long enough to stop Dad from making a sucking sound against his teeth when Bea suggested inviting him to their wedding. "Journalist, love," he said, and that was that conversation finished. On the whole, I've always liked Andy…or at least, I did until I saw the way his eyes lit up when the Brother dropped his clanger about me and Aidan.

Ever the journalist, he doesn't pull his punches – not

SCAVENGERS

even waiting for me to answer his first question before he jumps in with another one. "I didn't know you and Haydn Swift were friends…"

"Oh, you know. *Conventions.*" It's my best dismissive shrug – and I can tell from the look on his face that it's nowhere near dismissive enough.

"He's been to a couple now, hasn't he?"

"Umm. He's done programming at two for us – plus I think he tagged along with his publicist to one before that. I'm not sure."

"I heard you were the reason he got a slot on the programme to begin with. Lucky him – and quite the prize for your father."

This is fishing. Digging. Fish-digging…and I'm not giving him anything.

How can I, when I don't even know where Aidan and I really stand; when I don't know what we are or where we are? There've been emails, sure, but I know I've been distant. All that courage I thought I could summon: where did it get me? Wanting to feel closer to him and yet keeping him at arm's length because I'm too scared to do anything else. Way to go, Lexi.

And despite my trying very, very hard not to, I miss him.

"You've seen the push Eagle's Head are giving *Piecekeepers*," I laugh. "And *I* saw the special feature you ran on it last month – so don't give me that."

"Your dad should be proud of you, Lex. I hope he realizes what a natural you are at this," Andy says with a wink. I *definitely* like him a little less now.

"Natural? Nah. I learned from the best." I hand the envelope with his press pack and schedule across the table. "Dad's over in screening room two with Otto at the moment if you want to stick your head in and say hello? He's always pleased to see you."

"Mmm. Listen, Lexi – can I ask you something?" He leans forward ever so slightly; Sam – who until this point has been making a big show of adjusting her Catwoman claws – also leans forward ever so slightly as Andy glances over his shoulder to check nobody else is listening in. "Seeing as you know Haydn, what do you think of the photos from Italy?"

"Sorry? Photos?"

"We had a couple of photos in the other day – they went online this morning. Looks like he's been keeping busy."

"Oh?"

Suddenly my skin feels like someone has sprayed me with powdered ice. It prickles and stings and is so very, very cold – and when I speak, I can barely feel my lips; barely move my tongue.

"You haven't seen them?" Andy is a lot more casual and offhand than he was a moment ago. He hasn't taken his eyes off me the whole time; whatever he's saying, he thinks this is a story and he wants to see how I'll react. "You might want to have a look, you know, as a friend. Him and the lead actress from the *Piecekeepers* film...the one who's been cast as Ali."

NO.

The word is so loud inside my head that I only catch the very end of what he says next.

"...very cosy over breakfast in that hotel in Naples."

No. No, *no*. Because I know him. I *know* him.

Did Andy just tell me that Aidan's been with somebody out in Italy? An actress from the adaptation? So not only does she fit into Aidan's Haydn-world in a way I never could, she's playing the girl who started it all for him. *Ali* from the adaptation. Of *all* the people it could be, it's *her*?

*Hotel, breakfast, cosy.*

Because that's what it sounded like.

My skull fills up with the sound of my heartbeat; the sound of my blood rushing around my system. Only instead of the dull *thud-thud-thud* of my heart, it sounds like *breakfast-actress-breakfast-actress-breakfast-actress-Ali-Ali-Ali*.

"I guess you'd have to ask Haydn about that," I say, an idiot grin welded onto my face. "Or maybe his publicist? I don't have his Italian publisher's details but I can give you Jenna or Lucy's email at Eagle's Head if...?"

"No, no." Andy jerks away; steps back from the table.

His voice is smiling and jokey again. "I just thought…you know, if you were friends…"

"Like I said – conventions." And my voice is smiling and jokey too, and I'm playing the game because that's what you do when you're on this side of the table. Even more when you're a girl; even more than that when you're your father's daughter.

Inside, though…

Inside, I am not Lexi Angelo.

Inside, I'm just me.

And I am in pieces.

Andy gives us a cheery wave and sets off up the corridor towards the convention area lift, opening his press pack and peering into the envelope as he goes. Beside me, Sam pulls off her mask.

"You didn't mention anything about this after you and Aidan mailed yesterday!"

"No. No, I didn't. And *weirdly*, neither did he."

# ALL THE BROKEN PIECES

It would have to be the actress playing Ali, wouldn't it? Andy's words ricochet around my head like a stray bullet as I hurry down the corridor away from the registration desk. Sam can handle it, scavenger hunters and all.

We mailed. Yesterday. We pinged messages back and forth and not once did he casually say, *Hey, Lexi, guess what? I hung out with a couple of guys from the film. Including film-Ali.* But if he *had* said that, I would have thought it was absolutely fine and had no problem with it whatsoever, because why should I?

Because, obviously, I wouldn't. I don't.

Do I?

Because I didn't mean to, don't mean to…and yet this feels an awful lot like I do.

Inside, deep down inside where no one can see it, I think I do. I have a problem with it.

Lexi Angelo, are you *jealous*?

I thought he liked me, that's all. In his room in York, I thought…

After all, it was *me* who pulled away. I was the one who took a step back. I don't have any right to be jealous – and yet, I don't know…maybe I expected it would take a little longer for him to turn around and go after someone else. So no, not jealous, exactly. I guess I just expected… more. I expected he'd be upfront with me about where we are – or where he is, anyway, because there isn't really an "us", is there?

Was I right…or was I an idiot? Either way, this sucks.

The ops room door is half-hidden, covered by a mirrored panel in a back corridor of the hotel – and as I reach to pull it open, my reflection meets me. She's not exactly "glamorous actress" material; not in the red convention staff T-shirt that has splashes of Bede's coffee on it, or with the crazy hair that comes from forgetting to pack conditioner and having to use the two-in-one conditioner and body lotion (how is that even a thing? Who thought that up?) in the hotel shower – or even, if you look past all that, the fingernail that's turning suspiciously black after she managed to hit it with a hammer during the art-show build. She does not look like the sort of person you'd lean towards during breakfast on the balcony of a hotel on the Amalfi coast.

*Leaning. Balcony.*

Nobody said anything about leaning *or* balconies; Mirror-Lexi has come up with that one all on her own.

Thanks, Mirror-Lexi. Thanks for nothing.

I yank the door open.

Ops is even more chaotic than usual because, by some miracle, Dad's team is overstaffed. Just for once we have enough people to actually run a convention and make sure everyone gets breaks and time off and food. When I told Nadiya and Bede, they actually high-fived. And cackled. I don't know whether Dad, in a fit of post-honeymoon bliss, overbooked people, or whether everyone was so keen to meet this new, mellow version of Max Angelo that they all showed up (they never *all* show up). But either way, the ops room is absolutely stuffed full of people.

Which is not what I want.

What I want is for the ops room to be empty so I can sit down in peace and quiet until the pounding in my head and the shredded feeling in my heart go away – but no such luck. I'm barely through the door when the walkie in my pocket barks into life.

"We've lost the *Doctor Who* writers," says Nadiya through the speaker. I sigh, and fumble the radio out of my pocket.

"What do you mean, 'lost' them? Lost them where?"

"They've all gone down the pub for lunch."

"What…*all* of them?"

"Yep."

I grab a schedule from the table, running a finger down the columns until I find the item I want. I look at the clock. Right.

"But we need them for their soundcheck in ten minutes..."

"That's *Doctor Who* writers for you. They said they'd be back in time..."

"I can't decide if that was supposed to be a really bad joke or not."

Across the ops room, Marie looks up from the banquet list she's ticking off. "Don't worry. I know where they've gone. I'll get to the end of this page and then I'll fetch them."

"You will? You're amazing, Marie, you know that?"

"I do." She tries to look serious, but then ends up smiling anyway as she shuffles the pages of her list together and tucks them into her bag on the floor. "Won't be a sec..."

As she steps out, the sounds of the convention drift through from the corridor – more distant than normal, but still there. The sounds I normally love. Laughter and the rise and fall of voices; a smatter of applause from one of the panel rooms and music from one of the activity rooms (formal elvish dancing, by the sound of it). Today though, between that and the chatter all around me, I can't take it. I need to be on my own. Let someone else – *anyone* else –

take care of the convention for a while. I need to take care of *my* life. Putting the walkie on the table, I slip out of the room again. Nobody seems to notice – or at least, nobody *asks* me for anything, nobody *tells* me anything, nobody *says* anything.

I know where I'm going – there's a spot under a table in the empty banqueting hall with my name on it.

Halfway down the corridor, I'm overtaken by Bede and Mike – one of Dad's senior staff (The One Who Gets Things Fixed) racing past. Mike doesn't run very often. Mike is *running* now, and leaving a trail of curses so substantial behind him that the air virtually turns pale blue.

"Bede!" I shout after them, and Bede turns – still jogging backwards.

"Lift broke!" he shouts back.

"The *lift*?" Unlike a lot of hotels, this one has a single lift serving the lower floor of the convention area, and I've been worried about it from the start. Sam's been using it at every available opportunity, just in case it did break down with her inside it and she had to be rescued by firemen. "Shit."

"Mike's going to shout at someone."

"Who?"

"Anyone he can find! Want to come watch?"

"You go. Make sure he doesn't get us thrown out, okay?"

Bede hurtles off in pursuit of Mike. They don't need me; in the big picture, Mike's higher up the food chain than I am and this is what he does. Besides, he can shout a lot louder than I can. He used to be an actor and apparently it's something to do with breathing from the diaphragm…

The further I follow the corridor, the quieter the convention gets. The banquet hall here is at the front of the hotel overlooking the bay, the tables all set out ready for tonight. One of the staff hears me come in and pops his head around a pillar – he has an empty tray tucked under his arm and an invisible hand reaches into my chest and squeezes my heart because it makes me think of Aidan…

Outside, the rain lashes against the plate-glass windows. I'm sure there's the whole of Cardiff Bay out there somewhere, but from here it's just a great big wet grey smear. Like my soul.

I check the waiter's gone and clamber under the nearest table, letting the tablecloth drop down behind me. Only then – when I know I'm alone – do I slip my phone out of my pocket. There's no reception (as usual; why would anyone in a hotel want anything as boring as for their phone to work?) so I connect to the hotel Wi-Fi and open Instagram, typing *Haydn Swift* into the search bar…or *gadtyn aqift* as it comes out, because apparently that sausage I dropped on my phone at breakfast made more of a mess than I realized. Fortunately for me, my phone knows who I mean, and suddenly my screen is filled with blue.

Blue skies, blue seas. A lemon tree. What looks like a

medieval fortress, perched up on a rock – and everything washed in the most brilliant, buttery sunlight. I can almost feel the warmth of it from here – despite the sound of the rain beating against glass.

Sea salt and sun. If he were here now, if I could bury my face in the side of his neck and breathe him in, that's what Aidan would smell like. But he isn't here. He's there. Dozens of him, small enough to fit into the palm of my hand over and over again.

He's on a stage in front of a green backdrop, his eyes laughing behind his glasses as he sits on a wooden chair with a copy of his book in his hand.

He's gazing out over an azure sea, the wall he's leaning against painted ochre-red.

He's posing in front of a bookshop; the old-fashioned bow-fronted window artfully arranged with copies of *Piecekeepers – Capolavoro*, they've called it there. I don't know if it even means the same thing – can it? And is it the same book if it has a different title? If the name is something else…can it *be* the same?

A salmon-pink sunset over a harbour wall.

A row of vast, glittering motor yachts; all of them glossy white with glistening steel rails. Lights under the surface turning the harbour water a glossy green.

Aidan – Haydn – again, on the deck of one of those boats as it leaves a tiny port; behind him a washed-out mountain looms over a misty coast. The caption below the photo reads: *Working hard, playing hard in Ischia. Keeping an eye on Vesuvius though. Just in case…* followed by a load of tags. Thankfully, he hasn't included *#blessed* or *#nofilter* because the Winky Face of Idiocy is quite bad enough.

At least there's no sign of any actresses in these. That helps.

Except…who took the photos?

Not him.

Who was with him? At the bookshop and the festival, probably someone from his publisher. But on the boat? Who was that?

I can't bear to look for the photos Andy was talking about. It would be so easy – but then could I ever unsee them? Would they be better or worse than I imagine? As long as I don't see them, I can tell myself what I want. As long as I don't go looking, I'm still in control.

I guess it doesn't really matter, does it? This is Haydn, not Aidan. This is public, not private. This is the famous bestselling author with his game face on (yes, it's a bestseller already; no, of course I haven't been checking, whatever would give that impression?), not the guy who spills UHT milk all over himself in the early hours of the morning. Not the one who's allergic to lilies. Not the one who stood on the roof of a Brighton hotel with me and told me I knew him, even though I barely knew him at all…

And yet, however hard I tell myself that, there's still this *feeling*.

I can't control this, can I? People can't be managed by to-do lists and feelings don't stick to the plan. I can solve any problem you give me at a convention, any puzzle…but I can't solve this.

I can't solve him.

I took a risk, and what did it get me? This scraping sensation down the inside of my ribs; the feeling rattling down my arms that everything is too small and too imperfect and too stupid for words…

*It's all him…not me.*

He said that himself. Aidan and Haydn aren't the same. They aren't. They *aren't*. I tell myself that and I stare at the screen, at the tiny, tiny Haydns lined up in their neat little grid. These aren't Aidan. They're projections of him; ghosts. Masks and mirrors and what he wants the rest of the world to see. But they aren't him. They aren't what *I* see.

What was it Mum said? Stand up for myself? Be proud of who I am.

Right. So, I solve problems. I'm proud of that. It's what I do.

And there's only one way to solve this one: I'm going to call him.

Because Aidan *is* my problem.

I'm going to call him and talk to him and I'll feel like I've done something useful, instead of sitting here under a table stalking him from halfway across a continent. If it matters, he'll tell me who took the photos, he'll tell me what happened at breakfast. He'll tell me because I know him.

*And if he doesn't?*

Shut up, Lexi.

I scuttle sideways out from beneath the table – and frighten the life out of one of the cleaners wiping the windows. He actually drops the cloth he's using – I didn't think I was *that* scary. I do feel better though. Lighter. This is good. This is a *positive* thing. I'll speak to Aidan, and then I'll catch Dad and ask him if we can talk. He's been in such a perky mood that he might even say yes – and it's not like he can tell me we don't have enough staff for both of us to spare ten minutes for a chat, is it? I'll tell him how much I love the conventions, how much I love what we do…but I need to look beyond them too, and work out who I am when I'm not being Max Angelo's perfectly organized, perfectly in-control daughter. I'll have to do it sooner or later – might as well make it sooner, right?

If I can keep out of the way of the scavenger hunters, this might even turn out to be a good day.

I'm almost at the door when I hear footsteps – running footsteps – and suddenly Sam bursts through the doors into the banquet hall.

"Lexi."

She's out of breath; she's been looking for me.

"What? If it's about the lift, I know and—"

"It's not the lift." She shakes her head. "You'd better come. The ambulance will be here any time…"

"Stop. Ambulance?" Oh, god. One of the convention members has had an accident. That must be it. How many first-aiders have we got? Where did I put the insurance forms? Do we have any doctors around or do I need to call the hotel one? Dad'll know. "Okay. Is Dad there already or do I need to call him?" Bugger. Left the walkie in the ops room. We'll have to run back there to fetch it…

Sam's face turns ashen. "You don't know. Oh god."

"Know what?"

"Lex, it's your dad. The ambulance is for *him*."

My phone slips from my fingers and something cracks as it hits the floor – but what that is, I simply don't know.

# SIREN SONG

Inside the ambulance, everything is bright. Too bright. It burns.

Dad is strapped to a stretcher, and against the red blanket his skin looks sallow and saggy. His eyes have sunk deeper into their sockets and somewhere along the way he seems to have banged his head and there's a shiny, tight look to one side of his forehead. It must have happened when he fell.

The paramedic leans over Dad and holds out something small and white. "Max? Max? I'm going to spray something under your tongue."

Obediently, Dad opens his mouth…and at that precise moment I understand both how scared he is, and that I've never seen him scared before. Not of anything. Not at all.

He was already on the stretcher and trolley when I got to the lobby; the blanket pulled right up to his chin as the paramedics wheeled him out through the open doors. There

364

were people everywhere – hotel staff, convention staff and members…a sea of faces staring blankly at my father. Sam barged them out of the way and shoved me in front of her. "Wait! She's going with you!"

The second paramedic stopped and looked at me. "Are you his next of kin?"

"I'm his daughter."

"Come in the back." He ushered me with him to the open doors at the back of the ambulance.

"Sam!" I shouted back to the doors. "Call Bea! Her number—"

"I'll find it. Go." She held up a hand in goodbye as I climbed in behind the stretcher and somebody slammed the ambulance doors shut.

"Mr Angelo?" The paramedic is holding a clipboard and pen, peering at Dad.

"I'm perfectly…just need…" Dad's voice is thin and wheezy – and ambulance or not, he's obviously not listening to a word.

The paramedic gives up. "Do you know if your father has any allergies?" He's talking to me now, isn't he? And it's the weirdest thing, but all I can think is that *I* should be the one with a clipboard because that's what I do. Nobody else gets to hold the clipboard. It ought to be me.

"Penicillin, I think?" My voice sounds shaky and small, smothered by the siren speeding us on our way.

"You think?"

"I'm not sure. He's got this story about how he was given it when he had tonsillitis or something when he was a kid and he came out in a huge rash, and because it was summer he just walked around the house in his swimming trunks."

This was probably not the kind of information the paramedic was looking for.

But it's my dad. This man doesn't understand. It's my dad. My dad. That's who he is: stories and anecdotes and… *my dad*.

He taps the end of his pen on his clipboard and nods. "I'm going to put probable allergy for now. The hospital staff can confirm it when he's feeling a little more *robust*."

"Is he…what…?"

From the stretcher, there's a snort. Whatever the paramedic gave Dad is obviously starting to work. "I'm not going to die, Lexi. Don't panic."

"Dad, you collapsed in the middle of the lobby."

"I told them – I just got a bit short of breath. All I needed was a sit-down…"

The siren finally switches off and the paramedic clips his notes onto the end of the stretcher, picking up a pen-torch. He leans over Dad again, peering at him. "That, Mr Angelo, was a little more than getting short of breath. It sounds like it was most likely angina, but now we've got you, we're going to take you in so the doctors can run a few tests…"

"Nonsense. Too many sausages at breakfast. Bit of indigestion. I'll be fine – you can take us back…"

"Mr Angelo, I'm afraid—"

Angina. The word is strange – and right now, strange is scary. More than scary – petrifying. "What's angina?"

"It's a chest pain. Nothing," Dad says from his stretcher – obviously to me, before carrying on at the paramedic. "I really can't apologize enough for wasting your t—"

"Dad!"

Silence, other than the rattling of medical equipment in cupboards and drawers as we hurtle over a speed bump. Everything has that hospital disinfectant smell, rubbery and sour; cardboard and clean metal. Everything tastes of fear.

*Today might actually be a good day.*

I really had no idea, did I?

The ambulance turns a corner and slows. "All right, Max. Looks like this is our stop," says the paramedic – and a moment later, the doors are opening and the smell of rain fills our little metal box. I step down – right into a puddle – and follow Dad and his clipboard as he's wheeled through wide automatic doors from the hospital ambulance bay into the building. There's a long, high desk built along one wall, the top covered with in trays and bottles of hand sanitizer. A nurse peers over at us and calls "Triage 2!" – and Dad is wheeled through a wide brown door. I try to follow, but Desk Nurse yells at me. "Excuse me! Hello? You can't go through there!"

"But…he's my dad." I point at the door – which has swished shut behind the trolley. "I'm his daughter…" I add – just in case she hadn't figured that out from the whole "dad" thing.

Her stern expression softens. "You're better off out here. Let them take a good look at him and someone'll be out to talk to you. Is there anyone you want to call? Your mum?"

"They're divorced."

"You want to call her anyway?" She pushes a phone towards me across the top of the desk.

"She lives in France…would that be okay?"

The nurse nods, then picks up the handset and punches in some kind of code. "Just keep it short – or you'll get me in trouble."

I dial Mum's number from memory. For a moment, I didn't think I'd remember it  – I've always called it from the contacts in my phone…which is currently lying on the banquet hall floor back at the hotel. As the phone rings, I wonder if Sam remembered to go back for it and call Bea – and whether, when she switches it on, the first thing she'll see is my attempt at stalking Aidan.

"*Allô?*"

"Leonie?"

"Lexi! How are you?"

"I'm…I need to talk to Mum."

"But what's happened? Are you all right?"

"I'm fine. It's not me – is Mum around?"

"Of course, I will fetch her. Wait…"

There's a rustling sound, and I hear Leonie calling Mum's name; a pause, then a rapid burst of French. Footsteps, then the phone being picked up again.

"Lexi. Is something wrong? What's the matter?"

"Mum. It's Dad. You always ask if it's him. This time, it is."

"What? Is everything okay?"

"He's in hospital."

I hear her take a deep breath, as though she's steadying herself, and I carry on.

"I don't know much – he collapsed and they said it's angina and I don't know. They won't let me in with him and I don't know and…"

"Angina. Oh lord. It was your grandfather's heart that killed him. Is Bea there? Does she know?"

"Sam's calling her."

"Okay. Okay. Good." Her voice is quiet and tinny, as though it's coming from somewhere even further away than France…but it's still her voice, and I feel better for hearing it. "And your father? How is he now?"

"He was okay in the ambulance. They gave him something and he seemed a lot better."

"What was it?"

"I don't know. They sprayed something under his tongue."

"That sounds right. Good."

"You keep saying that. It's *not* good!"

The nurse behind the desk clears her throat and looks at me pointedly, making a *shhh* gesture with her finger to her lips.

When Mum speaks again she's calm, her voice clearer. "Lexi. I know. I know. But listen to me – your father will be fine. This is nothing, just a scare, okay?"

"But…"

"*Just a scare.* Okay?"

"Okay." I grip the handset so hard I'm afraid it will shatter under my fingers. The nurse clears her throat again. "I have to go. I'm using the hospital's phone. I left mine in the hotel."

"Of course, you go. Leonie and I are home all day – call me when you can, when there's news, okay?"

"Okay."

"And don't *panic*. I've known your father a very long time – longer than you have, remember. This isn't even going to dent him."

"I know, Mum. I have to go. Love you!"

"I love you too, sweetheart. Speak to you later."

I drop the phone back into its cradle and slide it over to the nurse. "Thank you," I say – and I mean it.

"You're welcome, love. Take a seat over there – I'll let the doctor know you're waiting when she comes out. It might take a while – we're a little understaffed today." She points me at a couple of rows of moulded plastic chairs along the wall. They're just the same as the ones in the dining hall at college – only blue instead of red. Halfway along the row is a battered coffee table with a stack of well-thumbed magazines on the top and a couple of children's picture books with the covers torn off. A flat-screen TV is mounted on the opposite wall, tuned to a news channel with the sound turned down and the subtitles switched on. I flop into a chair next to the table and pick up the top magazine from the stack, just to take my mind off *everything* – and when I straighten it out and look down at the cover, it's Aidan's face that looks back up at me. Of course it is.

I toss the magazine back on the pile, tip my head back against the wall and close my eyes.

And I wait.


I always thought hospitals were meant to be quiet places – you know, to help with healing. But they're not. Or at least this one isn't; it's actually noisier than most conventions. There's a constant buzz in the background – people walking in or out or through the brown door one way or another, ambulances pulling up and driving off, shouting, trolleys rattling, machines beeping… Just so much noise. How does anyone cope here? It's not that I'm not used to noise, but there's something so…desperate about it here. Something so hopeful and so sad all at once. And it seems completely chaotic too. People talk about conventions as chaotic, but they're not. There's a flow to them – people move out of one event and into another, or out to get lunch or a drink with friends. They rise and fall, drift and ebb. You can read them as easily as a clock if you know how.

Not here.

But then, nothing about a convention's life or death, is it? It's all just play.

Unless you're Dad.

It's not play to him, is it? It really is life and death – his life's work… And it's put him in the hospital.

The automatic doors to the outside world swish open again – and this time there's a rush of footsteps, and someone walks in front of me and sits in the chair beside me. "Lexi?"

Sam.

She grabs my hand, and I open my eyes.

"How is he?"

"I don't know – he seemed okay when we got here. They told me to wait, so I'm waiting."

She's still wearing the bottom half of her Catwoman costume – but with an old, baggy purple hoodie pulled on over the top. "Bea's coming. Here's your phone, by the way."

She pulls it out of her hoodie pocket and passes it to me. A jagged crack runs right across the screen. "Sorry. It was like that when I found it – must have broken when you dropped it. It still works fine though." She watches me rubbing my poor broken screen with my thumb. "Well. Fine-ish," she adds.

"You didn't have to come."

"We wanted to. I practically had to hold Mum and Dad back until I'd finished on the phone with Bea." She nods at her parents, who are talking to Desk Nurse.

"How is she? Bea?"

"Scared, but other than that…" Sam shrugs and settles back into her seat – then almost immediately leans forward again and wriggles. "For a waiting room, you'd think they'd spring for better chairs. What with people having to wait here and everything. Jesus." She fidgets some more and swears a couple of times under her breath before finally sighing and sitting still. "By the way, seventeen, in case you're wondering. Sev-en-teen scavenger hunt photos. I'm not even joking."

She didn't have to come…but I'm glad she did.


When Bea arrives, she's a whirlwind. The doors fly open ahead of her and she strides in, handbag under her arm and those bangles rattling with every step – and I've never been so happy to hear them. Instead of walking right past me to the desk like I expect her to, she comes straight over.

"Are you all right?" she asks. It's the first thing she says – not "How is he?", but am I okay. I nod.

"I don't know how Dad's doing. The doctors—"

"I've already spoken to them," she says, setting her handbag on the floor. "He's fine. I can't believe they wouldn't let you in with him – what nonsense. He's your *father*."

"Wait...you've spoken to them?"

"I called them from the train. After the eighth time, they decided it was probably a better use of their resources to put me through to the right room, rather than have me clogging up the switchboard."

"And?"

"There's still one or two tests they want to do, but everyone seems confident it was angina."

"That's what the paramedic said."

"Well then. They should have just asked *him*, shouldn't they? Instead of keeping poor Max stuck in here all afternoon and taking up a bed that could be used by someone who actually needs it."

"So...can I see him?" A vision of my dad strapped to the trolley in the ambulance and looking thin and grey – and, yes, old – flashes before my eyes.

"Better than that," says Bea, rubbing my arm. "We're going to break him out."

"But you said there were more tests?"

"And there's no reason they can't be done at home. There are perfectly good hospitals there, after all." She stands up and brushes imaginary dust from her hands. "Right. I'm going in."

She strides towards Desk Nurse – who looks up. From where we're sitting, I can't hear what either of them are saying – but I can still tell that Desk Nurse is losing. If Sam was right and Bea genuinely was scared, she's either really good at getting past it or her Game Face is second to none. Poor old Desk Nurse doesn't know what's hit her – as I could have told her, Bea has a habit of getting what she wants and it's impressively terrifying (or terrifyingly impressive – I'm not sure which) watching her at work. After a couple of minutes of heated debate – in which Desk Nurse valiantly stands her ground but Bea swings round to flank her, before surprising her with a brutal axe swing to the head and beheading her (I have spent too much time around LARPers), Bea walks back over.

"We can take him as soon as the paperwork's ready. They're bringing some medication over from the pharmacy and I'll go and find him now. Do you want to call a taxi for us all?"

"No need." Sam's dad turns away from studying the

subtitles on the television. "We came in our car, so there's plenty of room for everyone."

"Yes," mutters Sam, shaking her head. "Come ride in the minivan of despair. And pray he turns the radio off, or your brain'll be dribbling out of your ears before we even leave the car park."

"Your dad's taste in music's not that bad…" I whisper as Bea nods and vanishes through the brown door.

"No, sure. If you like the 1970s. And not the good bit of it." Sam snorts.

"There was a good bit to the 1970s?"

"I heard that," says her dad, raising an eyebrow at me.

Sam snorts again. "See? Lexi thinks the same."

"Then you can *both* walk back to the hotel, can't you?" But he says it with a smile.

Desk Nurse clears her throat a little too loudly. "Prescription for Max Angelo?" She's waving a small paper bag.

"I'll take it," I say, and bound over to the desk. "Thanks."

"You're welcome."


"I should ring my mum," I tell Sam. "I'll just be outside, okay?" I consider asking Sam to hold the medicine, but as I still haven't forgotten what happened when I asked her to look after the key to the storage cupboard where we were holding all the membership lanyards in Glasgow last year, I think better of it. (Personally, I thought everyone looked lovely walking around with their handwritten labels on ribbons we managed to source from the art shop down the street from the hotel…) Instead, I tuck it into my pocket as best I can and dial.

Mum answers on the second ring. "Any news?"

"They're letting him out."

"Thank heavens for that. And you're okay?"

"I'm fine. I think. Apparently there's still a couple of tests or something, but everyone keeps saying it was angina."

"Mmm."

"What does that mean, anyway – was he having a heart attack?"

"Not quite, no. It's…look at it as an early warning."

"So he *could* have a heart attack?"

"I don't know, sweetheart. Maybe, if he doesn't slow down a little – and almost certainly if he keeps eating those awful takeaways you two have…"

"Ummm."

"Stop. Stop panicking, darling. He'll be absolutely fine, I promise. Now, these tests…?"

"I'll ask Bea when she comes out. She's in with him now."

"She's there already? That's good. Well, if she knows then it's probably better I speak to her myself."

"You want to talk to her? Won't that be a bit…you know…weird?"

"Lexi, Bea and I have been speaking to each other regularly for months now. I thought you knew that?"

"You? You and Bea? You're…friends?"

"It was your father's idea, actually – for once, he thought of something sensible. And, yes, it was uncomfortable at first, but it turns out we get along quite well."

"But…why?" I wonder if she can hear that distant *BOOM* sound down the phone. Because that's the sound of my mind, blowing.

"You, mostly."

"Me?"

"Look. Your father and I didn't work. We tried, and in the end we just didn't, but there's a very good chance he and Bea will. They seem like a much better fit than we *ever* were. And she's very fond of you. We all have you in common. Whatever I feel about Max – your father – you're still *our* daughter. We're all family, however messy that is – and Bea's a part of it too."

Mind. Blown.

Bits of me, littering the entrance to the hospital. Just… scattered all over the place.

Wow.

Thankfully, before I have to get any further into this earth-shattering, mind-blowing (and not-a-little awkward, if I'm honest) conversation, Sam calls my name – and when I look round, through the big windows I can see Dad, coming through the brown door. He looks wobbly and tired, and he's still so very, very pale except for the bruise on his head which is now turning a fine shade of purple, but it's him and he's *walking* and he's *there*.

"I have to go – Dad's out."

"Give him my love, would you? He can give me a call himself when he's feeling up to it."

"I'll tell him."

"And Lexi?"

"Mmm?"

"Don't let him work too hard."

"I don't think Bea'll let him…"

"When it comes to conventions, both you and I know that there's only one person he'll listen to…and it's not his wife."

There's a faint click as she cuts the connection, and I'm already back through the entrance doors and throwing my arms around Dad – who almost does a convincing job of pretending he hates the fuss…but not *quite*.

"You scared the shit out of me," I mumble, not really meaning for him to hear – but he does.

"Language," he says sternly…then laughs and adds: "I scared the shit out of me too."

Bea smiles and picks up her handbag, bracelets jangling,

and Sam trails after her dad, arguing about why she can't pick the music in the car, while her mum goes off to pay for the parking…and before I quite know I've done it, I've dialled another number on my phone. There's a funny ringing tone, and then a click.

"Hello?" says the voice on the other end.

"Aidan. It's me."

# OCTOBER

## EDINBURGH

ANGELO EVENTS PRESENTS

# FANTASTICON
# HALLOWEEN
# MASKED BALL

## SATURDAY 28th OCTOBER

THE 19TH ANNUAL

One of the most popular Fantasticon
traditions returns!

Dance the night away in our bewitching ballroom.

This year's theme is "Black and White Magic"
– come dressed to impress and prepare for the
grand unmasking at midnight.

The enchantment begins at 8 p.m. in the
Grand Ballroom.

Refreshments available.

For further information or for access requirements,

# TRIBES

Despite the fact that there is nothing whatsoever wrong with his legs, and every sign that the medication the hospital gave him after his angina attack is working, my father has taken to walking with a cane.

My father being my father, of course, this is not just any old walking stick. Oh no. This…monstrosity is a glossy black thing, topped with a solid silver dragon whose tail winds down and round the top half of the cane. ("Custom-made by an old artist friend," he tells anyone who stands still long enough to hear.) This is equal parts blessing and curse: on the hard floors of a hotel lobby, the brisk click of his cane hitting the ground is a useful warning that we all need to look busy before he comes around the corner and actually sees any of us; however, it has also given him something with which to *gesture*.

"That picture needs moving…" POINT.

"If we move *this* table over *here*…" SWOOSH.

"Right down the end of that corridor…" JAB.

After an hour yesterday helping him supervise the traders' room set-up, Bede came back muttering about giving him a whole new place to keep his cane.

"That's my dad you're talking about, you know."

"And the fact he's your dad is the only reason I haven't snapped already and broken the fecking thing in half over his head."

"Not because he's your boss, then?"

"Shut up, Lexi."

So here we are. Last convention of the year, and it's the big one. Halloween.

(Except that because Halloween has inconveniently chosen to happen midweek, it's an almost-Halloween convention this year. But as long as we're all pretending – which we are – it'll be fine.)

October has always been Dad's favourite convention – growing up I used to think that was because it meant everything was in place and winding down, and he even got a holiday afterwards; a couple of weeks to just...stop. (He never did, of course – hence: angina!) And I know he's still excited about it this year, but things are suddenly different, and not necessarily in a bad way. And it's all because of Bea. I was afraid she would interfere, that she would take my place in some weird way – but that's not it at all. She's still away a lot, but when she's around Dad laughs, and they cook actual meals together (no more reheated takeaways) and she rolls her eyes when Dad interrupts dinner with yet another convention idea, and somehow it's okay. It feels right. It feels almost like she's just filling the space that was always there for her and we never knew it.

That's not to say there's any less work – not for this convention anyway. I thought I knew tired. I did – but now I think Tired and I might just have been waving at each other from opposite ends of the street. Three days a week, I've been getting up and checking the convention emails, having a shower, having breakfast, answering yesterday's emails on the bus to college, trying not to fall asleep in my classes, answering my morning's emails on the bus on the way home, doing my coursework, eating dinner (or pretending to, if Bea's away and Dad's taken it upon himself to make something), and then going through everything with Dad to make sure I'm not doing something horrendous which will stain the family's name and honour for the next seven generations, before I fall into bed.

On the other four days it's pretty much exactly the same – except there's no college and I don't have to try and type on a bumpy bus. (My spelling is *much* better those days.)

And best of all, it *works* – better than it has done before.

With one small problem: I can't stop thinking about Aidan.

It feels like more than months since I saw him; it feels like years. Since Dad's little…hiccup, I've had time – *made* time – to talk to Aidan again, to pick up the phone and call him and stop hiding behind my laptop keyboard. Even when I didn't mean to, it was him I called, like he's somehow taken up residence inside my brain and there's no shifting him now. He's moved in. And slowly, it's started to feel like we've found our way back to where we were. But courage or not, I still haven't been able to ask him about those photos Andy mentioned, and I definitely, definitely haven't been brave enough to look for them. He hasn't brought them up, and I just…can't. Maybe if I leave it long enough, I won't have to?

Baby steps.

Brave little baby steps.

"I think I'm jet-lagged." I balance on the edge of the freebie table, holding one end of a long string of paper ghosts against the wall. "Where's the Blu-Tack?"

"Sam took it to do the decorations in the lobby. Here – have mine." Nadiya climbs out from behind the registration desk and half-passes, half-throws a large ball of it at me. "And you can't be jet-lagged from flying to Edinburgh from London."

"Only Dad and Bea flew. I got the train," I groan.

"The train?" Nadiya's voice rises in shock and she stares at me, totally ignoring the lovely couple in matching *Star Wars* T-shirts trying to pick up their membership lanyards. "Why?"

"Worked out better for college," I say, pressing a wodge of tack against the wall. It falls straight off and lands on the carpet. "Naaaaadiyyyaaa…"

"I'm coming, I'm coming." She picks it up and gives it back to me. "But the train's got to be, like…"

"Eight hours, forty-five minutes."

"No! It can't be that long?"

"It is when you get told the train you're booked on suddenly won't be going to Edinburgh any more and you get diverted and have to change at Leeds and get the super-packed slooooow train that stops *everywhere*. There's fluff all over this tack now."

"That's all I've got." She sits back down again behind the desk. "Eight hours. Wow. What did you *do*?"

"Mostly wish I was dead?"

That's not entirely true; somewhere around Berwick-upon-Tweed, I was fairly sure I was *already* dead and in hell. Mostly because my seat was right next to the toilet. And it was a busy train.

The rest of the time…well, the rest of the time I was thinking. Thinking about being brave, and what a braver Lexi could do.

Thinking about who I am, what I want, what comes next. (And fine, sure; maybe *who* I want.)

Back in April, I wasn't expecting to have an existential crisis by the end of the season; but then I wasn't expecting my dad to get married – or to have a heart attack. Well, a nearly-heart-attack anyway. I wasn't expecting to meet Aidan either. I wasn't expecting *anything*. Everything in my life was laid out in neat little columns: conventions, college, Dad, friends…

And now?

Now I don't know. I don't know what comes after this. It's a blank page, ready to be written on.

The surprises keep coming too: two days ago, Control Freak Dad passed me a pile of CVs and said, "Take a look."

"Yes. This one's used the word 'passionate' four times in eight lines. What am I now, a proofreader?"

"I'm hiring an assistant."

"You have an assistant. His name's Davey, remember? He works in the events office and you ring him up to shout at him a couple of times a day – which, by the way, makes you a *terrible* boss." He glared at me, so I added, "Which I would know absolutely nothing about because personally I find working with you a complete *joy*."

"Not for the main business. For the conventions."

"You're hiring a me?"

"Hopefully, I'm hiring someone who will give me

significantly less backchat than you – but otherwise, yes."

"Oh." I didn't know how I was meant to feel about that. "You're *replacing* me?"

"Lexi." He took the CV I was holding out of my hands. "As my daughter, you are irreplaceable. But I've been thinking. You need to have your own life. Your own space. You need to do what *you* want – not just what I want."

"Have you been talking to Mum?"

"What makes you say that?"

"Nothing. Nothing at all." I tried not to laugh.

"You have your exams coming up, and then there's your whole future. Have you thought some more about going to university?"

"Daaaaaaad…"

"Whatever decision you make, that needs to be your focus. I've been unfair and asked too much of you. So, I'll get a convention assistant and you can dip in and out of the planning when you have time…and we'll talk again. Maybe you could come back and work for the company full-time after you graduated?"

"But if I went to university, that's" – I counted in my head – "four years away!"

He smiled and nudged me. "You're my daughter, Lexi. I've seen what you can do in four *days*. Just imagine what you could do in four years."

Four years.

That's, like, 1,460 days.

That's a *lot* of time.

That's a lot of me to make up…

Still, whatever happens, we have one more convention to take care of this season and I'm going to enjoy it. Just as soon as I get these ridiculous ghosts stuck to the wall.

The walkie-talkie on the table squawks, and Nadiya picks it up. It's Dad.

"Lexi, can you come over to the ops room, please?"

My table wobbles dangerously. "Tell him I'm busy," I hiss at Nadiya.

She tries.

He doesn't listen. "Nadiya, can you tell my daughter it's about a *pineapple*?"

"Shit."

The walkie goes dead, and Nadiya frowns at it – then at me. "Pineapple?"

"I'd better go," I say. "We've probably got a ghost running amok or someone's turned into a pumpkin or something." My head feels like somebody stuffed it with soup. "Are you *sure* you can't get jet lag from a train?"

Nadiya just blinks at me. She has a very expressive face, Nadiya.

I jump down from the table – it's more of an elegant fall really, but who's checking? – and drag myself along the corridor. A couple of the event rooms are along the way, their doors standing open – and there, right through the windows, is the castle perched up on its hill. Last year, one of the panel moderators actually asked if we could close the blinds in their event room, because everyone was too busy staring at the castle illuminated against the dusk to actually watch the panellists…

Suddenly, I feel a pang of jealousy. I don't want to share this – let alone with a stranger. A replacement me. I've always known how much I love all this, how much it matters to me…but I've never actually thought about how much I'd miss it if I stopped.

I'd miss the corridors, the running (so much running!). I'd miss the ever-changing wallpaper of hotels – but maybe not the hotels' wallpaper. I'd miss Bede's moaning and Nadiya's frowns and even the late nights – and that particular, breathless silence of the ops room before breakfast. I'd even miss the inevitable, infamous "rubber chicken" of the banquets. Probably.

I'd miss this world, because it's mine.

Everything else feels like I have to share it, but this… even though there are hundreds of other people here, most of them know exactly who I am. This is my place, my home, my family.

It's *mine*.

It's *me*.

But maybe it doesn't have to be *all* of me?

Behind the frosted glass of the ops room door, I can see figures moving around – and given how many people are in there, it must be one hell of a crisis.

Right, then. Brace yourself.

I shoulder the door open – and there's Dad and Sam. Both of them look serious.

And then they step apart, and behind them is a suntanned face and a mop of black hair that's even curlier and less under control than it was last time I saw it.

Aidan.

"You're *here*!"

*Well done, Lexi. Always good to state the obvious in case people haven't noticed...*

"I said I'd be at this one, didn't I?"

"But...not till tomorrow!"

"I came up early." He grins and slips out from between Dad and Sam and pulls me into a hug – and there's the smell of him, the smell I've missed so badly late at night that it's hurt, and I realize that for weeks all I've wanted to do is touch him; feel the warmth of his skin under my fingers, run my hands through his hair, breathe him in, drown in him.

*About those photos*, whispers a voice in my head. I ignore it. Later. It's waited this long, and now he's here...

Dad taps his cane against the floor, and I pull away, embarrassed, and look up into Aidan's eyes.

They are all I can see.

"You, umm, didn't come up by train, did you?"

"No. Are you crazy – why would I do that?"

"Oh, no reason." All my concentration is spent on not reaching for him again, not drawing closer and closer until our edges blur and we overlap. So I could be saying *anything*. I probably am.

*Pay attention, Lexi.*

"You need to come get your lanyard. I didn't bring it with me because I didn't know you were here because if I'd known you were here I would have brought it but I didn't so you really need to come get it."

*Yes, Lexi. That's so much better. Bravo.*

Is it hot in here all of a sudden, or is it me?

Aidan actually has the nerve to look smug as he yanks the membership lanyard out from under his shirt. "This lanyard, you mean?"

Sam shuffles her feet. "Sorry. That was me – I knew he was coming up early so I snuck it out of the box. You might want to, umm, tick it off your list?"

No wonder she's been avoiding me all day. I thought I'd done something to upset her…but it turns out she just remembered how awful she is at keeping *anything* a secret. And she thinks I'm annoyed with her for actually managing to.

I pull away from Aidan and hug my best friend, feeling her relax as I do.

"So…you're not pissed off?"

"Why would I be? It's an amazing surprise! I didn't think he would—"

"Not *Aidan*. Obviously. I meant me messing up the membership box. I was only going to take his lanyard out, but then I had the box resting on the back of the chair and Bede—"

"Wait. Messing up the membership box?"

"I dropped it. I thought you'd realized…" She slips out of my grasp, safely out of reach.

"You. Dropped. It."

"And then you were coming right round the corner so I kind of shoved all the envelopes back in really quickly, and I think they're a bit…jumbled?" Her voice gets quieter and smaller with every word.

"I left Nadiya on her own at reg."

Sam's wide eyes meet mine, and she says it at exactly the same time I do.

"*Shit.*"

When we round the corner back to the registration desk, the membership queue stretches all the way to the hotel's front door.

"You." I point at Sam. "Fix this."

She nods meekly and slides behind the table alongside

Nadiya – barely even flinching when Nadiya cuffs her around the back of the head.

The day slips away, time stretching and concertinaing like it does at every convention, and instead of heading to one of the parties in the evening, we all collapse into a booth in the hotel bar – where Bede takes it upon himself to induct Aidan into the world of convention staff, even though I've repeatedly asked him to shut up.

"What you see before you, Aidan, is a perfect cross section of your typical late-night convention tribes." Bede, standing on the red velvet seat of the booth, waves an arm around the bar. "Most of the membership are either in the late-night panels they have paid to attend – or in bed, because they're losers. These? These are the convention hardcore."

"Bede!" I yank him back down to a sitting position. "Shhh. You'll annoy everyone!"

"No, I want to hear this," Aidan laughs, looking around the bar. "Go on?"

Bede gives a grin of triumph as Sam groans, Nadiya puts her head on the table and I pretend I'm very busy checking emails. If I protest any more it'll only encourage him. He pokes his head up over the top of the booth and nods at the table closest to the door. "Over there, in the black T-shirts?

With the beards? Those are the Old-Timey Sci-Fi Bros. They don't go to any of the panels or readings because they hate all the programming – but they've been to every convention since the Stone Age and they're not about to break the habit of a lifetime. They only read science fiction by dead white dudes – bonus points if said dead dudes hated women and were a little bit racist."

"A *little* bit?" chorus Sam and Nadiya.

Now it's Bede's turn to shush them – mostly because several of the group he was just describing have turned to look at him. He ducks right down again.

"Okay, so that's one," says Aidan. "What about them?" He points to a smaller table, this one surrounded by people tapping away on their phones.

"Easy. Agents."

"And that one?" Another, near-identical table a few metres away.

"Oh, they're the Hollywood lot."

"But they look just like the agents!"

"Nope." Bede shakes his head. "Look closer, youngling. The agents – as you will see – have a variety of empty cocktail glasses on their table. The Hollywooders? Mineral water."

Aidan snorts into his drink. I elbow him sharply in the ribs and he pulls a face of mock-indignation. "What? It's funny because it's true."

There's a shriek of laughter from a lively table near the bar. "The YA writers," Bede says with a knowing look. "And that massive group over there?" He indicates a table littered with empty wine bottles, so completely surrounded by chairs that anyone trying to get in or out is having to climb over everyone else. "They're the crime and horror writers. Nice bunch. Make me nervous, though – how can anybody who writes stuff like that be a well-adjusted human being?" We all turn to watch as a tall blonde woman clambers out from the middle of the group, laughing. "Nope. I don't trust them at all."

"And what about them? The ones next to the staff table?"

"How do you know that's the staff table?" Bede asks.

Aidan shrugs. "They all look knackered."

"He's lying," I say to the others with a laugh. "Although it's a pretty good rule of thumb that con staff always look knackered. But actually he can see my dad in the middle."

Aidan sighs dramatically. "Thanks, Lexi. There goes my reputation as someone with a keenly observant eye."

"You had one of those?"

"Reputation, or keenly observant eye?"

I'm about to snap back with a witty answer, but Bede's started making fake retching sounds so I let it go.

"They're the newbies. First time at a convention," I say, looking over at the little group of members clustered around the small table. "They don't know many people yet, so they kind of gravitate towards each other. Usually they'll end up sticking together." I stand up and wave at them. Two of them look over at me and smile back, while the others just look terrified. "Do you want to come over here?" I call. "There's loads of room!" I point at the booth. Bede immediately, magically, expands to take up twice as much room as he normally does. Sam pokes him in the side of the neck, and Nadiya groans from face down on the table. "Not more people. No more people."

Most of the newbies head our way, bringing their drinks with them. Two obviously decide that a table of slightly grouchy convention staff is not their idea of fun and wander off towards tonight's big event – the film-soundtrack karaoke party we're studiously avoiding – but the others shuffle into the spare seats in the booth and pull up chairs and smile at each other and at us.

"So, how's your convention going?" I ask. Nadiya makes a noise that sounds a little like a sob. "Ignore her," I add.

Our new-found friends are called Jen, Jenny, Amanda and Mandy (and as they introduce themselves I can almost hear the cogs in Aidan's writer-brain starting to turn) and Craig and Daragh – two best friends who've come from Dublin especially for the convention. They introduce themselves and talk about what panels they're seeing, and Daragh gets into a fact-off about pineapples – of all things – with Bede. ("Did you know that pineapples are traditionally served with ham because there's an acid in them that dissolves meat? So when you eat pineapple, that tingling feeling on your tongue is the pineapple eating you back?" "And did *you* know that…" And on we go…) But Craig can't seem to take his eyes off Aidan. This is fine – until Aidan notices.

"Hey there," he says with a slightly uncomfortable smile.

Craig doesn't say anything, but just keeps on staring.

"So…are you going to the Halloween ball thing tomorrow night? It, umm, looks fun, right?" Aidan mouths the words "Help me" at me. I smile and shake my head and am suddenly deeply interested in hearing Daragh explain how people used to rent pineapples for dinner parties.

And then, at long last, Craig speaks.

"You're…"

Uh-oh.

"You're Haydn Swift!"

"I am."

"Would you sign my arm?" Craig pulls out a marker pen and starts rolling up the sleeve of the shirt he's wearing.

Aidan shakes his head apologetically. "Sorry – I don't really sign *people*, but if you… Oh." He stops so suddenly that everyone – me, Sam, Bede, Nadiya and all the newbies – turn to see why.

Craig has rolled up his sleeve to reveal a tattoo of Aidan's *face* on his arm. At least, I *think* it's supposed to be Aidan –

it's a little lopsided and slightly squished. What makes me certain is when I recognize it as a copy of his head and shoulders from the notorious Glowy Ball photo shoot.

"Huh," says Aidan in a high-pitched voice, while Bede is suddenly overwhelmed by a coughing fit.

"I was hoping if you signed underneath...?" Craig says hopefully, but Aidan shakes his head.

"Sorry. I'm not trying to be a dick, I just...you know?" Seeing how crestfallen Craig looks, he adds: "But if you've got anything else you want me to sign, I'm really happy to. As long as it's not you, that's all."

"My copy of *Piecekeepers* is in my room – can I?"

"Sure. I'll be right here." Aidan's smile is genuine and warm. As Craig pushes his chair back to go fetch his book, Aidan points to his arm. "And you know, that's really cool. I'm honoured."

Craig beams and hurries off.

The Jen-Jennys take this as their opportunity to say goodnight, while Mandy and Amanda murmur something about the karaoke. All four of them leave, while Bede is too busy flirting with Daragh to notice *anything*. Aidan slides closer to me.

"That was...quite a thing," he says. "I'm not sure how I feel about that."

"He has your *face* tattooed on his *arm*. I'm not sure how *I* feel about that."

"Oh really?" He raises an eyebrow. "You think you should get a say in where my face goes?"

I feel the blood rush to my face. "Stop it. He's coming back."

Craig is indeed back, holding out a dog-eared copy of *Piecekeepers*. "I've read it five times already," he says proudly.

Aidan takes it from him and opens it out on the title page to sign. "You should talk to Lexi here. It sounds like you know it even better than she does. Am I making this out to you, or...?"

As Craig gives him detailed instructions on what to write ("Just to me – not, you know, 'me', but Craig – just Craig – only without the just") I see part of myself in him. Admittedly, without the someone-else's-face tattooed on my arm, but I see me, back in the spring. Reading that book, feeling like whoever wrote it had done it just for me, like it was the world I was meant to be in.

Craig feels the same way, and there's something magical about that. He's not stealing it from me, and nor is anyone else – how could they? It's as much theirs as it is mine. We're all part of Haydn's little tribe.

And that's when I realize: I will always have to share Haydn. Haydn goes on trips to Italy and Detroit and gets onstage and smiles and laughs and answers questions and signs copies of his books and has his photo taken. It's Haydn that people approach in hotel bars and say "You're Haydn Swift!" to.

*Haydn*, not *Aidan*.

It was Aidan, not Haydn, building towers out of pistachio shells under a table.

Aidan, not Haydn, sliding down a corridor on a tray and laughing.

Aidan, not Haydn, who makes me feel like the floor has tilted under me; like the *world* has tilted under me.

Aidan I get all to myself.

And I think that just maybe we are our *own* tribe.

# GHOSTS

"Who's the extra seat for?" Nadiya nods at the empty place setting at the breakfast table while she loads her plate up with toast.

"Oi! Leave some for the rest of us." Bede makes a snatch for the top slice and she smacks his fingers with a teaspoon.

"Keep your grubby little mitts to yourself," she says. "I know where those hands have been."

"Re-taping the microphone leads in panel room two, that's where they've been," he snaps back, waggling his fingers at her. She rolls her eyes and throws the piece of toast at him.

"Actually," Dad says, far too loudly, "I thought that Lexi might want a place for Aidan…"

The whole table – my friends, most of their parents and even bloody Rodney, sitting at the far end – all look at me and make "Ooooooooooooh!" noises.

"Another convention couple," says Mike. "Just like Marie and Paul."

I stare at Marie, who is smiling at Paul beside her. "You two *met* at a convention?"

"Yep. And went to another one for our honeymoon."

"Some people don't need the Seychelles," says Paul, peering down the table at Dad.

Dad nods. "And some people want their honeymoon to be peaceful," he mutters, and prods his breakfast. "Passes the sausage test."

"But enough about your honeymoon…" Bede chimes in.

This time, *I* throw the toast at him.

And this is what Aidan walks in on: all of us, in full convention-breakfast flow.

"Don't ask," I say, pulling back his chair for him.


I'm running through the to-do list as we finish breakfast. "Sam, can you go and check we've got all the leads from the karaoke machine back in the ops room? It needs to be returned to the rental place this afternoon and they'll charge us from the deposit if we lose any of the cables."

Captain America nods at me as she finishes her tea. "Sure thing."

"And when you've done that—"

"I know, I know. Put the mic stand back in reading room two. I *have* done this before."

"You *have*?"

"Oh, my sides." She puts her hands on her waist. "Oh, wait. Not even slightly splitting." And then she blows me a kiss and wanders off towards the ops room – right as the Brother walks in and makes a beeline for our table. But it's not Dad he goes for – oh no. It's Aidan.

"Mr Swift."

Aidan swivels in his seat to look up at him, his mouth still full of scrambled egg. "Mmmpffhhy?"

"Damien – we spoke briefly while you were in Detroit?"

"Oh, wow. Yes." He gulps down the egg. "Good to see you again."

The Brother has come to mark his territory.

(And Detroit? Really? The Brother kept that little gem to himself, didn't he?)

I'll be civil. "Hello again, Damien."

"Hey there, Laura."

"Lexi."

"Lexi?"

"Lexi. Not Laura. My name's Lexi."

"I don't…?"

"You always call me Laura, but it's Lexi."

"Oh. Oh, sure."

There's a pause, and I raise an eyebrow at Aidan, mouthing "Detroit?" at him. He looks like he wants the ground to swallow him whole.

"Well, brother…" Damien's lost interest in me, and now

it's back to Aidan. "We – the committee, that is – have been looking at the guests we'd like to invite to come on over to New Orleans next year. The official invites haven't gone out yet, but seeing as we're all friends here I don't think it would be too much of a problem for me to say that we'd love to bring you over as one of our guests of honour!" He rocks back on his heels slightly, waiting for…what? A round of applause?

There's a stony silence, punctuated by a tapping sound from the other end of the table as Dad aggressively stirs his coffee. The tumbleweed should be blowing through any second; either that or Dad and Damien are both going to throw down and wrestle for the title of Winning Convention Organizer. And now Dad's got his cane…

It's Aidan who speaks first though, smiling at the Brother as though they're the greatest friends in the world.

"I don't know what to say. That's…so generous. And such an honour. But – and I'd have to check the dates to be absolutely sure – doesn't New Orleans clash with Max's first convention of the year?"

The Brother opens his mouth and closes it like a goldfish that's fallen out of its bowl, and my heart is suddenly so full I'm almost sure it's going to burst.

Aidan, as politely as possible, continues: "Because, obviously, when it comes to conventions, Max has first call on my time after all the support he's shown me this year.

It's the least I can do." Under the table, the tips of Aidan's fingers brush my palm as he takes my hand.

Dad takes a sip of his coffee and looks – on the surface at least – completely unmoved. But I know what this will mean to him; above everything else, my dad cares about loyalty. It's why he has the same people around him that he's had for years. It's who he *is*. And Aidan has just bumped himself right to the top of his friends' list without even really trying.

More than that, it shows that Aidan understands. He understands all of it.

All of *me*.

And that, I guess, makes me an idiot for what I did after the wedding. For once, I'm okay with having been an idiot. I'm actually happy about it.

Well. As happy as I can be, given the circumstances.

Making a swift recovery, the Brother's smile is back. "Of course, of course. You have to do what you have to do. But if those dates don't work for you, brother, how about Miami? Or Dallas, in July? We were hoping you'd be able to let us in on some of the plans for your next book, give us a bit of a scoop, seeing as Max here got the jump on us and found you first…"

"You know I can't do that. I'm not telling anyone *anything*! But don't worry – they're all safe in here." Aidan taps the side of his head, then pats his phone on the table. "And here."

"You're a tease, brother, but I see how it is."

That conjures up a terrible, terrible mental image. Thanks for that.

The Brother shakes Aidan's hand and sighs. "You'll still get that email. Let us know, won't you? It'd be a pleasure to have you any time."

"You're too kind. Thank you."

Aidan lets go of Damien's hand, but Damien holds on just that tiny bit longer...and then releases him, disappearing across the breakfast room in search of another victim. Or breakfast, maybe.

I raise my eyebrows at Aidan. "Everything *Max* has done?"

There's another chorus of "Oooooooh!"s – and Dad splutters into his coffee.

"Aidan, I wanted to talk to you about something." Time to get all our cards on the table, clear the air... pick a metaphor: one way or another, I have to know.

"Sure." Oblivious, he slides a hand around my waist and pulls me closer, so I'm walking with him and it's the easiest thing in the world, like we were always meant to be in step. We're crossing the lobby; I'm about to open up registration for the day – and double-check that Sam's handiwork yesterday has been put right – and he's going to look in on the Writing the Strange panel. So it seems like a perfect time to talk. Of course it does. If it was a big deal, I wouldn't be asking this now, would I? It's just…casual. Yes.

"When you were away last month…"

"I still feel bad about that."

"You do?" Mild panic, nothing I can't handle. What does he feel bad about? What? What happened? Why should he feel bad?

"Not being around when your dad was taken to hospital. In case you needed…" He pauses. "Someone."

"That? That's not what I meant at all!" I realize how this sounds. Because of course my father being rushed to hospital in an ambulance doesn't matter. Nope. I try again. "I mean, thank you, *obviously*. But I really meant that I wanted to talk about the whole…photos thing."

"The photos thing?" He looks at me blankly, but it's too late to pull back now so I might as well charge straight on.

"Umm. So, funny story. Stupid, probably. But the editor of *SixGuns* came up to me at the time and asked if we were friends and, if we were, did I know anything about you and…whatsherface. From the film. At breakfast. Because there were photos of you together in Naples and there was breakfast and it was in a hotel? But I didn't, and I don't, and I just wondered whether it was anything I need to know about so…umm. That. All that."

*Smooth, Lexi.*

"You mean Carly?"

*Oh.*

Carly. Not "Carly Senekal, who's been cast as Ali". Just *Carly*.

Well. That's just dandy.

"She was down the coast shooting while I was there for the literary festival, and she wanted to meet up. She had some questions about Ali's backstory – stuff she wanted to bring into her performance or something. The only time we were both free was crazy early one day though, so she came up to the hotel."

"Mmmmph."

"Lexi?" He studies me carefully. "Photos?"

"It's nothing. I mean, I didn't even see them, so…" If I thought I could fit my entire fist in my mouth, I would do that now. I couldn't possibly look like more of an idiot than I already do.

"Hold up…you mean those shitty pictures where they'd cropped everyone else out? The ones that made it look like it was the two of…" He tails off. He understands.

"I…everyone else?"

"Hang on." Shaking his head, he slips his phone out of his pocket and scrolls rapidly through screen after screen of pictures. "Maybe this'll show you what I mean." He hands me the phone, flicking away a low battery warning as he passes it across.

I recognize the setting immediately from one of his Instagram photos: the stone balcony, the blue sky. Definitely Italy. But this one includes a starched white cloth across a table…and gathered around it, at least a dozen smiling faces. It wasn't just Aidan and Carly having breakfast; it was half the crew.

"That's Tony, the unit director," he says, pointing out a guy in sunglasses at the end of the table. "And Rhodri, the location scout. That's Tash and Anna, and Marina…and *that*" – he taps a handsome suntanned face at the very edge of the shot – "is Rufus, Carly's husband."

I blink at him. Luckily, he has no idea what's going on inside my head. Good. Instead, he's tucking his phone away – still talking.

"You'd love it out there. It's amazing. Naples, Ischia… you should go sometime." He pauses. "Maybe *we* could go sometime. You know, if you wanted?"

"Husband."

In my head, I'm casual and I smile and I dismiss the whole thing with a mere wave of my hand…but what actually comes out of my mouth is: "Husband."

I mean, forget the fact that *he just asked if I wanted to go to Italy with him,* because there are too many things in my head and not enough space for all of them.

*OH FOR GOD'S SAKE, LEXI. GET A GRIP.*

"Husband," Aidan repeats. "They're pretty private, and

she keeps it quiet – it's bad for her image or something. I don't know. But I can see how it might have sounded if you heard about it from *SixGuns*, of all places…"

"Sorry." I feel small and stupid, like a kid who doesn't want to share the toys at nursery.

I have to share Haydn. I know that.

But it's Aidan who lays his hands on either side of my face and gently – so gently – tilts my face up towards his; looks into my eyes like they're all he *wants* to see and everything else is just dust.

"Aidan Green? Dude! Is that *you*?"

Both Aidan and Haydn are snatched away from me by the stranger standing in the middle of the lobby, grinning and looking right at us.

"Nick?" Aidan's hands slip from my face.

"Ade! I thought it was!"

And now the stranger with a buzz cut and skinny jeans with too much stuffed in the pockets is striding towards Aidan, who is frozen to the spot.

Nick.

Nick?

Nick…

Nick, Aidan's friend.

Nick and…

Suddenly she's there and she's as annoyingly pretty as I expected she'd be.

She looks just like he described her in the book. Long, glossy hair. A perfect smile, eyelashes as long as my *arm* – and to add insult to injury, she's exactly the same height as he is.

*Ali.*

"Oh. Ali. Ali…hi." Aidan is blinking like a deer caught in oncoming headlights. Headlights attached to a *tank*. "What are you doing here?"

"Thought we'd come and check out the…convention." Nick leaves the slightest gap before the last word and sniffs after it.

I do not like Nick.

"Right, okay. I didn't think you came to conventions?"

I'm about to step forward, to say hello – to do anything – when Ali opens her irritatingly perfect-shaped mouth and blows me out of the water.

"Not exactly. But I was in the bookshop down the road and I saw a big poster in the window for *this*…" She holds up a very familiar book and my heart sinks. "And it just happened to have your photo at the bottom." She flips it open with a smirk. "Haydn Swift, hmmm? Oh, don't worry. Your secret's safe with me."

Is she…is she *flirting* with him? Despite the fact her other arm is *looped through Nick's*?

Christ, no wonder Ali ends up badly in the book. I always liked Lizzie better anyway.

"Hi, I'm Lexi."

*Clipboard up, smile on and Effie Trinket the shit out of it. This is your Hunger Games, Angelo.*

They both look at me, and then through me. I am invisible. I am nothing.

Well, you know what? Clipboard or not, bollocks to that.

"Are you here to pick up your convention memberships? Day memberships over to the left, full memberships to the right. Banquet and ball tickets should be in your membership packs…"

"We've already got ours, thanks. Just here for the day," says Nick, pulling a lanyard from his pocket and waving it at me.

"Fantastic." My voice is too shiny. Too sparkly, like glass on a pavement. "If you could wear those at all times that would be really helpful. Otherwise security might accidentally throw you out – and we don't want that."

All three of them are now looking at me like I've turned into a horse.

No, not a horse. An ass.

An actual, giant, talking *ass*.

So much for not having to share Aidan…

"I've got to run, okay?" I say to him. I have to scrunch my fingernails into my palms to stop myself from touching him, from laying some claim on him. "I'll catch up with you later."

I'm gone before he can answer, but as I walk away I hear Ali asking: "Who was *that*?"

"Sorry – that was Lexi. She—"

Nick cuts him off. "Nah, nah, never mind her – tell us what's been going on with you! What's up with this *book*?"

And then Bede runs up to tell me one of the inflatable ghosts in the ballroom has exploded, and I've never been so happy to see him in my life.

I spend my day scuttling between the ballroom and the ops room. I can't face checking in on any of the panel rooms, or the readings. I don't even walk the halls in case I run into *them*. Am I hiding? No. I'm not hiding. I'm working. Not hiding; working. There's a world of difference, even if my work happens to be keeping me in a closed room away from all the people. But I'm definitely not hiding. Instead, I busy myself with filling balloons from the helium cylinder. What was Aidan about to say? Was he going to tell them I'm a friend? A member of the convention staff? Nobody?

*Sorry – that was Lexi. She's nobody.*

No. He didn't say that.

Ali though.

Ali. The girl he wrote into a book.

I'm not sure how I'd feel if I were her (other than, you know, amazing because, well, *those eyelashes*.). About being written into a book, I mean, because it's not like it's the real her, is it? It can't be; could never be. All fictional Ali can ever be is Aidan's impression of her.

Which was obviously pretty good.

I am not helping myself.

Ali. Ali is here. The real Ali; walking around *my* convention. The girl he wrote a book for. *My* book.

The balloon I've been filling goes BANG, jerking me back to the ballroom and out of thoughts about people I don't even know. I overfilled it. I sigh, and peel the remains off the nozzle and reach for another one – just as Sam comes crashing through the door with a bag of ribbons.

"So this is where you're hiding!" She hurls the bag onto a table. It scoots straight over the top and lands on the floor; she looks at it for a moment, then shrugs. "It's fine there. I thought I hadn't seen you in ages."

"I've got a headache," I lie. "Figured being away from the crowd would be a good thing. I don't want to feel shitty tonight."

"Mmmm. And this 'headache'" – she makes finger quotes around the word – "wouldn't have anything to do with those friends of Aidan's turning up, would it?"

"How do you know about that?" I open the nozzle on the cylinder and the new balloon fills up with gas.

"He's looking for you." She takes the balloon from me and ties it, looping a ribbon and weight around it and letting it go. It rises, then drops, hovering a metre off the floor.

"He's with his friends."

"*You're* his friend. And if you ask me – which of course you will, because I'm me and I have many, many wise things to say as always – he's not that fussed about the pair of them. So leave me to do the balloons and stop moping."

"You sound like my mother."

"Your mother," she says, pointing a finger at me, "is my *guru*."

"You have no idea how disconcerting it is to hear a girl dressed as a superhero say that."

"Disconcerting…or *amazing*?" Sam pulls herself into a full-on power pose; chin raised, hands on hips.

"The first one. Definitely."

She's right. This is stupid. It's more than stupid; it's embarrassing.

"Here." I pass her the packet of balloons. "They all need doing."

She snaps into a salute. "Yes, ma'am. Now get out there!"

"What's that accent even meant to be? Texan? Because it wasn't."

"I have no idea. It just felt like the right thing to do." She clamps a balloon over the nozzle and fills it – then lets it go. It flies around our heads with a *prrrrrrrrrrrp* noise, and she snorts. "You know I'm going to keep doing this till you go, right?"

By the time I make it to the door, she's done it another three times.

The first person I see outside the ballroom is Aidan, walking straight towards me.

Alone.

I can feel my heart expanding a little more in my chest with every step he takes; by the time he actually gets to me, my heart will be too big for my ribs and will either explode or break out and go flying around the ceiling making a *prrrrrrrrrrrp* sound just like Sam's balloons.

"Hey," I say, and all I want to do is throw my arms around him.

But something's off. Something's not right.

"Lexi. I need to talk to you a minute."

"What's the matter?"

There's some tiny little sensor built into everyone that automatically responds to a particular tone of voice, a particular look in the eye, with "What's the matter?"

"My phone."

"You *cannot* be serious." He's joking. He has to be, after last time. It's his attempt at a particularly unfunny in-joke, right?

"Lexi, I'm completely serious. It's gone."

"Gone?"

"It's either been stolen or…" He stops; frowns.

"Or what?"

"Or Nadiya's lost it."

I don't understand. "Why would Nadiya have your phone?"

"You really want to have this conversation in public, Lexi?" Aidan gestures to the groups wandering past us. He's right. This isn't a conversation I want people to eavesdrop on, not if something's been stolen.

"Okay. Right. We'd better carry this on in the ops room."

"Lexi?"

"Yep."

"You should know – if anything from that phone gets leaked, I'm in real trouble."

*Uh-oh.*

"Trouble…how?"

"I've got emails on there about the film. Script drafts. Set photos. It's not just notes for the next book – although if those get out I'll be screwed anyway. But I've signed a non-disclosure agreement with the studio, so if *any* of the film stuff ends up online, I could be sued. For a lot of money."

*Yeah, that sounds like trouble to me.*

I rest my hand on the ops room door and stop. I don't look at him, because if I do that, it'll be too hard.

"Aidan, before we go in there, I need to know how serious this is. Is this Aidan-from-the-roof who's lost his phone again, or is this an author with an issue?"

"Does it matter?"

"Aidan, please. If there's a problem, I need to deal with it. If it's just you, and you're freaking out because you've forgotten your phone in your room or something, that's different." I pause. This is not going the way I expected: his expression is getting colder by the second. "It's not like this would be the first time you managed to lose your phone, would it?"

He lets out an angry laugh. "Fine. Well, if it's so important for you to fit me into a box on one of your little grids, I'm an author and I'm coming to you with a work problem. I have not left my phone anywhere – other than with Nadiya."

"Fine, then! That's all I needed to know." My reply is probably more prickly than it needed to be, and I push the door open.

Nadiya is in tears. I look from her to Dad to Rodney, then back to Aidan and the hotel's security guy.

"It was there. On top of my bag, under the registration desk."

"Okay, so tell me what happened."

Nadiya sobs again, her shoulders heaving up and down – and I can't bear it. This is my *friend*.

"Nadiya. Nadiya, it's okay. Nobody's blaming you."

"Actually I am," Aidan mutters sulkily.

I put an arm around her shoulders. "That kind of attitude isn't helping."

"Neither's Nadiya."

"Excuse me," I snap, rounding on him – if he's seriously accusing my friend of losing a phone which should never have been her responsibility, I don't have to be nice. "Don't you dare speak to our convention staff like that."

Even Nadiya stops sniffing.

"Perhaps you can help by telling us why, precisely, you thought it was appropriate to leave your phone with a member of staff?" I add. "Especially if it has so much sensitive material on it – surely that's *your* responsibility?"

Aidan rubs his face with the heel of his hand. "I left my charger at home. I was asking Nadiya if she knew where I could get one near the hotel and she said I could borrow hers. Seeing as there's a plug right behind the table, it didn't make a lot of sense to go all the way back upstairs. She said she'd keep an eye on it."

"Oh, right. And because she offered to help *you*, this is *her* fault?" This is bad. It's bad – but it's not down to Nadiya.

Nadiya's a mess. She keeps looking at Aidan and saying, "I'm so sorry. Aidan, I'm so sorry."

"It's just a phone," I say…but one look at Aidan tells me this comment isn't helpful. I've never seen him look so angry and he keeps rubbing his face and muttering "My agent's going to tear me apart when I tell her" to himself.

GHOSTS

"I'll have to scrap the whole of the next book and start again. I'll blow my deadline by a mile – and that's before I even have to deal with the studio guys. I swear, she's going to *kill* me."

My father has been listening to this quietly, one hand resting against his chin. "How would anyone know you had anything so important in your phone?"

"You mean anyone other than the everyone who *happened* to be in the breakfast room this morning and heard me talking? Gee, I don't know."

"Then maybe you should try keeping your mouth shut." So much for me being Professional Lexi talking to a convention guest. This is pure, concentrated Crazy Lexi yelling at crazy-making Aidan; the Aidan who invaded the green room and made everything so *complicated* – and who, after all the effort I've made to let down my guard, has clearly reverted to Prick Mode. He gives me a look so dark that all the light in the room fades to nothing, and slams out of the ops office.

As the door bangs shut, Nadiya visibly flinches in her seat and squeaks uncomfortably. Behind her, Dad has his lips pressed so tightly together that they're almost white. His whole face has assumed a general *Sort this out, Lexi* expression.

With another quick glance at Nadiya, I wrench the door open and chase Aidan down the corridor.

"Hey!"

I don't know whether he can't hear me or whether he's ignoring me.

"Hey!"

He slows just a little, but he doesn't stop and he doesn't turn – it's enough for me to catch up and duck in front of him though; I plant my feet and force him to look me in the eye. Everything about him is cold and unforgiving and suddenly he's a stranger. But I'm not exactly in a warm and forgiving mood myself – not after that.

"What's the matter with you? You were completely unfair back there…"

"Was I?" He cuts across me. "Was I really? What you said wasn't exactly nice. Is this how you'd treat anyone else with the same problem?"

"Look… Sorry…but you aren't anyone else though – are you? You're *you*. And that's the only reason Nadiya would have offered to look after your phone herself."

"Do you have any idea how important the stuff on there is, Lexi? To me? To my career?"

"Important enough for you to be a dick about it, clearly. It's just a shame it wasn't important enough to keep it safe, isn't it?" I draw myself up to my full height and stare straight at him. "You do not get to talk to my friends like that. I don't care what's lost. I don't care what goes wrong. There is literally no circumstance in which it is okay for you to be that way to the people I care about when they're doing you a favour. And don't you dare tell me I'm not doing my job right."

"Did I say that?" His voice has dropped to a hiss.

"You might as well have."

"Oh, here we go." He shakes his head angrily at me. "It always comes back to the clipboard, doesn't it?"

"What's that supposed to mean?"

"You know what I think, Lexi? I think you're using this – the conventions, the work, all of it – as an excuse. You act like it's a big deal, but the truth is you don't know what you'd do without it. It's easier to play the martyr than it is to actually go and figure out what you *want*. It's easier and it's a hell of a lot less frightening, so here you stay – a big fish in a little pond."

I have never been so angry in my entire life. The inside of my skin burns and bubbles. "Right. Sure. This coming from the guy who hides behind a fake name," I laugh.

He glares at me for a moment...and when he speaks, his voice is soft and it's nearly the voice I know, the voice that has become so familiar. It's almost that voice – but it isn't.

"I might be hiding behind a fake name, but at least I picked it myself. I didn't just use my father's. And I'd rather be doing that than clinging onto a clipboard with a bunch of lists on it, hoping it'll keep anything I can't control away from me.

It hurts so much that I can barely breathe. Every muscle in my body wants to fold in on itself.

It hurts so much – and even as the words leave his lips, I know.

I know.

He's right.

That's why it hurts.

Because after all this, he does know me – and this is the time he picks to prove it.

He *knows* me – and right now I hate him, because with him I have nowhere to hide.

And I am falling in love with him and have been for months, and I am falling too hard and too fast to stop without it tearing me apart.

We stare at each other.

"I shouldn't have been a dick to Nadiya," he says, after the longest time.

"No. You shouldn't."

"Tell her I'm sorry?"

"Tell her yourself."

He pauses. "What did you mean a minute ago – about Nadiya helping because of me being me?"

He doesn't get it and I don't know if I can risk any more hurt by explaining, after everything that's been said. I look away, then back at him – because how can I not?

Something flickers deep in his eyes.

This is not how it was supposed to go. But I guess that's life; things change and you have to figure out how to move things around to make it work. You can't control people like you can a programme; can't plot their emotions on a grid.

And just a moment too late, I realize he's worth the risk.

Aidan Green, here, now, in this hallway and with the clouds gathering over our heads, is worth risking something – risking *everything* – for.

"Nadiya wanted to help you out. She wasn't doing it for *you*. She was doing it for me – because everybody here knows how I feel about you."

*Say something, Aidan.*

*Don't just stand there.*

*Say something.*

*Say anything.*

We are locked into this moment, the two of us. Trapped in the middle of the electrical storm.

And it feels like it goes on for ever.

And it burns.

I have aged a thousand years before he says something, and I can barely hear what he's saying over the ripping sound in my head. He has told me the worst truth about myself – something I've known for a long time, inside… And that is the exact moment – of all the moments in the whole, glorious span of eternity – that I decide to tell him how I feel?

*Say something, Aidan.*

*Say anything.*

"Nick and Ali asked me to go out and get dinner with them tonight. Maybe I should go."

Over his shoulder, I can see one of the posters for the masked ball.

Tonight.

I guess that means he won't be there.

I will not let my heart break. I can't. Not when all I have to stick it back together with is Blu-Tack, and the world where I want to run for comfort is the one *he* created.

"Maybe you should."

"Okay then."

*Rip. Rip. Rip.*


I walk back to the ops room alone.

There, I find Dad crouched down in front of Nadiya, her hands in his. "Nadiya, nobody is blaming you. Not for a second – I want you to understand that."

She looks at him and nods.

He carries on. "These things happen. We can be as careful as we like, but sometimes these things happen."

Nadiya nods again. "I was only trying to—"

"I know. We all know. Now, I want you to think back over the afternoon. Is there any time – any time at all – somebody could have got near your bag?"

"No. I was there the whole time, and I didn't…" She shakes her head…and then she stiffens. "Wait. There was the guy who fell over."

Dad glances over at me, and on autopilot I pick up my clipboard and a pen and start writing as she talks.

"About half an hour ago – about quarter to five. This guy bought a ticket for the banquet tomorrow – and he dropped his change. And while he was picking it up, this other man came up and sort of…I don't know. Tripped over him? It was really weird."

"He tripped over him?"

"Right next to my bag." Her eyes widen and she knows, we *all* know, that's when it happened.

Dad's voice is low and calm and soft, and he's still squeezing her hands. "Think very carefully," he says. "Was he wearing a lanyard?"

Nadiya screws her eyes shut like she's trying to picture him, trying to remember.

"Yes. Yes, he was. He's a member."

I reach for the membership list. "Then we should be able to find him."

"I don't suppose you remember who it was?" Dad tries, but Nadiya shakes her head.

"Just…a guy. I'm sorry, Max. I wish I'd never offered Aidan my charger."

Dad doesn't say anything; he just nods as a strange

ringing sound fills the room. It starts quietly, then builds and builds. Everyone looks at everyone else.

"Lexi." Rodney glances up and nods at me.

"What?"

"I think that's your phone, pet."

"My phone?"

And sure enough, it is. With one tiny, feeble bar of signal, someone has managed to get my phone to ring. I yank it out of my pocket.

"Hello?"

"Lexi! It's Bede. Nobody's answering the walkie."

"I must have left it in the ballroom. We're kind of in the middle of a crisis here…"

"I know. That's why I'm calling. You and your dad better come through to the main hotel lobby. Pronto." And he hangs up. I stare at my phone, and then at Dad.

"Dad? It's Bede. He says he needs us."

"Can't it wait?"

"I don't think it can…"

Waiting for us at the hotel's main reception desk is a small group of people. Bede, the hotel's security guard, the Brother and – looking half-ashamed and half-defiant – Andy from *SixGuns*. And sitting on the reception desk in front of them is a phone. I pick it up and turn it on, and the cover of

*Piecekeepers* flashes up at me. It's Aidan's. I give Dad a nod, and turn to Bede.

"How did you do that?"

"It was all Damien actually." He nods at the Brother and folds his arms as the Brother beams.

"Well, brother, I was just heading to the room party up on the fourth floor…"

I note Dad's involuntary twitch at the mention of a room party, but he says nothing.

"And Andy here said he might have a scoop on the next *Piecekeepers* book – and would I be interested, seeing as I'd been talking to Haydn Swift about that very thing at breakfast?"

"He was eavesdropping?"

"So I told him I'd be interested, and he said he might be able to get hold of some information—"

Bede interrupts. "And then he came to find me. *Me*, you'll note."

The Brother shrugs wearily. "Brother, you were the first one I could find."

Bede looks a little put out, but Dad? Dad looks *furious*.

"Andy. What were you thinking? Have you lost your mind? It's unethical – never mind illegal – and most of all, it's deeply, deeply disrespectful of what we're trying to do at my conventions!"

"Dad!" Typical of him to put the emphasis on that.

"Oh, hush, Lexi." He waves the end of his cane at me, then peers over my shoulder to where Rodney has just materialized. "Rodney, would you escort this gentleman to the ops room, please? I'm sure we can make him comfortable while we have a little chat in private."

Rodney nods and clamps a hand the size of a boiled ham around Andy's arm. "This way."

The Brother turns as though he's about to go, but I call after him. "Damien?"

"Lexi?"

"You got it right!" I clear my throat and pretend I didn't say anything, hoping he'll think he imagined it. Dignity and all that. "Thank you. It would have been such a mess, for Aidan...*Haydn*...and for Dad."

At first, he narrows his eyes and tilts his head a little to one side as though he's measuring me. I'm not quite sure what I should say – or whether I'm even supposed to say *anything*. And then he smiles and says, "The thing about conventions, little lady, is that we're family. We fight and we try to outmanoeuvre each other and show off...but when it comes down to it, we're all family. And family always sticks together when it counts. Tell your boyfriend I look forward to hosting him next year."

And with that, he turns to shake Dad's hand and admire his cane – and the two of them walk off practically arm in arm, with the Brother telling him that, funnily enough, this has given him an idea for a game to run over the course of New York.

*Tell your boyfriend…*

I can't quite get the Brother's words to stop echoing in my head. They bounce off my heart like a handful of spiked pinballs, punching holes in me every time they touch. I already regret everything that happened with Aidan in the corridor. I was angry because he was right, and I knew it. I love conventions, I love this world…but even I know I've been using it as an excuse not to let people in when perhaps I should; not to take the risk and see what else, who else, is out there. Throwing myself into schedules and planning and running around (running away?). Shrugging and saying that the people at college are fine, but they're not *my* people… The truth, though – the truth I've been carrying inside and not wanting to see – is that I've been too scared to do anything else. I've never been brave enough to admit it because the rhythm of a convention, the routine of it, is like a comfort blanket I've grown up with and can't let go. I mark time by the number of days to the next event, the number of emails I send, or crates of books and flyers I unpack.

*Big fish, small pond.*

Who do I want to be?

Who do I want?

I already know.

And he called me on it and I was already so angry with him that I didn't stop and listen.

I couldn't admit to someone else, anyone else, what I've known deep down for a while.

That I need to stop hiding behind my clipboard and my father's name...and make my own.

Because I can be who and whatever I want to be.

It's just that a little bit of me was kind of hoping *he'd* be around to see who that turned out to be...

There's a decidedly unsubtle cough beside me. "Sorry to interrupt this...*moment* but, Lexi, the city needs us."

"Samira. Can it not wait, like, *five* minutes?"

"Nope," says Sam. "The guy in charge of the ghost tour won't let one of the cosplayers on his bus."

"Why not?"

"Because he's dressed like the alien from *Alien*, and he's just made one of the authors' wives cry in the lobby. The cosplayer. Not the ghost-tour guy. Obviously."

I give myself a moment to process this information.

Nope.

Going to need several moments.

Everything else can come later.

Everything.

*Maybe I should go.*

# GHOSTS

It hurts too much, and I don't have time.
Sam is waiting, hands on hips.
"Come, my trusty sidekick!"
"No." I fall into step beside her.
"My faithful—"
"Just no."

# ROOTS

The dress code for the ball is "black and white magic". It might as well be grey…no, *beige*. Boring, bland and beige. I've been looking forward to it for weeks, the way some people look forward to their end-of-year party at school or their prom. I guess that's what this is to me – or *was*, anyway. Because now? Now, it's just not the same.

More than anything, I wish I could call Aidan and tell him he was right. I'm not sorry – not for defending my friend, not for one *second* – but I'm sorry that I took my doubt and fear out on him. I wish I could call him and tell him…but I can't, because his phone's in my dad's pocket waiting for him to collect it, and that's what started this whole mess spinning anyway.

If we hadn't had that fight, if he hadn't stormed off…

Would I have admitted how I felt – how I really felt – on my own? I don't know. I was right though. I was right that it would hurt; I took a risk and it hurts more than I ever imagined. But then, I've never felt like this about someone, have I? I never thought I could.

Aidan knows me. He *knows* me, and I know him and I can read him like a book. Like *his* book – and I was right about that too, when I knew that it would change everything. Because reading that is like looking through a window and he is on the other side of it looking back. He is the reflection in the mirror. We match. We *fit*.

And somehow, we've managed to mess it all up.

Sam waited for me for as long as she could, but even her patience has limits – and besides, there are still jobs to do. She went downstairs while I was still in the shower, which does at least mean I can get ready without her popping in and out of my room every thirty seconds. The peace is what I need.

Time is what I need.

When we get home, I'll help Dad go through the CVs for his new assistant – and then?

I don't know.

College, definitely. Concentrating on that.

And then?

Whatever I want – because why not?

Because my world is bigger and has more in it than a convention hotel after all. It can be as big and as full as I want it to be.

For tonight, though, all I can think about is him.

I ache and shiver and burn. And all because, yet again, he isn't here and he should be.

When I picked my dress for the ball, I thought the tiny silver stars scattered across the black fabric looked whimsical; it reminded me of the Piecekeepers' banner, and I thought it would make him laugh. Now, I'll just be going to the masquerade as a Black Hole of Misery. I slip it over my head and pull on my shoes, and tie the ribbons of my mask behind my head before checking the damage in the mirror. I'll pass. Besides, Aidan or no Aidan, I've worked hard for tonight – and so have my friends. So my Blu-Tacked, messy, frightened heart and I are going downstairs and we are going *dancing*.

In the couple of hours since I left the ballroom, some kind of enchantment has overtaken it. The specially-laid floor, which was covered in dust sheets before, is now a chequerboard of black and white tiles that glitter in the light. Artificial candles in vast silver candelabra taller than I am line the room, their little bulbs flickering just like real ones in a breeze. Balloons bob along the ceiling and trail their ribbons just above our heads, while in the centre of it all is a tiny grove of real, living trees. Their slender stems and branches reach up above us, their pots are buried in a deep drift of soft green moss (which already has several people sitting on it and poking at it, laughing) while tiny fabric roses dangle from the branches on ribbons. The music seems to come from everywhere and nowhere all at once; it's just drifting in the air, as much a part of it as oxygen.

It takes my breath away.

"It looks wonderful..." I begin, but Dad comes clacking up with his cane and a black mask that covers the top half of his face. Combined with the black velvet suit and the silver waistcoat he's wearing, it's quite a look. Bea picked it out, of course, saying that even though she wouldn't be here, she wanted everyone to see that her husband was the most handsome man in the room. (I left at that point. Can you blame me?)

"It was Aidan's idea. He wanted it to be a surprise. You can't imagine what it took to get these trees in without you seeing." He shakes his head as Sam appears in the doorway. Her dress is the colour of spring leaves and looks like something Marie Antoinette would have worn – all silk and ribbon and lace. Her hair is piled on top of her head and streaked with gold and she looks *incredible*.

"Samira, I believe the dress code was 'black and white magic'. With the emphasis on *black and white*," says Dad, raising an eyebrow.

She puts one hand on her hip and smiles. "Mr Angelo? I think you'll find I *am* the damn magic."

She smooths down the skirt of her dress and steps around me to take my dad's arm. He's trying not to laugh when he offers it to her, and the pair of them saunter off to the dance floor. Halfway there, she looks back at me. "You know, you really should check out those trees, Lex…"

There are people walking across the dance floor, people standing in groups and chatting, people carrying their drinks. Some are even dancing. All of them are masked. All of them have made an effort – some are cosplayers in black-and-white versions of their favourite costumes, some are dressed like Regency princes or like kings and queens…and I'm sure I saw a couple of Jane Austens having a fight over whose dress works better. There are feathers and corsets and sparkling jewels everywhere…and that's just on the guys. I feel quite understated in my starry black dress…but I didn't fancy being mistaken for Cinderella again.

Nadiya waves from behind the trees, her silver dress and matching hijab making her glow in the shadows. And Bede – homing in on her from the other side – is being Mad Jonathan Strange, dressed in a black frock coat and wearing a wild wig, carrying a toy mouse tucked under his arm. He spots me and brandishes it, swinging it round by its tail. Very funny.

And, as if by magic, the crowd on the dance floor separates, pulling apart as neatly as waves drawn by the tide – and there he is.

# ROOTS

A man in black, sitting under the trees.

Black suit, black shirt, black tie, black shoes. A black mask just like mine covering his eyes.

He is a storm, a whirlwind, a hurricane.

And he came back.

I look at him and he looks at me – and he stands, and he bows.

He *bows*.

I could get used to this – not that I'm curtseying back or anything. That would be stupid.

"You're here," I say when we meet in the middle. It's all I can say, and I hope he hears everything I've packed inside those words.

"Turns out I didn't want to be anywhere else." Behind his mask his eyes are deeper and darker than ever – and then he lifts my hand to his mouth and presses a kiss against my skin.

"Can you even *see* anything without your glasses? I mean, how did you even know it was *me*?"

"Sheer blind luck," he says with a shrug. "But then you got close enough for me to see your feet clearly and I figured there would only be one person in this whole hotel who would wear black trainers to a masked ball."

"Ah, but they're *glittery* black trainers." I hold up one foot to prove my point.

"And that's how I knew it was you."

"Until I started talking, because—"

"Lexi?"

"Mmm?"

"Stop."

"Oh. Right."

I step back and look at him, and he looks at me.

"Earlier…" I say.

"I was a dick," he says at the exact same time – and we both stop. He peers past me, and I turn to see who he's watching; it's Nadiya. She gives me a double thumbs up and nods at him.

"I apologized to Nadiya," he says…and suddenly he's closer to me than he was a moment ago. I don't remember him stepping towards me, or me stepping towards him, but now I'm seeing him again I don't think we can ever be close *enough*.

"Good."

Bede has joined Nadiya, and behind Aidan's back on the other side of the trees, they are acting out an elaborate skit which seems to involve a lot of swooning and bowing and kissing of hands.

Oh, I get it.

I give them my sternest glare. The pair of them dissolve into hopeless laughter.

"And I'm sorry. What I said…"

"No." I make myself step back from him so I can look up

at his face, show him I mean it. "I think the reason I got so angry with you was because I know you were right. You were right about the conventions, you were right about my dad. It's just…if I'm not Lexi Angelo-as-in-Angelo-events, Lexi with the clipboard…who am I? If I stop being her, do I stop being *me*?"

"Of course not! Are you crazy?"

"You've got, you know, stuff. You've got your books – you said it yourself, it's your career – and *two* names. I don't even have one of my own. Everything is *this*." I wave a hand around at the ballroom. "My dad, my friends – even my name. They all belong here."

"And you do too. That doesn't change because you do *other* things as well. You don't stop being you. It's not…" He looks around – and I can see him trying not to smile. "It's not that black and white."

Well. Right.

Time to be brave.

"We never did get round to seeing each other outside of conventions…maybe I could come to Bath sometime. See you in the real world, you know?" I can't look at him. I can't. But I can't stop either. "Maybe you could show me that museum?"

"The Holburne? I'd like that."

When I risk a glance up at him, he's smiling; he's smiling like he means it.

"Only if you're sure. Because otherwise—"

"No, I'm sure. I could show you where the magic happens…" Above his mask, I see one of his eyebrows arch.

"Or you could just show me the museum."

His hair is even more ruffled than it was earlier, like he's been running in the wind. I try to picture him with a haircut like his friend Nick's, cropped close to his skull – and I can't. Aidan's storm cloud of hair is the only way I can imagine him.

"What happened to your friends? Dinner?" I ask, and already his hands are reaching for mine and mine for his; our fingers knitting together as though even they know what a good fit they are. What a good fit we are.

"I left." He draws me closer, and I am leaning into him and, slowly, I feel my heart stitching itself back together as I breathe him in, rest my cheek against him.

"You left?"

"Yeah. We were in the pub and…I don't know."

"But I thought you hadn't seen each other for ages and he's your best friend and everything?"

"Two years ago, maybe. And I thought the thing with Ali might be a problem at first…"

*Ali. Right.*

"But it wasn't even that in the end."

*Is that good? Bad? Middling to vaguely indifferent? I DON'T KNOW ANY MORE.*

"So...?" I try prompting him. I need to know, before I start to feel; before I *let* myself feel. I need to know.

"We were in the pub and having a drink...and they started making jokes, you know? About the convention. About everybody here. About Sam. They were pretty rude to her this morning and, the way they were talking about it, you'd think it was the best joke anyone's ever made."

"*Sam?* They were rude to Sam? She didn't say anything!" I'd thought I wasn't keen on them before. But now? Wow.

"Maybe it didn't even bother her, but it bothered me." His fingers tighten, ever so slightly, around mine. "While I was talking to them in the lobby, she came running up to ask if I knew where you were, and they..."

I get it. "Captain America. They were dicks about the costume, weren't they?"

"They were. And I got it. I got why you were so angry with me – and listening to the way they talked about it in the pub, I realized I didn't want to be there. I wanted to be here. And I wanted to be here with *you.*"

This, of course, would be the appropriate moment to melt into his arms; to let him sweep me off my feet and carry me up a vast curving staircase that will materialize out of nowhere. But unfortunately, I'm still me and it comes out before I can stop it: "I was worried you'd say I was nobody. When they asked who I was."

"What?"

I can hear the shock woven through his voice – as though he can't believe I'd even think something like that, let alone say it out loud.

This is…encouraging.

"That's why I left you with them. Because I didn't want to hear you say 'Oh, this is Lexi – she's nobody'. Because I'm not nobody. I'm me."

He grabs my hand again and he pulls it up to his face; curling his fingers around mine, he runs my knuckles across his cheeks, the line of his jaw, his lips. His other hand slides around my waist and pulls me in to him until his face fills my vision and he really is all I see – and then he ducks his head to one side and his lips graze my ear and I can feel him whisper it…

"You're you, Lexi Angelo. And that's…that's exactly why I've fallen for you."

The room spins, and we are at the middle of it; the only fixed point. Everything else whirls around us like shooting stars and the storm breaks about me. He smells like the sea seen from a rooftop in Brighton, like laughter in hotel corridors. Like magic and stories and streetlights – and lightning far off in the night.

This time, I don't – won't – pull away, and I raise my face

to his. Because he feels like a perfect fit…and he tastes like the courage it's taken me my whole life to find.

And he is – we are – worth every second of it.

"Here. I wanted to give this to you earlier – I was going to, but it ended up not being the time." From somewhere behind his back he produces a black rectangular wooden box, about the size of a book. "It's for you."

"What is it?"

"Well, generally the idea with presents is that you *open* them?"

So I do.

The lid of the box hinges up, and inside – resting on a black velvet lining painted with tiny silver stars, just like my dress – is a book. It's a copy of *Piecekeepers* – but it's different. Aidan takes the box while I take the book, and I really see what I'm looking at.

It's a new edition. A limited edition. On the very first page, a small silver stamp says:

*1 of 100*

"When the book really took off, Eagle's Head said it might be cool to do a special collectors' edition. I wanted you to have the first one."

I turn the page. The title is embossed in silver ink. It shines like it's alive.

I turn the page again – and almost drop the book, because the epigraph, and below it the line about meeting in jail that I accidentally quoted at him that day, has disappeared... and in their place is a new dedication.

*To Lexi, for the night we spent in jail.*

"You did *this* for me?"

"Why not? *You're* Lexi Angelo."

"Shhh. It's supposed to be a masked ball. What if you give away my secret identity?"

"Hard to say. The night's still young."

"Oh, you didn't just say that!"

And I take his hand in mine and we walk together across the dance floor where my friends and my family – my complicated, untidy, messed-up, unconventional convention family – are dancing and talking and laughing all around us, and I could almost believe in magic.

I could even believe in Haydn Swift and his Piecekeepers tonight...but I don't want to live in *his* world any more.

I don't need to.

I have my own, and it's bigger than I ever believed it could be. It's here and it's now and it's everything that comes after – and I have *no* idea what that's going to be. But I can't wait to find out.

# MAGIC TIME

## SUNDAY 29TH OCTOBER
## 2 A.M.

Sam's whisper has always been louder than she thinks, and when she near-bellows, "What are we *doing*?" everybody shushes her as one. This makes Nadiya even more nervous than she was before – and she keeps looking over her shoulder in case someone's following. "Are you sure we're not going to get yelled at by the night manager?"

"SHHHHH!"

We tiptoe along the corridor, leaving our shoes by the stairs for a quick getaway. Each of us is carrying a large, round, steel room-service tray, while on the other three floors of the hotel, several doors have neatly stacked piles of dirty plates sitting beside them on the carpet.

Aidan stops, surveys the corridor ahead of us. "Show them how it's done, Lexi." As I step forward, he adds: "Want a push?"

"Nope. I've got a better idea."

And, holding my tray, I back up a few steps…and I run. I run like my life depends on it and I run like I'm chasing all

449

the nows I ever cared about; everything that ever mattered.

Every time I was moving crates of books in hotel service corridors at midnight, every time I've hidden under a table, every single breakfast meeting with my dad…

Every phone call with Sam, every time I've groaned at Bede's jokes, every time Nadiya's told me exactly what I should be doing with just a twitch of her eyebrow.

Every time I've laughed.

Every time I've cried.

Every time I've sworn about not being able to get my homework done *and* plan an author reading schedule and somehow managed to do them both anyway.

Everything that makes me me; that makes me *her* – Lexi Angelo.

And I say "Okay" to all of them, because I know there's more to me than just one thing.

And when I'm running fast enough, I drop the tray and jump on, gliding to a stop to a round of applause. I turn to bow and pick up my tray…and am almost knocked flying by Sam – because of course she couldn't wait for me to get out of the way, but came barrelling down the corridor right behind me. Bede comes next, then Nadiya, clamping her hands over her eyes as soon as she's on the tray. Aidan comes last. He slides down the corridor towards us like he's carried on the wind.

And when he comes to the end and he jumps, I catch him.

# THE END

# PIECEKEEPERS

## BY
## HAYDN SWIFT

# CHAPTER 1

# MANTUA & VENICE

The air in the upstairs gallery had a peculiar smell; something like hot dust. It caught in the back of Jamie's throat and prickled. A PA system nearby crackled into life and a polite voice asked visitors to evacuate this section of the building – something about a fault with the air conditioning – but Jamie wasn't listening, because there she was.

The girl from the steps, striding through the room full of Raphael's paintings – impossibly confident; her coat flying behind her like a battle flag. She swept past him without a second glance and disappeared into room sixty-one.

Jamie watched the tourists shuffling past him in the opposite direction, heading back towards the stairs. And then he looked at the empty doorway she had walked through.

"Once again, we request that all visitors please evacuate this section of the building via the nearest exit. This area of the gallery is now closed. We apologize for any inconvenience."

With one last look at the exit, Jamie took a deep breath and headed for room sixty-one.

The girl had stopped in front of one of the Busati oil paintings. If she heard him come in, she didn't show it. Jamie cleared his throat, not entirely voluntarily: the hot dusty smell was stronger in this room, and the air felt thicker and heavier – like the morning after Bonfire Night.

She still didn't seem to know he was there, and it didn't look like she was planning on leaving any time soon; she was studying the painting closely, while pulling on a pair of delicate red leather gloves.

Jamie cleared his throat again. "Hi..." he said.

She looked round at him, her long dark hair flowing across her back as she turned, and she smiled. "You might want to get down."

"I'm sorry...?"

"Get. Down." She pointed to a bench in the middle of

the room as she turned away again, her attention already elsewhere.

"The bench? You want me to... What is that?"

He'd been hearing a faint hissing noise since he stepped into room sixty-one. Mostly he'd ignored it, assuming it was something to do with the faulty air conditioning... But now, it was louder. Nearer. And it didn't sound so much like air, as like sand running through an hourglass.

"Actually, I really think you should leave." Her back was to him, and her floor-length coat blocked his view of most of the painting – but not all of it. And even from where he was standing, he could see what was happening.

One of the two little cherubs painted at the bottom of the panel was...disintegrating. There was no other word for it – as he watched, pieces of it seemed to crack and collapse, turning to dust and tumbling out of the frame to land in a neat pile on the floor.

"The painting..." He couldn't manage any more than that: his voice simply stopped working. But the painting! Something was wrong with the painting – it bulged outwards in the centre, as though the paint was trying to pull itself away from the canvas it was bound to.

As though something was trapped behind it, and was forcing its way out.

"Are you still here?" She had to raise her voice over the

noise now, which had climbed from a hiss to a steady howl. Jamie opened and closed his mouth in protest, but nothing came out.

The girl shook her head and reached under her coat, pulling out a small, battered brown leather pouch on a long cord which she slung around her neck and across her body. "Don't say I didn't warn you..." She tugged the little bag open and reached in, pulling out a handful of black powder that trickled to the floor from between her gloved fingers.

The painting bulged even further; the roar around them was joined by the sound of splintering wood... And as Jamie dived for cover under the bench, the girl threw her handful of powder into the air.

When, later, Jamie looked back at what happened in that room, he could never explain it – not even when he knew precisely what she'd done. Because the first time he saw Lizzie at work was the first time he ever believed in magic.

The black powder hung there. It did not fall or drift; it simply stayed, even in the wind that seemed to have come from nowhere and was whipping her hair out in long, straight lines. From his spot under the bench, Jamie watched her lean into the gale, pull out another handful of dust from her bag and launch it into the air – where, just like the first, it hung motionless – and he watched the painting creak outwards, a long split appearing down the centre of it like doors waiting to open.

*This can't possibly be real. It can't.*

And just when he thought it couldn't get any stranger, she started to draw in the air; her fist making huge, sweeping strokes through the black cloud as she moved. It was like watching a dance, like watching an artist sketch on a giant canvas. She whirled this way and that, and everywhere her hands touched the air, it lit up.

The dust sparked, turning from black to brightest white until the air was thick with stars – a whole miniature cosmos hanging in the gallery – and, in the middle of it all, she stopped, and glanced over her shoulder…and winked at him.

And then she clapped her hands and everything – the room, the world, Jamie's whole life until that point – was lost in blinding, blinding light.


*Piecekeepers* is Haydn Swift's debut novel.
Haydn enjoys reading, writing and spends most of his time travelling between Bath and London.

# BEDE'S TOP FACTS ABOUT PINEAPPLES

 A pineapple plant only produces one pineapple every two to three years. Once a pineapple has been picked, it won't get any riper. (Though it will begin to perish after two days.)

 The top of a pineapple can be cut off and planted in soil. With some water, care, light and a bit of luck, a new pineapple plant should start to grow...

 A pineapple is not an apple, or a pine... It's a berry!

 The pineapple is native to South America, and Christopher Columbus became the first European to come across one when he visited Guadaloupe in 1493.

 Between the 17th and 18th centuries, pineapples were very expensive and a real rarity in Britain, and as a consequence, they were seen as a huge status symbol. They became an emblem of hospitality and a successful venture, dating from the times when sailors would bring home one of these exotic fruits on their return from a voyage. Placed on the front porch, the pineapple was a sign that they were safely returned and an invitation to friends who might like to visit.

However, given their expense, the pineapple was out of reach for all but the wealthiest, as well as these fortunate sailors. And, as a result, a booming pineapple rental economy developed – allowing the fashionable to hire pineapples by the day for the centrepiece of their social gatherings…

As a measure of its sought-after status, a pineapple can be seen atop the Wimbledon Men's Singles trophy, which was designed and made in 1887.

It is an urban myth that you can dissolve your fingerprints using pineapple juice. Pineapples contain an enzyme called bromelain, which breaks down protein. While continued exposure to a pineapple (or its juice) would mean that the bromelain might wear away the ridges on your fingertips, these ridges would continue to grow back.

June 27th is International Pineapple Day and is celebrated across the world.

# ACKNOWLEDGEMENTS

A book – any book – is like a house. To some people, it's just a building you pass on the street: it's got the usual house-related bits like a roof, walls, windows…maybe a few flowers growing outside…and that's it. But to others, that house is more than the sum of its parts: it's home. And it takes a lot of work from a lot of people to make a home.

This is where I get to thank them.

My wonderful editor Rebecca Hill, who leaned forward instead of backing away when I said: "So, I've got this idea…" and who understood Lexi in an instant. I'm not quite sure how you do it, so I'm just going to assume that you're magic.

Becky Walker, whose emails brighten the whole process, and who is always happy to rigorously discuss the most bizarre questions: did we ever decide whether moshing and pogoing *are* the same?

Juliet Mushens: agent and hand-holder; cheerleader,

oracle and voice of sanity. You really are a war-time consigliere and I don't have the words. (You might see this as a plus.)

Enormous thanks to everyone at Usborne: to Sarah, for pointing out when I've been an idiot and making me do something about it; to Kath, Will and Sarah C for turning a bunch of words into an actual book (more magic!); to Amy D, Stevie and Alesha – geniuses all the way down to the last pineapple bullet point. Thank you, too, to Helen Crawford-White for a beautiful, beautiful illustration: if books are judged by their covers, this one's in good hands.

Special thanks to Will Hill – who was the only person I told about this book for the longest time, because he gets it *all* – and to Non Pratt and Melinda Salisbury for not even hesitating when I asked them to be a part of it. (Read their books. They're brilliant.)

To my convention family: you know who you are and you know what you mean to me, even if we don't see each other as much these days. We'll always have 2 a.m.

To my actual family: I love you. Thank you for…well, all of it, really. Because any home would be nothing without you.

# MEET MAGGIE HARCOURT

Maggie Harcourt writes about a lot of different things. She also reads about a lot of different things, and will always be a fan girl at heart. Maggie lives in Bath with her family.

**1) WHAT'S YOUR FAVOURITE BOOK, MAGGIE?** Either *Jonathan Strange & Mr Norrell*, or *The Three Musketeers*. (I think *Strange* just wins.)

**2) WHAT'S THE BEST THING ABOUT CONVENTIONS?** They're all about celebrating something you love – with other people who love it too.

**3) IF YOU COULD SPEND ONE NIGHT ON A ROOF WITH ANYONE, WHO WOULD YOU PICK?** Someone who's as much of a geek as I am. And has brought a blanket.

**4) WHAT'S YOUR FAVOURITE THING ABOUT FALLING IN LOVE?** Falling in love makes us see the world (and ourselves) differently for a while.

# THE LAST SUMMER OF US

## by Maggie Harcourt

The air smells of hot, dry grass trampled underfoot.
It smells of diesel, of cider and cigarettes and burgers
and ice cream and the ends of things.
The end of the summer.
The end of us: of Steffan and Jared and me.

This is the story of a road trip.
The story of three best friends crammed into
a clapped-out car full of regrets and secrets,
on a journey that will change their lives for ever.

*A story of love, lies, grief, friendship and growing up.*
*A story you'll never forget.*

ISBN: 9781409587699

"Exquisitely sad and yet touchingly beautiful.
And so, so real."
HOLLY BOURNE, AUTHOR OF "AM I NORMAL YET?"

EVERYONE'S A FAN OF SOMEONE...OR SOMETHING!

AND IF YOU'RE A FAN OF UNCONVENTIONAL,
WE'D LOVE TO HEAR FROM YOU.

WHAT DID YOU
LOVE MOST ABOUT
THE BOOK?

GOT ANY GOOD
CONVENTION
STORIES?

TOTALLY WANT TO READ
PIECEKEEPERS
FOR REAL?

# #UNCONVENTIONAL

GET IN TOUCH ONLINE:

 @USBORNE

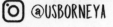 @USBORNEYA

 USBORNE YA

FOR MORE FABULOUS USBORNE YA READS, NEWS AND
COMPETITIONS, HEAD TO USBORNEYASHELFIES.TUMBLR.COM

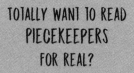